Readers are loving *The W...*

'BRILLIA...

'**Superbly written** with wonderful, well-developed characters you can relate to and so easy to read'

'Another **excellent** read by Lesley Eames. I love all the characters' different personalities and storylines and **definitely recommend**'

'I was only two pages in when I knew this would be a **5-star read** . . . I honestly can't put my excitement into words at the thought of reading the next one'

'A **real page-turner** for me and I can't wait for the next in the series'

'Loved this book. A **comforting** read with trials and tribulations of WWII and families. **Difficult to put down**'

'The spirit and sense of community shone throughout and **I was left wanting more**'

'Another lovely book that **drew me in and kept me wanting more**. It has a fab story and characters that bring it to life'

*Also by Lesley Eames*

The Runaway Women in London
The Brighton Guest House Girls
The Orphan Twins
The Wartime Singers

*The Wartime Bookshop* series
The Wartime Bookshop

# LAND GIRLS AT THE WARTIME BOOKSHOP

Lesley Eames

PENGUIN BOOKS

TRANSWORLD PUBLISHERS
Penguin Random House, One Embassy Gardens,
8 Viaduct Gardens, London SW11 7BW
www.penguin.co.uk

Transworld is part of the Penguin Random House group of companies
whose addresses can be found at global.penguinrandomhouse.com

Penguin
Random House
UK

First published in Great Britain in 2023 by Bantam
an imprint of Transworld Publishers
Penguin paperback edition published 2023

A CIP catalogue record for this book
is available from the British Library.

ISBN
9781529177367

Typeset in New Baskerville ITC Pro by Jouve (UK), Milton Keynes.
Printed and bound in Great Britain by Clays Ltd, Elcograf S.p.A.

The authorized representative in the EEA is Penguin Random House Ireland,
Morrison Chambers, 32 Nassau Street, Dublin D02 YH68.

Penguin Random House is committed to a sustainable
future for our business, our readers and our planet. This book
is made from Forest Stewardship Council® certified paper.

To my beloved daughters, Olivia and Isobel,
bringers of joy and happiness
(and sometimes chocolate too).

# CHAPTER ONE

## Kate

### APRIL 1941
### *Churchwood, Hertfordshire, England*

It was a bright Monday morning in early spring and, like many English villages, Churchwood was going quietly about its daily business – until a scream shattered the calm and froze passers-by in their tracks. Having just emerged from the bakery, Kate Fletcher was one of them, though she froze for only a moment. As another scream lacerated the air, she whirled around to see the tall, lanky figure of Marjorie Plym waving her arms hysterically as she ran down the path from the church. *What on earth . . . ?*

Kate was tall too, and, having worked on a farm all her life, she was both fit and dressed in practical breeches with her long chestnut hair secured in a no-nonsense plait down her back. She wasn't the only person who moved towards Marjorie, but she was by far the quickest, throwing her shopping basket down beside her bicycle, then racing across the village green to catch Marjorie as she stumbled through the churchyard lychgate and collapsed in tears.

'What is it, Marjorie? What's happened?' Kate asked, easing the older woman to the ground.

1

Marjorie was too hysterical to answer.

*Oh, heck.* Kate wasn't good at this sort of thing. She hadn't had the practice. As a member of the notoriously rough Fletcher family, Kate had been shunned in Churchwood for most of her life. As a result, she'd always treated her neighbours with bold-eyed disdain, despite loathing her family just as much as anyone. Only since Alice Lovell had moved to the village and befriended her had Kate's sharp edges softened. Gradually, she'd welcomed the village into her life just as, with Alice's influence, the village had started to welcome her – even gossip-loving and rather silly Marjorie, once one of her snootiest critics. Despite that, Kate was still out of her depth when it came to dispensing comfort and sympathy.

She glanced around desperately and was relieved to see Alice, now her best friend, approaching through a gathering sea of other faces. Alice might be a slight, fair-haired little thing but she was both clever and compassionate. She'd know exactly how to handle Marjorie.

'I've no idea what's going on,' Kate told her. 'Can you take Marjorie while I investigate?'

Alice looked at Marjorie's prostrate form then sent Kate a sympathetic glance as she got down beside her and reached for the older woman. 'Come to me, Marjorie. Kate needs to get up.'

Whimpering, Marjorie slithered over to Alice, who nodded at Kate to suggest it was fine for her to go now.

Relieved that Marjorie was quietening already, Kate scrambled up and ran along the path to the church. St Luke's had been built from mellow stone and flint in Victorian times and the entrance was an old oak door. Kate passed through it and stood for a moment to adjust her eyes to the shadows within. There was a central aisle with pews and pillars on each side, an arched roof overhead and an altar at the front. All was hushed quietness, motes of dust flickering in the light from the high stained-glass windows.

'Hello?' Kate called.

No one answered and she could see nothing amiss. She set off along the aisle, glancing from side to side and still seeing nothing untoward. Reaching the front pews, she paused and called out again. 'Hello?'

Silence, but Kate noticed that flowers were scattered beneath some sort of pedestal flower holder. Had Marjorie come in to arrange them only to drop them? A minor accident hardly appeared to justify screams – unless she'd been stung by a bee hiding in the petals? April was early for bee stings but still possible, and it would be typical of Marjorie to play up a sting to make herself look interesting in the eyes of the village.

Kate could see no bee now. Gathering up the flowers, she returned them to the pail in which Marjorie must have brought them. She turned away to leave – and gasped.

A foot was sticking out of the half-open vestry door. It was wearing a black sock and a shoe with a hole in the sole. Kate took a steadying breath and walked over to see the rest of the Reverend Septimus Barnes lying on the vestry floor as though he'd fallen backwards, arms outstretched.

It was obvious that the ageing, white-haired vicar

3

had said his last prayer in this life because his eyes were open in a glassy stare, but Kate kneeled down beside him anyway and, after a moment's hesitation, touched his cheek. It was icy, with none of the softness of living flesh.

Not being a churchgoer, she'd never got to know Septimus Barnes well, but he'd seemed a decent sort of man and Kate felt sadness for him. Perhaps, though, he'd have been pleased to end his days in the church he'd served for so many years.

She returned to Alice. 'Reverend Barnes,' she said, and was glad to see that Alice understood immediately.

'Could you fetch my father?' Archibald Lovell was a retired doctor, and though Septimus Barnes was beyond earthly help, Dr Lovell would know what was best to be done. 'Better fetch Naomi too,' Alice added.

Kind but bracing Naomi Harrington was Marjorie's oldest friend and the best person to comfort her.

Kate set off at a run back over the green to where she'd left her bicycle outside the bakery. 'What's going on?' a woman asked.

'Sorry, Mrs Hayes. Can't stop.' Kate retrieved her basket from the ground and hung it over the handlebars; then she pedalled off at speed towards The Linnets, the picturesque cottage where Alice and her father lived on the edge of the village. There she skidded to a halt, dashed up the short path and banged on the door.

Dr Lovell blinked at Kate like an ageing cherub when he finally opened it. A widower, he'd retired from his London medical practice the year before last and was spending his days studying civilizations from the distant past. Doubtless she'd distracted him from ancient Greece, Egypt or another such place.

'Alice needs you,' Kate said, only to regret her choice of words when she saw the alarm in his eyes.

'She's fine,' Kate assured him hastily. 'It's Reverend Barnes who's . . .'

'Unwell?'

'Beyond unwell, I think.'

'I see. Let me get my things.'

'He's in the church. I need to fetch Naomi too. It was Marjorie Plym who found the vicar.'

'Ah, Miss Plym.' No further explanation was needed.

Kate rode the bike across Brimbles Lane and between tall gateposts on to the drive of Foxfield, the grandest house in the village, where Naomi lived. Middle-aged Naomi had once been Kate's arch-enemy, and where she'd led the rest of Churchwood had followed, but, thanks to Alice and a dawning appreciation of each other's better qualities, Kate and Naomi had become firm friends.

Gravel flew into the air as Kate skidded to another halt. It must have alerted Naomi, whose sitting room overlooked the drive, because she came into the hall just as her maid Suki opened the door to Kate's sharp rap.

'Thank you, Suki,' Naomi said, and the little maid retreated.

'It's Reverend Barnes,' Kate said. 'He's . . . um . . .'

'Oh, heavens.' Naomi touched a hand to her chest.

'Marjorie found him.' Again, no more needed to be said.

5

'I'll come straight away.'

'You won't mind if I go on ahead?'

'Of course not. My dumpy little legs will never keep pace with your long ones.'

Kate returned to Alice, passing Dr Lovell on the way. 'Your father's almost here and Naomi won't be much longer.'

Alice sent her a thankful look. Marjorie was still in a state of collapse, though the hysterics had subsided to moans and occasional shudders.

'Is there anything else I can do?' Kate asked.

'Keep people away? They all mean well but Reverend Barnes deserves his dignity, and I don't think he'll get that from being stared at by half of the village.'

'Understood.'

'Could you also tell people that the bookshop won't be opening today?'

Doubtless Alice thought that was a matter of respect too, as the bookshop was held in the Sunday School Hall. 'I'll put a notice on the door,' Kate agreed.

The church, the vicarage, the hall and the elementary school stood next to each other along one side of the triangular-shaped green, the other sides being home to shops and cottages. Kate entered the hall, located a pen and paper amongst the bookshop stores and wrote: *Today's bookshop session is cancelled out of respect to Reverend Barnes.* She paused before adding, *We expect to reopen soon,* for surely that was the case.

She pinned it to the door, spent a few minutes encouraging people to leave the scene and then returned to Alice. 'My father is in the church,' Alice told her.

6

'Good. I wrote that we'll open the bookshop again soon.'

Alice nodded. 'I can't imagine Reverend Barnes would wish us to pause for long so perhaps we could reopen on Wednesday. Do you think you might be able to come a little early for a meeting with the others?' Alice, Kate and Naomi ran the bookshop alongside Janet Collins, May Janicki and Bert Make-piece. 'We should talk about how we want to mark his passing as he was such a staunch supporter.'

Kate suspected he'd only supported the bookshop in its early days because Naomi was involved and he treasured his invitations to Foxfield. But over time he'd come to appreciate it on its own merits. 'This is a splendid way of bringing the village together,' Kate had heard him say.

'It would be nice to honour him in some way,' Kate agreed, though she had no suggestions. Alice was much better at the niceties of life than she was.

'We need to talk about next month's programme anyway, and . . .'

Kate waited but no more words came. 'And what?' she prompted.

Alice looked as though she wished she'd stayed quiet, though why she should—

*Ah.* 'You're not worried the bookshop won't survive without Reverend Barnes's approval?' A new vicar was bound to be different from an old one, but surely he wouldn't want to change a bookshop that had become the beating heart of the village?

'I'm not worried,' Alice assured her, 'but it can't hurt to think about the future, can it?'

Kate supposed not, but the very idea of change had jolted her. The bookshop hadn't only become the beating heart of the village, it had also become a crucial part of Kate's existence. After years of being on the outside of village life, she'd been reluctant to get involved at first, but Alice had encouraged her to give it a try and Kate had never looked back. The bookshop had brought her friends and a wonderful sense of belonging. She learned all sorts of things there too – from the books, magazines and newspapers she borrowed and from the people she met. The bookshop was also fun, especially when it threw parties! The thought of slogging on the farm day after day without those bursts of joy . . . it frightened her.

'Do you think you might be able to come on Wednesday?' Alice asked.

Kate pulled herself out of her gloom. 'I can try.' It was always difficult for Kate to get away from the family farm.

'Why not go home now?' Alice suggested. 'Get ahead on your work?'

'You don't need me for anything else?'

'You've done plenty already. And look. Here comes Naomi.'

Huffing and puffing from walking quickly on her stout little legs, Naomi was red in the face. She exchanged nods with Kate and Alice then bent towards her friend. 'Now, now, Marjorie. You've had a shock but it's time to get up.'

Marjorie groaned. 'If you only knew what I've been through.'

'I understand it's been difficult. But sitting on the ground and lying across poor Alice isn't helping.

Come along. Up you get and I'll take you back to Foxfield for a cup of tea.'

The proposal acted on Marjorie like a tonic. 'Perhaps I can manage to get up now.'

Kate lingered long enough to help haul Marjorie to her feet. The older woman's shoulders always drooped but she also swayed a little today. 'Big breaths, Marjorie,' Naomi instructed. 'That's the ticket.'

'I'll see you on Wednesday,' Kate told Alice. 'If I can get away.'

Cycling homewards, Kate's thoughts returned to the bookshop. Started by Alice as a way of bringing the Churchwood community together, it was so much more than an ordinary bookshop. It opened several times a week and was a place to come for tea and companionship. For entertainment too. Stories were read out loud, sometimes for children, sometimes for adults. Activities and talks were held, from knitting and fashion to Digging for Victory in village gardens. Then there were the social gatherings with beer and dancing, often attended by staff and patients from the nearby military hospital. And if anyone needed help due to illness or some other reason, the bookshop was the place where aid would be arranged.

Surely there could be no reason for changing something so wonderful? But perhaps it really was just a case of deciding the best way of helping a new vicar to understand the bookshop's merits.

Brimbles Farm was more than a mile away along the lane that ran between Alice's cottage and Naomi's Foxfield. It was never a pleasure to return there. Why would it be? Only a few months old when her mother

9

died, Kate had been brought up as a skivvy to her four obnoxious older brothers and her surly father, a man she'd only ever called by his given name of Ernie because he allowed none of his children to call him Dad or Father, probably because he preferred to keep them at an emotional distance.

She'd been an unpaid skivvy until recently when Alice's threat to help Kate build a new life elsewhere had enabled her to negotiate a tiny wage of two shillings a week – recently renegotiated to three shillings – and time off to spend with her friends.

Not that taking time off was easy. There was always too much work, for one thing. And for another, Ernie and her brothers begrudged every minute she spent away from the farm, still seeing her as the spinster daughter who should devote her entire life to running the house and working in the fields.

Kate had no intention of staying on the farm for ever, but she wasn't looking to forge a new life elsewhere just yet. Having found friends only recently, she was in no hurry to leave them. She needed to save some money before she ventured into the wider world too. And she also felt she was contributing to the war effort by helping to grow food for the country's tables. Until she was ready to leave, Kate was keen to keep some sort of peace at home and give her father no excuse for stopping her wages or trying to keep her from her friends. It meant she often laboured from the crack of dawn to well into the evenings.

Reaching the farm, she locked the bicycle in the barn to keep it safe from her brothers' mischief and carried her basket into the kitchen. Expecting to find the room empty, she came to a sudden halt as she saw that all five Fletcher men were there, the atmosphere so taut that it felt like electricity was crackling around them.

'What's wrong?' she asked.

'Ask this pair of idiots.' Ernie smacked the ginger heads of his youngest sons, twins Fred 'n' Frank, then pulled a chair from the table to sit down with his back turned to them in fury.

'They've joined up. That's what's wrong,' Kenny, the eldest son, told her.

'Joined the army?' Kate stared at the twins in shock. Despite their size they looked like naughty school-boys dragged before the headmaster.

'Both of 'em,' Vinnie crowed. He was the second eldest, and even in a crisis he couldn't contain his glee at seeing his younger brothers in trouble.

Kenny glowered at him. 'I don't know why you think it's funny.'

'Vinnie's an idiot too,' Ernie spat. As ever, the only emotion he was allowing himself was anger, though he had to be feeling more than that. After all, he valued his sons far more than his daughter.

'He *is* an idiot,' Kenny agreed. 'Because it means there's going to be a lot more work for the rest of us.' He stared hard at Kate. 'That includes you.'

'I always do my share.'

'Your share just got bigger. All our shares just got bigger, so don't start feeling sorry for yourself.'

Was she feeling sorry for herself? Not exactly. Uppermost in her mind was fear for the twins. She couldn't like them as people, but she loved them as brothers and shuddered at the thought of them being injured – or worse.

11

The possibility of harm coming to them hung in the air like a presence – sharp and jagged, stoking up anger because none of the Fletchers could express softer emotions. Except for Kate. 'I'm sorry you're putting yourselves in danger,' she told the twins and for perhaps the first time in their lives they looked grateful to her.

Kenny was still raging. 'What's the point of being exempt from military service if you go and join up?' he fumed.

'It seemed a good idea in the Wheatsheaf last night,' Frank confessed sheepishly.

'An adventure,' Fred added.

'*Adventure?*' Kenny was apoplectic. 'There's no adventure in getting shot or blown up!'

'It was the beer that made it seem . . . sort of glamorous,' Fred admitted.

'Drunken idiots,' Ernie spat.

'But why enlist this morning when you'd sobered up?' Kenny demanded.

'We got a lift from Billy Cheeseman and Tommy Boyd,' Frank said. 'They enlisted too.'

'And you were afraid of what they'd say if you went back on what you'd agreed last night,' Kenny guessed. 'Pathetic. That's what you two are. Pathetic.'

The twins exchanged more embarrassed looks.

Kate placed the bread in a cupboard then closed her eyes and breathed in deeply. She too was worried about what the twins' departure would mean for those left behind. They might be short on brains but there was no doubting their brawn. Even if they wasted a great deal of their energy in larking around, the farm's prosperity still owed much to them.

Without them that prosperity would suffer and doubtless Kate's wage would be the first casualty of any cutbacks in spending. If that happened, she'd be plunged back into the dark days when her only clothes were worn and patched cast-offs from her brothers. And with no time to see her friends, desperate loneliness would engulf her again.

She too would have a battle to fight after the twins left. A battle to keep some sort of life of her own.

# CHAPTER TWO

## *Alice*

It had been a rush to prepare the Sunday School Hall for the Wednesday bookshop session and still leave time for a meeting, but they'd managed it. Books, magazines, newspapers and comics were laid out on tables around the edge of the room. Still more tables stood in the centre with chairs around them so people could sit together and chat. Toys lay on mats on the floor ready for the children, and in the kitchen, cups, saucers and biscuits awaited teatime. Looking around, Alice registered smaller details too: the basket in which people could place items for future fundraising, from jars of preserves to lavender bags and hand-made wooden toys; the noticeboard on which they could advertise things they needed or wished to sell, swap or give away, and the plate on which they could donate a few pennies towards running costs if they could spare them.

As always, the sight of the bookshop warmed Alice with pleasure. She was proud of it. Grateful to it too, as it had given her a much-needed sense of purpose.

This wasn't the time to stand idling, though. 'Shall we begin?' she asked.

They settled at a table – Alice; Naomi; bear-like market gardener Bert Makepiece; homely long-term

14

Churchwood resident Janet Collins; and tall, elegant May Janicki, a newcomer who'd moved from London shortly before Alice, bringing with her three Polish refugee children who were the nieces and nephew of her husband, Marek. Like Alice's fiancé, Daniel, and Janet's youngest son, Charlie, Marek was away at the war.

Just then Kate arrived too, and hastened to a seat. 'Sorry I'm late.'

Alice guessed from her anxious expression that Kate had found it particularly difficult to leave the farm today. Alice half wished she'd urged her to stay at home. But while Kate could be spirited – her glares could make people quake – her confidence was still fragile at times so Alice hadn't wanted to exclude her.

'I thought it would be helpful to have a quick word about Reverend Barnes as he was a good friend to the bookshop,' Alice said. 'Have any of you heard about plans for his funeral?'

She looked particularly at Naomi, who'd known him best.

'I telephoned his niece to offer condolences and she told me she'd prefer to hold the funeral near her home in Bristol instead of Churchwood,' Naomi said.

The old vicar had long been a widower and had never had children, so his niece was his closest relative. Even so, Alice had expected him to be buried in Churchwood. From the looks on their faces, so had the others.

'He was our vicar for thirty years,' Janet pointed out.

Naomi shrugged. 'His niece doesn't plan to come here at all. She's going to arrange for removal men to clear the vicarage for the next incumbent. She was businesslike about the whole thing.'

'We could still send flowers as a gesture of thanks for the way he supported us,' Alice suggested.

'Better than nothing,' Bert agreed, but it was clear that they'd all have liked to do more.

'There's something else you should know,' Naomi said.

'Oh?' Alice had put Naomi's sombre mood down to the death of her old friend but perhaps there was more to it.

'I heard Cecil Wade talking.'

There was a collective grimace. Cecil Wade was a newcomer to the village, a pompous man with a high opinion of himself and a low opinion of so much else – especially women and the bookshop. He'd only visited the bookshop once, spending no more than ten minutes looking around at what was a typical bookshop scene: young mums with babies in their arms; small children playing merrily; older women laughing over a romance novel that featured a dashing duke on the cover; and older men teasing each other over dominoes. 'I'm afraid I have more important calls on my time,' he'd announced, sneering, and he'd never returned.

'You all know that Cecil replaced me when I stood down as churchwarden,' Naomi continued. 'Apparently, he's already been in touch with the Diocese about Septimus's replacement.'

'That feels rather quick,' Alice said. The old vicar was barely cold.

'I heard him in the Post Office telling Arthur Fellows about a telephone call he'd made to the archdeacon. It seems the archdeacon feels the timing of the vacancy is fortuitous in that he knows of a minister who's just what Churchwood needs. I explained to Cecil that I'd been unable to help overhearing and asked for more information. All he'd say was that the man the archdeacon has in mind is a splendid chap.'

A moment of quietness followed as everyone thought it over. 'Was it Cecil or the archdeacon who described the man as splendid?' Alice asked, because Cecil's idea of a splendid chap was likely to be radically different from theirs.

'I believe it was the archdeacon.'

'Then the man really might be splendid, though to be honest – and it still feels early to be talking about Reverend Barnes's successor – I'd like to see Adam Potts in the role.'

'Me too,' Bert said. 'Young Adam's been a curate over in Barton for several years now. He must be due a parish of his own.'

Adam had sometimes taken services at St Luke's when Reverend Barnes was away or unwell and he supported the bookshop enthusiastically, visiting often and joining in with storytelling, crafts and even tea-making.

'Adam would be perfect,' Janet agreed.

Naomi nodded. 'None better.'

'I don't go to church, but I think the world of Adam,' May said. 'He's wonderful with the kids and so kind too.'

'Kate?' Alice asked. 'I know you're not a churchgoer either, but what are your thoughts on Adam?'

Kate looked startled, as though her thoughts had

been elsewhere, but she rallied herself to say, 'He'd be great for the village.'

'Then we're all agreed.' Alice felt pleased but also concerned because an anxious frown was cutting through the smooth skin on her friend's forehead. The bookshop had done wonders for Kate's self-esteem so any threat to it was certain to worry her, but was something else troubling her too?

Alice turned back to Naomi. 'You may not be a churchwarden any more, but you still sit on the council at St Luke's.' The Parochial Church Council helped with the management of church affairs. 'Will you be involved in appointing the new vicar?'

'I believe appointments are decided jointly between parishes and the Diocese. Vacancies are often advertised so there can be several candidates.'

'There's no reason why Adam shouldn't be one of them?'

'Not as far as I'm aware.'

'Then I suggest we encourage him to apply. The archdeacon's man may be splendid but so is Adam.'

'Good idea to give the lad a nudge,' Bert said, to nods all round because Adam's natural modesty might stop him from putting himself forward.

'Shall we talk to him about it the next time we see him?' Alice asked Naomi.

'Yes, let's,' Naomi agreed. 'There's a meeting of the church council tomorrow evening. I'll speak up for Adam then. For the bookshop too, of course.'

'Thank you.'

Voices reached them from outside. The happy voices of people arriving for the bookshop session.

Kate got to her feet. 'I have to get back to work. I

wish Adam and the bookshop well, but I might struggle to stay involved in future.'

No wonder she looked depressed. Something bad
had happened, but what?

'The twins have enlisted,' Kate explained. 'It's
going to mean a lot more work for the rest of us.'

'Oh, Kate!' Alice cried.

'Surely the twins are exempt from military service,'
Naomi said, and Kate's mouth twisted.

'They chose to join up.'

'I'm sorry—' Alice began but Kate was already
through the door. Sympathy always turned her prickly.

Bert shook his head. 'Don't anyone try to tell me
those Fletcher boys joined up to serve King and country. They just let beer and bravado drive whatever
sense they had out of their tiny minds.'

And as a result poor Kate was under more pressure
than ever.

With an effort, Alice turned to welcome the arrivals.
'Glad to see you're over your cold, Mrs Hutchings . . .
Yes, you can play with the hobby horse today,
Tommy . . . You're on tea-making duty today, Mrs
Hayes . . . That's right, Edna, May and Janet are collecting clothes for families who've been bombed out
of their homes in the Blitz . . . Bert's going to lead a
session on making toys for Blitz children and Churchwood children alike, rag dolls and toy trains, things
like that . . . An embroidered tray cloth will make a
lovely raffle prize, Pam . . .'

Phew! As everyone settled, sitting near friends and
calling out to others, Alice felt another burst of pride.
The bookshop was wonderful and the possibility of a
new vicar sweeping it away on a tide of change was

surely slight. Even so, it panicked her a little because Churchwood needed the bookshop, and Alice needed the sense of purpose it gave her,

Three hours later the session ended and Churchwood's residents filed out, calls of 'Thanks!' and 'See you next time' ringing in the air. Alice helped to clear up then walked home to the cottage.

It felt quiet after the bustle of the bookshop. Waiting in the kitchen for soup to heat on the stove, Alice stared out of the window at the back garden. The cottage had been empty for a year before her father bought it, and the garden had been neglected. Now it was bright with spring flowers – yellow daffodils, red tulips and purple irises. There was also a large vegetable patch and a coop for Alice's chickens, Audrey, Constance and Louisa. Both vegetable patch and chickens had been Kate's idea and she'd been a great help in getting them started.

Poor Kate. Alice felt a spurt of anger towards the twins for leaving Brimbles Farm in the lurch and going off to the war.

Thoughts of the war led inevitably to Daniel, currently serving in North Africa after being rescued from the beaches of Dunkirk the previous year. Alice touched the ring he'd given her when they'd become engaged last summer – a central aquamarine with diamonds on each side. 'An aquamarine matches your eyes and reminds me of the sky on a sunny day,' he'd explained. 'That's how you make me feel, darling girl – as though the sun has come out and painted the sky a glorious blue.'

Alice felt the same way about Daniel. Not that their romance had been plain sailing as Daniel still blamed himself for an accident that had injured her hand and left her unable to work – so far, anyway. Alice hadn't blamed him at all, but for a frighteningly long time she'd pushed him away, suspecting he only wanted to marry her to rescue her from dependence on her father. That misunderstanding was behind them now, but Alice still wished desperately to find paid work so she could prove to Daniel that he needn't worry about her. Much as she loved the bookshop, she didn't earn a penny from it.

Becoming self-sufficient was important to Alice's pride as well. Even as a child she'd worked for her father after school, at weekends and during the school holidays. She'd enjoyed it, and the activity had saved her from loneliness after the death of her mother. She'd also loved the fact that she'd earned extra pocket money. It had given her spirits a real boost to know that the gifts she gave to her father at Christmas and on his birthday were bought with money earned through her own efforts. To know, too, that she could buy books or other small items for herself, and that when she gave to charity, she was donating from her personal money.

After leaving school at the age of sixteen she'd worked for her father full-time until his retirement. She'd made appointments for him, looked after his patients, typed his letters, paid his bills, ordered his supplies and kept his account books in order. She hadn't earned a lot of money as her father also paid the running costs of their home, but it had been enough to give her the independence of buying her own clothes and paying for her other expenses.

Alice hated the fact that, far from moving on with

her life, she was back to being supported by her father and marking time until Daniel supported her instead. Her father was all generosity, but Alice knew his retirement funds were modest. He'd been a kind and careful doctor but not one for mollycoddling patients who liked to be fussed over and were prepared to pay for the privilege. As a result, his practice hadn't been the most successful in London and it upset Alice to know that the more she drained his funds, the less he'd be able to afford the comforts and small luxuries he deserved after working hard for so many years.

Daniel would be all generosity too, but Alice wanted to enter the marriage with a little money of her own behind her. With a sense of pride and achievement too.

She exercised her hand daily but it would always be weak and her fingers would always be prone to painful cramping. She was managing tasks such as cooking that had once been impossible, but she was still slow and needed help with lifting anything heavy. It seemed that no one wanted to employ a secretary who could no longer type, and Alice's injury made her unsuitable for more physically challenging work.

Opportunities for employment in Churchwood were few anyway as it was a large village rather than a town. She'd still applied for jobs in neighbouring towns, keeping her applications secret because she didn't want anyone to feel sorry for her when they were rejected – as thus far they always had been. A jewellery shop had refused to employ her because, even though the job involved no heavy lifting, her injury made fastening and unfastening clasps difficult. An office manager had declined to employ her as a supervisor because he considered her too young – barely twenty – with no recent experience. Another office manager had rejected her as a bookkeeper because she struggled to lift the heavy accounts books. Alice was determined to keep trying, though.

She put her hand through a few exercises now, Daniel's ring sparkling amid her scars. He'd kissed them tenderly when he'd placed the ring on her finger, assuring her that *they* were beautiful because *she* was beautiful. Their ugliness bothered her much less these days, but she still chafed at being unable to work.

After the soup lunch, she washed the dishes and got ready to walk to the military hospital where she volunteered several times each week. It was the patients' need for books that had initially sparked the idea of the village bookshop. Now hospital and bookshop regularly came together for social events that made everyone feel part of the Churchwood community.

Alice's route took her past Brimbles Farm where Kate lived. There was no sign of her in the fields but perhaps she'd be out later when Alice returned. Kate needed friendly faces around her just now.

Arriving at the hospital, Alice exchanged smiles with Tom, the middle-aged porter who'd become a friend. 'I hear you've had a death in the village,' he said.

'Reverend Barnes.'

'Old chap, was he?'

'In his seventies, I should think.'

Tom nodded and Alice guessed he was thinking that a death that followed a long, fulfilling life was sad but the natural way of things. In contrast, the hospital patients were mostly young. Some would recover their health in full but others faced lifetimes of challenges while an unlucky few wouldn't survive at all. It was the wish to improve the men's lives that kept Alice coming to volunteer in all weathers.

Parting from Tom with another smile, she made her way to Ward One. Stratton House was a grand Palladian-style mansion that had stood empty for several years before being taken over by the military. Now it was a bustle of activity, the rows of iron beds and hospital equipment contrasting with the elegance of floor-to-ceiling French windows, wood-panelled walls and chandeliers.

Matron was in the corridor. 'Good to see you, Alice. We've a couple of new faces in. I'm sure you'll do your best to cheer them up.'

Alice had found Matron rather stern in the early days, but they'd developed a warm regard for each other.

'Got any books today?' Corporal Mikey Allardice called the moment Alice entered the ward. He had a leg injury that was taking a long time to heal.

'I expect I'll have some later.'

Alice consulted the notebook in which she kept a record of the books which were out on loan to patients and the books which they wanted to read next. A circuit of the three wards yielded nine books that patients had finished reading and Alice distributed them to other men. Returning to Ward One she smiled at the new patients, Privates Law and Webster, but neither seemed inclined to talk. Patients often took time to thaw from the shock of their injuries. 'Let me know if you ever want books,' she told them.

Billy Barker waved to catch her attention. 'If you've time, I'll be glad if you could write a letter for me.'

He'd damaged his arm but was glad to be out of the war and counting down the days until he could return to his wife and little boy.

Alice wrote a letter for Billy, chatted to some of the men who liked to laugh and joke, then read a couple of stories out loud, finally leaving the hospital to friendly calls of 'You're a ray of sunshine, Alice!' and 'Come back soon!' It was rewarding work but, like her bookshop activity, it was unpaid.

Once again Alice failed to spot Kate in the fields on the walk home. The Fletcher men didn't welcome visitors, but unless Alice saw her friend within a day or two she'd brave their disapproval and visit anyway. It wouldn't be the first time Alice had defied the Fletchers' hostility. Not that she could provide any practical help to Kate, but a visit would show that her friendship was valued.

Alice reached home to find two envelopes on the doormat. She wasn't expecting a letter from Daniel as she'd heard from him only two days ago, so she felt no particular flurry of anticipation as she carried them into the kitchen. The topmost one was addressed to her in handwriting she didn't recognize. Bookshop business? Or a letter of rejection in reply to one of her job applications?

Alice tore the envelope open and drew out a single sheet of notepaper. It had been sent from an address in St Albans.

*Dear Miss Lovell,*
*Thank you for applying for the role of part-time assis-*
*tant with regard to my memoirs. I should be obliged if*
*you would call on me one morning next week (week*

*beginning 14 April) to discuss your application
further.
Yours sincerely,
Hubert Parkinson*

Alice gasped. She had an interview! An actual interview!

She'd seen the advertisement in the *Hertfordshire Echo*: *Person wanted to assist with curating papers for a family memoir. Ten hours per week. Salary to be discussed. Apply setting out relevant experience to* . . .

Of course, her application might go no further if typing skills were required, but perhaps they wouldn't be. Alice was more than capable of reading and recording papers, photographs and the like. She had plenty to offer, even with a damaged hand.

Turning to the second envelope, she felt a jolt of surprise followed by a fizz of excitement as she realized Daniel had written again after all. He must have news for her. Was he coming home on leave?

*Dearest Alice,
I've heard that I'm being granted leave! I don't know exactly when I'll be back in England. If I can let you know, I will. Otherwise I'll simply turn up on your doorstep.
   I can't wait to see you, darling girl. In fact, I'm floating on air at the thought of it* . . .

So was Alice. Despite her worries, joy was fizzing through her veins. Daniel was coming home!

# CHAPTER THREE

## *Naomi*

Oh, dear. Naomi looked around at her fellow members of the St Luke's church council – known locally as simply the church council – and felt trepidation trickling through her like cold rain down a window. She'd spoken confidently at the bookshop meeting when she'd agreed to champion both Adam Potts and the bookshop, but all along she'd doubted her ability to be of any use. The reason for that doubt sat at the head of the table in a natty little bow tie, smiling smugly and doubtless congratulating himself on his greatness in the world – Cecil Wade, self-appointed chairman of the meeting now Septimus Barnes was dead.

If only Naomi hadn't stood down as churchwarden! She'd have been chairing the meeting herself instead of sitting on the sidelines, but she'd had no idea that Cecil, so recently arrived from Brighton, would put himself forward for the position, then set about dominating everyone else through a combination of belief in his own superiority and a way of making other people feel small.

Naomi was supposed to be communing with the Almighty, giving thanks for the life of Septimus Barnes during the moment of silence Cecil had

ordered. Instead, she was seething at Cecil's hypoc-
risy, for he'd held the old vicar in contempt and rarely
taken the trouble to conceal it. Yes, Septimus had
been foolish at times. Occasionally he'd been tiresome too, in the way he'd sought invitations to
lunches and dinners, especially at Foxfield. But his
heart had been in the right place, and he deserved
more than Cecil's sneers.

A cough from Cecil signalled the end of the silence.
They'd already discussed the wreath the council
would send to the funeral. Now Cecil rubbed his
hands as though consigning Septimus to history while
relishing his own starring role in the future he was
planning.

'I'm pleased to report that I've drawn up a rota of
visiting ministers to lead our church services while
the position of vicar is vacant. I've also been in touch
with the Diocese about the vacancy and I'm hopeful
that it won't be long before we have a new vicar in
place. The archdeacon already has someone in mind.
A first-rate fellow, from what I hear.'

Cecil loved sucking up to Church bigwigs.

'What can you tell us about this candidate?' Naomi
asked.

Cecil sighed and glanced around at the other council members – all men – inviting them to share his
exasperation in being interrupted by the silly woman
in their midst. 'Reverend Forsyth is recently returned
from Africa but I know no more at present,' he said
with exaggerated patience. 'It's early days in the
appointment process, Mrs Harrington.'

He never called her Naomi though he called

28

everyone else by their first names. She guessed it was his nasty little way of making her feel an outsider.

'*Very* early days,' he added, his tone suggesting that anyone with a modicum of intelligence would know that and not be asking asinine questions.

'I look forward to hearing more about Reverend Forsyth,' Naomi said, hoping she wasn't blushing. 'I believe other ministers can apply for the role if they, too, wish to be considered for it?'

'I can assure you that proper procedures will be followed. The Diocese has vast experience of these things.'

'No doubt. And we have experience of our village. We've built up the sort of community that works for everyone. We should ensure that the Diocese understands that and supports all aspects of it.'

'You're thinking of your so-called bookshop,' Cecil guessed, wrinkling his nose in distaste.

'Partly. The bookshop has become an important part of village life. It's also played a role in getting more people to attend church services.'

'You don't believe the work of this council and the late Reverend Barnes has had anything to do with increasing church attendance?'

'I didn't say that. I'm simply pointing out that the bookshop has made a difference too. People feel relaxed coming on to church property when visiting the bookshop. It's made some of them decide to try church services too.'

She looked around at her fellow council members again and suspected there wouldn't be an ounce of fight in any of them. Her gaze fell on Seth Padgett, the second churchwarden, but he took fright and looked away. Naomi was sure Cecil had only invited Seth to serve alongside him because he was an easy man to dominate.

Once again she wished she hadn't stepped down and let Cecil take over, but she'd had her reasons. For years Naomi had tried to compensate for her insecurities with bossiness, but while she'd certainly done some good in Churchwood, it hadn't made her much liked as a person. Gradually, she'd come to realize that people tried to ingratiate themselves into her company only because of her status as the richest woman in the village with the best house to which invitations were much coveted. Possibly, some people had been a little afraid of her too.

Recognizing that Alice's more democratic approach to getting things done was better for all concerned, Naomi had changed her ways and learned to relax her control on things. As a result, she'd formed truer friendships and grown happier. Standing down as churchwarden had been part of that retreat from bossiness. Unfortunately, she hadn't anticipated Cecil Wade stepping into her place.

'I'm thinking of encouraging Adam Potts to apply for the job,' she said now. 'Several of us feel he'd be an ideal fit for Churchwood.'

She was pleased when Wilfred Phipps said, 'Nice young man is Adam.'

Perhaps Wilfred had some backbone after all, but everyone else looked too wary of being belittled by Cecil to say a word. Not that Cecil would abuse them exactly. He simply had a way of sighing – more in sorrow than anger – then letting silence fall and stretch on and on until the person who'd challenged him could bear it no longer and muttered that perhaps they'd been mistaken. Satisfied that his will would prevail after all, Cecil would smile and, gulping in relief, the offender would mop perspiration from their brow.

'Young, though,' Cecil pointed out. 'Inexperienced.'

'He's been the curate at Barton for several years,' Naomi reasoned. 'He's always been popular when he's stood in for Reverend Barnes. He knows our ways, too.'

'He certainly knows *your* ways, Mrs Harrington.' Cecil's smile suggested that she only wanted Adam so she could wrap him around her finger.

'You won't object if I encourage him to apply?'

'It isn't for me to object,' Cecil said, with a modesty he clearly didn't feel. 'I'm sure all applications will be considered on their merits.'

Naomi didn't approve of violence but her hand itched to slap the smugness from his face.

They discussed a few more matters, and then the meeting concluded. 'It'll be good to have Adam Potts taking the service on Sunday,' Wilfred Phipps said to Naomi as they left the Sunday School Hall.

'It will. I'll have a word with him then about applying for the Churchwood role.'

'Good luck,' Wilf said.

Naomi felt encouraged. Perhaps she could win support from other council members if she approached each one privately rather than hoping they'd stand up to Cecil in meetings. If several supported her, she might convince them that there'd be safety in numbers from Cecil's displeasure.

Pushing that awful man from her mind temporarily, she spared a few moments of sympathy for poor Kate – how typical of her brothers to join up without consideration for anyone else – and then turned her thoughts to Alexander.

'I'll be home tonight,' he'd told her on the telephone.

'How nice,' she'd replied, keen to maintain the appearance of a happy marriage even if the past year had brought her to the realization that it was a loveless one.

At twenty Naomi had been plain, tongue-tied and hampered by a father she adored but who was considered a common little man by the society into which he hoped to introduce himself and his daughter. When dashing Alexander Harrington took an interest in her, she'd been hugely relieved. And when her father died unexpectedly – her mother having died many years earlier – Naomi had been glad to marry the man who swore he loved her.

She'd fought a long battle with disillusionment over the years that followed but had finally stopped resisting the obvious and accepted that the only thing Alexander loved was the fortune she'd inherited from the sale of her father's quack tonics business. Not that she'd been half as rich as he'd hoped.

Naomi had still tried hard to make the marriage happy, and it saddened her to know she'd been unsuccessful. She was particularly grieved that they'd had no children. Still, as long as they treated each other with respect, she was content for the marriage to limp on. Alexander had his career and his golf. Naomi had her friends and the bookshop.

Suki must have been on the watch for her because she opened the door as her mistress reached it. 'Mr Harrington has arrived, madam.'

Doubtless a friend with a mysterious supply of petrol had dropped him off. Alexander's own petrol ration was nowhere near enough to get him to and from his London office each day, let alone around the country for golf. As a result, he'd decided to live mostly at the London flat as he wasn't the sort of man to demean himself on trains and buses if there was any way of avoiding mixing with the rough and ready sections of humanity. Naomi hadn't had the use of the Daimler since the beginning of the war, of course.

She handed her coat to Suki, accepted the maid's offer of tea, and went into the small sitting room where she spent most of her time. There was a mirror over the mantelpiece and she used it to check her appearance and tidy her hair. Not that she had any hope of Alexander finding her attractive, but a woman had her pride. Satisfied that at least she looked neat, she patted the head of Basil, her mournful-looking English bulldog, then left the room to tap on the door to Alexander's study.

'Come in,' he called.

Naomi entered and he glanced up from his desk, nodding by way of a greeting. Even at fifty he was a good-looking man with clean-cut features and the sort of sharp blue eyes that could scare people a little.

'Good journey home?' she asked.

'Giles Dawning dropped me.'

'It's good to see you. About dinner . . .'

'A tray will suit me best. I need to work.' He gestured to the papers on his desk.

'Of course.' Naomi hadn't really expected him to eat with her. 'Suki is making tea.'

'I've already told her I don't want any.' He'd poured himself a glass of whisky from the crystal decanter he kept in the room.

'Septimus Barnes passed away on Monday,' she said.

'Oh?'

'It's believed his heart gave out.'

Alexander nodded but clearly wasn't interested, having only ever felt contempt for the vicar's fawning ways.

'I'll let you get on,' she told him. 'I think I'll have my tea upstairs. It's been a busy day and I'd like to rest my feet before dinner.'

Alexander only grunted.

Suki appeared with a tray as Naomi left the study. 'Could you take it upstairs, please?' Naomi asked.

'A rest before dinner. Just the ticket.' Suki was a sweet little thing.

Naomi fetched Basil and followed Suki upstairs. After the maid had left, Naomi kicked off her shoes with a sigh of relief. She had wide feet that ached often. Plumping up her pillows, she climbed on to the bed while Basil settled on the rug she kept beside it especially for him. But she'd left her book downstairs. It was a romance involving a pretty girl called Louella and a handsome Adonis called Raul. Nonsense, really, but Naomi was enjoying it, even if the characters' torrid emotions highlighted the coolness that existed between herself and Alexander.

She heaved herself off the bed, made her way down the carpeted stairs in her slippers and retrieved the book from behind a cushion in her sitting room. The chances of Alexander going in there had been small, but Naomi still hadn't wanted to risk him seeing the book and giving one of his lip-curling sneers. Not wanting him to catch her with it now, she retraced her steps, walking as quietly as she could manage, given that she was no lightweight.

She was passing the door to Alexander's study when she heard laughter. Alexander's laughter, but not his usual hard bark. This laughter was soft. Intimate. And it stopped her in her tracks.

Heart beating faster, she moved closer to the door and heard him speak. She couldn't make out the words but, again, the tone was . . . tender? Seductive?

No, it couldn't be. The solid wooden door must be distorting the sound.

She stiffened as she heard movement in the kitchen. Not wanting to be found eavesdropping, Naomi hastened upstairs. But she didn't read a word of Raul and Louella's story. Her mind was too full of what she'd heard – or thought she might have heard.

But it was ridiculous to suspect Alexander of an affair. Not for a moment had he ever given her cause to wonder if there might be someone else, and even in the early days of their marriage he'd shown little interest in physical intimacy. He was too austere. Too cold.

Or was he only austere and cold with her? Might there be another side to the cool, irritable man she knew? A warmer side he showed only to the woman – or women – he saw behind Naomi's back? After all, he'd always had plenty of opportunity, having spent much of his time away from home even before the onset of wartime petrol shortages. Only rarely had a week passed without him spending one, two or even three nights in the London flat as he'd often worked late or entertained clients. Weekends, too, had frequently been given over to clients or golf. In fact, some of his golfing tours had lasted a week or more.

But no. Alexander simply wasn't a philandering sort of man. Naomi reached for her tea but the doubts crept back, carving a hollow of uncertainty inside her. It was one thing to know their marriage was loveless. Naomi could live with that. But could she live with the insult – the disrespect – of being betrayed, especially while Alexander continued to enjoy her money?

Basil let out a whimper as though sensing her distress and Naomi reached down to caress his ugly head. 'What am I going to do?' she asked him.

The sensible thing was surely to do nothing because she was letting her imagination take flight over something she might simply have misheard. It wasn't going to be easy, though. Naomi could feel the worm of suspicion burrowing into her head even now. *Alexander might be having an affair,* it whispered.

'Oh, shut up!' Naomi told it out loud, startling poor Basil.

She turned her thoughts to the bookshop instead. What a difference it had made to her life. It had brought her friends. Real friends, who kept loneliness at bay and made her feel a valued member of the community instead of a woman who stood on the sidelines barking orders at others. It made her feel useful, too, because the bookshop helped people and Naomi was part of that. It also made her smile and laugh and enjoy the sort of carefree fun she'd never known before. It would leave a huge hole in her life if it closed.

A picture of Cecil Wade came into her mind. When Basil shuffled closer and gave a sorrowful whine, Naomi felt he was speaking for both of them.

# CHAPTER FOUR

## *Kate*

Breakfast at Brimbles Farm had always been an unpleasant experience for Kate. A typical day involved the Fletcher men grabbing the food with filthy hands and scattering crumbs in all directions as they crammed it into their mouths. Fred 'n' Frank would fight over something or other. Vinnie would indulge his spitefulness by spilling tea or smearing butter over the table. Meanwhile, Ernie and Kenny would talk grumpily about farm matters. Today was worse, though. Today all was grimness.

Ernie hunkered over his plate, glancing up only occasionally to glare at the twins and mutter, 'Idiots!'

Vinnie's malice was in temporary abeyance following a slap round the head from Ernie, while Kenny stared gloomily into space and the twins sulked because they were in disgrace.

Kate was glad when they all went outside to work, though as she pegged out washing she could hear distant complaints about a problem with the tractor. Broken machinery would be all they needed to make a bad time worse.

The twins' wild and selfish behaviour had long appalled Kate, but it chilled her to think of them going into danger. This must be how Alice, May and

Janet felt, for all three had loved ones involved in the war – a fiancé, a husband and a son. The constant dread of bad news was going to be terrible.

Realizing her name was being called, Kate looked around to see Alice over by the orchard and went to join her.

'I was calling you for ages,' Alice said.

'Sorry.'

'You've a lot on your mind.'

True, but Alice had a lot on her mind, too, and rarely complained about it. Following her example, Kate attempted a smile. 'On your way to Stratton House?'

'Yes, but I've been thinking about how you're going to manage here. Has your father considered getting other help in?'

Kate's smile turned to a grimace. 'Can you imagine Ernie paying proper wages?'

'It'll be better for him to pay wages if it keeps the farm in profit,' Alice pointed out, 'but I'm actually thinking of the Women's Land Army.'

'Land girls?'

Alice nodded. 'They might be cheaper to employ than men.'

'True, but I can't see women wanting to work in this pigsty of a place.'

'What's the alternative?' Alice could always cut straight to the heart of the matter. Kate didn't have an alternative.

'Your father and brothers may be repellent but *you're* not.' Alice continued. 'You could help land girls to settle and feel comfortable.'

'You really think so?'

'I do, and I also think you should leave no stone

39

unturned in trying to preserve your time off and wages.'

'I could make some enquiries,' Kate agreed, though she was still struggling to imagine land girls being happy on Brimbles Farm.

'Naomi has offered to make the enquiries for you since she has a telephone. Shall I tell her to go ahead?'

'Yes, please, though I'll have to speak to Ernie before I commit to anything. How *is* Naomi? Has she had any luck with the church council?'

'Cecil Wade isn't helping.'

'That man is a pompous clown,' Kate declared.

'Smug with it, and one of those men who doesn't like women much.'

'An idiot, then.'

Alice smiled. 'Hopefully, not too powerful an idiot. Naomi plans to speak to all the council members personally about getting the right man in post as vicar. As for Adam, he'll be leading the service on Sunday morning so we're both going to talk to him about applying for the job.'

'That's good to hear.'

'Well, I won't keep you from your work any longer.'

Alice was always sensitive to the needs of others. Kate was about to thank her when she realized there was something particularly sparkling about Alice today.

'You've heard from Daniel?' Kate guessed.

'He thinks he'll be granted leave soon.'

'That's wonderful!' How typical of Alice to keep her good news to herself for fear of rubbing Kate's nose in her relative misfortune. 'I'll keep my fingers crossed for him.'

40

Alice began to move away. 'Think about those land girls, Kate.'

'I will.'

Kate did think about them. 'We need more help on the farm,' she announced when the family gathered for lunch.

Kenny rolled his eyes at this statement of the obvious and Vinnie snorted with enjoyment because he loved conflict in the family when it didn't involve him.

She took no notice of either of them. 'I have an idea for how we might get that help.'

'What's that, genius?' Kenny drawled.

'Land girls.'

'Slips of girls?' Ernie scoffed.

'I'm not suggesting they could do the same amount of work as Fred 'n' Frank but they could do *some* work.'

'They'd be useless.'

'Like I'm useless?' Kate retorted. 'If that's the case, I might as well stop working now.'

'You'll do your duty, girl. And watch your lip.'

'We won't cope without help,' Kate pointed out. 'The farm will lose money.'

Skinflint Ernie didn't like the thought of losing money. He shifted in his chair.

'Who's got a better idea?' Kate demanded.

No one answered.

'These land girls. They'd want paying?' Kenny asked.

'I expect so. But I also expect that, being female, their wages would be lower than men's.'

'Would they be local?'

'I doubt it. We'd need to put them up and feed them.'

'Put them up where?' Fred demanded.

'In your room.'

'Our room?' Fred 'n' Frank exchanged outraged looks. 'Where would we stay when we're home on leave?'

'You should have thought of that before you joined up,' Ernie pointed out.

'You could sleep in the barn,' Kenny told them.

'Wouldn't be much fun in winter,' Frank complained, but the twins had caused this mess and no one thought they were due any sympathy.

'Shall I look into the possibility of getting land girls?' Kate asked.

She wasn't expecting an answer and she got none. The Fletcher men would as soon credit her with a good idea as they'd learn how to waltz, but their silence was agreement enough.

Kate's mood lifted. Land girls might not only help on the farm and allow Kate some life of her own – they might also be fun.

But would they want to come to a rough place like Brimbles Farm? Would they even be allowed to come? The Women's Land Army surely wouldn't send them to any old dump. Time would doubtless tell.

# CHAPTER FIVE

## *Alice*

By mutual agreement Alice and Naomi set out for church early on Easter Sunday morning. 'Let's warn Adam that we'd like a word after the service so he doesn't rush off,' Alice had suggested. Not that Adam was the sort of person to rush off without good reason. He made time for people.

As they walked through the village now Alice saw that lines of strain were etched into her friend's forehead. 'I hope you're not taking it too much to heart if Cecil Wade is being unpleasant,' Alice said.

'He's always unpleasant. To me, anyway.'

'To most people, because he thinks he's better than the rest of us. But it won't be your fault if the church council goes along with whatever he suggests. People like Cecil have influence because they make people afraid of looking small.'

'We'll see,' Naomi said, but her frown remained.

They found Adam in the vestry.

There was nothing impressive in his appearance. He was small and slightly built with an abundance of unruly dark hair that always looked to be in urgent need of a cut. His suit was old and shiny with wear, while his equally ancient shoes looked to be strangers to shoe polish. But his brown eyes were kind and his smile sweet.

'I was sorry to hear about Reverend Barnes,' he said.

They spent a moment talking respectfully of the former vicar then stood aside as three choirboys entered, grinning and calling, 'Hello, Adam!'

He was a great favourite with Churchwood's young people. With the village's older people too, many of whom wanted to mother him by smartening him up and feeding him.

'Might we have a word after the service?' Alice asked.

'Of course.'

More chattering choirboys came in.

'Look, Adam. My brother gave me some marbles . . .'

'You must come and see my puppy, Adam . . .'

'Adam, my shoelace has broken . . .'

Leaving him to the merry chaos, Alice left the vestry with Naomi, declaring, 'He'll be perfect for Churchwood.'

'If we can get him.'

At that moment Marjorie Plym arrived and waved to catch Naomi's attention, clearly wanting her friend to witness what she doubtless considered to be her moment in the spotlight.

'Yes, it was me who found poor Reverend Barnes,' Marjorie began saying to anyone who would listen. 'Such a shock! Naomi had to revive me with sherry . . .'

Hiding a private smile, Alice walked off to sit down and soon the service began.

Afterwards, everyone appeared to want to speak to

Adam, but eventually the crowd thinned and he invited Alice and Naomi back to the vestry.

'Lovely service,' Naomi said.

'Thank you. I'm sure you missed Reverend Barnes, though.'

In truth Adam was far more popular than Septimus, but it would have been unkind to the old vicar to say so.

'Now Reverend Barnes is no longer here, many of us in Churchwood would welcome you as our new vicar,' Alice said.

'Really? How kind!'

'Do you think you might apply for the position?'

'I'd love to come to St Luke's if you really want me, but I'm not sure I'd be the Diocese's first choice.' Adam smiled crookedly. He wasn't one of the those dignified, High Church men who stood on ceremony. He lived life simply and kindly. To Adam, kicking balls around with children was more important than steering clear of mud, while holding the hands of sick parishioners all through the night was more important than sprucing himself up.

'We *do* really want you,' Alice assured him, and Naomi nodded.

'Then I'll certainly give it some thought.'

Movement at the vestry window caught their attention. Marjorie Plym was looking in on them, obviously curious about what they were saying. It was time to leave.

Outside, Alice said, 'It wouldn't hurt for us to write to Adam so he knows we're serious about wanting him to apply.'

'We should ask as many people as possible to write

45

to him,' Naomi agreed, then made a visible attempt to brace herself as Marjorie approached.

'There you are, Naomi. I wondered where you'd gone.'

Alice sent Naomi a sympathetic smile and went on her way.

'I'm thinking of going to St Albans tomorrow,' she told her father when she reached the cottage. 'Is there anything I can get for you while I'm there?'

'I don't think so, my dear, though I appreciate the offer.'

Alice visited St Albans occasionally on bookshop business. This time she planned to call on Hubert Parkinson about the job he'd advertised, but there was no point in setting her father up for disappointment by mentioning it to him. He already felt guilty about moving to Churchwood where job opportunities were few, and she had no wish to add to that guilt.

Mr Parkinson lived in a substantial Edwardian house in Avenue Road, a short walk from the bus stop. A maid opened the door to Alice's knock, bade her to wait on a nearby chair and then walked towards the back of the house. Alice duly sat and looked around. The hall was square and spacious, but also museum-like with a dark wooden coat stand, a brass pot for umbrellas and shadowy oil paintings on the walls. Portraits of Mr Parkinson's ancestors?

'This way, please,' the maid said, reappearing.

Alice followed her into a room that contained walls of glass-fronted bookcases, a sturdy mahogany desk and boxes of what looked to be old papers on the floor around it.

The man who got up from behind the desk was around the same age and height as Alice's father, but his dark hair, dark spectacles and dark suit gave him a more solid, sober appearance. 'Good morning, Miss Lovell. I'm Hubert Parkinson.'

'Thank you for seeing me.'

They shook hands, then Alice was invited to sit. Now she was closer to the boxes she could see that some contained notebooks and photographs as well as old documents, but she didn't like to stare at them.

'I'm writing a history of my family,' he told her. 'I believe I mentioned it in my advertisement.'

'You did, and it sounds interesting.'

'Some of it, certainly. I've never been much of an adventurer myself, but other members of the family have been more intrepid. A great-uncle took part in Shackleton's expedition to the South Pole and was stranded there for more than a year. A distant cousin was a Member of Parliament and even my grandmother was celebrated for her watercolour paintings. That's one of hers over there.'

Alice looked round and saw a painting of a countryside scene. 'It's beautiful.'

'I feel the history of the family shouldn't be lost and now I'm retired I'd like to record it. Not for publication and not for my own children as I have none, but for nieces, nephews, cousins . . .'

'I understand.'

'I need help with organizing diaries, letters, photographs, newspaper reports and that sort of thing. You mentioned in your application that you organized your father's medical practice.'

'I did, though he's retired now too.'

'And since then?'

'I help to organize a bookshop in the village where I live, though the word *bookshop* doesn't quite describe what we offer.' She told him about the talks and activities. 'I also volunteer at the local military hospital where I run a library, read stories and write letters for patients who can't write themselves.'

'You wouldn't find the work here tedious? It would involve looking through old paperwork and photographs. Keeping careful records of them too. And much of the time you'd be working alone.'

'May I see?' She gestured to one of the boxes.

'Please do.'

Alice took out some of the contents and they talked about them for a while. Then Alice suggested cataloguing them in several ways – by item type, by date and by the family member to whom they related. 'Only if that suited your purposes, of course.'

'It would suit my purpose admirably,' he said, and Alice was thrilled.

But then Mr Parkinson brought her spirits crashing down to earth. 'You'd need to decipher my handwriting, of course, so you could type out my notes and manuscript.'

*Ah.* 'I used to be a competent typist,' Alice told him, 'but I can only type a little now due to an injury.' It was a painfully slow process as she could only use one hand.

He appeared to notice her scars for the first time. 'What a pity,' he said, his tone making it clear that she hadn't got the job, after all.

Disappointment swooped in on her. Would she ever get paid work again? 'I could manage the other

48

aspects of the job,' she pointed out, then chided herself for sounding desperate. She was probably embarrassing the poor man.

She got to her feet. 'I'm sorry I wasted your time.'

Alice left quickly but the bus home wasn't due for more than an hour and she wasn't in the mood for shopping. She walked around for a while, trying to get on top of the setback by reminding herself that she wasn't going to starve or struggle to keep a roof over her head. Besides, Daniel would be home soon and nothing could diminish her joy in that. But it was still a crying shame she'd be unable to tell Daniel and her father that she had a job. They'd worry about her less if they knew she was moving forward in her life, and Alice's own self-esteem would fly high.

She came to a halt in the street, ashamed of her self-pity. She was outside a cinema and, though she had neither time nor inclination to sit through the feature, she decided to go in to watch the Pathé newsreels about the war. She was just in time to see a film about the Blitz on London. Newspapers had pictured the damage aplenty, but the film brought the attacks to devastating life, recording searchlights scouring the sky for enemy planes, explosions, buildings burning or reduced to rubble, homeless families picking their way over the debris . . .

Compared to their suffering, rejection from a job was a trivial matter. Tears came into her eyes at the thought of the people who were enduring night after night of bombing, often losing loved ones and homes. If a stray tear was for herself, Alice refused to admit it.

# CHAPTER SIX

## *Naomi*

'Hmm,' Bert Makepiece said as Naomi stepped out of the Post Office.

She'd kept up a show of cheerfulness inside the shop but allowed her expression to slump on leaving and Bert had caught her out. Several days had passed since she'd heard Alexander laughing in the study but, try as she might, she'd been unable to purge it from her mind. With uncertainty over the bookshop and her frustration with Cecil Wade worrying her too, Naomi's sleep was suffering and she knew she must be looking as haggard as she felt.

But the last thing she wanted just now was to talk about her problems, even to a good friend like Bert. She especially didn't want to talk about the Alexander situation. After all, she wasn't yet sure that there *was* an Alexander situation.

Bert wasn't an easy man to fool, but she tried it anyway, summoning a smile. 'Sorry, Bert, I was away with the fairies just then. How are you?'

'I'm fine and dandy. It's you who isn't.'

'Me?' Naomi faked surprise.

'Yes, you, woman.' He folded his arms over his bulky middle and stood with the air of someone who'd wait all day for an answer, if that was what it took.

Sighing, she opted for the truth, even if it wasn't the whole truth. 'I admit I'm not feeling my best. Cecil Wade . . .' She let the explanation hang in the air, hoping it would be enough.

'He's an idiot.'

'He is. But don't worry. I won't give him the satisfaction of browbeating me.' Fighting talk, but it made no impression on Bert.

'Hmm,' he said. 'Like that again, is it?'

She didn't want to ask what he meant but *not* asking would be tantamount to admitting that it was indeed like that again. 'Like what, Bert?'

'You bottling up your problems instead of sharing them with your friends.'

Naomi feigned puzzlement again. 'I've just shared my problem. Cecil Wade.'

Bert only rolled his eyes. 'Spare me the playacting, Mrs H. It wasn't Sanctimonious Cecil as put that look on your face.' He looked at her for a moment longer, then threw his arms into the air as though giving up the inquisition. 'Have it your way.'

*Thank goodness!*

'For now,' he added.

Bert's tone was ominous, but, grateful to be allowed even temporary relief from his questions, Naomi asked one of her own.

'Have you managed to write to Adam Potts about his application?'

'I have, and I'm just about to post the letter. For good measure, I've also written to the church council to let them know that, as a churchgoer, I'd welcome young Adam as our next vicar. Yours shouldn't be a lone voice in the council wilderness.'

'That was an excellent idea, Bert. I appreciate it. Well, I'd better get on.'

'Going home to ponder whatever's troubling you?' he asked. 'That's an excellent idea too. And while you're pondering, remember you have friends who'd like to help. Be seeing you, Mrs H.' He shambled off towards his truck.

Naomi felt sudden tears prickle her eyes. Kindness could ambush a person when they least wanted it, especially when they were feeling tired and fragile. Breathing deeply, she blinked to drive the prickles away and then turned for home.

*Be seeing you, Mrs H.*

Bert called her Mrs H when he wanted to take a poke at her pride because, back in the past when she'd taken her dignity too seriously, she'd insisted on being called Mrs Harrington. She'd known Bert Makepiece since moving to Churchwood not long after her marriage but as a scruffy market gardener he hadn't moved in her circle. Only in the last year or so, after Bert had practically dragged her on to the bookshop's organizing team, had they become friends. In the process he'd made her take a long, hard look at the bossy, snobby person she'd become and for that Naomi would always be grateful.

But it wasn't pride that had her keeping her suspicions to herself. Well, perhaps there was *some* pride involved. No one liked to be made a fool of, after all. But mostly what she was feeling was hurt. It might be groundless hurt, though, and, instead of prematurely rushing into confidences, Naomi wanted to settle in her head whether she had cause to suspect Alexander and, if so, what she should do about it.

Reaching Foxfield, she sat in her sitting room to think. She'd certainly heard laughter in Alexander's study but had it really been as soft and intimate as she'd thought? She'd asked herself that question numerous times over the past few days but she still couldn't fix on an answer.

She could try to get to the truth by confronting Alexander, of course, but Naomi shuddered at the thought of that. Their relationship might be remote and empty, but if he were innocent of an affair, an accusation could stir up all sorts of anger and resentment from which their marriage might never recover. And if he were guilty . . . Even if he promised to give up his lover and never take another, Naomi's trust in him would be broken. And what if he didn't promise? Was she prepared for a separation, a divorce, a scandal . . . ?

She didn't feel prepared for anything. The safer option still appeared to be to put the soft laughter from her mind. But Naomi had tried that and, thus far, it hadn't worked. So what was she to do?

Nothing yet, she decided. It would be foolish to rush into an action she might later regret. Better to bide her time and see how her feelings developed, though she needed to keep a tighter guard on them if she was to stop them from showing in her face and worrying her friends.

Enough brooding for now. Naomi reached for the notes she was making of her conversations with individual members of the church council.

'Adam Potts is a pleasant young man,' Reuben Bates had agreed. 'But Cecil says the Diocese may have even better candidates for us to consider. After all, the Diocese has the parish's best interests at heart.'

'I like young Mr Potts too,' Lionel Smith had told her. 'But Cecil says we shouldn't offend the Diocese by giving the impression that we won't welcome their contribution to the selection process.'

It was the same with the other four council members to whom she'd spoken so far: Adam was very much liked, but *Cecil said . . .*

They were all awed by Cecil.

She made a mental note of the council members she had yet to approach, then turned her thoughts to Kate and the problems on the farm. Alice's suggestion of employing land girls was a good one – they wouldn't make up completely for the absence of those strapping twins, but they'd surely be of some use, and it might be nice for Kate to have female companionship.

Naomi picked up the phone to call the Women's Land Army.

# CHAPTER SEVEN

## *Kate*

Looking around the farmhouse kitchen, Kate wondered if there was a more wretchedly inadequate bunch of people in all the world.

The twins stood on one side, awkward yet defiant as the minutes ticked down to their departure. Ernie and Kenny stood on the other side, angry and stiff but blinking and swallowing often. Standing beside them, Vinnie appeared to realize this wasn't the time for malicious tricks but, having little experience of anything else, he looked out of his depth and unsure of how to behave.

'Oh, for goodness' sake!' Kate burst out, crossing the room to hug the twins. 'Look after each other, and keep yourselves safe,' she instructed them.

'We'll be fine,' Frank said.

'Yeah, fine,' agreed Fred, but it was bravado speaking – neither of them could know what the future held.

'Here.' She handed each twin a parcel. 'Sandwiches, ginger beer and cigarettes. And in case you're wondering . . .' She turned to Ernie. 'I paid for the cigarettes and ginger beer myself.'

'Nice!' Frank said.

The rumble of a truck announced the arrival of the

twins' friends Billy and Tommy. Billy's cousin was taking them all to catch the train. 'We'll be going then,' Frank said.

Picking up their bags, the twins headed outside.

The rest of them followed, watching as the twins swung their bags on to the back of the truck.

'Well?' Kate demanded of her brothers.

Kenny gave a self-conscious cough and walked across to offer a hand to Frank.

'Eh?' Frank said, unused to social etiquette in the Fletcher family.

'He wants to shake your hand, idiot,' Fred said, grinning, though he was pale now.

Kenny shook Frank's hand and then took hold of Fred's. 'Good luck,' he told them both before stepping back, looking uncomfortable and unsure of what to do next.

'Vinnie?' Kate prompted.

'Good luck!' Vinnie called, but she nudged him forward and, sheepishly, he made his way to his brothers and play-punched each one on the shoulder. 'Good luck!' he repeated.

It was too much to expect Ernie to follow suit, but he nodded at the twins and Kate saw that he was holding himself rigidly, as though fighting to keep his emotions inside in case they made him look weak.

The twins climbed into the truck and everyone except Ernie waved as it rumbled away. 'Be safe,' Kate whispered.

'Back to work,' Ernie barked when the truck was no longer in sight, but he headed for the lavatory where Kate guessed he'd battle to get on top of his feelings.

Returning indoors, she went up to the twins' room and stood at the door, looking in. It was a medium-sized room containing two narrow beds with iron frames, two chairs – one with a leg missing due to some tomfoolery on the twins' part – a chest of drawers and a tall cupboard. None of the Fletchers owned much in the way of possessions but the twins had still managed to leave their marks behind in the form of a sock sticking out from under Fred's bed, empty beer bottles on the window ledge, an ashtray overflowing with cigarette butts on the chest of drawers, discarded underwear hanging from Frank's bed and cold, scummy water in a shaving bowl.

There was an unpleasant odour of sweat and old tobacco. Kate crossed to the window, encountering the stickiness of spilt beer underfoot, and opened it wide. Fresher air entered and began to drive out the staleness but for a moment Kate was tempted to close the window again to keep the smell of her brothers in the room for a little longer. Brimbles Farm wouldn't be the same without them. Kate would miss them and fear for them until the day they returned. But in the meantime, the farm needed extra workers urgently. That meant land girls – who needed a decent place to sleep. Even cleaned up, this sorry room might not satisfy them but Kate would do her best to make it habitable.

She noticed someone waving over by the orchard. Alice. Kate waved back, then hastened downstairs to go and greet her.

'I'm on my way to Stratton House,' Alice said, 'but Naomi asked me to tell you she has information from the Women's Land Army for you.'

'I'll call in on her, though I've been looking at the twins' room and I can't imagine girls wanting to sleep in there.'

'I'm sure you can make it clean and tidy, even if you can't change the furniture.'

'I'll certainly try.'

Kate called at Foxfield while out shopping. With Naomi's help, she wrote an application for two land girls to start as soon as possible.

'You took your time,' Ernie complained when Kate reached home again. He was sitting at the kitchen table, oiling shears as he waited for his lunch.

'That's because I've been busy. You need to sign this.'

She put the application in front of him along with a pen.

'Eh?'

'I'm asking for two land girls – if we can get them. Or would you rather I didn't bother?'

'How much will I have to pay them?'

'At least twenty-eight shillings a week each.'

Ernie almost choked. 'Twenty-eight shillings a week for slips of girls!'

'That's ten shillings a week less than you'd have to pay a man. Fourteen shillings can be kept back for board and lodging, but I'll need that for their food. And while we're on the subject of money, I'll have another pay rise.'

'You won't!'

'I will, or I'll register for war work somewhere else. I'll settle for seven and six a week. That's still much less than land girl wages. If we can get the land girls, that is. The inspector may take one look at this place and declare it fit only for pigs.'

Vinnie had come in and caught the end of the conversation. 'You're not going to let Kate speak to you like that?' he demanded.

'Oh, shut up,' Ernie told him. Snatching the pen up, he scribbled something that would hopefully pass as a signature.

Kate posted the application in the village later that afternoon, calling at Alice's cottage on the way home. 'I just wanted to let you know the application has been sent and to say hello as I might not have another chance for a while now the twins have gone.'

'I'll keep my fingers crossed for you getting land girls soon,' Alice said.

Kate hesitated, and then asked, 'Naomi was wonderfully helpful, but she didn't seem herself to me.'

'Cecil Wade is making things difficult on the church council. I've told her she can only do her best to persuade the council to champion Adam and the bookshop, but I'm not sure I'm getting through to her.'

'I wish I could do more to help.'

'You're in a tricky situation. We all understand that.'

It occurred to Kate then that Alice was looking out of sorts too. 'Have you heard when Daniel's arriving?' Surely Daniel would bring the sparkle back to Alice's eyes?

'Bad news, I'm afraid. His leave has been delayed due to sickness. Not Daniel's sickness, thankfully, but other men have gone down with some sort of bug, and he can't be spared until they're better.'

'I'm sorry.'

'Hopefully, it'll only mean a short delay.' Alice

smiled but she always put on a brave face in bad situations and Kate knew her disappointment must be intense.

As ever, work on the farm awaited Kate and prompted her speedy departure. Cycling home, she reflected that it wasn't only so she could enjoy the company of her friends that she hoped her application for land girls succeeded. Without help with her workload, Kate would find it impossible to be a good friend in return.

# CHAPTER EIGHT

## *Alice*

**Still no news of my leave,** Daniel had written.

> *If you're half as disappointed as me then you're very disappointed indeed. But it's postponed rather than cancelled so I hope to be with you soon. Please don't feel you have to go to any trouble to entertain me. I'm looking forward to enjoying simple things – working in your vegetable patch, feeding your chickens, walking around the lake . . . I'm looking forward to visiting the bookshop and getting to know your friends better, too. I'll have to see my parents, of course – also my godmother – but I hope to spend most of my time with you, darling girl. Just tell me if I get under your feet!*

Alice would love to have Daniel cluttering up the cottage and getting under her feet. She pictured him in her head – fresh-faced with a warm smile and dark eyes that softened when he looked at her with affection or desire . . .

Impatience swept through her, but all she could do was endure the waiting.

Alice had other worries too. Two weeks on from her failed interview with Mr Parkinson, she'd seen no other jobs advertised for which she stood even the slenderest chance of being considered. She was also concerned about both Kate and Naomi. Then there was St Luke's. It would be reassuring to know the new vicar would support the bookshop.

With no magic wand to wave over her problems, Alice could only concentrate on preparing for the future as best she could. As a precaution against Cecil Wade speaking badly of the bookshop, she was collecting favourable testimonials and the number of them was growing.

*I am a widow and the bookshop gives me comfort and companionship in difficult times,* Edna Hall.

*It was only because I missed a bookshop session that people realized I was unwell and rallied round to help,* Ada Hayes.

*It was attending a bookshop talk on Digging for Victory that got me started on growing vegetables. Now I can afford to feed my family nutritious food,* Mary Webb.

*Going to the bookshop gets me out of the house when I am feeling low,* William Treloar.

*I've learned to sew at the bookshop and am proud to have made my little granddaughter a dress she badly needs. I used old curtains as fabric,* Joan Lamb.

*I am a refugee from Poland. The bookshop helps me to learn English so I am doing well at school,* Rosa Kovac, age 11.

*I've made new friends at the bookshop,* Michael Palfrey, age 7.

*I was at the bookshop when I mentioned that my cooker had broken. Straight away people came round with hot soups and offered me the use of their stoves.*

*One of them even managed to fix my stove's problem,* Margaret Webster.

*I am a patient at Stratton House military hospital, having been injured in the service of my country. I know I speak for my fellow patients as well as myself when I say that visiting the bookshop for talks and socials cheers us up no end,* Private Wally McAndrew.

*I am unable to afford books or magazines. Reading them at the bookshop has taught me all sorts of useful things, from what is going on in the world to tasty recipes,* Maria Gibb (Miss).

*I am the matron at Stratton House military hospital and can say wholeheartedly that the bookshop does wonders for the spirits of the patients. It also provides an opportunity for staff to meet village residents and enjoy their time off duty,* Maureen Peters.

Hopefully, the bookshop wouldn't need defending, but it was no bad thing to have a record of how it was helping. She might even show the testimonials to Daniel. She'd already told him about the death of Septimus Barnes and her hope that Adam would become the new vicar but, not wanting Daniel to worry, she hadn't mentioned the problems with Cecil Wade.

Already three weeks had passed since Reverend Barnes's departure from the world. Naomi had warned that replacing him could take months but with Adam and the archdeacon's man waiting in the wings the process might be quicker. With luck, by the time Daniel arrived, Adam would have been appointed and the future of the bookshop assured.

After filing the testimonials in her bookshop folder, Alice set out on the long walk to the hospital. She saw no sign of Kate on Brimbles Farm but wished her well anyway.

Arriving at Stratton House, she collected and distributed books, wrote three letters for patients and then pulled up a chair read a story out loud.

Called 'The Enemy in Room 46', it was about a German spy who was caught thanks to the intrepid intervention of Private Harry Baggins, who happened to be passing through London on his way home on leave.

'That was a cracker of a story,' Larry Porter told her.

'Three cheers for Harry Baggins,' Ben Dodd said.

'And three cheers for Alice for reading to us,' said Wally McAndrew. Seeing Matron hovering, he corrected himself rapidly. 'What I meant to say was, three cheers for Miss Lovell for reading it to us.'

Walking past, Matron sent Alice a wink.

'When is the next bookshop social?' Wally wanted to know.

'Hopefully soon,' Alice told him, amid murmurs of enthusiasm from other patients.

Alice had been dragging her heels about arranging another social, not wanting to disappoint the men should the new vicar take a dim view of gramophone records, beer and dancing on church property. But as she walked home, she wondered if it might be possible to squeeze a social event into the calendar before any decision about the new vicar was made. After all, they might lose their chance of a party if Cecil Wade had his way.

She glanced across at Brimbles Farm again in passing. She could see the Fletcher men gathered around the tractor but there was still no sign of Kate.

Alice ate a quick lunch then headed for the bookshop, pleased when Adam Potts came in, dishevelled after cycling five miles from Barton.

'Can I persuade you to read a story?' she asked.

Adam was almost as good at reading out loud as Kate.

'I'd love to.' He took the book she offered.

'Bicycle clips,' Alice reminded him, and, laughing, he bent to pull them off his trousers.

He got down on a rug with the children and one little girl worked her way on to his lap to sit sucking her thumb. Two others leaned against him, and all the others gathered as close as they could manage. They all loved Adam and he loved them.

'Today's story is "The Littlest Raindrop",' he announced. '*Once upon a time, a tiny raindrop lived in a cloud high up in the sky . . .*'

He didn't stop when the outer door to the hall opened and closed, assuming a latecomer had arrived, but then unfamiliar voices could be heard in the vestibule. A moment later the inner door opened and three people entered, only to pull up short in surprise. 'Goodness, what have we here?' one asked.

Adam scrambled to his feet. 'Archdeacon! This is an unexpected pleasure.'

'So it would appear.' Archdeacon Francis Rudge looked Adam up and down, clearly noting his unpolished shoes and untidy hair, then sighed as though the curate always disappointed him.

Alice felt defensive on Adam's behalf. It wasn't his fault that little Joshua Taylor had smeared half-eaten biscuits down Adam's front, and anyone could have a button hanging loose now and then. Naomi and Bert stood nearby, sharing Alice's concern, judging from the looks on their faces.

The archdeacon turned to the couple who'd entered with him and made introductions. 'Reverend Julian Forsyth and his wife, Lavinia. Julian is newly returned from ministry in Africa. This is Adam Potts, the curate at St John's, Barton.' Clearly, he thought Adam would rise no higher in the church.

'Pleased to meet you,' Adam said, offering his hand, which the Forsyths took with fastidious distaste as though they suspected that the biscuits which had made a mess of Adam's front were also smeared on his fingers.

'So . . . ?' the archdeacon said, gesturing to the room then raising an enquiring eyebrow at Adam.

'This is the Churchwood bookshop,' Adam explained.

'I'm afraid I don't know . . .'

'It's a place for people to come to buy and borrow books, hear stories, get involved in activities and that sort of thing. Today, it's story time for younger children.'

Julian Forsyth spoke up. 'Bible stories, I assume.'

'Sometimes. The children love the story of Noah's Ark. All the animals, you see? They like the story of David and Goliath too and—'

'The stories that *aren't* from the Bible. They're still Christian stories?'

'Erm . . .'

'Good grief!' Lavinia Forsyth stepped forward and snatched a child's comic. 'The *Beano*?' She looked towards the archdeacon, who took the comic she offered and leafed through the pages.

'Big Eggo, Contrary Mary, Lord Snooty and his Pals . . . This is all nonsense.'

'It's just harmless fun,' Adam said gently.

'It's far from harmless,' the archdeacon snapped. 'Young children need moral guidance. Wholesomeness. Not this rubbish. *Lord Snooty*, indeed. In a building that's supposed to be dedicated to God. How disrespectful!'

'Archdeacon.' Lavinia Forsyth caught his eye and nodded towards Betty Oldroyd, who was holding a copy of *The Count's Embrace*, a rather torrid romance that Naomi had donated.

The archdeacon sucked in air and strode to Betty, who looked like a guilty child. She handed the book over as though it had begun to burn her fingers.

'How do you explain this, Potts?' The archdeacon held up the book to show the cover on which a tall, handsome man held a pretty girl in his masterful arms as though about to kiss her. Very thoroughly. 'This sort of disgusting fiction causes discontentment and undermines happy marriage.'

'It appears we've arrived not a moment too soon,' Lavinia Forsyth said.

'We're certainly needed here,' her husband agreed.

'As I said before, you'll be forces for good if you take on St Luke's,' the archdeacon told them.

Alice and Naomi exchanged looks of dismay. Alice could sense similar glances being traded around them. The Forsyths would be disastrous for the book-shop and for Churchwood too.

Alice rose to her feet. 'I think you've formed the wrong impression of our bookshop, Archdeacon Rudge. It brings great benefits to the village, and the local military hospital too. Gathering people together in an informal setting like this relieves loneliness and provides companionship. It helps us to support each other through life's trials and tribulations, and—'

'I'm all in favour of bringing parishioners together, Miss – er . . .'

'Lovell.'

'But bringing them together for Bible study is what's needed. The answer to all of life's problems can be found in the Bible.'

'Doubtless. But we're reaching out to people in need and making sure no one slips through the net of our community.'

'All perfectly achievable through Bible study.'

'I'm afraid not everyone in the community will come to Bible study.'

'Then it's the church's job to draw them in. Cheap gimmicks like children's comics and novels of ques-tionable morality have no place in a Sunday School Hall.'

Naomi intervened. 'It's the very informality of the bookshop that appeals to people. They can relax. Have fun. Chat together.'

'Moral example is what's needed, Mrs – er . . .'

'Harrington.'

'Am I to understand that Reverend Barnes approved of this . . . this venture?'

'He understood the value of it, yes. He saw for him-self the good it does in the village.'

'Septimus Barnes was a fine man in his day.' Obvi-ously, the archdeacon believed that day had passed long ago and standards had slipped. 'Fortunately, Reverend Forsyth and his delightful wife are here to lift Churchwood up again.'

'Excuse me, Archdeacon, but isn't there a process for appointing a new vicar?' Naomi asked.

'Oh, certainly.' But it was clear that the archdeacon considered the process to be a mere formality.

'We're hoping that Adam might apply for the pos-ition,' Alice said.

'Indeed? If Potts wishes to apply, his application will be considered.'

But if the archdeacon had anything to do with it, that application would be found wanting.

'Good day to you all,' the archdeacon said then. 'I look forward to visiting Churchwood again in the not-too-distant future and hope to find things . . . improved.'

Goodbyes were muttered in return as he gestured to the Forsyths to follow him outside, and then silence fell.

'You've got to apply for the job of vicar now,' Alice told Adam after the door had closed behind the visitors.

'I'd be wasting my time.'

'It isn't necessarily the archdeacon who decides on the new vicar,' Naomi pointed out. 'The Diocese might appoint someone else to represent it. The church council also has a say.'

'I believe the council appoints two representatives to consider the applications and take part in the interviews,' Adam agreed. 'But if Cecil Wade is one of them . . .'

'Promise you'll at least apply for the job,' Alice urged.

Others urged him, too, but it felt as though a dark cloud had settled over the bookshop's future.

# CHAPTER NINE

## *Naomi*

Much as she disliked the thought of it, Naomi decided she'd have to expose herself to Cecil Wade's belittling contempt by pushing herself forward. 'I'd like to be involved in selecting the new vicar,' she told the council meeting, and waited for Cecil to wither her with scorn.

He smiled smugly. 'It's the duty of all council members to be involved in the selection of the new vicar.'

As if she didn't know that! 'I mean I'd like to be one of the people who consider the applications and interview the candidates.'

'I see.' Cecil made a steeple out of his fingers and rested his chin on them. Then, with obviously fake regret, he said, 'I've received some support for taking on that role myself.'

His smile suggested that he'd been begged to take the lead, though the truth was that he'd almost certainly suggested it himself and made it difficult for people to refuse him.

'I believe two people from the parish can take on the roles,' Naomi pointed out.

'Indeed. Several of us share the opinion that Arthur Fellows is the ideal man to work alongside me. He's lived in the parish all his life while I'm a more recent addition so we'd represent both old and new interests. Rather a good balance, I think.'

Naomi looked at Arthur but he couldn't meet her gaze. Doubtless Cecil had bullied him into the role – Arthur wouldn't say boo to the proverbial goose.

'Arthur would be grand,' Wilf Phipps said, 'but I'm sure he won't mind if I point out that Naomi could represent female interests. That would be an even better balance.'

Naomi sent him a grateful look, but Cecil was unmoved. 'Will the vicar be a woman?' he asked. 'Are any of the bishops women? Were any of the twelve disciples women? Certainly not, yet the Church cares for its female members as for all members.'

He let out a titter as though congratulating himself on his wit and Naomi blushed despite herself.

'Though now you've brought up the female perspective,' Cecil continued, 'perhaps that's something we should address now by taking a moment to consider the sort of person we'd like to see as our new vicar. A married man with an active wife would be ideal, would he not?'

In other words, a married man like Julian Forsyth. Not a young bachelor like Adam Potts.

'I don't think the new vicar needs a wife,' Naomi said. 'It's more important that he's the right man for St Luke's.'

Ignoring her, Cecil picked up his pen and drew his notebook closer. 'I think it would be helpful for us to list the sort of attributes we want to see in our new vicar. I'm sure we all agree that a strong faith should come first on our list.'

He wrote *A strong faith* in his pretentiously decorative handwriting.

'He needs to be kind,' Naomi suggested. 'Tolerant too.'

Cecil's smile implied that her suggestions were minor irritants like midges hovering in the sky on summer evenings. His pen didn't move.

'Kindness and tolerance are excellent qualities,' Wilf said.

As though he had to take notice now a man had spoken, Cecil wrote them down.

'Good with children,' Naomi added.

'Our vicar needs to be good – as you put it – with all parishioners,' Cecil replied, clearly thinking she was stating the obvious. 'I think an enthusiasm for Bible study should come next on our list.'

'I'd prefer a decent person to a scholar,' Naomi argued.

Cecil sighed. 'The knowledge of how to be a decent person comes from the Bible, does it not?'

'We need someone who listens too,' Naomi persisted. 'Listens to the village, I mean.'

'Obviously, the new vicar will need to get to know his parishioners, but the important thing is that *we* listen to *him*. He'll be our spiritual leader, after all.'

And so it went on – a sparring match between Naomi and Cecil with Wilf speaking up occasionally but everyone else staring down at the table.

Afterwards, Naomi headed outside with Wilf at her side. 'I appreciate the support,' she told him.

'You might be worrying over nothing. Julian Forsyth may be the archdeacon's choice but the bishop might have other ideas.'

'Let's hope so.'

Arthur Fellows emerged from the hall, looking nervous. 'Naomi, I hope you don't think I set myself against you in there? Nothing could be further from the truth. But Cecil thought—'

'I know what Cecil thought.'

'We all want the same thing: the best possible vicar for St Luke's.'

'Indeed. I've done what I can to get him and now the responsibility for choosing the right man lies with you, Arthur. So does the responsibility for saving the bookshop.'

Arthur's wife was one of the bookshop's most enthusiastic visitors. He paled and swallowed hard; then he scuttled off, possibly wishing he need never come back.

Naomi walked on, frustrated with herself for letting everyone down despite her efforts – Adam, the bookshop, her friends and even Churchwood itself. She could encourage more bookshop supporters to write to the Diocese but would it do any good?

Reaching home, she sank into her favourite armchair, feeling exhausted. Of course, the appointment of the new vicar wasn't her only worry. There was also Alexander, and Naomi was no closer to deciding what – if anything – to do about him. No sooner would she conclude that he really was too austere to pursue an affair than the doubts would sidle back.

Who might she be, this other woman? If there *was* another woman. His secretary? Miss Seymour was slender and beautiful, with fair hair and blue eyes. She'd always struck Naomi as rather cold, but that coldness could be an act she used to deflect suspicion on the rare times Naomi met her. Or might Alexander's lover be a warm, sultry woman with a voluptuous figure and seductive voice?

Naomi was doing herself no good with all this speculation. It was torturing her while changing nothing.

She still baulked at the thought of confronting Alexander, but might there be another way of discovering if something was going on? By finding receipts for intimate dinners? Bills for gifts that hadn't come Naomi's way? Love letters or notes?

The very notion of searching Alexander's things terrified her but the situation was robbing her of sleep and making it increasingly hard for her to function when she was awake.

It was too late to search Alexander's things now. Night was falling and she didn't want to signal her presence in his room by putting lights on. Morning would be a better time. If she could find the courage.

Naomi slept hardly at all that night. Every time she thought of what she planned to do, sickly dread twisted in her stomach.

She couldn't do it.

She *had* to do it.

'I think I'll read in bed for a while,' she told Suki when the maid brought Naomi's early-morning tea.

'Good idea, madam. I know it isn't my place to say such things, but you've been looking peaky recently. A rest will do you good.'

Naomi waited for the maid to go back downstairs,

then heaved herself out of bed, pushed her feet into slippers and put on her salmon-pink quilted dressing gown, suppressing the memory of having bought it some years ago in the hope that it might please Alexander. He hadn't even noticed it.

Creeping to the door, she listened to be sure no one was in the hall downstairs before tiptoeing on to the landing and along towards Alexander's room. She paused outside it, breathing deeply in an effort to steady her nerves, then she opened the door and stepped inside.

The bedside cabinets seemed a good place to start. Naomi moved over the thick-piled carpet, wishing she was built on less sturdy lines so no one in the room below would hear her movements. It was the dining room. Unused at this time of day, but who knew when the staff would take it upon themselves to go in and polish the silver?

The cabinets had two drawers each. Naomi slid open the top drawer in the first cabinet and saw dyspepsia tablets, a handkerchief, spare glasses, a pen and a small notebook. Picking up the notebook, she leafed through the pages but only the first of them bore any handwriting. *Matheson 1.15 Connaught* could refer to an appointment with a client. Alexander had also written *Ring dentist.*

The drawer below contained a scarf, a pair of driving gloves and a traveller's atlas of Great Britain.

The second cabinet held only programmes from long-ago golf tournaments. Naomi crossed to the dressing table. There were silver-backed men's hairbrushes on top along with a bottle of cologne. A drawer held a comb, an unopened bottle of the same cologne and a stock of handkerchiefs. A second drawer held a silver box containing cufflinks and tie pins, none of which looked new. There was also a nail file.

Turning, she moved to the large walnut wardrobe. It was full of handmade shirts and shoes, bespoke suits, golfing clothes, and a dark coat with a velvet collar. Doubtless Alexander had more clothes in London. A trawl of pockets produced only a few coins and a cloakroom ticket. Nothing of interest.

Was that reassuring? Not really. Naomi realized she shouldn't have expected to find anything incriminating in here because this room was cleaned regularly by the staff. If Alexander had anything to hide, it would be in his study. He didn't like the staff to go in there unless he was present himself. 'I bring papers home from the office,' he'd said after he'd bawled at poor little Suki for absent-mindedly entering without permission. 'Confidential papers relating to clients' private financial matters. It would hardly be appropriate for servants to see them.'

Naomi had thought him over-cautious, but she wondered now if that caution arose from having other secrets to hide.

A door opened downstairs, making Naomi's heart leap in her chest. How would she explain being found in here?

Panicking, she stood rigid for a moment but, hearing no footsteps on the stairs, she tiptoed to the door and peeped out. The landing was clear so she sped along to her own room as fast as her short legs would carry her, then threw herself on to her bed and willed her heart to stop racing.

She reached for her teacup but it trembled in her hand, so she returned it to its saucer before she spilt liquid over her bedcovers. As a spy she'd be hopeless. She hadn't the nerves for it. But had she enough nerve to search Alexander's study? Not now the staff were up and about, but another day?

# CHAPTER TEN

## *Kate*

'No,' Kate told Kenny.

'What do you mean, "No"?'

Kate sighed as though talking to an unintelligent child. 'I mean no, I won't help you in Five Acre Field this morning. The inspector from the Women's Land Army is coming. I need to get the house ready.'

Kenny appealed to their father. 'Tell her, Ernie. Tell her the farm's more important than prettifying the house.'

'Prettifying?' Kate scoffed. 'There's nothing pretty about this place and there never will be while you animals live here.' She stared at their father. Hard. 'Do you want the land girls or not? If you make me work with Kenny this morning, I'll assume you don't want them. After all, we're managing so well without the twins, aren't we?'

They weren't managing at all, and tempers were boiling over.

'You can spend the morning in the house, but you'd better make up for it this afternoon no matter how long it takes.'

'So you won't mind going without dinner tonight?'

Vinnie had been watching the argument with his usual glee, but the thought of an empty stomach turned him serious. 'I'm not going without my dinner! Tell her, Ernie. Tell her she's got to cook dinner.'

'Oh, shut up, the lot of you,' Ernie told them.

It signalled the end of breakfast. Grumbling, the Fletcher men headed outside, Ernie pointing a warning finger at Kate and saying, 'All this cleaning nonsense had better not be a waste of time.'

As if it would be her fault if Brimbles Farm failed the inspection!

Rolling her eyes, she raced to clear up the dishes. She'd been working her way around the house, giving it a thorough clean, ever since the twins' departure three weeks ago. She'd washed windows and paintwork, scrubbed floors, and cleared out cupboards. But with mud trampled in several times a day, the house needed a final spruce. Not that it would look appealing even then because it was shabby and unloved, but Kate was determined to make the best of it.

She dusted and swept the little-used sitting room, wiped and scrubbed the kitchen, and made up the beds in the twins' room with sheets and blankets that were worn but clean. With the twins' belongings stored in the barn, the room was tidier and fresher now. Kate gave it a final touch by filling a jug with greenery and placing it on the chest of drawers.

She tidied herself next. She'd washed her hair the previous evening, dipping her head under the pump in the yard until her ears rang and her teeth hurt from the cold water. Now she stripped off the ancient shirt that had once belonged to her brothers, washed herself and put on the only woman's blouse she possessed.

It was a simple cream shirt she kept for special occasions like bookshop events. The inspection by a representative of the county office of the Women's Land Army felt like a special occasion, or at least an important one. Hopefully, there'd be enough warmth from the early-May sun to mean she wouldn't need to put anything over the blouse as her only two jumpers were more shabby cast-offs from her brothers. She also put on her best breeches, though she couldn't hide the fact that they were patched and limp with age.

Her hair was in its usual single braid, but she unplaited it, brushed it and plaited it again. Studying herself in the flyblown mirror, Kate couldn't understand why Alice and others called her beautiful. Yes, she was tall and slender with clear skin and dark eyes but there was nothing special about her.

More worryingly, she looked nothing like the sort of cosily domestic farmer's wife or daughter who was likely to reassure the inspector that her land girls would be in good hands. Kate could only hope that the inspector understood the difference the land girls could make to Brimbles Farm and its ability to contribute towards the country's food supplies.

She'd just finished setting out the cups and saucers she'd borrowed from Alice when she heard the sound of a car engine. Crossing to the window she saw an old but stately vehicle enter the farmyard and come to a halt. A middle-aged woman dressed in tweed got out, holding a large handbag and what looked to be a folder of papers. Kate hastened to the door and opened it.

'Miss Fletcher?' the woman asked. 'I'm Hilary Donovan. Mrs. Women's Land Army county office.'

They shook hands and then Kate said, 'Please come in. Would you like tea?'

'Perhaps later. Let's get down to business, shall we?'

They sat at the kitchen table. 'This is an arable farm, I believe,' Mrs Donovan began.

'We don't keep animals apart from chickens.'

'That's good. Did you know that an acre of land growing potatoes can feed forty people? An acre given over to grazing for animal fodder can feed only two.'

'I didn't know.'

'With German attacks on our shipping, we can't import as much food as before, so we need to make the best possible use of the land.'

'We're growing as many crops as possible, but we're struggling to manage them without more labour.'

'Which is why you've applied for land girls, of course. Now then, land girls are outside workers. They can't be expected to work indoors in a domestic capacity as well.'

'I look after the house and the cooking,' Kate assured her.

'The girls' hours of work are forty-eight in winter and fifty in summer. Minimum payment is twenty-eight shillings per week although you can keep back fourteen shillings for bed and board – assuming they'll be billeted here rather than in the village or somewhere else?'

'Here,' Kate confirmed. 'I can show you the room.'

'All in good time. The girls will bring their ration books, of course. They'll hand them to you if you're the lady of the house?'

'My mother died many years ago.'

Mrs Donovan nodded, but then hesitated. 'Please understand I'm casting no aspersions when I say this, but we've heard of a case where the lady of the house sold some of the girls' rations on the black market. Meat and sugar, I believe it was.'

Kate was appalled. 'I'd never do that.' And she'd make sure Ernie and the boys weren't tempted either. 'I know the girls will need feeding well if they're doing labouring work.'

'I meant no offence,' Mrs Donovan said. 'Any questions so far?'

'You mentioned hours of work. What about holidays? Time off to visit families and that sort of thing?'

'The girls sign on for the duration of the war. There's no requirement for holidays at present.'

Kate was surprised. Not everyone's family was a dead loss like the Fletchers. It felt harsh that girls who were doing war work had no automatic right to go home now and then.

'Of course, we may look at requiring the girls to be given time off in the future. We don't want to dissuade them from joining because the conditions are too harsh.'

'What about clothes?' Kate asked.

'The girls will be kitted out with uniforms.' Mrs Donovan consulted a list. 'Three fawn shirts, two green pullovers, two pairs of breeches, three pairs of fawn socks, brown brogues, brown hat and brown coat.'

Kate was relieved. She couldn't imagine Ernie paying for clothing.

'Any more questions?'

'I don't think so.'

'Then let's have a look around.'

Kate showed Mrs Donovan the house first. Notes were made along with murmurs that varied from brief 'Hmm's to 'I see'. But nothing was said to indicate whether the house was passing muster.

'It isn't a luxurious house,' Kate admitted, 'but I'll do my best to make the girls comfortable.'

'I'm sure. Let's head outside now, shall we?'

Kate led Mrs Donovan into the farmyard. 'Chickens over there, as you can see. Here's the barn. Obviously. We keep equipment and stores in here.'

'Hmm.'

They moved to the growing bed at the back of the barn. 'This is where I grow vegetables for the family,' Kate explained. 'Potatoes, onions, carrots, beans, turnips, cabbages and that sort of thing. Soft fruits too, when the time is right.'

'So it's a kitchen garden.'

'I suppose that's the proper name for it.' But the Fletchers had never bothered with niceties.

Kate gestured towards some trees. 'Over there is the orchard. Apples, pears, cherries and a few plums. And there . . .' Kate waved her arm again. 'The fields.' She was glad to see three figures in the distance as it meant that none of the Fletcher men were nearby. The last thing Kate wanted was to expose Mrs Donovan to their charmless company.

'The girls will be expected to do whatever outdoor work is required of them, I suppose?' Mrs Donovan asked.

Kate listed the first tasks that sprang to mind. 'Ploughing, sowing, planting, watering, fertilizing, harvesting . . . That sort of thing. Then they'll be needed to pack crops into crates for transport, and help with maintenance. Like mending fences.'

More notes were written. 'I think I've seen enough,' Mrs Donovan finally said.

'Time for tea?' Kate wondered, hoping the answer would be no because the longer Mrs Donovan lingered, the more likely she was to come face to face with the Fletcher men.

Mrs Donovan consulted her watch, then, to Kate's relief, said, 'I'm afraid I need to press on. I've another appointment today.'

Kate walked the inspector to her car. 'Are you able to tell me whether we've passed the inspection? It will help us enormously with planning the workload if we know we're getting help.'

'Well, as you said yourself, Miss Fletcher, this isn't a luxurious sort of place but there's a war on and the country desperately needs to feed its people. In principle I'll recommend that two girls be placed here, though I don't know when they might arrive. It depends on the situation locally. Some areas have a shortage of girls while in other areas girls are having to go home after their training to wait for placements to open for them. It's the farmers, you see. Some won't entertain the idea of female labour. Terribly unenlightened. Without female labour they might see their crops rotting in the fields. A crime during wartime, to my way of thinking.'

Luckily, money had motivated Ernie and her brothers to accept female labour.

Kate waved Mrs Donovan off, then went indoors to slump in a chair and let the tension of the inspection drain away a little.

'Well?' Ernie demanded, entering a few minutes later.

'We may be allocated some girls or we may not. It depends if any are available.'

'Humph.'

Kenny and Vinnie entered too, wanting their mid-morning tea. 'What do you think you're doing, lazing about indoors while we're working?' Kenny demanded.

'Trying to get some help, you idiot.'

'Are we getting help?'

'Maybe.'

He made a disgusted sound. 'Is the kettle on? We've no time to sit around waiting for it to boil.'

Kate dragged herself back to her feet and lit the gas on the stove.

'If we get some girls, make them pretty ones,' Vinnie said with a disgusting leer that would surely have any decent girls packing their bags and running straight home.

And there lay Kate's second problem. Getting the girls was proving hard enough. Keeping them was likely to be even harder.

# CHAPTER ELEVEN

## *Alice*

Alice took her father's tea into the study then returned to the kitchen to pour cups for May and herself.

'I don't see what more we can do,' May said. 'Adam's applied to be vicar and we've written to both the church council and the Diocese to show our support for him and the bookshop too.'

'I included the bookshop testimonials with my letters.'

May nodded approvingly. 'Good idea. Do you know how many applications have been received?'

'I don't know much at all,' Alice admitted. 'It might be a simple choice between Adam and Reverend Forsyth, or there may be several candidates.'

'Any vicar would be preferable to Julian Forsyth.'

'It's hard to imagine a worse one,' Alice agreed. 'Even Naomi is struggling to find out what's happening. Cecil Wade is playing his cards close to his chest, and as for Arthur Fellows, if he ventures out of his house at all, he scurries back in at the earliest opportunity. I swear he actually ducked behind the war memorial to avoid Naomi yesterday.'

May smiled ruefully but then turned serious again.

'Poor Naomi. I think the strain is taking a toll on her health.'

'I think so too, though she insists she's fine.'

A thoughtful silence descended and then May said, 'Changing the subject, have you heard any more about Daniel's leave?'

'Not yet.'

'I had a letter from Marek a couple of days ago. He sounded cheerful but I don't know if he was pretending for my sake. He must be worried sick about his family in Poland. It's been months since we had any news of them.'

'How are the children coping?'

More than a year had passed since a family friend had smuggled Rosa, Samuel and Zofia Kovac out of Poland while their parents and grandparents stayed behind. The need to keep them safe while her husband fought in the war had forced May to give up her much-loved job designing and manufacturing clothes in London and move to Churchwood instead. It had been a wrench for her and for a while she'd struggled, but May was wonderful with the children now.

'They're all doing well at school and their English is remarkable,' May told Alice. 'But they're sad at times, especially Rosa. Being the eldest, she has the clearest memories of her parents and her old life. Being the youngest, Zofia's memories are hazier, and I suspect England feels more like home to her now than Poland. As for Samuel, he's somewhere between the two.'

'They're lovely kids.'

'They are.' May took a sip of her tea before asking, 'How's Kate? Any news of her land girls?'

'Not as far as I know. Hopefully—'

Alice's words were cut off by the sound of the post landing on the doormat out in the hall. 'You don't mind if I . . . ?'

'Course not. You might have a letter from Daniel.'

Picking up the post, Alice saw that she had indeed received a letter from Daniel. She tore it open – and let out her breath in a long sigh of relief. At last!

'He's finally got leave,' she said, returning to the kitchen.

'Wonderful! When will he arrive?'

'Wednesday.'

'Today's Monday so I expect you need to rush around getting ready. Which means it's time for me to go. Thanks for the tea and the chat.' May stood up; then she paused and said, 'He'll be here for the book-shop social on Saturday. That'll be nice.'

Alice hoped he wouldn't be too tired to enjoy it.

News of the social had been met with enthusiasm in both the hospital and the village. 'I assume we're not asking the Diocese for permission to hold it?' Bert had said.

'And give the archdeacon a chance to say no? Until someone actually bans the bookshop, I think we should carry on as normal,' Alice had replied.

'Quite right.'

She saw May to the door, told her father when Daniel was expected and then tidied the house before setting off for the hospital. Daniel's impending arrival buoyed her up with warmth, but it was a pity she couldn't tell him she had a job. Perhaps one day soon she should return to St Albans and knock on the doors of as many businesses as possible in the hope that someone would see she had something to offer despite her injured hand. She might not find anything half as interesting as Mr Parkinson's memoirs, but any job would be better than none.

A job felt especially important now the bookshop was in danger. Even though it was unpaid, her work on the organizing team still helped Alice to feel useful. Aware of that, Daniel would be troubled for her sake to hear that it was under threat, and she didn't want it to cast a shadow over his visit. She'd just have to persuade him that she was going to be happy focusing her energies in other directions – on the patients at Stratton House, her friends and acquaintances in the village, her vegetable patch and chickens . . .

She was ready and waiting for Daniel long before it was reasonable to expect him. He was travelling by boat, train and bus, and the bus wasn't due to arrive in the village for an hour. Even so she began looking out of the cottage windows in the hope of seeing his tall, trim figure approaching, just in case, by some miracle or other, he happened to be early.

Naomi had offered him a room at Foxfield but had understood Alice's need to keep him close at The Linnets instead. The spare room was small, and the sloping ceiling meant he'd have to be careful to avoid hitting his head, but Daniel wouldn't mind that. He'd laugh about it. And at least the room was sparkling clean and fresh in readiness for his arrival.

Alice's room was next to Daniel's and last night she'd lain in bed and smoothed her hand down the wall that separated them, excited to think that tonight he'd be lying just a few feet away from her.

When she could bear the waiting no longer, she told her father she was going out and headed into the village. She exchanged a few words here and there with the people she passed. Marjorie's Plym's eyes lit up at the sight of her, doubtless scenting fuel for her beloved gossip.

'Your young man is coming today, I believe,' Marjorie said.

'All being well.'

'You're waiting for the bus?'

'Mmm.'

'Staying with you at The Linnets, is he?'

'That's right.' Alice let speculation gleam in Marjorie's eyes for a moment then added, 'My father is very fond of Daniel.' In other words, there'd be no hanky-panky under the roof of The Linnets.

Alice hid a smile as the gleam in Marjorie's eyes went out like a snuffed candle and wistful disappointment took its place. 'Oh, I'm sure.'

Marjorie wasn't a bad person, but like everyone she had her weaknesses and hers was a love of tittle-tattle.

'Here comes Naomi,' Marjorie said then.

Alice turned and saw Naomi walking up from Foxfield. How tired she looked! She really was taking on too much personal responsibility for the survival of the bookshop. It must be a blow to her self-esteem to know that her opinion counted so little with the church council when it had once counted so much.

'Alice is waiting for her young man,' Marjorie announced. 'He's coming on the bus and staying at The Linnets. With Dr Lovell, of course. I wouldn't like to suggest anything improper.'

Naomi shared a wry smile with Alice because they both knew Marjorie would have loved to report on something improper. 'I hope Daniel arrives soon,' Naomi said. 'I'm looking forward to seeing him again, but only when it's convenient. I'm sure you'll want some time to yourselves first. Marjorie, I think we should leave Alice to enjoy a private moment with her fiancé, don't you?'

'Oh.' Marjorie looked like a child who'd been refused a slice of cake.

'Come along, Marjorie.' Naomi sent Alice another smile then nudged her friend away.

Feeling grateful, Alice crossed the road to the village green, wanting to be alone when Daniel arrived so she could savour the moment. A few people waved and Alice waved back but thankfully no one came over.

Her heartbeat quickened as the bus rumbled into view. Surely he was on it? The thought that he might have been held up on his journey was too terrible to contemplate. The bus lurched to a halt outside its usual stopping place by the baker's and several passengers stood up to alight. Alice caught a glimpse of brown or khaki through the windows – Daniel's army greatcoat? – but it was instantly swallowed up by other people's clothing. The bus door faced the opposite side of the road to where Alice stood but she watched as passengers moved past the bus itself to go about their business. When a tall, trim figure appeared, her heartbeat quickened even more.

He looked around, doubtless wondering if she was nearby or waiting for him at the cottage. 'Daniel!' she called.

He turned, saw her, and even at a distance she could see the glow in his dark eyes. He stared at her for a long moment as though drinking in the sight of her, then jogged across the road, his kit bag slung over his shoulder.

'It's a little more private on this side,' she told him.

'Then let's not waste this opportunity.'

He drew her close and kissed her, and Alice sighed with pleasure, delighting in the tall shape of him next to her own slender frame. But she didn't want to make a spectacle of herself in public. With a small, giddy laugh she drew away.

Daniel smiled down at her. 'That kiss will keep me going,' he reassured her, then his eyes twinkled and he added, 'Even if it's only for a little while.'

Alice blushed but didn't protest. She wanted him to kiss her again soon. Thoroughly and deliciously.

'It's so good to be here,' Daniel told her.

'Waiting has been torture.'

'For both of us.'

He placed an arm around her shoulders, and they set off for The Linnets, waving to people along the way.

'I was devastated when your leave was postponed, but in one way it's worked out well,' she said, deciding to tell him about the bookshop before he heard the news from someone else. 'There's a bookshop party on Saturday so you'll be able to come along.'

'Sounds wonderful.'

'We're hoping it'll be a good one because we're not sure what will happen to the bookshop when the new vicar is appointed.'

'Surely its future can't be in doubt when it does so

much good? Anyway, aren't you hoping Adam Potts will be the new vicar?'

'The Diocese may have other ideas. The archdeacon brought another candidate to visit St Luke's and I think they both thought the bookshop wasn't pious enough for their tastes.'

'The village has a say in who's appointed, though?'

'Through the church council. But Naomi isn't a churchwarden any more and the man who replaced her is . . . Let's just say the words *arrogant* and *pompous* could have been invented for him.'

'It would be mad to close the bookshop down. It would disappoint so many people.'

'We're fighting the idea, of course.'

'I'd expect no less of you.' Daniel smiled his approval.

'But we may not succeed so Saturday's party could be a final celebration.'

'You'll feel the loss of the bookshop keenly if it closes, darling.' He was frowning now.

'Of course. But I've plenty of other activities to keep me busy. Visits to friends, visits to the hospital—'

'Yes, but the bookshop brought the whole community together. *You* brought the whole community together.'

'Hardly alone. I had masses of help.'

'Even so.'

They'd reached the cottage. 'I *will* be disappointed if the bookshop closes,' Alice admitted. 'I'll be upset for the people it helps and upset for myself. But I'll cope.'

Daniel's eyes softened as he reached out to cup her cheek and smooth his thumb over her skin. 'You're a fighter, Alice Lovell.'

'I am. So you needn't spend this visit worrying about me.'

'I'd like to spend it kissing you.' He lowered his mouth to nuzzle her lips again. 'Part of it, anyway,' he whispered.

Alice kissed him back, but then stepped away in case her father was looking through a window. 'I'm glad that's settled. Now, what do you think of the cottage garden?' The white lilac was out. So too were bluebells, peonies and lily of the valley.

'Almost as lovely as you,' he said, 'but not quite.'

They exchanged grins. 'Come in and say hello to my father,' Alice said next, glad that the bookshop problem was out in the open, even if she suspected that Daniel would still worry.

Her father must indeed have been on the lookout for them because he opened the door smiling with sincere pleasure. 'Welcome, dear boy.'

'I'm glad to be here at last,' Daniel said.

The men shook hands and they all went inside. 'A letter came for you,' her father said, passing an envelope over.

The spiky handwriting was familiar, but Alice couldn't quite place it . . .

Oh yes, she could. A month had passed since her interview with Hubert Parkinson. She hadn't expected him to write to confirm the sorry outcome but realized he must like to observe social niceties in business as well as life. What rotten luck that she should receive his letter while both Daniel and her father were standing beside her. If she opened it now, they'd wonder why she hadn't mentioned the interview before and would worry she was upset at having failed.

'Oh, that,' she said, as though she knew the letter would be of no great significance. 'I'll put the kettle on, shall I?' Heading for the kitchen, she dropped the letter behind the wooden box in which bread was kept.

Daniel came in behind her. 'Need any help?'

Had he seen what she'd just done? If so, he'd think it odd. Suspicious, even. Turning, she was relieved to see no sign of puzzlement in his face. 'Not just now, thanks. Dinner won't be ready until later but I'll make you a sandwich – if it'll be welcome?'

'I'm famished,' he admitted.

'Is cheese and pickle all right?'

'If you can spare it. Please don't use precious rations on me.'

'We've plenty of food.'

'Whatever you serve will be better than army food. Anyway, I'm more interested in spending time with you than being fed.'

He kissed her again, then lingered in the kitchen, watching as she made the sandwich and a pot of tea.

'You won't mind if we sit in my father's study?' Alice asked. 'He's been looking forward to your visit.'

'And you're glad to get his nose out of books and into the living world?'

'Exactly, though he's much more sociable than he used to be. When we first came here I thought he'd be happy if he never saw any neighbours, but Churchwood has dragged him into village life anyway, if only in an occasional way.'

'He also has a loving daughter who wants the best for him.'

Alice did indeed want the best for him. She'd

96

understood that he was worn out with years of being at the beck and call of patients all day and often all night too. She'd also understood that, having served as a doctor in the 1914 war and seen its terrible impact first hand, he'd wanted to distance himself from a second war. But she hadn't wanted him to end up isolated and alone, especially if she forged a life elsewhere.

Alice loaded the tea and sandwich on to a tray. 'If you want to be useful, you could carry that into the study while I take this apron off,' she said.

Daniel lifted the tray and, watching him go, Alice breathed out slowly, relieved that Mr Parkinson's letter could remain a secret.

The study was actually the cottage drawing room, a large and lovely room with French windows opening into the garden. Alice's father was clearing piles of books and papers from chairs when she entered. He looked happy, his white hair floating around his face like a dandelion clock. 'Sit down,' he urged.

She poured the tea and let her father occupy Daniel for a while. It gave her pleasure to watch Daniel being so respectful, courteous and kind to the older man. She took pleasure in Daniel's appearance too – his well-shaped head with the glossy dark hair, his clear skin, his dark eyes that could soften with affection one moment then dance with humour the next . . . Studying him now, Alice felt a swell of love for him.

'Do you have any thoughts on how you'd like to spend your leave?' her father asked him eventually.

'I need to see my family. My godmother too. Mostly, I want to spend time with your lovely daughter.'

'Don't let a dry old stick like me keep you from her. Go on. Off you go. You've spent long enough with me.'

Daniel laughed. 'I'll see you again soon,' he told the doctor.

Alice collected the tea things together, and Daniel carried the tray back into the kitchen where she washed the dishes and he dried them.

'The vegetable patch is looking good,' he said, inspecting it through the window. 'How are the chickens?'

'All laying well so you should have at least one egg for breakfast.'

They moved into the garden to say hello to the chickens and give Daniel a closer look at the vegetable patch. 'I'm looking forward to working in it,' he said. 'Did my things come, by the way?'

He'd had a parcel of clothes sent so he didn't have to spend his entire leave in uniform.

'They did. I put the parcel in your room. It's only a small room, but I hope you'll be comfortable.'

'I don't care about the room. I care about you.' His darkening eyes told her he wanted to kiss her again, but he followed her gaze to the cottage windows and realized she was afraid her father might see. He grinned. 'I'd better be on my best behaviour or your father won't trust me under his roof.'

In bed that night she touched her hand to the wall that separated their rooms and wondered if he'd reached out to the wall on his side. If he had, their fingers would be only inches apart.

# CHAPTER TWELVE

## *Naomi*

It pleased Naomi to set out from Foxfield to walk into the village and see Alice and Daniel arm in arm over by The Linnets. Admittedly, it also cost her a pang of regret over the state of her own marriage – a pang of loneliness too – but she suppressed those bleaker emotions quickly. Alice and Daniel were lovely people who deserved to be happy.

She wasn't quite so pleased to see that Bert had pulled up his truck beside the young couple and was chatting to them through the open window. He was a lovely man and a valued friend, but he had a way of seeing through her pretences and it would unsettle her to be with someone who'd guess she had troubles in her life when she was trying so hard to keep them private. If she searched Alexander's study and found evidence of an affair . . . Perhaps then she'd confide in Bert. But if she didn't find evidence, she wanted to be able to lay her suspicions to rest with no harm done. At least, she hoped she'd feel able to do that.

For a crazy moment she considered ducking back into her garden and hiding there. But, knowing Bert, he'd already have spotted her in the truck's mirrors. Besides, she was forty-six years old. Far too mature for such craven childishness.

Walking on, she came to a halt by the truck. She greeted Bert with a nod and then focused on the young couple. 'It's good to see you back in Churchwood, Daniel. Looking in fine fettle too.' The African sun had browned his skin.

'It's good to be amongst friends, especially my darling Alice.'

The warm look he gave his fiancée rekindled Naomi's own sense of loss. No one had ever looked at her like that – not even Alexander when he was pretending to love her. But, aware that Bert was watching, Naomi roused herself. 'I won't keep you from Alice now, Daniel, but I hope to see more of you while you're here. You're always welcome at Foxfield.'

'Thank you. I hope to have the pleasure of twirling you around the dance floor at Saturday's bookshop social.'

'I dance like a hippopotamus,' Naomi warned him. 'I'd fear for your toes.'

'You dance well,' Daniel said gallantly.

'Flatterer! I hope you'll have a truly happy leave.'

Naomi moved on, nodding at Bert again while hoping she could reach the shops before he too parted from the young couple and caught up with her. Unfortunately, she hadn't gone far before she heard the truck approaching. She walked faster but realized her dumpy little legs must look ridiculous and make it obvious to Bert that she was trying to escape him.

'Hop in,' he said, pulling up beside her.

'I've only a few more yards to walk. It's kind of you to offer, though.'

'I'd like a chat,' he said.

It was the last thing Naomi wanted.

'Don't look so scared, woman. I mean a chat about the bookshop.'

Even so . . . 'I'm busy today. Perhaps another time, we could—'

Too late. He'd swung his substantial frame out through the driver's door and walked around to open the passenger door for her.

Fearing he might offer his shoulder to boost her broad posterior up into the truck, she insisted, 'I can manage,' and scrambled up in an unladylike manner that only added to her fluster.

'Apparently, two people have applied for the post of vicar,' Naomi told him as he got in beside her. Hopefully, she could make this chat a short one.

'Young Adam and Julian Forsyth?'

'I know Adam has applied because he's told me so. I can only assume the other applicant is Julian Forsyth.'

'Cecil Wade being all mysterious, is he?'

'Applications are confidential, even from council members – the ones who aren't involved in selecting the vicar, that is.'

'Cecil Wade wouldn't give you as much as a hint anyway. Too pompous by half, that man.'

Cecil had taken great pleasure in refusing to reveal information. 'I've been placed in a position of great trust, Mrs Harrington. It would be wrong of me to breach that trust.'

'Do you know who'll be representing the Diocese in the process?' Bert asked then.

'No, but I hope it isn't the archdeacon. He's bound to choose his own man.'

'With luck, it'll be someone impartial who'll take notice of the letters we've sent.'

'Indeed. Oh, look. Marjorie is waving.'

'Here to rescue you from Big Bad Bert, is she?'

Naomi chided him with a disapproving look. 'Don't be silly, Bert. I'd better go and see what she wants, though.'

'Naomi . . .' he began, and his tone was serious.

She could never fool him. 'Not now,' she pleaded. 'Please not now.'

He nodded slowly. 'All right. But I've said it before and I'll say it again. You have friends in Churchwood and I'm one of 'em. I may not be a doctor, but I know when someone's looking peaky, and right now that someone is you.'

There was no point in denying it. 'I'm a little . . . troubled,' she admitted.

'But not ready to talk about it?'

'There may be nothing to talk about. I may be worrying over nothing.'

'It still doesn't hurt to talk. Bottling things up tangles our thoughts like knitting wool. Talking smooths them out.'

'You're probably right, but I'd still like a little more . . . certainty first.'

'Fair enough. You know where to find me when you're ready. I'll let you go now in case Marjorie decides I've kidnapped you and rushes off to announce it to the village. One last thing, though. You know you can trust me to keep any confidences to myself?'

'I do, Bert. And I appreciate it.' Naomi's throat tightened and the tears she dreaded prickled in her eyes. She realized she couldn't recall a single occasion when she'd been held in someone's arms while she cried her heart out. Swallowing, she managed a small smile of farewell and then climbed out of the truck.

She was glad to have a moment to blink the tears away before Marjorie reached her. Then her conscience stirred as she saw how pleased her friend looked at this encounter. Naomi had been neglecting Marjorie of late but, silly and tiresome as she was, she'd been a loyal friend for almost a quarter of a century and deserved better.

'Out shopping?' Marjorie asked.

'Just picking up some stamps.'

Marjorie followed as Naomi walked into the Post Office. She'd stick to Naomi's side all day unless shaken off by force. 'I'll walk back with you as far as Foxfield,' Marjorie said, once the stamps had been bought. 'Stretching my legs will do me good.'

It was a none-too-subtle hint that she hoped to be invited for lunch and Naomi hadn't the heart to dismiss her when they reached the Foxfield gateposts. 'I'm sure Cook won't object to stretching lunch to include you,' she said.

'How kind! We don't seem to lunch together half as much as in the past.'

Before Alice came and set the village buzzing, Marjorie meant. Naomi knew her old friend was torn between jealousy and admiration for the new interloper.

'Perhaps we should treat ourselves to a sherry,' Naomi offered.

As expected, Marjorie's eyes brightened with anticipation.

Cook was accustomed to Marjorie turning up, often uninvited, so made no fuss when asked to stretch the luncheon to include her.

Naomi poured glasses of sherry and braced herself for an hour or two of chatter. 'I saw Alice out with her young man this morning,' Marjorie began. 'He makes a handsome soldier, doesn't he? Perhaps he'll dance with me at the bookshop social.' She let out a giggle that mixed self-mockery with longing.

As a girl, Naomi hadn't been popular at balls and dances but at least she'd been considered an heiress and sought out for that reason. Equally unattractive, poor Marjorie had been further disadvantaged by her family's dwindling fortunes. Doubtless her parents had hoped to marry her off to a man who could support her comfortably, but it had never happened and now Marjorie lived alone on the barest of incomes, the glories of her family's former splendour having passed into history.

Daniel was kind. He wouldn't mind if Naomi suggested he spare five minutes to dance with Marjorie.

An hour became two and threatened to become three. Marjorie's silliness wore on Naomi's nerves. She needed some time to think and perhaps to take action too – if, bolstered by sherry, she could find the courage. 'Goodness, look at the time!' Naomi finally said.

'Three o'clock,' Marjorie observed, but the hint that it was time to leave had passed over her complacent head.

'I have to make some telephone calls.'

'I don't mind you making telephone calls.'

'I wouldn't dream of expecting you to endure such

boredom.' Naomi reinforced the hint by getting to her feet.

At last the message got through and Marjorie stood too, though reluctantly. 'Thank you for the lunch. And the sherry, of course.' The alcohol had reddened Marjorie's cheeks.

Naomi saw her to the door; then she stuck a stamp on a letter and rang the bell for Suki.

'Would you mind popping into the village and posting this for me, please? I'd like it to catch the next post.' The letter was unimportant but Naomi wanted Suki out of the house.

'Be glad to, madam.'

'You might also call at Mr Corbett's and ask if he's reheeled my shoes yet. They're not due for collection until tomorrow, but if you happen to be passing . . .'

Suki nodded and set out a few minutes later. Cook was already upstairs taking her afternoon rest, while the cleaning lady had gone home hours ago. There'd never be a better time to search Alexander's study. Naomi took another gulp of sherry before creeping across the hall.

It was a rather grand study with a large mahogany desk by the window. The surface was inlaid with dark green leather tooled in gold and everything was neatness on top – the blotter, the silver inkwells and the tray for Alexander's pens and pencils.

She moved to the desk drawers, opening them quietly. One contained only stationery – notepaper, envelopes and spare bottles of ink. Another contained Alexander's business cards together with cards he'd received from other people. Flicking through them, none leapt out as being suspicious.

On to another drawer and what was this? Last year's diary! Naomi turned the pages – games of golf; fittings with a tailor; work meetings; several lunch and dinner engagements . . . Ignoring the engagements with men's names beside them, she concentrated on the female names. *Mrs Greatorex – 1 p.m. Claridge's.* Naomi knew Mrs Greatorex to be in her eighties. *Lady Stratfield – 8 p.m. Rules.* Naomi knew Lady Stratfield was no spring chicken either. *Millicent F. – 1.30 p.m. Savoy Grill.* Naomi stared at that one, then decided that, if Alexander had to remind himself which Millicent he was meeting by adding the first letter of her surname, he was unlikely to be having an affair with her.

She was more troubled by the entries that mentioned only initials – *AB, SK, LM, GT* . . . She had no way of identifying those people.

Time was marching on so she moved down to lower drawers, finding a cash box, unlocked, with around thirty pounds inside it; old golfing gloves; golf tees and balls; more programmes from golfing tournaments . . .

A bookcase held dull-looking books on golf, wine, antiques, tax and finance. Naomi inspected one book but it was exactly what it said on the cover and there was nothing hidden within its pages. She took out a second, a third and a fourth book from different shelves but they too were exactly what they appeared to be.

A cupboard revealed spare golf clubs and golfing shoes. Hanging up were golfing clothes.

Only a three-drawer filing cabinet remained unexplored. The first drawer held files relating to Foxfield and the London flat – tradesmen's invoices for repairs, maintenance and insurances. A separate file related to the Daimler.

The second drawer held general financial papers. Naomi glanced through some of them but found no receipts for intimate dinners or hotel accommodation.

The third drawer contained only relics from Alexander's youth – school reports, newsletters his university sent to former students, medals for cricket and cross-country running, and a university scarf.

Was she pleased that she'd found nothing incriminating? Not really, because it might only prove that Alexander was too careful – too clever – to be caught.

Her gaze fell on the blotter on his desk. She lifted a corner. Looked underneath and saw nothing. But something was tucked into the side of the leather case in which the blotting paper sat. Pulse racing, she teased out a small card and saw that it was a receipt.

*Alderton's, Jewellers and Watchmakers*, she read. *Chancery Lane, London*. Underneath was a handwritten note. *To: replace broken 18-carat gold clasp with new 18-carat gold clasp.*

Her heart leapt up into her throat at the sound of gravel crunching. Suki must be returning along the drive. She'd walk round to the kitchen entrance but would pass by the study window. Naomi tucked the card back into the blotter then hastened to the door. She glanced rapidly around the study to ensure that the room looked undisturbed, then moved into the hall and on into her sitting room, whisking herself out of sight just in time.

She sank into her armchair, her hand over her stampeding heart. Hearing Suki coming through the hall from the kitchen, Naomi reached for one of her lists.

'I got the letter in the post but your shoes weren't ready, madam. Mr Corbett sent his apologies.'

'Tomorrow will do very well for the shoes.'

'Tea, madam?'

Brandy would have been better but tea would be welcome. 'Yes, please, Suki.'

The maid left and Naomi realized she'd been holding her list upside down. Luckily, Suki had given no sign of noticing. Naomi set the list aside and thought about the receipt. A gold clasp could be the fastener on a woman's necklace, bracelet or a brooch. Could it also be the fastener on a badge? A golf club badge, perhaps? It felt unlikely that an ordinary golf club badge would be made from gold but Alexander might have won a special one as a prize. Or he might have broken the fastening on a watch.

Deciding there might be a way of finding out, Naomi waited for Suki to leave after bringing the tea and then reached for the phone. She hadn't made a note of the telephone number of Alderton's but there couldn't be more than one jeweller of that name on Chancery Lane. She asked the exchange to put her through and waited with a dry mouth for the connection to be made. 'Alderton's. How may I be of assistance?' a voice asked. Male.

Naomi spoke softly. Just above a whisper. 'My name is Harrington. I believe my husband left an item with you for repair. The clasp was broken. He's had appointments all day so I haven't been able to ask him directly, but has the – er – item been collected yet?'

'Harrington, did you say?'

'Alexander Harrington.'

'If you wouldn't mind waiting a moment . . . ?'

Naomi waited.

'Mr Harrington collected it last week,' she heard then.

Naomi had hoped for a mention of the actual item – the necklace, the bracelet, the brooch . . .

'May I help you with anything else, madam?'

'Er, no. No, thank you.'

Naomi rang off, frustrated but feeling that her suspicions had deepened. Not into certainty – not nearly – but enough to make her want to go on looking for evidence. There might be more to find in the London flat. Alexander would feel safer there. After all, Naomi hadn't visited the flat in more than a year. Should she take a trip to London soon?

# CHAPTER THIRTEEN

## *Kate*

Kate ripped open the envelope without even bothering to wash her hands first. Who cared about a bit of grubbiness when so much else was at stake?

The letter tore a little as she tugged it out, but she was more concerned with its message than its appearance. She read it through, then closed her eyes and let out her breath in a sigh.

Rousing herself, she dusted the worst of the dirt off the letter, washed her hands and set about preparing lunch.

Fifteen minutes later, Ernie, Kenny and Vinnie trooped in, spreading filth and bad temper. The brawn of Frank 'n' Fred was being sorely missed.

'You need to get along to South Field this afternoon,' Ernie told Kenny.

'Can't. Tractor's playing up again. I need to have another go at fixing it. Vinnie can help in South Field.'

'Can't,' Vinnie said. 'Haven't finished in Five Acre Field yet. Don't blame me. Blame the twins.'

Ernie scowled and cursed.

'You'll be pleased to hear we're definitely getting some help,' Kate announced, serving up the soup.

'Eh?'

'Two land girls.'

For a moment no one spoke but Kate hadn't expected enthusiasm or relief and she certainly hadn't expected gratitude.

'Land girls!' Ernie finally said, shaking his head as though female workers could only be nuisances.

Kate wasn't fooled. He simply didn't want to admit that they might be useful and that his daughter had done a good thing in applying for them.

'Let's hope they're pretty,' Vinnie said.

'They're coming to work,' Kenny pointed out harshly.

Ernie stabbed his finger in Kate's direction. 'They'd better not be useless.'

'When are they coming?' Kenny asked.

'I don't know yet, but I'm told it's likely to be soon. I'll be sent another letter.' She paused, then said, 'Talking of letters, I've heard from the twins.'

No one answered because no one could admit to caring. The letter was typical of the twins. It was short – a single page – and a complete mess. Frank had started it but Fred had taken over. Then Frank had drawn arrows leading to added snippets alongside Fred's writing and Fred had drawn more arrows leading to extra bits alongside Frank's writing.

Deciphering it had been tricky but Kate had managed to tease out Fred's story about Frank being tricked in a card game – *Not true!* Frank had scrawled – and Frank's story about a sergeant major whose moustache was wider than his head. There were requests for *ciggies and grub*.

*Hope you're missing us*, they'd squeezed in at the end, which Kate took to mean that they were missing the family but didn't know how to say so.

111

She placed the letter on the table. Ernie, Kenny and Vinnie all looked away but moments later she saw all three of them trying to read it surreptitiously.

'Any messages to send back?' Kate asked.

More silence.

'Tell 'em the gate's broken in West Field again,' Ernie said. 'They were supposed to have fixed it.'

'Kenny?'

'You could tell them the tractor's playing up.'

'Tell them about the land girls too,' Vinnie suggested with a giggle. 'They might come running back to take a look at 'em.'

All code for *stay safe, you're missed*, Kate assumed.

'Would anyone like to contribute towards a parcel for them?' she asked, but that was stretching goodwill.

The three Fletcher men returned to work without another word.

Kate cleared up and went outside too, keen to stay on top of her own work. The land girls should have done a few weeks of training before their arrival but even so they were likely to make Kate's life harder before they made it better. It would take time for them to settle in and learn the ways of Brimbles Farm, and it was Kate who'd have to teach them.

The kitchen garden, as the inspector had called it, was Kate's sole responsibility. She set to work uprooting weeds while thinking about the sorts of meals the girls might expect. Kate didn't regard herself as a bad cook considering she had to work with whatever ingredients the farm produced, supplemented by whatever she could buy on a tiny housekeeping budget. But the girls might expect better food, even in wartime. She'd need the full fourteen shillings a week allowance for each girl's bed and board if she was to feed them well, and if Ernie had visions of withholding it, Kate might personally murder him.

She paused at the sound of a distant motorcycle. Bikes and even cars occasionally used Brimbles Lane to get to the hospital as it was something of a short cut, but this motorcycle seemed to be drawing nearer instead of passing by along the lane. Kate walked around the barn to investigate just as the motorcycle entered the farmyard.

It was being ridden by a man wearing the short brown leather flying jacket of the Royal Air Force together with a leather helmet and a pair of goggles. The jacket hung open, showing the blue of an RAF uniform underneath. Not that Kate had seen a man in RAF uniform before, but she'd seen photographs in newspapers and magazines. He brought the machine to a halt, kicked the stand into place, then pulled off his goggles and helmet to reveal tobacco-brown hair and blue eyes that were full of amusement. 'I hope you're not planning to attack me with that,' he said, nodding at the gardening fork she still held. 'I know farmers don't always welcome trespassers on their land, but please believe me when I say I come in peace.'

Kate was torn between foolishness for standing there with the fork as though repelling the enemy and awareness that those laughing blue eyes were extraordinarily attractive. Caught between the two feelings, she couldn't think of a way to respond.

'Flight Lieutenant Leo Kinsella,' he added, swinging his long legs off the bike and coming towards her. He was wearing gauntlet gloves but tugged one off to offer a hand.

Kate found her voice at last. 'Not a good idea,' she told him, showing him the dirt on her hands.

He grinned and said, 'Pity,' which brought sudden warmth to her cheeks.

He was several inches taller than her, which was unusual. In fact, beside him Kate felt almost delicate instead of thinking she resembled an awkward giraffe.

'I'm looking for a place called Stratton House,' he said. 'According to a map I consulted, this lane leads to it but all I can see ahead are trees and bushes. Are you able to offer directions?'

'Keep going and you'll see a track. It's wide enough for a horse and cart or even a car so you should be fine on a motorbike.'

'Perhaps you're more competent with a horse and cart than I am with a bike,' he said. 'A pilot in the Royal Air Force almost getting himself lost is shameful.'

'What matters is whether you're any good with an aeroplane,' Kate pointed out, then blushed again.

Luckily, Leo Kinsella laughed. 'I seem to be managing all right in an aeroplane.' He paused then added, 'I hope you don't mind me asking, but are you a member of the Women's Land Army?'

'A farmer's daughter.'

'This is a very pretty part of the country.'

Was he really talking about the countryside being pretty? Or was he talking about her? The gleam dancing in his eyes suggested the latter. Again, Kate didn't know how to reply so stayed silent.

'I've told you my name, but you haven't told me yours,' he said then.

'It's Kate. Kate Fletcher.'

He nodded as though her name met with his approval. 'Well, I can see you're busy and my cousin is expecting me to visit. He's a patient at the hospital.'

Kate felt a burst of sympathy. 'I'm sorry.'

'He's going to be fine. Eventually. It's going to take a while, though.'

'I hope you find him well.'

'Thank you.' He looked at her for a thoughtful moment, then returned to the bike, not bothering to replace his helmet, goggles or gauntlets, presumably because he didn't have much further to travel. 'It's been a pleasure to meet you, Kate Fletcher of Brimbles Farm, Churchwood. Perhaps I'll be along this way again.'

He fired the bike into life, circled to face the way he'd come and sketched a salute, which he accompanied with a warm smile.

Goodness. Kate watched him ride away and was still standing there when her father appeared. 'Turned into a statue, have you? Leaving the work to the rest of us?'

Kate snapped out of her trance. 'I work as hard as anyone.'

'Who was that on the motorbike?'

'Just someone wanting directions to the hospital.'

'They should put up a sign. Save busy folk from being bothered.'

What a misery Ernie was. Kate returned to work but all through the afternoon found her thoughts drifting back to Leo Kinsella. He'd made her feel feminine despite her dirt. He'd made her feel attractive.

She looked up at the sky as it began to rain, but the weather had no power to trouble her today.

*

115

'You're too busy to come and say hello to me, Kate, so I've come to say hello to you,' Alice's Daniel said.

Alice was with him, holding on to his arm and looking happy to have him close.

'My beloved girl is on her way to Stratton House,' he explained. 'I didn't want the patients to be deprived of her company just because I'm here, so I decided to walk up with her.'

'It's good to see you,' Kate told him.

'I hear two of your brothers have joined up and left you in a pickle.'

'Mmm, but I'm hoping we'll be allocated a couple of land girls soon.'

'Is there anything I can do to help for an hour or two until Alice returns?'

How kind of him! Kate would be glad of some help, though her father wasn't exactly welcoming to strangers. He was downright rude, in fact. Was it fair to expose Daniel to that?

'Oi!' As if on cue, Ernie's foul-tempered voice cut across the field. A moment later he walked over, fixing Alice with a glare. 'You again! What trouble are you causing now?'

Alice only smiled. She was never cowed by Fletcher hostility. By the look on Daniel's face, Alice had warned him what to expect, but his eyes had narrowed at the disrespect Ernie was showing to his beloved.

'Mr Fletcher, I assume,' Daniel said. 'I'm Alice's fiancé and a friend of your daughter's. Convention suggests I should say it's a pleasure to meet you, but I wouldn't wish to make a liar of myself. However, I'm here to help if you'd like assistance.'

116

'What do you know about farming?' Ernie sneered, because even in his oldest clothes Daniel looked tall, trim and smart.

'Not a lot, but I can take instruction. And I do know engines. More than you know, judging from the awful noise that tractor is making.'

Alice had definitely given Daniel a lesson in how to handle the Fletcher men.

'Do you want me to take a look at it?' Daniel asked.

'Nothing else to do with your time, eh?' Ernie made it sound as though Daniel were some sort of idle aristocrat instead of a serving soldier and, before that, a successful engineer who worked with racing cars.

Daniel merely shrugged. 'Doesn't bother me whether I look at the tractor or not. It isn't my tractor. And it isn't my work that's being held up.'

Ernie looked unsure how to reply without having to swallow his pride. '*She* wants you to look at it, I suppose,' he finally said, waving a dismissive hand at Kate.

As if he cared what his daughter wanted!

With a final sneer, Ernie walked away and Kate could only be thankful that he hadn't spat at Daniel's feet.

'Well, I was warned,' Daniel said, laughing. He turned to Alice and kissed her. 'Go and cheer those patients up. I'll see you on your way back.'

Alice went on her way and Kate gestured towards the tractor. 'Shall we?'

Within half an hour Daniel had fixed it. Ernie only grunted but Kenny managed a brief nod that could have signified appreciation. Thankfully, Vinnie was

117

still over in Five Acre Field so Daniel was spared his uncouth company.

'What else would you like me to do?' Daniel asked Kate.

She asked if he could help to repair an outhouse door and he set himself to the task with energy. 'I hear there's going to be a bookshop party tomorrow,' he said, after taking a nail from between his lips. 'You'll be coming along?'

'Probably not. The workload here . . .'

'Do try to come. Everyone needs a break, and it may be the last bookshop event.'

'We don't know yet that it will definitely have to close,' Kate pointed out.

'No, but it might. More's the pity.'

'Are you worrying about Alice? She'll be disappointed if the bookshop closes. We all will. But Alice is strong. The strongest, bravest person I know. If the bookshop closes, she'll focus on the hospital patients – there are more and more of them as the war goes on – and I'm sure it'll only be a matter of time before she has another idea for helping the village.'

Daniel smiled proudly. 'That's my Alice. But I'm sorry she may have to go through disappointment first, especially as I won't be around to comfort her. Blast this war, eh? How are your brothers getting on?'

'I think the discipline is a shock to their systems. The twins have always been on the wild side.'

'I'll bet that goes down a treat with their sargeant major. Don't worry, Kate. Discipline could be the making of them.'

'Let's hope so.' As long as they survived to put it to good use . . .

When Alice returned, Daniel told her that he'd encouraged Kate to go to the party.

'Do come,' Alice agreed.

'I'll try.' Kate thanked Daniel for his help then watched him walk away, arm in arm with Alice again. It must be lovely to have found a soulmate.

The memory of Leo Kinsella's face floated into her mind, but she dismissed it instantly. She'd only met the man for a few minutes! Even so, he'd made her feel good about herself. Was it possible that she might meet a man who loved her one day?

Enough daydreaming. She'd only set herself up for disappointment if she entertained ideas of a romantic nature. Kate got back to work.

The following morning brought her another letter. Two land girls would arrive on Monday.

Kate felt a celebration was in order and when Ernie threw a torn jacket at her and grunted, 'Needs patching,' she told him, 'All right, but it'll have to wait.'

'Eh?'

'I'm going out.'

'Out where?'

'To enjoy myself.'

'Kate!' Alice cried, as Kate walked into the Sunday School Hall that evening. 'It's so good to see you!'

'I've left a lot of work behind but we're getting two land girls next week.'

'That's certainly worth celebrating.'

Other people had smiles for Kate too. Naomi was the next to come over. 'You've been missed.'

'Couldn't be helped. Sorry I haven't been around

119

to help with the bookshop.' Poor Naomi still looked tired from it all.

Then May approached. Janet too. And Bert Makepiece said in his dry way, 'Good to see you, young Kate.'

Daniel was giving Marjorie Plym a turn around the dance floor. She looked flushed with pleasure though she had no sense of rhythm and kept saying, 'My word!'

The record came to an end. Daniel kissed Marjorie's hand, making her flush an even deeper shade of puce, then came over to Kate as Benny Goodman's 'Sing, Sing, Sing' came on the gramophone. 'Will you do me the honour?' he asked, holding out an arm in invitation.

'I'm no good at dancing.'

'Practice makes perfect.' He swept her on to the dance floor.

Daniel had a way of making people feel comfortable and Kate enjoyed dancing with him, even if it wasn't always Daniel's dark eyes that she saw in her mind but Leo Kinsella's laughing blue ones. Was he as good a dancer as Daniel? Kate suspected he was. There was something about Leo that suggested he grabbed life with both hands.

It was lovely to be amongst friends again, and Kate had high hopes for getting more time off when the land girls came. She especially wanted to be a better friend to Alice and Naomi. Both were throwing themselves into the party atmosphere with all the appearance of merry abandon, but Kate knew how bereft Alice was going to feel when Daniel returned to the war, and Naomi looked as though she hadn't slept well in weeks.

'*Sing, sing, sing, sing,*' Daniel crooned, twirling Kate around.

She glanced round at the partygoers – residents old and young, hospital patients and staff . . . No one knew what the future held for any of them, but this was a moment in time in which the bookshop was flying high and offering fun to all of them. It felt wrong not to make the most of it. She smiled at Daniel, took a deep breath and began to croon along with him. '*Sing, sing, sing, sing . . .*'

The land girls were travelling to Churchwood by train and bus. When Monday came, Kate took the cart into the village to collect them, hoping her friendliness would go some way to making up for the roughness that awaited them back at Brimbles Farm.

She felt a mix of excitement and relief when the bus rumbled into view. Passengers began to alight and, amid the regular coats and jackets of Churchwood residents, Kate caught sight of two land girl uniforms – breeches, cream shirts and green jerseys. Jumping down from the cart, she went to greet the young, female strangers who were wearing them. 'Hello! You must be Ruby and Gertrude.'

She was smiling, but as they turned to look her up and down, Kate felt the first stirrings of unease. Might there be trouble ahead with these girls?

# CHAPTER FOURTEEN

## *Kate*

To be fair, her unease arose mostly from just one of the girls. Kate knew that land girls must come in all shapes and sizes so wasn't taken by surprise by the fact that this girl stood no more than five feet in height and had an extremely curvy figure. No, it was her glamour that was disconcerting – the hair dyed to startling near-whiteness, the bright red lipstick and other cosmetics, and, above all, the manicure. How were such long and beautifully tended nails going to survive toiling in the fields?

Something in her look and manner made Kate's instincts tingle too. Was it confidence? Challenge? Guardedness? It was hard to gauge, but, having grown up being judged unfairly herself, Kate was the first person to recognize that appearances and first impressions could be misleading. 'I'm Kate Fletcher,' she said. 'I'm delighted you're coming to Brimbles Farm.'

She offered a hand, holding it midway between them so the girls could choose who shook it first. She wasn't surprised when the shorter girl took the initiative. If Kate was reading the situation correctly, it was this girl who was the leader of the pair, the other girl being her loyal follower.

'Ruby Turner,' the shorter girl said. 'Charmed, I'm

sure.' Her voice held a hint of the Cockney accents Kate had heard on the radio.

'You're very welcome, Ruby,' Kate said, and then turned to the other girl who waited for a nod from her friend before springing forward like an eager Labrador to crush Kate's fingers in her grasp. 'Gertie Grimes,' she said cheerfully, 'but call me Pearl. It means we're Ruby and Pearl, do you see?'

Two jewels, though it was hard to imagine a name that suited this girl less. Kate wasn't short but Gertie – or Pearl – was at least six feet tall. Broad in the shoulder and wiry in build, she had exceptionally large hands and feet, and not even the kindest person would have called her pretty. Her nose was too large and her complexion too red, while her hair was short, limp and a nondescript shade of brown. But if Pearl was the name she preferred, Kate was happy to go along with it.

'It's lovely to meet you, Pearl.'

'Gosh.' The big girl stuffed her hands into her pockets, looking both ungainly and embarrassed.

Guessing she wasn't used to approval, Kate felt a flash of sympathy for her. Of gratitude too, because at least Pearl looked as though she'd take farm labouring in her stride.

'I'll be working alongside you both,' Kate said, hoping to build some rapport.

'Are you a land girl too?' Ruby asked.

'No, I'm . . . Brimbles Farm belongs to my family.'

'You mean your family is in charge?' Ruby looked struck by the information.

'My father's in charge.'

Ruby nodded thoughtfully then smiled again.

'Well, Kate, it's kind of you to meet us. Are you ready to go, Pearl? We don't want to keep Kate and her father waiting.'

Kate felt as though she'd gone up a notch in Ruby's estimation. 'The farm is a little way out of the village, so I brought the cart,' Kate said, gesturing towards the wooden vehicle. 'The pony is Pete. He's been with us for years.'

Ruby set off towards the cart, leaving Pearl to manage the bags.

'Need any help?' Kate asked, but Pearl merely picked them up and slung them over her shoulders.

'Strong as an ox, me,' she said, walking to the cart and dropping the bags into the back.

Ruby had already climbed up on to the bench seat at the front. Kate got up on one side of her to take the reins, and Pearl the other.

'What are those buildings over there?' Ruby asked, pointing across the village green.

'St Luke's Church, the vicarage and the Sunday School Hall.'

'And the fourth building?'

'The elementary school.'

Ruby gave a thoughtful nod, and continued looking around. 'And along here are shops.' She gestured around the other sides of the triangular green where a mix of shops and cottages stood.

'There's a Post Office so you'll be able to send letters home without too much trouble,' Kate told her. 'Grocer, greengrocer, cobbler, baker . . .'

'I like the sound of the bakery,' Pearl said. 'I love a slice of cake or a bun.'

Kate smiled, hoping again that Ernie wouldn't

124

cheat on the housekeeping money so these girls could be well fed.

They left the village green behind. 'At the moment a lot of village life centres on our bookshop, which is open several days and evenings each week in the Sunday School Hall,' Kate said, aiming to reassure the girls that Churchwood was a good place to live. 'We call it a bookshop but we also have talks, story times and social events.'

'Hear that, Ruby?' Pearl said. 'Social events.'

'Nice,' Ruby said, but her thoughts appeared to be on other matters.

'What sort of social events?' Pearl asked.

'Music, dancing . . . That sort of thing.'

'You'll like that, Ruby,' Pearl said.

'Oh, certainly.'

'They're mostly attended by village residents,' Kate continued, 'but patients and nurses from the nearby military hospital often come too.'

She paused; then, feeling an obligation to be truthful, she added, 'There's a chance that the bookshop might have to close, though.'

'Shame,' Pearl said.

Kate steered Pete on to Brimbles Lane, past Alice's cottage on one side and Naomi's Foxfield on the other. 'We're around half an hour's walk from the village. Less if you walk briskly. I have a bicycle I can lend you to make it even quicker. From the village you can catch the bus to other places.'

She didn't mention that the buses were slow and infrequent. Instead, she told them a little about the management of Brimbles Farm. 'Have you worked on farms before?' she asked.

'We've had six weeks of training,' Pearl answered.

It was better than nothing, though Kate was at a loss to understand how Ruby's smart nails could have survived six weeks of labouring.

'That was where we met,' Pearl explained. 'Hit it off straight away. Didn't we, Ruby?'

'We did.'

A thought crept into Kate's head. Had the friendship been born of Pearl's need for a friend and Ruby's need for someone to help with her workload? It would explain how Ruby had managed to keep her nails looking so immaculate.

Kate had no experience of city life, but Ruby struck her as the sort of person who'd thrive amongst bright lights, dance halls and pubs. From making parachutes to driving ambulances, she could have chosen war work that kept her close to that hub of life and perhaps paid better too. Farm work in the middle of nowhere felt an odd sort of choice for her, though doubtless Ruby had her reasons. She might be escaping an unhappy home life, fleeing a scandal over a married man, fleeing a different sort of man who wouldn't take no for an answer . . .

Whatever the reason, Ruby's presence remained a mystery.

A few minutes later, Kate began to point out the Brimbles Farm fields, boundaries and orchard.

She drove the cart into the farmyard and on into the barn where she jumped down and began to take Pete out of harness. Pearl jumped down too, gave Pete a cautious pat and grabbed the bags from the back. Ruby climbed down more slowly and moved out into the yard where she stood looking up at the farmhouse, thinking . . . Kate had no idea what Ruby was thinking.

With Pete restored to his field, Kate led the girls into the house and put the kettle on for tea. 'The accommodation is pretty basic, I'm afraid,' she said, watching their reactions to the scuffed, shabby kitchen. Pearl looked contented enough. As for Ruby, Kate was sure the girl was taking note of every detail, though she gave nothing away in her expression.

'Want some help?' Ruby asked suddenly.

'Oh!' Kate was startled. 'Thanks for the offer but you're not supposed to do indoor work.'

'Who cares about silly rules like that?'

Kate cared. If Ernie and her brothers thought that rules could be broken, they'd soon try to exploit the girls by piling on work out of hours and maybe even withholding some of their wages. She didn't want to get into trouble with the Women's Land Army officials and neither did she wish to set a bad example.

'It's sweet of you to offer but I'd like to do things properly. Sit down and relax.'

Ruby did so and Kate suspected she was secretly pleased, having only made the offer for show.

'Have you lived in the countryside before?' Kate asked.

'Not me,' Pearl said. 'I'm from Croydon. That's a town in Surrey.'

'I hope you won't miss it too much.'

'I'm glad to get away, to be honest.' Pearl did one of her awkward shifts from one big foot to the other before joining Ruby in sitting at the table. 'I reckon my mother's glad I've gone too.'

'Oh?'

'She and my sister are dainty. I take after my father, who's a big sort of chap. Six feet five inches, can you believe? My mother and sister still try to steer me into the most frightful dresses, then despair when I look awful. I'm nagged all day long at home.' Pearl began to mimic the voices. ' "Stand up tall, Gertrude. Stop slouching. Take your hands out of your pockets. You're not on an army route march so take smaller steps. Change those awful trousers for a dress before the neighbours see you." '

Kate felt a pang of pity for Pearl. 'Where do you call home, Ruby?'

'London.'

'She's from Poplar,' Pearl said.

Kate had a vague idea that Poplar was near the docks in the city's East End. Not prosperous compared to other parts of London. Quite poor, in fact, and in places even squalid. Was it possible that Ruby simply craved the clean air and open spaces of the countryside?

Kate placed bread and butter on the table along with a jar of jam she'd made and hidden away for special occasions now shop-bought jam was rationed. 'What work have you done before?' she asked, thinking that both girls were probably three or four years older than her so likely to have had at least one job in the past. She also hoped the question would lead to some sort of insight into why Ruby was here.

'I tried a few things to please my mother,' Pearl said. 'I was companion to an old lady for a while, but she found me too big and unsettling. She said I wasn't conducive to rest. My mother says, "You're a cart-horse, Gertie, more's the pity." She's right. I tried working in an office after that and then in a shop but I wasn't right for them either. I preferred my next job – helping in a kennels. I like dogs and they seem to like me. My mother and sister weren't happy, but they'd given up on trying to marry me off by then, so it didn't matter. As if any chap would want to marry me!'

'I don't see why not,' Kate said, but Pearl only laughed – loudly, and perhaps a little wistfully.

'Ruby?' Kate asked then.

Pearl answered for her. 'Ruby's done all sorts of things. She was in service until the mistress decided she didn't like the way the master looked at her.'

Or had the mistress not liked the way Ruby looked at the master?

'She worked in a factory making biscuits after that, then went into shop work, selling cosmetics and perfume.'

That sort of work sounded much more suited to this coiffed and painted girl whose appearance obviously mattered to her. Ruby simply smiled.

'Farm work will be a new challenge for both of you,' Kate said.

Tea finished, she offered to show them to their room.

Unsurprisingly, Pearl carried both bags upstairs. 'I'll take the bed by the window,' Ruby announced when they reached the twins' room where Kate had put another jug of fresh greenery.

'Chamber pots under the beds. Other facilities in the yard,' Kate said. 'There's space in the drawers for your things. I'll leave you to unpack and wait for you downstairs.'

Kate left the room but, glancing into it as she walked downstairs, she saw Ruby throw herself on to the bed and lie back with her arms making a pillow for her head, a cat-like smile playing on her lips. It intrigued Kate while at the same time making her a little nervous, but she was still determined to give the girl every chance to prove herself.

Downstairs, Kate put the kettle on again and made tea for her father and brothers, slicing bread and piling it on to a plate. Ernie was the first to arrive. 'Well?' he demanded.

'The girls are unpacking.'

'Humph.' His grunt suggested they were shirking work already.

Vinnie appeared next. 'Are they here?' His ferrety eyes were bright, though it was hard to know whether he was excited because the girls might be pretty or gleeful because Kate would be in trouble if they proved useless.

Footsteps sounded on the bare wooden stairs. The girls were coming down.

Kate made the introductions.

'It's a pleasure to meet you, Mr Fletcher,' Ruby told Ernie. 'I hope I'm going to be an asset to the farm. Producing food in wartime is important, isn't it?'

Was Ruby sucking up to Ernie? If so, she'd be disappointed in him because Ernie rated pounds, shillings and pence above charm and cajolery.

Sure enough, all he gave Ruby was a hard stare and a warning. 'I only pay for work that's actually done.'

He sent another hard stare in the direction of

Pearl, who turned even redder in the face, then he sat at the table and began to read a newspaper.

Kate glanced at Ruby, curious to see her reaction, but the girl saw she was being watched and kept a smile in place.

Kate introduced Vinnie next. He'd looked startled at the sight of Pearl – she was taller than him and possibly capable of crushing him – but now he was leering at Ruby.

She met it with another smile but it was bland and distant. Kate couldn't blame her for being unimpressed with Vinnie.

But then Kenny walked in and Ruby's eyes widened. She was seeing his good looks, of course, not yet having been exposed to the morose personality that cancelled out – drowned out – the advantages Mother Nature had given him. Besides, he'd never shown an interest in mere females.

At least, he'd never shown an interest before now. He too looked taken aback by Pearl but when his gaze fell on Ruby his surprise became mixed with an obvious awareness of her attractions.

Kate made the introductions again and was sure there was more warmth and even huskiness in Ruby's voice when she said, 'It's a pleasure to meet you, Kenny.'

He coughed suddenly, as though snapping himself back into his customary dourness. Sparing the girls no more than a nod, he turned to Ernie and began talking about the price of fertilizer.

'We've had our tea so I'm going to show the girls around the farm,' Kate announced.

131

'We can't wait to see it,' Ruby said, but Kenny had his back to her and didn't respond.

Kate was relieved. The last thing Brimbles Farm needed was a flirtatious romance.

But as she gestured the girls outside, she saw that Kenny's head had turned just enough for him to watch Ruby's swinging hips leave the kitchen. *Oh, heavens.*

# CHAPTER FIFTEEN

## *Alice*

The first face Alice saw when she walked into Ward One on Tuesday belonged to Babs Carter, a nurse who – along with fellow nurse Pauline Evans – had become her good friend over the past year. 'That was a great social on Saturday,' Babs said. 'I've never danced so much in all my life. The patients loved it too. Did you see Percy Tomkins dancing in his wheelchair?'

'I did, and I was thrilled for him.'

'I can't believe the bookshop might close when it does so much good. Surely making people feel part of a community and helping one another is living the Bible, not just preaching it?'

'If only you were choosing our new vicar, Babs.'

'I'd choose Adam. He danced with me twice on Saturday. Such a sweetheart!' Babs smiled at the memory then turned serious. 'It'll be a tragedy if the bookshop closes but there's nothing a stuffy old vicar can do to stop you bringing books and reading stories to the patients here. You'll still be helping people, Alice. Just not as many.'

'I know.'

Babs hesitated, then, wincing as though she knew it

was a difficult subject, she said, 'Daniel got off all right, did he?'

Alice had to swallow to keep the sudden rush of emotion in check. 'I walked him to the bus stop yesterday.'

'Parting is hard.' Babs patted her arm and went to see to a patient.

'We can say goodbye here,' Daniel had offered before leaving the cottage. It would have kept their farewell private with no need to put on brave faces for anyone else, but Alice had wanted to spend every last second with him, for who knew when she'd get to see him again?

They'd held each other tightly until the bus conductor had said, 'Can't wait any longer for you, mate. Either you get on now or wait for the next bus.'

'I'm coming,' Daniel had said, because he had a train to catch.

He'd kissed Alice for one last time, told her he loved her to the moon and back, then swung his bag over his shoulder and stepped on to the bus.

Alice had stood waving until the bus had trundled out of sight.

'Doesn't get any easier, does it?' Janet Collins had said, pausing on her way to the shops. With her son a serving soldier, Janet knew all about the distress of partings.

'It certainly doesn't.'

Not wanting to be caught crying in public, Alice had hastened home and gone up to the bedroom where Daniel had slept. The tears had been flowing freely by then – and they flowed even more when she discovered a note he'd left on his pillow.

*Dearest Alice,*

*By the time you receive this, I'll be on my way back to the regiment and our time together will be receding into the past. But know that it's a time I'll always treasure and memories of it will comfort me over the months to come. Enjoying that slap-up meal at the restaurant in St Albans when you came with me to see my godmother . . . Holding you in my arms as we danced at the bookshop social . . . Collecting eggs . . . so many joyful memories!*

*I'm sorry the future of the bookshop is so uncertain. You're being brave about it, but I know you'll be devastated if it closes. Please don't keep your feelings to yourself. I want to help.*

*Meanwhile, please write often. A letter from you turns the darkest day cheerful.*

*Please give my love to your father and our Churchwood friends, but know that most of my love is for you, my darling Alice.*

*Daniel x*

Alice had read it twice then lain down on the bed, placing her head where his head had rested and feeling bereft at his absence. But, as ever, the world kept turning and in time she'd got up and gone about her day, glad to have the memories Daniel had described and more besides, not least the time at the bookshop social when Miss Gibb had told him that she despised all men but for him might make an exception, while ancient Mrs Clegg had told him he could hold her knitting wool for her any time because, even with cataracts, she could tell he was handsome. He'd rolled up his sleeves and made tea for everyone, taking the

135

cups round like a waiter to give everyone a taste of tea at the Ritz. Then he'd sung a comic duet with Adam Potts that had everyone cheering and clapping.

Now she was here at the hospital, Alice was putting on her best show of cheerfulness for the patients, accepting compliments about the social from those who'd attended and answering, 'Let's not jump to conclusions prematurely,' when a patient who hadn't been well enough to attend complained in outraged tones, 'What's this I hear about the bookshop closing? I was so looking forward to the next social!'

She read a story about a group of hikers who were lost in thick mist in the Scottish Highlands before being guided back to safety by something unseen. 'A Scottish kelpie?' the story suggested.

'Or the Loch Ness Monster,' Private Ben Dodd said, and other patients laughed.

Alice paused for her usual brief chat with Tom the porter on her way out. He read newspapers and listened to the wireless keenly so was always a good source of war news.

Lunch was overdue by the time she reached home. The kitchen was tidy but Alice hadn't wished to waste Daniel's leave on cleaning so she'd let standards slip a little. She made cheese on toast for her father and herself, then set to work to give the kitchen a thorough going over.

Moving the bread box, she noticed something behind it. What was . . . Of course! The letter from Hubert Parkinson. Alice had forgotten all about it – which had been stupid of her as it could easily have been found by Daniel or her father.

Usually, she used scrap paper for writing shopping

lists or starting fires but she didn't want to leave this letter lying around again. She reached for the box of matches to burn it in the sink but paused, deciding she should at least read what Mr Parkinson had written before destroying it. Tearing the letter open, she pulled out the single sheet of paper.

*Dear Miss Lovell,*

*Thank you for coming to see me and for your interest in the position I advertised. On reflection, I feel I was too hasty in concluding that your injury made you unsuitable. I was struck by your enthusiasm, organizational abilities and not least your neat handwriting, and it has occurred to me that I could use a secretarial agency for typing the manuscript once you had helped to make it legible. On that basis, I am offering the position to you. Please let me know by return of post if you wish to accept it.*

*Yours sincerely,*

*Hubert Parkinson*

Alice gaped down at the letter. *Let me know by return of post . . .* Instead she'd allowed the letter to lie hidden for almost a week. Doubtless the position had now gone to someone else.

She wanted to scream and cry and stamp her feet.

# CHAPTER SIXTEEN

## *Naomi*

If Cecil Wade had been a peacock, he'd have been preening his feathers and strutting proudly.

'To summarize,' he told the church council. 'We're not advertising the position of vicar because two strong candidates have already applied and advertising will only delay matters. The interviews will be conducted by the bishop, the archdeacon, Arthur and myself.'

He smiled, as though savouring the triumph of being a very important person, then continued. 'I need hardly remind you – at least I hardly need to remind *most* of you – that information relating to the applicants and their interviews is confidential.' His gaze lingered on Naomi, signalling his belief that she was the weak link in the chain of privacy, being both a woman and a gossip.

Refusing to rise to the bait, Naomi said simply, 'The bishop and the archdeacon have seen the letters written in support of Adam Potts and the bookshop?'

'I can assure you that no relevant information is being withheld, Mrs Harrington,' he told her, which didn't actually answer her question.

She turned to Arthur, who was gripping the edge of the table in a way that suggested he was trying to anchor himself in place when what he really wanted to do was flee. 'You'll make sure the letters and testi-monials are given proper weight?' she asked him.

His gaze flickered to Cecil, who merely smiled to indicate that he wasn't going to let the implied insult unsettle him.

'Arthur?' Naomi prompted, and his Adam's apple bounced up and down like a child's toy boat.

'Um, well, as Cecil said, nothing will be held back.'

But Cecil had referred only to relevant information – relevant according to him.

The meeting broke up and Arthur raced for the door, doubtless hoping to avoid being caught by Naomi. She followed him outside, feeling that once again she hadn't done enough to champion Adam or the bookshop. She was trying her best, but lack of sleep had turned her brain to fuzz – just when she needed it to be sharp and incisive.

Most of the council members were retired so the meeting had taken place late in the morning rather than the more usual evening. Naomi headed home for lunch but was soon retracing her steps to the Sunday School Hall for an afternoon session of the bookshop, having warned the others that she'd be late because of the council meeting.

She found the bookshop in full swing and, stand-ing in the doorway to observe it for a moment, she felt the familiar tug on her heart that came from being part of a community. Over in the kitchen Janet and her friend Betty were dispensing tea and biscuits with smiles here and kind words there. Alice was rock-ing a baby in her arms to allow the child's mother some much-needed rest. May was showing a group of women how to alter a dress to fit a larger child. Bert was playing dominoes with a group of men who cheered loudly at something or other. And here and there groups of people chatted and laughed.

'Naomi!' Hilda called. 'Come and settle an argument.'

Naomi went over.

'Those books about a man and his servant. You know. The ones that make us laugh. I say the servant is called Jeeves and the man is called Bertie Wooster. Iris says their names are Jones and Wooster.'

Naomi smiled. 'Sorry, Iris, but Hilda is right with Jeeves and Wooster.'

Ada Hayes was next to call Naomi over. 'My Peggy has just had her third. Another boy.'

'How lovely!'

Then someone commented on last Saturday's bookshop party and soon everyone seemed to be talking about how they'd enjoyed it – the music, the dancing, the food . . . Lily Larkin even got up to demonstrate some dance steps. 'There's still some life left in this old girl!' she laughed, finishing to a round of applause.

It was wonderful to be a part of this. Oh, people would still be friends if the bookshop closed but this togetherness would suffer terribly. She really had to do better with the council.

Bert sidled up and spoke quietly in her ear. 'How was the meeting this morning?'

'Cecil was his usual self.'

'Bad as that? And the other – er – business?'

By which he meant Naomi's private troubles.

'I'm . . . making a little progress.'

'Try making it faster,' he advised. 'You're looking peakier than ever.'

With that, he walked away, leaving Naomi torn between frustration at being given advice she hadn't asked for and knowing Bert was right.

She might make some progress if she went to London, yet she had been putting it off because she was afraid of what she might find in case it rocked her world off its axis. But the alternative was to put her suspicions behind her, and that was proving impossible. She needed to stop dithering.

Walking home later, Naomi decided she could at least prepare the ground for a London visit. Handing her coat to Suki, she winced and touched her jaw.

'Toothache, madam?' Suki asked sympathetically.

'It comes and goes.'

'Cloves might help. My ma always puts cloves on teeth when they're hurting.'

'Thank you, Suki. Perhaps I need to see a dentist too.'

'You don't mean go all the way to London? Not with the bombs?'

'Mr Garland has been looking after my teeth for many years and understands me. And there's been no bombing to speak of for almost two weeks. Apparently, the Germans might have sent their planes elsewhere. To Russia, perhaps.'

'The planes might come back.'

'We'll see. I won't make an appointment just yet.'

She needed to stiffen her backbone first.

# CHAPTER SEVENTEEN

## *Kate*

For perhaps the first time ever, Kate was glad of Ernie's surliness. He dumped his teacup on the table, wiped his wet lips on the back of his hand and got up, saying, 'No one gets paid around here unless they work. I don't pay shirkers.'

He looked at no one as he spoke but Kate guessed the message was intended for Kenny and Vinnie as well as the girls. The girls had arrived on Monday. Now it was Friday, and the buzz in the air between Ruby and Kenny hadn't diminished. Mostly he appeared able to resist her, especially when working, but Kate suspected he was losing the battle to withstand Ruby's charms. And, as though he didn't want to be left out, Vinnie had begun larking around with Pearl. Work on the farm was suffering and it didn't help that, as Kate had feared, Ruby and farming just weren't a good fit.

Oh, she made all the right noises. 'Fancy,' she'd say, when Kate pointed something out to her, or 'How interesting,' or 'I'm so enjoying working here,' and even 'Leave it to me.'

But leaving work to Ruby mostly meant leaving it to Pearl. More than once Kate had caught Ruby scowling at the idea of doing anything that might threaten her manicure, and as soon as Kate's back was turned the work slowed down considerably, probably because Ruby eased off and Pearl had to continue alone.

Not that Pearl was complaining. She appeared to be so overwhelmed by her good luck in having a friend at last – a friend, moreover, who was glamorous and confident – that she considered it an honour to do Ruby's work as well as her own.

Ernie was clearly as fed up as Kate and turned at the door now to roar, 'Get to work!'

Kenny and Vinnie both jumped up and headed after him.

Kate washed and dried the breakfast dishes quickly while Ruby sat at the table smoking a cigarette with Pearl beside her.

'Give it another try,' Ruby said, and Kate guessed she'd passed the cigarette to Pearl because a moment later Pearl began coughing.

'Keep at it and you'll get used to it,' Ruby advised.

Kate hoped not. It was bad enough having the house fugged up by Ruby and the men smoking without Pearl joining in. But Pearl had said Ruby looked sophisticated with a cigarette in her hand so Kate wasn't hopeful.

She dried her hands then turned to the girls. She'd given them only light duties so far to ease them into life on Brimbles Farm but it was time they started pulling their weight. 'Let me show you the compost heaps.'

She caught the beginnings of a grimace on Ruby's face before it was covered with a smile.

'Compost is important,' Kate explained. 'It feeds the crops and reduces the need to buy fertilizer. We

143

don't have pigs so don't collect pig swill. We put most of our food waste on the compost heaps instead. Vegetable peelings, eggshells . . . things like that. We sometimes put scrunched-up newspapers in there too. The paper rots down eventually, but until then it creates little pockets so the air can get in and break the compost down.'

'Come on then, Pearl,' Ruby said, getting up with a show of enthusiasm Kate was sure she didn't feel.

They collected spades from the barn then made their way to the compost heaps. 'We have three,' Kate explained, 'mature, still maturing and new. We turn them regularly to keep the air and worms moving but we're only using the mature compost at the moment.'

Ruby had shuddered in distaste at the mention of worms.

'They do most of the work in breaking everything down,' Kate added. 'Have either of you turned compost before?'

'Not me,' Pearl said.

'Me neither,' said Ruby, and Kate guessed that it was an experience she'd gladly forgo.

*Why, oh why, hadn't she chosen to work in a factory or shop?*

Kate demonstrated what to do then stood by as Pearl got to work with vigour and Ruby dipped a spade into the very edge of the heap as though fearing she'd become contaminated if she moved too close.

'I need to hang some washing out, but I'll be back soon,' Kate told them.

She'd left the laundry soaking in the dolly tub after giving it a good scrubbing before the girls were up.

144

She rinsed it at the sink, carried it to an outhouse to put it through the mangle, then pegged it out on the lines that were strung across the gap between farmhouse and outhouse. The farm had better places for drying but Kate used this spot because the Fletcher men were less likely to pass by and move the washing out of their way with dirty hands.

She was away for as short a time as possible but returned to the compost heaps to find Pearl working and Ruby leaning back against a nearby fence. 'Problem, Ruby?'

'Just taking a breather. I only put my spade down a moment ago. Didn't I, Pearl?'

'Only a moment ago,' Pearl confirmed.

Short of calling them both liars, there was nothing Kate could do. 'We need to load some of the compost into wheelbarrows so we can spread it on the lettuces, strawberries and raspberries I planted.'

'I need to visit the little girls' room first,' Ruby announced, and she walked off as Kate and Pearl began loading the wheelbarrows.

'You seem to enjoy farm work,' Kate said, after a while.

'Beats getting in a tizz over not holding a china cup the right way and not plucking my eyebrows.'

'I suppose it must.' Kate paused, then she added, 'Is Ruby enjoying it too?'

'Course she is.'

Was Pearl's tone a shade too defensive? Perhaps. Kate understood why Pearl should wish to protect her friend. After all, by the sound of things Ruby was her *only* friend and loyalty probably felt like the least Pearl owed in return, even if it meant being flexible with the truth. After all, she was trying to make up for Ruby's shortcomings by working doubly hard herself – when she wasn't larking around with Vinnie.

It was frustrating but Kate couldn't condemn Pearl for it, knowing from her own experience of loneliness how precious friendship could be. But she still wanted to know what had brought Ruby here to the farm. 'It must be a big change for her after living in London,' Kate said.

'Yes, but she wanted to breathe fresh air after the smoke and smog of the city. Not that the air on a farm is always exactly fresh.' Pearl grinned at that thought. An open, honest grin.

'It isn't always fragrant,' Kate agreed, thinking that, if Ruby had other reasons for leaving home, she hadn't confided them to her friend.

Movement on the edge of Kate's vision had her looking up to see Ruby sashaying back across the yard while Kenny stood nearby and followed those inviting hips with his gaze. As Kate watched, Ruby sent him a smile. Kenny didn't smile back but possibilities still tingled in the air between them like electricity.

Reaching the compost heaps, Ruby's expression took on an edge of defiance as she realized Kate had seen her performance. The thought of the land girl becoming even harder to handle made Kate's heart feel heavy.

Later, over lunch, Kate announced, 'I have to go into the village to shop this afternoon. Perhaps you could supervise Ruby and Pearl, Ernie?'

Ernie grunted but didn't actually object.

'I'd like to help you with the shopping, Kate,' Ruby offered.

'Kind of you, but I think you'll be of more help on the farm.'

'I need to visit the shops anyway.'

'If you tell me what you want, I can add it to my list.'

'What I need is . . . personal.' Ruby smiled in a cat-like way. Perhaps she knew Kate wouldn't want the conversation to move in an embarrassing direction in front of the Fletcher men.

Kate swallowed down more frustration. 'Very well. But don't forget, you're free to go into the village in your time off in future.'

The girls had a half-day free as well as Sundays and Kate had made sure that the half-day would fall on a day when the village shops were open. The half-day had fallen yesterday, in fact, but Ruby had chosen to spend it lounging in the kitchen and up in her room.

'Oh, of course,' Ruby said airily.

She made a few half-hearted comments about the farm as they set out, then settled down to her private thoughts while Kate seethed quietly beside her, resenting the fact that she'd been manipulated.

'I'm going in the grocer's,' Kate said when they arrived, and Ruby followed her inside, looking around at the goods on offer.

Marjorie Plym bounded over. 'This must be one of your land girls,' she said, clearly thrilled at being the first resident to meet her.

'Ruby, this is Miss Plym. Marjorie, this is Ruby Turner.'

'You look too pretty to be a land girl,' Marjorie told her.

'We all have a duty to help the war effort,' Ruby said piously, which almost made Kate choke.

'Have you come far from home?' Marjorie asked.

'From London.'

'Fancy! What kind of work were you doing there?'

Ruby was looking bored. Vexed, even. 'This and that,' she said, then faked surprise: 'Oh, what's that?'

She stepped away though there was nothing special about the display of custard powder she went to investigate.

Kate bought several items and Ruby bought nothing.

'Bye, Ruby!' Marjorie called, but Ruby sent her only a small, tight smile.

'What an awful old gossip,' she said when she and Kate were outside.

There'd been a time when Kate would have agreed. But having learned that Marjorie's gossip was mostly the lonely woman's way of making herself feel important, Kate found herself feeling protective of her. 'She has her good side.'

Ruby wasn't listening.

Kate visited the Post Office next to buy playing cards to send to the twins. She used her own money because skinflint Ernie wouldn't take kindly to his money being spent. Ruby studied the shelf of newspapers and magazines. Was this her idea of buying something personal? A magazine about fashion or film stars?

Kate was surprised when Ruby marched up to the counter to pay for a copy of the *Beano*. 'It's for my little brother,' she said, defensively, when she caught Kate's stare of surprise. 'He's an evacuee and . . . well, I like to keep in touch.'

'That's nice,' Kate said, meaning it.

Rolling the comic up, Ruby bought a wrapper of brown paper and a stamp and sent it off.

Kate's last call was the bakery. Afterwards they headed home, neither saying much to the other.

'Did you have fun?' Pearl asked Ruby on their return.

'It's hardly London, Pearl.'

Which brought Kate back to the same old question: why on earth was Ruby here? Kate didn't want to judge her unfairly, but she was finding it impossible to trust her. Yet later, after Kate had carried clean laundry upstairs, she remembered Ruby's kindness in treating her little brother to the *Beano*. The girls' bedroom door was open and, passing by, Kate glanced in to see a framed photograph on the window ledge by Ruby's bed. It showed a boy of around seven years, far from good-looking, but with an endearingly cheeky grin.

Might there be a nicer, more genuine side to Ruby than Kate had seen so far?

# CHAPTER EIGHTEEN

## *Alice*

Gravel crunched on the drive behind her and, turning, Alice was pleased to see Adam Potts approaching Stratton House on his bicycle. She waited for him to catch up and smiled as he dismounted to walk the last few yards at her side. 'I heard you'd promised to visit,' she said.

'Some of the patients I met at the bookshop party told me I'd be welcome so here I am. Stratton House is in Holy Trinity's parish over in Epsley, but the vicar there doesn't visit because he hasn't a car and, to use his own words, his cycling and hiking days ended years ago. He told me I wouldn't be treading on his toes if I visited instead.'

'I'm sure the patients will be delighted to see you.'

Adam smiled. 'They'll certainly be delighted to see *you.*'

'Here's hoping we can both do some good.'

They agreed that the best way to reach more patients was to split up and go to different wards then change over. 'If you have a spare moment, I'd like a word before you leave,' Adam said.

'Of course.' It was always a pleasure to talk to Adam and he might have good news about his application.

Even so, Alice hoped he wouldn't keep her talking

for long. She had a reason for wanting to leave promptly today and it wasn't just so she could get to the bookshop.

She headed for Ward One and, seeing that all the nearby patients were awake, called, 'Good morning. Who's got a book to return? And who'd like a new book?'

She redistributed books, read a story out loud, then wrote letters for one patient whose hand was out of action and another for a patient who was capable of writing but preferred Alice to write on his behalf. 'My parents complain they can't make out at least half of anything I write,' he explained. 'I was never good at schoolwork. I preferred to be out and about on the moors, watching the birds and otters.'

'There weren't any otters where I lived in London,' Alice told him.

'You must have seen wild and exotic creatures in London Zoo, though. Not that seeing animals in cages is the same as seeing them in the wild.'

He glanced around the ward and she wondered if he was feeling caged in himself. 'I've got a book about an otter,' she told him. '*Tarka the Otter*. A patient in Ward Two has it but I can pass it on to you when he's finished reading it.'

'That would be grand, miss. My reading is better than my writing. A bit slow, but I get there in the end.'

Moving into Ward Two, she found Adam surrounded by a group of four or five patients, one in bed and the others on chairs or in wheelchairs. Their laughter made a lovely sound in the midst of so much suffering.

'Sorry. Are we being loud?' he asked.

151

'Not at all.'

She moved further along the ward to the patient who had *Tarka the Otter*. 'I've only a few pages left,' he told her. 'I'll finish them now so you can pass the book on to the other chap.'

Alice left him to it and went to have a chat with Bob Tucker, a sergeant who was one of the older patients in the hospital.

More laughter from Adam's group rippled down the ward. 'I like that Adam Potts,' Bob said. 'He doesn't try to force religion down a man's throat. That's the fastest way to turn folk against religion, by my reckoning. Adam's kind to everyone, saint or sinner – and that's far more likely to make men wonder if there might actually be something in this religion business.'

Alice agreed. But would the bishop see through Adam's scruffiness to the diamond inside? Would he also see that, while Julian Forsyth might be perfect for some places, Churchwood needed someone like Adam?

She spent a while longer in the ward before returning to Ward One with *Tarka the Otter*. Afterwards, she headed up to Ward Three, passing Adam in the corridor.

'What time are you leaving?' he asked.

'In about half an hour.'

'Let's meet in the hall.'

He was waiting when she came downstairs and accompanied her outside. 'I have an interview on the second of June,' he told her.

'That's wonderful!'

'I think my chances of being appointed are

negligible – that isn't false modesty talking, just an honest assessment of the situation – but I'm touched by the support I've received, and I want you all to know that I intend to do my best.'

'I understand. But don't despair, Adam. The archdeacon and Cecil Wade might favour Julian Forsyth but the bishop and Arthur Fellows both have votes to cast. I can't believe the bishop can ignore all the support you've received, and while Arthur may not be the bravest of men, he knows he'll upset the village if he doesn't vote for you.'

'You're an optimist, Alice, but rest assured I'll be trying my hardest to win them round.'

'No one could ask for more.'

'Now you need to get home to your lunch and I have more patients to see.'

He smiled, touched her arm companionably and walked back into the hospital.

Alice looked across at Brimbles Farm as she passed. She didn't see Kate but there were figures in a distant field. Did two of them belong to the land girls?'

Alice hoped they were settling in well, for their own sakes as well as Kate's, though one of them sounded surprisingly unlike Alice's mental image of a typical land girl – if Marjorie was to be believed. No one would call Marjorie a reliable source of information, but the report had come through May who said Marjorie had sounded awed instead of disapproving.

'The girl looked like that film star I've seen in magazines,' Marjorie had apparently said. 'She had the same colour hair. Not white like an old person but fair the way a hairdresser might dye it.'

'Jean Harlow platinum blonde?' May had asked.

'That's right, Jean Harlow hair, though this girl was shorter and rounder in her figure. She wore cosmetics too. Face powder, red lipstick and varnish on her nails.'

'Doesn't sound like a typical farm girl,' May had told Alice.

Perhaps not, but as long as she was a hard worker . . .

For a moment Alice toyed with the idea of heading up to Brimbles Farm to welcome the girls to the village. More than a week had passed since their arrival and they couldn't have formed a favourable opinion of Churchwood if the only people they'd got to know were the Fletcher men and Marjorie. But Alice didn't want to disrupt the farm routine and besides, she was eager to reach home quickly today.

She arrived just in time to greet the postman who'd called with the second post of the day. 'Looks like a book for your father,' he said, handing over a parcel.

'Thank you. Anything else?'

He smiled indulgently. 'I brought a letter from your young man yesterday.'

'Yes, but—'

'Oh, there is something else. Here you are.' He handed over a letter, though it wasn't from Daniel.

'Thank you!'

Hastening into the kitchen, she ripped the envelope open, read the letter then sank on to a chair. The world might be full of uncertainties and cares, but she'd just been given a little burst of joy.

# CHAPTER NINETEEN

## *Naomi*

It was early when Naomi set out for the bus stop. She was allowing plenty of time for her mission and also hoping to avoid seeing anyone she knew on the bus, her nerves not being up to a lot of chattering today, however well meant. Her steps faltered when she saw that Alice was already at the stop and for a moment she considered turning around and postponing her mission to another day. But it would be hard to explain her sudden return to her staff, and besides, lovely Alice didn't deserve to be snubbed.

Continuing onwards, Naomi fashioned her lips into a smile. 'Good morning, Alice. I didn't expect to see you out and about this early.'

'I didn't expect to see anyone either,' Alice told her. 'Apart from people going off to work, of course. Are you out for a walk or catching the bus?'

'Catching the bus then the train into London. I want to see my dentist about a tooth that's been niggling me.'

'I didn't realize you've been having toothache!' Alice's tone was a mixture of sympathy and understanding, as though toothache might go some way to explaining why Naomi's spirits had been so low recently.

'It comes and goes.' The toothache was an invention, of course. Naomi hoped she wouldn't be struck down by real toothache as a punishment for lying.

'I'm glad you're having it checked,' Alice said, 'but take care in London.'

'I will.'

The bus arrived, and they got on and sat side by side. 'You didn't say why *you're* out so early.' Naomi steered the conversation away from her imaginary ailment.

'I have a job,' Alice said proudly.

'A job?'

'For a gentleman who's researching his family history. It's going to involve thousands of old letters, photographs, diaries and the like, and he wants me to help to organize them. It isn't a full-time job. Two days a week, I think, though I'll know more after I've seen him today.'

'Where does the gentleman live?'

'St Albans. I'm looking forward to the challenge and I'll enjoy earning some money of my own again.'

'Then I couldn't be happier for you. But I didn't know you were looking for work.' Had Alice only sought work because she needed something to do if the bookshop closed? The thought made Naomi feel even guiltier over her failure to influence the church council.

'I've been keeping an eye out for opportunities for a while actually, though only in a casual way. To be honest, I thought I'd lost the chance to work with Mr Parkinson because he wrote to offer the job when Daniel was here and somehow the letter was overlooked.'

Alice blushed slightly, presumably at the implication that she'd been so caught up in the pleasure of Daniel's company that little else had seemed important. Naomi felt another pang of regret for the absence of such overwhelming love in her own life.

'I wrote back to Mr Parkinson as soon as I rediscovered the letter,' Alice continued. 'I thought I'd be too late – he could have offered the job to someone else by then. Luckily, he hadn't, so here I am.'

'I'm sure you'll be an asset to him.'

'As I said, it's only a part-time job. I'll still have time for the hospital and bookshop.'

'If we still have a bookshop,' Naomi said soberly.

'Don't take it to heart if we don't,' Alice urged. 'No one could have done more to keep the bookshop going than you.'

'If I hadn't stepped down as churchwarden and left the position free for awful Cecil Wade . . .'

'You weren't to know what he'd do and how he'd conduct himself. You'd been churchwarden for years. You were due a break. No one blames you for anything, Naomi. Adam is full of praise for all the support you've given him with his application.'

But would it be enough when the archdeacon and Cecil Wade were so much in favour of Julian Forsyth and his haughty wife?

'Even if Reverend Forsyth *is* appointed, we shouldn't assume the bookshop is at an end,' Alice argued. 'He might be a different man when he's away from the archdeacon and no longer trying to impress him.'

Did Alice really believe that or was she simply trying to make Naomi feel better?

'In any case,' Alice continued, 'the Forsyths might

157

think twice about closing the bookshop if we show the strength of opinion in favour of it.'

Alice would be wonderful at mobilizing local opinion, but Naomi felt as weak as a prematurely born kitten. Sleepless nights were continuing to take their toll, though after today, she might have a clearer picture of what – if anything – was going on with Alexander. The thought of what might lie ahead made Naomi feel nauseous.

The bus reached St Albans at last. Alice went off to her job and Naomi headed for the train station.

After the relative quiet of Churchwood, London felt loud and full of bustle. Many people were in military uniforms – army khaki, air force blue and the darker blue and white of the navy. There were other uniforms too, declaring to the world that their wearers were fire wardens, bus conductresses, members of the Women's Voluntary Service and the like. The facial expressions and bearing of the people she saw ranged from bold and chirpy to tired and beaten after months of air raids.

Other signs of the war abounded – gaping holes where buildings had once stood; other buildings that were boarded up to await demolition or repair; newspaper sellers offering the latest war news; shop windows advertising goods to send to servicemen who were far from home; posters reminding people to carry gas masks or appealing for clothing for the homeless . . .

Amidst it all, life went on.

Naomi went to her dentist in Harley Street first. Alexander was a patient of Mr Garland too and Naomi didn't wish to be caught out in a lie if he chanced to go for an examination and Mr Garland mentioned that he hadn't seen Naomi in an age. She hadn't told Alexander she was coming to London yet but had decided it would be wise to mention it to him so it wouldn't feel odd if he happened to hear of her visit from someone else. She'd mention it later, though, as she didn't want him rushing back to the flat to hide anything incriminating.

'It's just an intermittent discomfort,' she fibbed as Mr Garland peered into her mouth.

'I can't see anything that could be causing it. Let's keep an eye on things. In the meantime, you could pay more attention to your gums. They're important at any age but especially important as we get older.'

Naomi didn't like to be reminded of her age, especially when she felt even older, but she thanked him for his advice, paid his fee and then took a taxi to St John's Wood, where she asked the driver to pull in to the kerb just before they reached James Mansions, the large apartment block where she and Alexander owned a flat on the first floor.

It was probable that Alexander was in his office or out meeting clients, but she still looked around to be sure he wasn't nearby before she paid the driver and got out, feeling horribly exposed as she stood on the pavement. She walked towards James Mansions cautiously.

The block was set behind a low stone wall and a small garden. Naomi was surprised to see humps rising out of the grass until she realized they were Anderson shelters. There were four of them, not large enough to shelter all the residents but doubtless of some use for those residents or passers-by who hadn't managed to get into cellars or underground stations after the sirens sounded.

Still half hidden by the neighbouring building, she counted off windows until she reached those that belonged to the flat. There were no shadowy figures inside that she could see but – just in case Alexander were home, or heard later that she'd come to the flat – Naomi had a cover story prepared to explain her visit: she was here to look out books she could donate to the bookshop.

She took a deep breath and, doing her best impersonation of a confident woman, marched to the gates, passed between them and walked along the short path to the impressive entrance doors and on into the hall. She expected to see one of the old concierges at the desk – smiling Jonny Paulson or cheeky Mickey Dobson. Instead, she saw a young woman rise to her feet behind the desk. Fair-haired and smartly dressed in a silver-grey suit, the woman was cool and self-possessed, with all the warmth of a glacier. She put Naomi in mind of Alexander's secretary, Miss Seymour.

'May I help you, madam?'

'No, thank you. I'll go straight up.'

'Are you a resident?'

There was nothing wrong with the question but the accusing look that accompanied it made Naomi feel as though she was doing something wrong. Besides, even though she had her cover story prepared just in case Alexander found out that she'd been here to the flat, she hoped that he wouldn't actually learn of it. The cover story felt weak – so weak that Alexander might wonder if she'd begun to suspect him of an affair. Forewarned, he might take extra care to conceal it and Naomi might never get to the truth.

'Harrington. Flat sixteen,' Naomi said reluctantly, summoning up the imperious manner of old.

The young woman didn't blush or apologize but some of the edge had left her voice when she said, 'I haven't seen you here before.'

'My husband and I have property in Hertfordshire where I spend most of my time. You're new, aren't you?'

'I've been here for three months.'

'Hmm.' Naomi's tone suggested the young woman still had a lot to learn.

'Will you be taking the lift?' The young woman walked around her desk, perhaps with a view to helping.

'I'll manage, thank you.' Naomi pulled the lift's outer cage and inner door open then stepped inside, closed them again and pressed the button for the first floor. The lift rose upwards.

Had she made a mistake in retaliating to the younger woman's hostility? Might it lead to a complaint to Alexander? Good grief, might the young woman be Alexander's lover? He was too old for her, but perhaps she was willing to overlook his age in return for gifts and fine dining. The broken clasp came back into Naomi's mind. Had it been attached to a gift Alexander had given to this young woman? The gold locket she was wearing now, perhaps? Was there a picture of Alexander inside it?

Pushing the thoughts aside, Naomi let herself into the flat. She had every right to be here, especially as it was likely that her money had paid for much, if not

161

all, of it. Even so, the idea of snooping made her feel furtive and a little unclean.

The floors were wooden – beautiful parquet – but pale blue Persian carpets covered much of them, absorbing the sound of footsteps so that Naomi felt almost spectral as she moved inside and made for the drawing room.

The curtains here were made from heavy damask the colour of old gold, matching the upholstery on the sofas and chairs. A sideboard, a bookcase and various small tables completed the furnishings but yielded nothing of interest to Naomi. She took three books from the bookcase but, still hoping to keep her visit here secret, disguised their absence by spreading the others along the shelves.

Next door was a dining room, which doubled as Alexander's study. Naomi found nothing of interest in there either. Clearly, he kept most of his papers elsewhere.

Reaching the master bedroom, Naomi paused. Was it her imagination or was there a scent in the air? Something flowery? Naomi picked Alexander's cologne off the dressing table and sniffed it. Familiar sandalwood. Not flowery.

There were no tell-tale signs of a mistress on the surface of the dressing table or in its drawers. One bedside cabinet contained spare reading glasses, a hair comb, handkerchiefs, and an old wallet with a small amount of cash inside. The other cabinet contained only a book. It was an Agatha Christie crime novel. Alexander didn't usually bother with fiction. Had someone else sat reading in this bed, perhaps filling time as Alexander got ready for work in the mornings? Impossible to say.

Opening the wardrobe door, Naomi saw a selection of Alexander's clothes. There was nothing in the pockets except for a stray shilling. No, wait. What was this? A button. Plain black and not especially large. A woman's button? Again it was impossible to say, but Naomi's imagination still supplied a scene in a nightclub in which Alexander's dark-haired mistress looked long, lissom and sophisticated as they danced together. 'Oh, bother!' the woman said suddenly. 'I've dropped a button. Be a darling and pick it up, then pop it in your pocket for me. I've left my bag by the table.'

The spare bedroom was empty of all but the furniture. Perhaps the bathroom would give more insight into Alexander's life. His satin dressing gown hung on the back of the door, the pockets empty. His shaving set sat next to the sink along with another comb. Inside the cabinet were pills for dyspepsia, eye drops, plasters, cotton wool, toothpaste, Brylcreem, a toothbrush and . . . Naomi backtracked.

There were two toothbrushes in the glass tumbler. It wasn't like Alexander to have two brushes in use at once. Did the smaller one belong to his mistress? Or was it simply a toothbrush he'd picked up while overnighting elsewhere because he'd left his own toothbrush at home?

Naomi made her way back along the hall to the kitchen. It was pristine because Alexander never cooked. The only supplies were champagne, wine, jars of olives and cherries, and tea, including Earl Grey, which Alexander disliked. The packet was unopened, though, so perhaps it was left over from a hamper that had been sent by a grateful client at Christmas.

There was a box of chocolates too – another item from a hamper? – and this *had* been opened. Three chocolates were missing. Alexander rarely indulged in chocolate, but it was possible that he'd come home late one evening and, finding nothing else to eat, had snacked on the chocolates himself. It was equally possible that someone else had eaten them. The dark-haired mistress floated back into Naomi's mind, her voice low and seductive. 'Pass the chocolates, there's a dear. Oh, look. A strawberry cream. My favourite . . .'

Naomi returned to the drawing room and breathed deeply. Experimentally. There it was again. That flowery smell. Of course, Alexander's cleaning woman might be using a flower-scented polish, but the scent was surely too feminine and too expensive for furniture polish. Naomi's imagination might be running away with her, though.

There was nothing to be gained by staying longer. Having taken care to leave no obvious fingerprints or footprints in the carpets, she was locking the flat door when a thought occurred to her. The cleaning lady only came to the flat twice a week. Might Naomi find something of interest in the wastepaper baskets? Returning to the drawing room she found only a couple of empty envelopes. In the bathroom there was a soap wrapper, but the soap was Alexander's usual brand. In the bedroom there was a pair of men's socks, worn through and discarded. Underneath were two strips of card that, upside down, looked like tickets. Naomi pulled them out and turned them over. Tickets indeed – for an evening performance of *Down Cherry Blossom Lane* that had taken place a few days earlier at Winfield's Theatre on St Martin's Lane.

Had the tickets been for the opera, or the ballet, or a serious drama, Naomi might have thought Alexander had been entertaining a client, though she couldn't recall Alexander ever having mentioned taking a client to the theatre before. But *Down Cherry Blossom Lane*? It sounded . . . frivolous.

Naomi replaced the tickets and left the flat. Riding the lift down to the entrance hall, she roused herself enough to sweep past the concierge with a cool 'Good day to you.'

'Good day, Mrs Harrington.'

Only once she was out of sight of James Mansions did Naomi allow herself to slump. She hated this cloak-and-dagger business. It wrung her nerves like wet dish rags. She still had no firm evidence that Alexander was betraying her, but the case was surely building against him: the laughter, the jeweller's receipt, the toothbrush, the perfume, the tickets . . .

She took some steadying breaths and headed towards a telephone kiosk. A few minutes later she was talking to the crisp Miss Seymour and after a further minute or two Alexander came on the line. 'What is it, Naomi?'

'I'm sorry to ring you up in the middle of the working day but I'm here. In London.'

He didn't answer. She imagined he was surprised. Irritated, too.

'I had a touch of toothache so I went to Harley Street to see Mr Garland.' No need to mention that she'd visited the flat afterwards. 'Now I'm here, I wonder if we might meet for lunch or—'

'I already have a luncheon engagement. Really, Naomi, you can't expect me—'

'I'm not expecting anything. I only rang in case you happened to be free. Clearly, you're busy.'

'I'm busy this evening too.'

'Then I'll see you when you next come home.'

She wasn't disappointed because she couldn't have faced him today. She was merely covering her tracks.

It would be mid-afternoon at the earliest before she reached Churchwood, so Naomi went in search of a solitary lunch, ordering soup, lamb cutlet and a fruit cobbler at a nearby hotel, though her appetite was non-existent and she'd have to force the food down. She wasn't the only person eating alone. Two men sat at separate tables but they looked purposeful, as though they were in London on business and would go home to their families at the end of the day. Naomi felt self-conscious and lonely.

She ate her meal and left a tip despite the indifferent service, then took another taxi to Selfridge's where she searched for that elusive flowery scent at the perfume counter. Was this it? Parisian Spring? Maybe. But Naomi couldn't be sure.

Outside, she saw a newspaper seller. *War latest!* his placard announced, but when she bought a copy she took it into a side street and turned straight to the entertainment pages. As well as a listing there was an advertisement for *Along Cherry Blossom Lane*. One critic had described it as *the best musical in London's West End*. Another claimed that it offered *a feast of musical entertainment*, and for yet another critic the show promised *romance at its best* with *a wonderful performance by London's sweetheart, Gladys Walker.*

It sounded the sort of show that Alexander would have scorned to attend with Naomi, but maybe no sacrifice was too great for a different woman.

Perhaps the time had come to talk to Bert.

# CHAPTER TWENTY

## *Kate*

The sound of laughter reached Kate as she headed for East Field where Ruby was supposed to be helping Vinnie. Kate had separated the girls so Ruby couldn't leave all the work to Pearl, though both girls had grumbled about it. 'I don't see why we can't work together,' Pearl had complained, clearly not wanting to be parted from her friend.

'We can get jobs done faster when there's two of us,' Ruby had added, though the cheek of it had almost taken Kate's breath away. Not only was Ruby leaving the lion's share of the work to Pearl when she thought she could get away with it, she was also distracting her friend into chatting so neither girl was working efficiently.

Kate hadn't argued. She'd simply let her silence tell them she expected them to follow orders and they'd finally gone where directed. Sulkily, though, which Kate found exasperating as she was hardly overloading them with work and was generous with the time she allowed them for breaks.

She was still trying to be friendly, though, not liking to be seen as a hard taskmaster and hoping to establish a pleasanter working relationship with the girls instead. She hoped she was making progress with

Pearl, though the tall girl's loyalty to Ruby clearly came first, and in Pearl's eyes Ruby could do no wrong.

With Ruby, Kate had made no progress at all. In fact, the more Ruby drew Kenny under her spell, the less she appeared to feel the need to impress Kate, though she was still putting on an act of being a good worker in front of Ernie. Kenny wasn't actively encouraging Ruby's attentions yet, as far as Kate could see, but there was no doubt that he was increasingly fascinated by her because he stole glances at her at every opportunity.

Not knowing what else to do, Kate did her best to keep the girls well fed and feeling welcome, taking an interest in their lives as far as they'd let her. 'Is your brother happy as an evacuee?' she'd asked Ruby, to be told, 'No. He's staying with a family that doesn't want him and doesn't give him enough to eat. He's made to play outside even if it's raining, and when he's finally allowed indoors, he scarcely dares to breathe for fear of getting yelled at.'

'I'm sorry.'

Ruby had only shrugged and turned to watch Kenny through the kitchen window, the sly, cat-like expression back on her face.

Following the sound of the laughter now, Kate came round a hedgerow and saw Ruby and Vinnie leaning against the tractor and smoking cigarettes. She hadn't expected to find them throwing themselves into the work – two idle people who were already leading each other astray – but placing Ruby with Vinnie had felt a better option than putting her with Kenny.

'What do *you* want?' Vinnie demanded, aggressive because he'd been caught shirking.

'I'm simply checking that Ruby is all right.'

'She's fine,' Vinnie said, casting a leer in the land girl's direction.

Ruby smiled back, but the leer bounced off her. Kate guessed she only tolerated Vinnie because he gave her cigarettes and a chance to idle away the working day.

'There's nothing wrong with taking a break for a couple of minutes,' he added.

But there were the butts of several cigarettes near Vinnie's feet.

Kate hated being a nag but if the girls didn't justify their wages, Ernie would get rid of them and then what would happen? Even without working as hard as they might, the land girls were still of some use, especially Pearl. Without them, tempers at Brimbles Farm would be savage again, and as for time off . . . Kate might as well expect a treasure chest full of diamonds to appear at her door.

She lingered until they'd returned to work. 'Lunch in an hour,' she said.

Pearl and Kenny had nothing to say to each other and were working well, thank goodness.

Kate returned to the house to find a letter had come for her. The envelope had been addressed by hand but might still be from the Women's Land Army. Was Kate expected to report on the girls' progress? If so, should she ask to swap Ruby and Pearl for two other girls who might work harder? Unfortunately, there was no guarantee of being allocated more useful girls and it would be hard to complain about Ruby and Pearl when Kate's own brothers were leading them astray.

She opened the letter, her eyes widening when she saw it had been sent from RAF Hollerton in Bedfordshire, and widening even more as she read its contents.

*Dear Miss Fletcher – or may I call you Kate?*

*I've been thinking of you often since we met. A five-minute conversation doesn't amount to a long acquaintance, but it was enough for me to wish for another, longer conversation.*

*Of course, you may be frowning as you read this, wondering who on earth I am. I hope you haven't forgotten me but, just in case, let me remind you that I'm the RAF officer who came into your farmyard seeking directions to Stratton House. Is that ringing a bell with you? A welcome bell?*

*It may seem forward of me to ask to see you again when we've barely been introduced but I'm asking anyway. Blame the war. I'm not exaggerating when I say that being a fighter pilot makes my future deeply uncertain. It means I want to grab at life with both hands. Not that I intend to grab at you (that really would be forward of me!) but I'd very much enjoy spending more time in your company.*

*Might you make time to see me on Sunday afternoon? I'll be happy to fit around your convenience, whether you have time for a ride out on the motorbike, a picnic or just a walk.*

*I've included a telephone number at the top of this letter so you can leave a message for me. If that isn't possible, I'll pass by anyway.*

*Yours hopefully,*

*Leo Kinsella*

Goodness. Leo had been sliding into Kate's thoughts often since he'd come to Brimbles Farm. It had given her a wistful sort of pleasure to remember how his blue eyes had danced with humour and glowed with warm appreciation when he'd looked at her. But it had never crossed her mind that he would get in touch and ask to see her again.

Now emotions jostled for space inside her. Surprise and delight were uppermost but there was awkwardness too. Kate had come a long way over the past year or so. She'd learned to feel comfortable with people and strike up conversations. But those people were known to her. Leo was a stranger and a handsome stranger at that. He must cross paths with many young women who knew how to be witty and how to flirt.

Kate had no experience of such things. What if she met with him only to bore him? The humiliation would be dreadful.

There were other complications. For one, Kate had fought a battle to win grudging permission to see her friends, but she was sure her father and brothers would see a handsome young man as a threat to the lifetime of skivvying they had planned for her and do everything they could to make it difficult – even impossible – for her to meet him.

And for another, the thought of exposing Leo to the rude, uncouth awfulness of her family filled Kate with horror. He'd be disgusted. Appalled. And he'd wish himself a million miles from her.

Yet Kate wanted to see Leo again. Very much.

Time was passing so she pushed the letter into her pocket and set about preparing the meal. But her mind wasn't on the job and only when she carried the soup to the table did she notice that she'd forgotten to put out bowls.

'Daydreaming about a handsome lover?' Vinnie mocked, not realizing how close he was to the truth.

'I'd dream about anything to get away from you,' Kate retorted, hoping she wasn't blushing.

Vinnie didn't bother to respond but Kate was aware of Ruby watching her thoughtfully.

If Kate did meet Leo, she'd have to hide it from the land girls as well. She certainly couldn't trust Ruby to keep quiet if she noticed Kate leaving the farm looking . . . not dressed up exactly, but having made some effort with her appearance. Ruby might even try to use it to her own advantage – 'Stop nagging me about work or I'll tell what I saw.'

It wouldn't hurt to throw Ruby off the scent in the meantime. Today the interviews for the new vicar were being held, and Kate was desperate to see Alice to learn the outcome. She made no secret of the fact that she was going out when evening fell. She changed into her best blouse, brushed her hair and made sure she was clean, the idea being to make it appear as though she often smartened herself up when she saw her friends.

'Where do you think you're going?' Ernie demanded in his usual surly tone.

'Into the village to see Alice.'

Kate fetched her bicycle from the barn and set off along Brimbles Lane, pushing Ruby from her mind and allowing Leo Kinsella to come back into her thoughts. What would Alice say if she heard about his letter? Doubtless, she'd urge Kate to take a chance and meet him on the grounds that if nothing was ventured, nothing could be gained. Then she'd spend time trying to boost Kate's confidence by insisting that she was a lovely girl who was clever, kind, interesting and fun – everything a sensible young man could possibly want. Unfortunately, Kate's confidence never lived up to Alice's expectations.

Reaching The Linnets, Kate leapt off the bicycle, leaned it against the wall and knocked briskly on the door.

'Kate!' Alice said, on answering. 'I'm so glad you're here. We're in the dining room.'

*We?* Alice was already leading the way inside. Following, Kate saw that the other members of the bookshop organizing team were there, and so was Adam Potts. 'It isn't good news, I'm afraid,' Adam told her. 'I tried my best, but it wasn't enough. I'm not going to be your new vicar.'

Dismay swept through Kate. Would this be the end of the bookshop and the lifeline it offered to so many people, Kate included?

'Adam couldn't have done more to support us,' Alice pointed out gently and Kate roused herself, afraid she must look as though she blamed him.

'I'm sorry, Adam. I didn't mean . . . Thank you so much for trying. Does this mean that other man got the job?'

'Reverend Forsyth. Yes, it does.'

'Favouritism,' Kate declared. 'The deacon or archdeacon or whoever he was wanted his own man from the beginning. You didn't stand a chance.'

'The archdeacon was certainly keen on Reverend Forsyth but it would be wrong of me to suggest I wasn't given a fair interview. I don't think I'm breaking any confidences in saying this, but the bishop was actually very kind. He told me I'd made a strong application, but he didn't feel he could pass over a man of Reverend Forsyth's calibre and experience. Also, Reverend Forsyth was available to start immediately while I'd have to give notice to leave St John's.'

'Humph.' As far as Kate was concerned it was the outcome that mattered, not the flowery language that excused it. 'So it's the end of the bookshop?'

'Not necessarily,' Adam told her. 'The bishop said it sounded a worthy community venture.'

'But this Reverend Forsyth will change it out of all recognition – unless someone stops him. Do you have any ideas for stopping him, Adam?'

'Churchwood isn't my parish. Septimus Barnes always made me feel welcome, but I can't tread on the new vicar's toes. He has to be given a fair chance. Once he's settled in and seen how Churchwood and the bookshop fit together . . .'

'He'll still want to change them. So will his wife.'

'Kate's right,' Alice said, 'but I'm not sure we'll stop them by going into battle with them. A battle might even be counter-productive if they dig their heels in on principle. Maybe subtlety will work better.'

'What do you have in mind?' Bert asked.

'Doing everything we can to make them welcome, so they feel part of the village and part of the bookshop too. If they don't feel under attack, they might come to see the value of the bookshop themselves.'

'I agree,' Naomi said, and Kate noticed again how tired she looked. The triumph of awful Cecil Wade must be hard for her to bear.

175

'I agree too,' declared Bert. 'Let's pile on the niceness and tell the Forsyths how much we appreciate their kindness – and wisdom – in letting the bookshop continue.'

May nodded. 'Flattery. It's got to be worth trying.'

'Definitely,' said Janet.

'Kate, you're fidgeting,' Alice said. 'Does this mean you disagree?'

'It means I need to get back to the farm. I'm not the right person to decide on the best way of dealing with Church people – no offence, Adam, you're one of us – so I'll leave it to the rest of you. Let me know if I can do anything to help, though at the moment . . .'

'Things are difficult even with the land girls?' Alice asked.

Kate shrugged.

'We understand,' Alice said then, and everyone gave Kate sympathetic looks.

Kate got up but then hesitated, thinking about Leo again. She still wanted to see him, but would it really be worth the effort of trying to sneak away from the farm under the noses of the Fletcher men and Ruby, not to mention the fury that would rain down on her head if she were to be caught with him? Her head told her 'no', but her heart screamed '*yes*'.

Whether she decided to meet him or not, she needed to telephone him, otherwise he might turn up at the farm and that would be mortifying.

How to ring him, though? She could use the telephone in the Post Office but that would be glaringly public. Or she could ask to use Naomi's telephone, which would be more private but leave her feeling awkward if she didn't explain why she needed to do so. Kate wasn't ready to tell anyone about Leo yet.

Unable to reach a decision, Kate simply said good-bye to everyone. 'I can see myself out,' she said, but Alice followed her to the door anyway.

'I've got a job,' Alice told her.

'A job?' Kate hadn't expected this.

'Only for a few hours each week. I'm helping to organize the papers of someone who's writing a family memoir.'

'I didn't even know you were looking for work.'

'I've been keeping an eye out for opportunities, that's all.'

'Then I'm glad for you. If it's what you really want,' Kate said.

'It is. I want to do something useful and earn a little money of my own.'

Kate understood the importance of having money – and of earning it independently too – but Alice was already doing useful things with her hospital visits and the bookshop.

'I'll still have time for the bookshop and the hospital,' Alice said, as though reading Kate's mind.

But Kate still wondered if Alice saw the bookshop's closure on the horizon and was taking steps to fill the gap it would leave behind. Alice was Kate's favourite person in all the world and thoroughly deserved her opportunities and happiness, yet Kate couldn't prevent a pang of loneliness at the thought of Alice having less time for their friendship. Not that Kate herself was free to see much of Alice just now, but she was trying hard to create space for them to be together.

Shrugging the selfish thoughts aside, she folded Alice into a hug. 'Congratulations. It's wonderful news.'

Racing back to the farm, Kate's feelings were in turmoil again. She was worried about the bookshop, which had done so much to bring her together with her friends. She was worried about the farm, which, thanks to the flirting between her brothers and the land girls, wasn't running half as smoothly as it might. And she was still in a dilemma over the best way to respond to Leo's letter.

Trying to hide her feelings, she walked back into the farmhouse kitchen and took up some sewing. Pearl was teasing Vinnie and he was teasing her back. Ruby was being cleverer in her pursuit of Kenny. When he was near – Ernie too – she put on an act of helpfulness. 'Why don't I make a pot of tea?' she suggested now. 'I know it isn't my job, but we should help each other, shouldn't we? Ernie, you're looking tired. I'm sure you'd welcome a cup of tea.'

Ernie scowled but there was no doubt that she was making a good impression on Kenny.

It rained the following morning. Ruby walked into the kitchen and came to a halt, wincing and touching her forehead, just as she reached Kenny. 'What's up?' he asked, looking alarmed.

Ruby looked up and gave him what Kate supposed was meant to be a smile designed to melt the hardest heart. 'Just a headache. I'm sure it'll pass. Eventually. I know there's a lot of work to be done and I don't want to let you down.'

'You shouldn't,' he said. 'Work, I mean. Not if you're sick.'

He looked towards Kate, frowning as though to prompt her into doing the right thing.

'You really shouldn't work if you're sick,' Kate repeated, feeling guilty that part of her struggled to believe this headache was real. This was the trouble with Ruby. She didn't inspire trust.

'Well, if you insist, I'll stay indoors today,' Ruby said, and she lowered herself into a chair as though her fragility made her as vulnerable to breakage as a porcelain figurine.

Unsurprisingly, she recovered in good time for the evening. It was a triumphant evening for her because she somehow manoeuvred an invitation for herself and Pearl to walk down to the Wheatsheaf with Kenny and Vinnie.

More days passed and Kate's indecision about Leo escalated to panic. Time was running out. It was Saturday and if she didn't telephone him today he might simply turn up at the farm tomorrow, or assume she didn't want to see him and move on to some other girl. And that, Kate realized, would be awful.

Her mind was made up. Leo was worth the risk.

Luck played into Kate's hands for once when Pearl accidentally knocked over the last of the day's milk. 'Oops! Sorry! Shall I walk into the village and buy more?'

'I'll be quicker on the bike,' Kate said.

She waited for Ernie to produce some money and then left, but instead of turning towards the village at the bottom of Brimbles Lane, she raced through the Foxfield gateposts to hammer on Naomi's door.

'It's all right, Suki. I'll deal with this,' Naomi said

from inside the house. She opened the door and blinked. 'Kate! You look flustered. Is everything—'

'Everything's fine. But I wonder if I could use your telephone?'

'Of course.' Naomi led the way into the sitting room and gestured to the phone. 'Would you like tea? A glass of water?'

'Thanks, but really, I'm fine.'

Naomi nodded and withdrew.

Kate had only ever used a telephone twice before, both times on farm business. She looked at the number Leo had sent and wondered who would answer it – if anyone answered at all. She picked up the telephone and hesitated, still unsure what was best to be said. But she couldn't delay any longer – Naomi wouldn't stay away for ever.

She gave the number to the woman at the exchange but was so caught up in her thoughts about what to say that she missed the name of the person to whom she was put through. 'May I leave a message for Flight Lieutenant Leo Kinsella?' she asked, flustered.

'Go ahead.'

Oh, heavens. Was there some sort of secret code that young women used when leaving messages for RAF officers? Kate didn't want to get Leo into trouble if he wasn't actually allowed personal messages.

'Hello?' the voice prompted.

'Sorry. This is . . .' She'd have to take a chance. 'My name is Kate Fletcher. I'm due to meet Flight Lieutenant Kinsella tomorrow. Could you suggest he comes to Beech Lane, near the big sycamores?'

'Beech Lane. Big sycamores. Time?'

'Four o'clock?' she asked.

'You tell me, miss.'

'Yes, four o'clock.'

'Anything else?'

'I don't think so.'

'Goodbye then, miss.'

'Thank—'

The call had already ended.

Kate paced the room until Naomi returned to ask, 'Did you manage to get through?'

'Yes, thanks.'

Naomi was too tactful to ask whom she'd called but Kate felt uncomfortable about not volunteering the information. Perhaps Naomi had other things on her mind, though. She was looking exhausted. 'I hope you don't mind me asking, but are you feeling unwell?' Kate said.

'Touch of toothache, that's all.' Naomi patted her jaw.

'Sounds horrible.'

'It isn't too bad, and the dentist is keeping an eye on it.'

Kate nodded. 'I'm sorry if I interrupted when you were resting.'

'Don't worry, you didn't.'

Toothache was far from being Naomi's only problem, Kate suspected. The bookshop situation was probably dragging her down too. But Naomi appeared reluctant to talk about her worries just as Kate was reluctant to talk about Leo. Maybe everyone had their little secrets. Even Alice hadn't mentioned wanting a job until she'd found one either.

Goodbyes were said and then Kate continued into the village to buy milk.

All through the rest of Saturday and into Sunday she wondered if Leo had received her message and, if so, how he felt about it. Did he think it had been bossy of her – presumptuous even – to issue orders about when and where they should meet? He must have his fill of orders in the RAF. Would he even bother to turn up? It would be humiliating if he didn't. Worse than that, it would be hurtful because Kate only had to think of Leo to feel a spark of excitement.

What should she wear? It would look suspicious if she went out in a dress, so she'd have to go in her usual outfit of breeches, shirt and sweater, though she'd make sure they were clean. She'd been wearing breeches when he came to the farmyard, and they hadn't put him off her. Then again, would he expect her to make more effort if they were meeting by design?

Grgh! Kate was clearly hopeless when it came to romance. Even so, she set off to meet Leo with anticipation fizzing in her veins.

# CHAPTER TWENTY-ONE

## *Alice*

Weeds were growing quickly now June was under way and Alice was taking advantage of a spare few minutes after Sunday lunch to tidy the cottage's front garden when a swish of movement made her straighten. Kate had turned the corner from Brimbles Lane and was cycling past at speed. 'Kate!' Alice called, but her friend had already moved on.

Strange. Even bending towards the weeds Alice would have been visible if Kate had glanced over. Why *hadn't* Kate glanced over? Had something happened at Brimbles Farm to put her in such a fury that she needed to get away before she exploded? The Fletcher men would drive anyone to distraction but were the land girls to blame? Alice had seen little of Kate since their arrival, but it was clear that the land girls weren't working out as well as had been hoped.

Alice had met them only once so far. She'd been preparing to walk into the village on Thursday afternoon when she'd heard female voices approaching along Brimbles Lane. A glance out of her bedroom window had shown her the land girls.

Ruby was riding Kate's bicycle but not enjoying it. 'This road's full of ruts and holes,' she grumbled. 'They're making my bones shake.'

'Shall I ride the bike while you walk?' Pearl asked. 'I hate walking too.'

Alice ran downstairs and left the cottage just as the girls rounded the corner on to Churchwood Way. 'Hello,' Alice said, smiling. 'You must be Ruby and Pearl. I'm Alice, a friend of Kate's.'

They came to a halt and Alice offered a hand to Pearl as she was closer. The tall girl bounded forward to take it. 'Pleased to meet you,' she said, grinning and sounding as though she meant it.

Alice tried not to wince at the pressure of Pearl's grip. She found herself warming to this big, ungainly girl. Something about her awkwardness was endearing.

Alice offered her hand to Ruby next and found it taken for barely a moment though the glamorous girl's words were polite enough. 'A pleasure.'

Hmm. Alice hated to jump to conclusions about people, but she found herself understanding why Kate felt uneasy about Ruby Turner. While Pearl looked the picture of uncomplicated openness, Ruby gave the opposite impression. The word that drifted into Alice's head was *scheming* though she instantly felt bad for entertaining it when she had no cause for believing it to be true.

'Are you walking to the shops?' Alice asked, wanting to get to know the girls better. 'You won't mind if I walk with you?'

Pearl looked to Ruby, who shrugged and said, 'Course not.'

The answer appeared to please Pearl and they set off walking, Ruby pushing the bike at her side until she winced as her ankle knocked against a pedal.

'Shall I take that?' Pearl offered and the bicycle duly changed hands.

'How are you finding Churchwood?' Alice began.

Pearl looked to Ruby again as though it was the natural order between them for the blonde girl to take the lead.

'It's pretty,' Ruby said, and the answer set the tone for the rest of the conversation.

Churchwood was pretty, Kate was nice, both land girls were glad to do their bit for the war effort . . .

Alice couldn't help wondering if Ruby was merely saying what she thought Alice wanted to hear.

They reached the Post Office. 'Nice talking to you,' Ruby said, and went inside.

Pearl stayed outside with the bike and Alice took the opportunity to talk to her alone. 'Kate speaks highly of you.'

'Does she?' Pearl sounded surprised. Pleased too, as though compliments came her way rarely.

'She says you're very good at the work and a great help to her.'

'Gosh.'

'No one works harder than Kate, so praise from her really counts for something.'

'Golly.'

'She's glad to have Ruby too, of course,' Alice added, fibbing in the interests of keeping the peace. 'Perhaps you'd both like to call at the cottage for a cup of tea and a chat one day.'

'Love to,' Pearl said. 'I'll tell Ruby.'

Apart from trying to befriend the girls and make them feel part of Churchwood, Alice had no idea how else to help poor Kate.

Watching Kate cycle into the distance now, Alice dusted off her gardening gloves and decided to call a halt to her weeding. She was due to visit Hattie Maddocks, who'd been unexpectedly absent from the bookshop on Tuesday. Young widow Hattie lived some way out of Churchwood with her mother and three young children. She had no near neighbours so after the bookshop closed for the day Alice had gone to check that she was well.

'Thank goodness you've come,' Hattie had said. 'I've got both Mum and Sally sick. I haven't been able to get to the shops or anywhere else.'

'I'm here to help,' Alice had assured her.

She'd returned to the village to buy some supplies for the family, then insisted on looking after Mum, Sally and the twin little boys while Hattie caught up with some much-needed sleep. Afterwards, Alice had drawn up a rota for helping Hattie and taken it along to the bookshop, where people had gladly signed up to it.

Arriving at Hattie's cottage today Alice was delighted to see that Hattie and her family were looking much better. 'Thanks to you and everyone else who helped,' Hattie said.

This was the aspect of the bookshop that the Forsyths appeared not to understand. Could they be brought to understand it? Alice hoped so. After all, a job had seemed unattainable not so long ago, but now she was gainfully employed. Anything was possible.

Thoughts of her job warmed Alice as she walked home again. She was grateful for the sense of achievement and the wage it was delivering – ten shillings each week! – and had also been delighted to have something positive to tell Daniel in the same letter in which she'd shared the depressing news that Julian Forsyth was to be Churchwood's new vicar.

*Of course, we're all disappointed that Adam wasn't given the position* [she'd written], *but we've decided to make the Forsyths welcome and hope to persuade them to leave the bookshop largely unchanged. We might have to make some concessions to their ideas, but a compromise may be possible. We'll see.*

*I have more news! I have a job!*

She'd explained about Mr Parkinson and his memoirs, and stressed her satisfaction in bringing order to a muddle of old papers. *It's a new interest for me and you know how I like a challenge. I work for ten hours each week, over two days, and I can choose the days that suit me best. My father is happy for me. I hope you're happy for me too.*

When Monday dawned she had no trouble getting up early so she could tidy a few things at home before setting out for work. Arriving at Mr Parkinson's house, she spent some time summarizing diary entries so Mr Parkinson wouldn't have to read them all, added some photographs to her growing list, then copied out several pages of his manuscript, deciphering his scrawl and rewriting it in her neater handwriting so the typist from the agency would be able to read the words more easily. It was twenty minutes after her agreed finishing time when she reached the end, but Alice liked to get the job done well. She took the pages over to Mr Parkinson. 'In case you want to read them through,' she explained.

He began to read as she put on her coat.

'A word, Miss Lovell,' he said, and with some dismay she realized he was frowning. 'Have you changed some of the text I wrote?'

Oh, heavens. 'Only in a few places when I thought it didn't read quite smoothly,' she admitted.

But she should have asked him first. It had been presumptuous of her – arrogant, even – to think that she knew best. Was she about to lose her job already? Daniel and her father would pity her and worry about her and so would her friends. Alice wouldn't be able to bear it.

# CHAPTER TWENTY-TWO

## *Naomi*

A narrow lane – little more than a track – ran between Naomi's Foxfield and Bert's market garden. On his side there was a hedge and, looking over it, she could see him digging in a growing bed. He turned, saw her and leaned on his spade to give her a considering look.

'About time,' he finally said, and he nodded her towards the gate that was positioned a few yards away.

Meeting her there, he held the gate open so Naomi could pass through, then led the way to the house. 'In you go,' he said when they reached the kitchen door. 'Give me a minute to get these boots off.'

They were ancient work boots. The laces didn't match, and he'd glued a patch over the toe section of one of them.

Naomi waited in the kitchen. It was old-fashioned, faded and worn by decades of use but it was also warm and gave the most extraordinary feeling of comfort. The simple cupboards were painted cream. A dresser stood against one wall, holding pretty but mismatched crockery. A plain table occupied the kitchen's centre with equally plain chairs arranged around it. Armchairs were positioned each side of the hearth and

Bert's cat curled up contentedly on the homely rug that lay between them.

He stepped into the kitchen after her and Naomi noticed he had a hole in one of his socks. No one would call Bert Makepiece smart, but he didn't care a jot because fine clothes and feathers impressed him not at all.

He slid his feet into slippers and put the kettle on the stove to boil. 'Sit yourself down.' He waved towards the armchairs.

She sat in the chair that must have once been occupied by Bert's wife, Mary, dead long before Naomi came to Churchwood. A photograph on the dresser suggested she'd been a pleasant-looking woman with a big heart.

Nerves fluttered through Naomi's stomach. Had she done the right thing in coming here? It was going to humiliate her to talk about Alexander's possible infidelity but Bert had said something about bottled-up thoughts becoming tangled like knitting wool and Naomi's thoughts felt exactly like that. She needed someone to help her to move forward. He brought cups of tea over and sat in the opposite armchair. But he didn't begin by questioning her. Instead, he picked up his cat, Elizabeth, and stroked her, leaving Naomi to begin when she was ready.

She fidgeted with the clasp of her handbag, then, irritated with herself, put the handbag on the floor. 'I think Alexander might be having an affair,' she said.

There. It was out.

She'd expected him to look shocked but he didn't even look surprised. Perhaps he'd guessed all along that her troubles were related to her marriage.

'I'm sure you have your reasons for suspecting him,' he said.

'They're not very substantial reasons.' She told him about the laughter, the jeweller's receipt and the theatre tickets.

'You're forgetting another reason,' he said, then, at her puzzled look, added, 'Instinct?'

'I'm not sure my instincts count for much. If Alexander really is having an affair, they've been letting me down for years.'

'The point is that your instincts sprang to life the moment you heard the laughter.'

'Perhaps. You don't think I'm being . . . well, foolish? To suspect him, I mean?'

Bert pulled a sceptical face. 'If you asked me was it foolish to keep your worries to yourself for weeks or even months, then I'd have to say yes, you've been an idiot, woman. But foolish to suspect that long stick of ice you married of an affair? Hardly.'

Naomi breathed out in relief. She'd dreaded being considered a needy, melodramatic sort of female who might be going through the change of life. She should have trusted Bert to know her better than that.

'The question is, why does it matter to you if he's having an affair or not?' Bert asked.

She blinked. 'You don't think infidelity matters?'

'It matters to *me*,' he told her forcefully, 'but it doesn't matter to everyone. Some couples are happy to live separate lives. I'm asking why it matters to you because your answer might lead you to the next step of deciding what you should – or shouldn't – do about it.'

Naomi understood what he meant. All along she'd been wary of opening Pandora's box in case all the Furies leapt out to stir up troubles and consequences beyond her control – something she might later regret. 'It matters to me because even though Alexander and I aren't close, there should be respect between us. Honesty. Honour,' she explained.

It was one thing for Naomi to know that Alexander wasn't interested in *her*. It was quite another for him to be cavorting with someone else behind her back, possibly at her expense.

'An affair would mean he was making a fool of me,' Naomi continued. 'He'd be treating me as though I don't matter.'

'So there's pride in there, and there's also hurt,' Bert concluded.

It was a fair summary. 'No one likes to be treated with contempt,' Naomi said.

'I suppose talking to the man isn't a possibility?'

Naomi shuddered at the thought of Alexander's cold fury. He'd toss her flimsy evidence to the floor and grind it to nothing with his heel. 'No.'

'Then you need to gather more evidence.'

'How, though?'

'Hmm.' He stared off into space for a while and then said, 'If you've done all you can by yourself, you need someone else to gather evidence on your behalf.'

'Who?' Naomi barely knew Alexander's colleagues or friends, and she couldn't imagine any of her old charity committee acquaintances being willing to help, even if she could bring herself to ask them.

'What about one of those private detective chaps?'

Goodness. If Alexander found out, his rage would be incandescent.

'Where's the harm in just talking to one of them? It needn't commit you.'

True. But how did a person go about finding one? 'I don't suppose you know of any private detectives?'

'You don't suppose correctly. I've never had call to use one. But they want people to employ them so I assume they advertise. Let's have a look.'

Putting Elizabeth down, he got up and went into what looked like a scullery, returning with a handful of old newspapers. He passed one to her, then sat down and opened one himself. 'Let's try the classified ads,' he said.

Naomi flicked through her newspaper until she reached the pages of classified advertisements. There were columns for all sorts of things, from situations vacant and situations wanted to items for sale, pawnbroker services, painters, decorators and plumbers . . . In which column were private detectives to be found?

'Here we are,' Bert said, folding his newspaper and holding it out to show her a particular page. It included a column of advertisements dedicated to enquiry agents promising confidentiality, discretion and rapid results in matters of a delicate nature. 'Just what you need,' he said.

'Perhaps,' Naomi conceded, though the thought of actually confiding her private business to one of those agents repelled her. She pictured the detective as a thin, oily man with knowing eyes, a dark moustache and a fawn raincoat belted at the waist. Doubtless, his wiriness came in handy when he shinned up drainpipes to take photographs of husbands or wives in compromising positions with their lovers. The photographs would be presented in brown envelopes to cuckolded partners with a note of the detective's bill. Unless he'd been paid in advance. Yes, it felt likely that he'd have required to be paid at least some money before he set to work.

'I can see you don't like the idea,' Bert said, 'but what's the alternative?'

Naomi didn't know.

'At least take it and think about it.' Bert thrust the newspaper towards her. 'Another few nights of no sleep and you might find the idea grows on you.'

She really must be looking haggard.

Naomi took the newspaper and tucked it inside her bag with a shudder of distaste.

Bert then turned the conversation to the bookshop, concluding with the comment 'It's a pity we can't stop the Forsyths from coming to Churchwood but there it is.'

Walking home, Naomi wondered if he'd chosen his words carefully to highlight the fact that, while there was nothing to be done to keep the Forsyths away, there was something she could do about Alexander. Bert was a plain, outspoken man but shrewdness lurked beneath that scruffy appearance and he could be subtle.

# CHAPTER TWENTY-THREE

## *Naomi*

Standing at the bus stop watching removal men load furniture and boxes into a van, Naomi thought there was something forlorn about the vicarage now it was being emptied of Septimus Barnes's earthly possessions. It still didn't feel right that the former vicar should be erased from the village without his thirty years of service being marked in some way, but at least Septimus would live on in people's memories.

Would the vicarage look less forlorn if it was being cleared so Adam Potts could take up residence? The pretty Victorian house would soon have become untidy with Adam in place, but everyone would have been welcome and many a jolly gathering would have been held there. Naomi feared the opposite was likely to happen with Julian and Lavinia Forsyth in residence. Visitors would probably be welcome, but they'd feel stiff, nervous and judged.

Alice's plan to win the Forsyths around with niceness was a good one. Naomi only wished she could be more confident of its chance of success. Of course, they wouldn't need a plan at all if she'd done a better job of swaying the church council in Adam's favour. No one was blaming her for that failure – her friends couldn't have been kinder – but Naomi still blamed herself.

From the bookshop to her marriage, she was finding life a struggle. But she was trying to fight back. She wasn't ready to take Bert's advice and involve a private detective in her personal troubles yet, but had decided to play detective herself – even though she had only the vaguest idea of what she'd do. Searching Alexander's London office was out of the question as there'd be too many partners, secretaries and clerks around, so he'd be sure to hear of her visit. But following him . . . she could certainly attempt it.

Her first step on arriving home from Bert's this morning had been to announce to Suki that she needed to visit the dentist again; her second to attempt to ascertain when Alexander would be at the office.

She'd rung him at his office in Clark Street in the City area of London. 'Do you have any interesting plans for this week?' she'd asked, hoping she sounded casual.

'Work, of course.' His tone told her he considered her question to be stupid.

'But will you be meeting anyone interesting? Or anyone I know?'

'Naomi, you know business matters are confidential.'

With that she abandoned her efforts, deciding that as he was at work today she should seize the moment to try to follow him when he left it.

Now she was waiting for the bus that would take her on the first leg of her journey. She hadn't long to wait. Turning away from the vicarage, she climbed on board and found a seat. From St Albans she caught the train into London and from the station she took a taxi to Clark Street, arriving shortly after noon and asking the driver to pull in to the kerb some distance from the office so she couldn't be seen from Alexander's window. Stepping on to the pavement, she looked around for a place to wait for him to emerge to go to lunch – assuming he was still in the office.

She hadn't told him about this second visit to London. He'd made no comment about her first visit and, hopefully, knew nothing of her visit to the flat. If he discovered she was here again, she'd repeat the toothache excuse but with luck it wouldn't come to that. The more often Alexander was aware of her presence in London, the more likely he was to take special precautions against being found out in wrongdoing. Naomi preferred to keep him in ignorance.

It was a pity it wasn't raining because Naomi could have hidden behind an umbrella. The day being fine, she scuttled into an alley that ran between two buildings on the opposite side of the street from the office, still some distance away, but with a decent view of the entrance if she stayed at the front.

London was a fast-paced and impersonal city, but she was still conscious of receiving occasional puzzled looks from passers-by. A middle-aged woman skulking in an alley was an odd sight, after all. She met the looks with smiles as though to reassure the curious that she was merely catching her breath or killing time before an appointment, but one bowler-hatted gentleman stopped to ask, 'Are you in need of assistance, madam?'

Naomi felt her cheeks redden. 'How kind of you to ask, but I'm merely trying to avoid blocking the pavement as I wait for my husband.'

He made a small bow and continued on his way.

When Alexander finally emerged, her heart bounced nervously, and she ducked further along the alley so he wouldn't see her. Unfortunately, that meant she couldn't see him. She shuffled forward again, peeped into the street and saw him walking in the opposite direction. Tucking her head into her neck in an effort to hide her face, she set off after him.

'Harrington!' someone called from close behind her, and Naomi's heart skittered in panic.

A man swept past, calling to Alexander again. Then Alexander turned to investigate the call and Naomi dived into the entrance of the nearest building, colliding with a young woman who was coming out. 'So sorry!' Naomi said.

'Humph!'

Perhaps Naomi's stout foot had trodden on the girl's slender toes. With an impatient sound, the young woman swept around Naomi, who was still standing in her way, too afraid of being seen by Alexander to move.

'Sorry,' Naomi said again, but the young woman was already striding off.

Naomi waited for a moment longer, then turned around to see Alexander shaking hands with the gentleman who'd called to him. They exchanged a few words she couldn't hear before walking away together.

Crossing the road, Naomi set off after them, trying to keep them in sight while also dodging other pedestrians and keeping close to buildings so she could step into a doorway or turn to a window if Alexander happened to glance back. It didn't help that she'd changed her cardboard gas-mask holder for a more robust metal one. Even in an outer bag, it banged against her legs if she walked quickly.

He rounded a corner and Naomi hastened after him, relieved to catch sight of him again, only to see him and his companion dodge nimbly through traffic as they crossed another road. Being less nimble, Naomi struggled to cross. She got over eventually, just as the men passed through a door. Which door, though? She was too far away to be certain. She made her way down the street until she reached several shops. A gentlemen's bespoke tailor, a tobacconist, a stationer . . . Risking quick glances through their windows, Naomi saw no sign of Alexander. She reached a restaurant called Hobson's – and saw Alexander being shown to a table with his companion. Were they meeting others? It appeared not. They settled at a table for two.

Alexander's lunch would surely take an hour at least so Naomi decided to find some lunch herself. Not because she had an appetite but because she wanted to rest her aching feet.

She found a simple café where she ordered tea and Welsh rarebit. After she'd finished eating she hailed a taxi to take her back to Clark Street, where she spent another hour in the alley before Alexander returned to the office. Again, he was alone.

What next? She couldn't stay in the alley all

afternoon. She spent the time walking around the City where the country's financial life was concentrated. Signs of the war were frequent in the form of uniforms, posters, sandbags and occasional bomb sites, which made her shudder. Mercifully some of London's more outstanding buildings had been spared serious damage. Thus far, anyway. St Paul's Cathedral and the Bank of England were two of them. It was heart-breaking to think of the people and businesses that hadn't been so fortunate. Set amongst a patchwork of pretty fields, little Churchwood felt a world away.

She had another cup of tea and by four-thirty was back in the alley. At five o'clock exactly, Alexander swept out of the building, hailed a taxi and was driven away. Naomi hailed a taxi too but lost precious minutes before an empty one came along. 'Where would you like to go, madam?' the driver asked.

'Straight on,' Naomi told him, hoping to catch up with Alexander.

But she was too late. She saw other taxis, but none had Alexander in them. Maybe he'd simply gone home. 'Could you take me to St John's Wood, please?' she asked the driver.

He fought his way through the traffic, and they finally reached James Mansions. 'Pull in there, please.' Naomi pointed to a space on the opposite side of the road.

The driver duly obliged and she sat forward, locating the flat's windows and waiting to see if she could spot signs of life inside.

Nothing happened.

'Erm,' the driver said, as though to attract her attention.

'Could you wait a moment longer, please? I'll pay.'

They waited for ten more minutes but there wasn't even a flicker of movement beyond the windows. Clearly, Alexander hadn't come home. He could be anywhere – at the theatre, in a hotel, in his lover's home . . .

She asked to be taken to the station.

'Thanks!' the driver said when they arrived and she added a generous tip to the fare.

The day hadn't finished with her yet. She got off the bus in Churchwood to see Cecil Wade outside the Post Office talking to Arthur Fellows. 'Ah, Mrs Harrington,' he said, his smug brightness contrasting with her weariness.

'Good evening, Mr Wade.' She wouldn't call him Cecil while he refused to call her Naomi.

'I have news.' He preened like a vain cockatiel. 'Reverend Forsyth and his dear lady will be with us next Monday.'

So soon!

'They saw no reason to delay the beginning of their ministry. I'm passing on the good news to all council members.'

'Thank you for telling me.'

He nodded then called to Seth Padgett, who was out walking his dog on the green. Seth came over.

As Naomi walked away, she heard Cecil share the glad tidings with him before adding, 'I'm hosting a dinner for them on the evening of their arrival. Simple fare in these times of rationing but I think it's important to welcome them and introduce them socially to some of the more – er – influential residents. I count you amongst them, Seth.'

Clearly, he didn't count Naomi amongst them. She disliked Cecil Wade intensely, but the humiliation stung her anyway.

# CHAPTER TWENTY-FOUR

## *Kate*

Ruby had been watching Kate ever since she'd returned from meeting Leo, so only when she was alone was Kate allowing her thoughts to turn to him. Stepping out into the evening air to unpeg the washing that had been drying on the clothes line since early that Monday morning, she allowed herself a smile that felt like sunshine bursting through grey rainclouds.

Her emotions had been in tumult yesterday when she'd cycled to the meeting place she'd suggested. She'd felt dread that Leo might not turn up, horror at the thought of boring him, and anger at the need to meet him in secret. But she'd also fizzed with excitement.

Not wanting anyone to catch her eye and ask where she was going, she'd looked to neither left nor right as she cycled through the village but kept her focus on the road ahead. There was no sign of Leo when she reached the sycamores on Beech Lane but she fought off disappointment by telling herself that she might be early or Leo might be a little late – if he'd managed to get away from the base at all. It wasn't as though he could have let her know if the arrangements were inconvenient. Of course, he might simply have changed his mind about wanting to see her, but Kate refused to jump to such an upsetting conclusion just yet.

She'd chosen Beech Lane because it was little used, but as a precaution she hid her bicycle behind a bush and then stood beside it, ready to duck down if anyone approached. Without a watch she had no way of knowing the time, but Kate decided she wouldn't wait for longer than what she'd estimate to be fifteen minutes or so. She already felt a fool, standing there facing the possibility of humiliation if he didn't appear.

But soon she heard the distant phut-phut of a motorbike and was thrown into panic. What would Leo expect of her? A kiss? Kate didn't know how to kiss and was bound to make a mess of it. But perhaps it was too soon for a kiss. She hoped so. After all, she'd only been in the man's company for five minutes before today.

The phut-phutting grew louder as the motorbike drew near. Realizing she'd look ridiculous hiding in the bushes, she ran across the lane and climbed a gate, hoping to appear more at ease sitting on top of it. But then it occurred to her that it might be someone else on the motorbike and she was tempted to run back behind the bush.

The bike came into view before she could reach a decision, and Kate felt lurches of both anxiety and joy as she saw that the rider was Leo, in his brown leather flying jacket. He brought the bike to a halt beside her and pulled off his goggles. 'You're a sight for sore eyes,' he said, smiling.

Blushing, Kate felt struck dumb with awkwardness.

Luckily, Leo gave no sign of expecting an answer. Instead, he grinned. 'Fancy a ride?'

'On that?' Kate had never been on a motorbike.

'Yes, on this trusty steed.' He patted the seat behind him.

Kate hesitated. A ride on the motorbike would mean sitting close to him. Holding on to him even.

'Not scared, are you?' he taunted.

'Of course not!' Pride made Kate scornful.

She jumped down from the gate, relieved she hadn't changed out of breeches because riding on a motorbike in a skirt would have felt indecent. 'I can't be out for long, though,' she warned him. 'I still have work to do.'

'On a Sunday?'

'Farms need attention every day of the week.'

'I suppose they do. Flying fighter planes isn't exactly a nine-to-five job either. Hop on, then.'

Kate climbed on to the bike, careful to avoid touching him.

'You'll fall off if you don't hold on,' he said. 'Put your arms around my waist.'

She hesitated, but all she'd be touching was the flying jacket. Reaching her arms around him, she kept some space between their bodies.

'Just shout if you don't enjoy it,' he said.

Kate was determined to do nothing so feeble. Even so, her stomach tightened as they set off, and instinct drew her closer to him.

A minute or so passed. Two, three . . . and Kate began to enjoy herself. There was something exhilarating in travelling at speed along country lanes with the wind catching the stray hairs that framed her face. Leo leaned into the bends in the road and Kate found herself doing likewise. They were circling Churchwood, she realized, Leo taking seriously her wish that they shouldn't travel far. She liked him for it. She liked the breadth of his shoulders too.

After ten minutes or so, he slowed and then stopped. They were near a wooded area. 'Time for some refreshments?' he asked.

'I haven't brought any. I didn't realize this was a picnic.' She couldn't have sneaked food out of Brimbles Farm anyway.

'Fortunately, I *did* bring some,' he said. 'Let's find a good place to sit.'

He unstrapped a bag from the back of the bike and they walked a short way into the trees, to a clearing from where they could keep the bike in view. Leo opened the bag and brought out bottles and something in a tin. 'Ginger beer and fruit cake,' he announced.

The cake looked and tasted delicious. 'Made with real butter without stinting on sugar and fruit,' she declared. 'Has rationing not reached the Royal Air Force?'

'It was a gift from my mother. She made it before the outbreak of war and kept it moist by regular soakings in brandy.'

That explained the rich taste and texture.

'Cheers,' he said, holding up his bottle. 'I take it you enjoyed the bike ride so let's drink to new adventures.'

Kate clinked her glass against his, wondering if his idea of new adventures also extended to meeting her.

'I knew you'd like the bike,' he said.

'Oh?'

'There's fire in your eyes.'

Once again Kate was conscious of warmth in her face and didn't know how to reply.

'Tell me about your life,' Leo invited.

'There's not much to say. I'm a farmer's daughter and I've only ever worked on the farm.'

'You make it sound dull but I'm sure it isn't. Tell me about the farm and your family.'

She described Brimbles Farm briefly, conscious that to someone who fought dog fights in the sky it really must sound humdrum. Then she told him – even more briefly – about her family, saying nothing about how awful they were.

'Your twin brothers joined up?' Leo questioned, puzzled. 'Weren't they exempt as farmers?'

'They were, but it didn't stop them.'

'Patriotism at work?'

'I'd like to say yes, but I think it was more a case of trying something new.'

Leo nodded, looking thoughtful, and she guessed he was hoping that Fred 'n' Frank wouldn't come to regret their decision.

'Has it left you short-handed on the farm?' he asked.

'Yes. There's always a lot of work, and with two men down . . .'

'You can't get help?'

'We've got help. Of a sort. Two land girls.'

'They're not turning out well?'

'I'm a little disappointed.'

'More than a little, I suspect.'

Kate shrugged, not liking to be pitied yet grateful for his understanding. 'Tell me about your life,' she

207

said, deciding it was his turn to supply information. 'Tell me about flying.'

She regretted mentioning flying as soon as the words were out of her mouth. She also regretted the way she'd poured scorn on the idea of being afraid of the motorbike as though fear was only for the weak. Who wouldn't be afraid flying fighter planes in wartime?

'Don't feel you have to answer,' she added quickly.

'No, it's fine,' he said. 'As for my background, I'm the only child of parents who live in Cheltenham. Both excellent people, though I think my arrival came as a surprise to them because they were older than most parents and had given up hope of having a family. They delighted in spoiling me rotten as a boy.'

He was none the worse for it, Kate thought.

'As for flying, I joined the RAF as a career even before the war. So did my best friend from school, Ralph. We joined together and trained together, and now we're flying in the same squadron. I love flying – the views, the open sky, the feeling of being up with the birds . . . I value my fellow servicemen too. Not only Ralph, though he's the best of them, but the others as well. They're a great bunch of chaps. Mostly. And when it comes to fighting, I feel I have right on my side. Men like Adolf Hitler and his gang of aggressors need stopping.'

'They do.' Kate told him about May Janicki and the Jewish refugee children she was looking after.

'I've met a few Polish pilots,' Leo said. 'They're great chaps too.'

He paused, then added, 'Downing enemy planes is essential if the Nazis are to be defeated but I get no pleasure from knowing I'm harming someone's son or brother or sweetheart. Not all Germans are Adolf Hitlers. I imagine plenty of them want peace as much as we do. Still, there's one good thing that comes out of living in dangerous times.'

'An appreciation of how much life matters?'

'Exactly. None of us know what the future holds so we should make the most of the present. But enough of the war. What do you do when you're not on the farm?'

Hating the idea that she'd sent Leo's spirits spiralling downwards, Kate made an effort to lift the conversation, telling him about the bookshop and how it helped the village. 'It's fun too. We have social events when staff and patients come from the hospital.'

'My cousin told me about the bookshop. Isn't it in some sort of trouble?'

'A change of vicar,' she explained.

'He doesn't appreciate fun?'

'No, but when he sees the good the bookshop does . . .'

'The fire's back in your eyes,' Leo said, smiling. 'If your friends are half as passionate about the bookshop as you, I'd say you stand a good chance of winning this new vicar around.'

'We'll see.' But Kate's passion was useless without time to support the bookshop.

This wasn't the moment to dwell on it, though. She wanted to entertain Leo, not depress him. Casting around her mind for something suitable, she told him the story of Elsie Fuller, who once laughed so hard during a bookshop visit that her false teeth flew into the lap of old Jonah Kerrigan. Leo responded with a story about some fellow airmen letting a pig into the officers' mess. From there other stories came naturally.

But time was marching on. 'You need to get home?' Leo guessed.

'I'm afraid so.'

'I won't argue because I don't want to get you into so much trouble that you refuse to see me again.'

He wanted to see her again? Kate's heartbeat quickened.

'I don't know when I can come back, though,' he said. 'You're not on the telephone?'

Kate shook her head.

'May I write?'

Letters were risky as there was a chance of her family seeing them. It was only down to good luck that Leo's first letter hadn't been seen by anyone else. But he had no other way of getting in touch.

'I could use an office typewriter to make the envelopes look businesslike,' he offered, and she realized he must have guessed that she didn't want her family to know about him.

'That would help.' Kate decided she'd try to intercept the postman each day so no one would see his letters, but just in case any slipped through, typed envelopes would be easier to pass off as bookshop business or communications from the Women's Land Army.

'Typed envelopes it shall be,' Leo said.

They packed up the remains of the picnic, Kate refusing another slice of cake as she wanted Leo to have it. Then they got back on the motorbike and rode back to Kate's bicycle. Leo dismounted the motorbike with her.

Did he intend to kiss her? Kate found herself torn between excitement and anxiety.

Breath caught in her throat when he stepped towards her, but he simply kissed her cheek, then smiled down at her warmly as though he'd sensed her nervousness. 'You're worth waiting for, Kate Fletcher,' he said.

Goodness.

'Thank you for the ginger beer and cake,' she told him, retrieving the bicycle from behind the bush.

'It was my pleasure to share them.'

'Goodbye then.' She set off pedalling and soon Leo overtook her on the motorbike, sending her a final wave before disappearing around a curve in the lane.

Kate realized she was worried for him. She was already concerned about the twins and now Leo had added another layer of anxiety – a deep one because, while no servicemen were safe, some were less safe than others. Flying fighter planes was a dangerous business and the number of young pilots who were losing their lives was terrible.

But Leo had been right in saying they should make the most of the present because none of them knew what the future held. Just now Kate's present included the prospect of seeing Leo again, and as she took the last shirt from the washing line and added it to the laundry basket, excitement bubbled inside her like champagne.

Her next job was going to be ironing so she picked up the basket and headed back towards the kitchen door. Halfway there, she frowned in sudden puzzlement. Was that music she could hear? The nearer to the house she drew, the louder it sounded, and when she opened the kitchen door the volume nearly drove her back outside.

The wireless was blaring out Glenn Miller as Kenny danced with Ruby, who was sending him provocative glances and emphasizing her feminine curves in the way she moved. Vinnie was dancing too – with Pearl – though they both looked clumsy and awkward, as though dancing came naturally to neither of them.

Where was Ernie? Kate couldn't imagine he'd approve of this sort of scene.

He stepped into the kitchen from behind her. 'You can pack this in right now,' he roared, stomping towards the wireless and turning the music off abruptly. Ruby pouted with disappointment.

'We were only having a bit of fun,' Kenny protested.

'Yeah, fun,' Vinnie echoed.

Ernie only sneered and sat down at the table. 'Where's my tea?' he demanded.

Kate put the washing basket down and began to make it, but not before noticing a look pass between Kenny and Ruby. An intimate look and, on Ruby's side, also a satisfied one. There was no doubt now that she'd succeeded in getting her claws into him. It didn't bode well for the smooth running of Brimbles Farm.

# CHAPTER TWENTY-FIVE

## *Alice*

'No!' Babs Carter said when Alice told her that Mr Parkinson had questioned the changes she'd made to his manuscript.

'It was my fault entirely. When I first spotted errors – a missing word here, a missing question mark there – I talked to him about them. I didn't want to keep bothering him, though, so I started correcting them myself. And then I got carried away, changing words he kept repeating, rewriting awkward sentences and even rearranging paragraphs. It was arrogant of me. Imagine if you decided you knew better than Matron.'

'She'd kill me. Or at least give me a dressing down,' Babs said. 'Mr Parkinson didn't fire you, I hope?'

'No, though I wouldn't have blamed him if he had. He actually said I wrote well and improved his writing.'

'That must have been a relief!'

'A big relief, though I wonder if I haven't let myself in for more work. He isn't being as careful with his writing now he knows I'm going to correct it, so I'm working flat out.'

'You enjoy it, though?'

Alice smiled. 'Very much.'

'I hope you don't work so hard that you've no time for the hospital any more.'

'I'll always make time for the hospital. I may even have more time for it if the bookshop closes.'

Babs took a bandage from a cupboard. 'It would be a foolish vicar who couldn't see the benefits of the bookshop.'

'I'm not sure Reverend Forsyth is foolish, but I do think he has fixed ideas on right and wrong,' Alice said.

'Here's hoping he turns out to be a lot less stuffy than expected.'

Alice smiled but struggled to share Babs's optimism. All things were possible, but Babs hadn't been present the day the archdeacon brought the Forsyths into the bookshop.

Unfortunately, many Churchwood residents *had* been present and had wasted no time in telling everyone else about the dim view they took of Julian Forsyth's appointment.

With the memory of those grumbles in her mind, Alice approached her next task with trepidation. Leaving the hospital, she walked into the village to check on the poster she'd put up in the Sunday School Hall.

*To welcome Reverend and Mrs Forsyth to St Luke's*
*we propose to present them with a hamper from our*
*community bookshop. Please add your name below*
*if you would like to contribute. Even very*
*small contributions are welcome.*

Churchwood was usually generous but the only

names that had been added so far belonged to Naomi, May, Janet, Bert and Alice herself. Deciding something needed to be done about it, Alice called on May as she lived close by. Making up in a small way for the career she'd left behind in London, May had become the Churchwood dressmaker. 'I like the challenge of making clothes on a budget, especially when the only fabric available comes from old curtains, sheets and bedspreads,' she'd said. She was a wonder at altering old clothes too, giving them a modern spin and adjusting them to fit new owners.

She was at her sewing machine now. 'Am I interrupting?' Alice asked.

'I need a break, anyway. Cup of tea?'

'I won't stay. I just want to let you know that no more names have been added to the poster.'

'No one wants to spare precious food for people who turn their noses up at them, especially when those people might be much better off financially.'

'I understand how everyone feels,' Alice said, for the Forsyths had indeed looked down on the residents while also having an air of financial ease about them. Perhaps they had family money at their disposal. 'But I still think our best chance of winning them around is by friendliness. We'll never get them on our side if they think we're hostile.'

'Then it looks as though we have work to do, doesn't it?'

# CHAPTER TWENTY-SIX

## *Naomi*

Did Alexander realize that he was eating some of Naomi's bacon ration as well as his own? He'd said nothing about the breakfast that had been served to him. He'd merely walked into the breakfast room muttering a cool 'Good morning' then arranged his newspaper so he could read it as he ate.

'Tea?' Naomi offered.

'Please.'

She poured a cup and placed it beside him. Alexander grunted and that was that. Conversation over – unless she forced him into speaking by asking questions, something she felt less and less inclined to do, and not just because she might incite his irritability. For years she'd kept up the appearance of a successful marriage to fool the staff, as well as herself, but she no longer felt she was fooling anyone. Even little Suki – not yet eighteen – gave Naomi sympathetic looks from time to time as though she knew her employer was unloved and unwanted. Except for her money, of course.

But it was one thing to be unloved and unwanted, quite another to be betrayed. Would she actually demand a divorce if she discovered Alexander was having an affair? One in a long line of affairs, perhaps? The thought of the earthquake divorce would trigger filled her with dread – the disgrace, the gossip, the division of assets and maybe even the loss of Foxfield . . . Naomi blanched at the thought. But she had to know the truth, even if she did nothing about it.

Should she follow Bert's advice and ask a detective to investigate Alexander's private life? The idea still felt grubby. Degrading. Even so, it would be prudent to prepare for the possibility of consulting such a man and that meant ensuring she had enough money to pay him. Naomi always carried a certain amount of cash but most of her bills were settled by cheque and Alexander had access to her banking records. She couldn't pay a private detective by cheque without risking Alexander finding out that she was investigating him. She'd have to pay in cash.

In the past she'd withdrawn cash from their bank in London as there was no bank in Churchwood, but now the war was on and she wasn't travelling so much she tended to ask Alexander to withdraw money for her, their bank being near his office. Perhaps it would be safer to stick to routine. 'I'm running a little short on cash,' she told him.

Alexander looked up from his newspaper. How cold his blue eyes were!

'My trip to the dentist ate up a fair bit with the train fare, taxis, luncheon and the like. I hadn't been to London in a while, so I made a few small purchases too.'

'How much do you want?'

'Let's say thirty pounds and I shouldn't have to trouble you for more for a while.'

He didn't argue. How could he when he spent so freely himself despite his talk of wartime economy? He simply finished his breakfast, went out to his study and returned with six five-pound notes which he placed beside her.

'Thank you.'

Within half an hour he'd been collected by a friend with a seemingly unlimited petrol supply, leaving Naomi to stare at the money and wonder what she was going to do with it.

# CHAPTER TWENTY-SEVEN

## *Kate*

Kenny stuck his chin out as though anticipating an argument he had no intention of losing. 'Ruby needs a day off,' he announced.

'She has a day off,' Kate pointed out. 'Sunday, as well as half of Thursday.'

'The buses don't run often on Sundays, and she needs a full day to travel to her little brother and back. He isn't happy where he is, and he's missing her.'

'What's this?' Ernie demanded, not wanting to be diddled out of a penny of the money he paid the land girls in wages.

'Ruby needs a day off and I've told her she can have one,' Kenny said. 'Don't worry. She'll make the time up.'

'Make it up when?' Ernie demanded.

'She'll work all day today instead of taking the afternoon off and she'll work for a few hours on Sunday too. You won't lose out.'

If Ruby's little brother was truly unhappy, Kate felt for him and would have had no problem with adjusting his sister's hours of work to accommodate a visit – had Ruby been a better worker and trustworthy too. But now Ruby was confident she had Kenny for her champion she'd given up entirely on pretending to please Kate and her work had slackened off even more. She still worked some of the time and kept up an act in front of Ernie – she wasn't stupid – but there was no doubt in Kate's mind that Ruby was taking advantage of Kenny's enchantment with her as well as Pearl's loyalty in covering up for her.

Kate even wondered if the brother's unhappiness was another invention to give the girl an excuse to down tools. Ruby might not intend to visit her brother at all but have a jaunt to London in mind.

Was it mean-spirited to harbour such suspicions? Kate hated feeling this way but couldn't shift the idea that Ruby had a motive for becoming a land girl that had nothing to do with farming or patriotism.

'Which day do you want off?' Kate asked.

Ruby had schooled her features into an expression of regret but couldn't hold back the triumph from her eyes. 'Friday.'

In other words, tomorrow.

'I only pay for work that's actually done,' Ernie reminded her sourly.

'Of course, Mr Fletcher, I wouldn't dream of not working hard.'

Kate walked away before she said something she might later regret.

'I'm going into the village,' Kenny announced the following morning. 'I'm out of Woodbines, and we're running low on oil for the tractor. While I'm there I can do the shopping for Kate if we need any. Save her a job.'

It would be the first time ever that Kenny had been

moved to save Kate a job, but he was simply trying to get her on his side. The person he really wanted to help was Ruby. 'I can give you a lift on the cart,' he told her.

'How kind.'

The conversation sounded rehearsed and Kate guessed they'd agreed the arrangement in advance.

'No work, no pay,' Ernie grunted.

'It's ever so kind of you to let me visit poor Timmy,' Ruby told him. 'I'll make up for it, I promise.'

She was wasting her time trying to win Ernie round. Unlike Kenny, he wasn't susceptible to her charms.

'Have you got a shopping list?' Kenny asked Kate.

'No, because we don't need anything, and I'll be going out for bread tomorrow anyway.' Kate hadn't time to make her own bread.

Kenny looked disappointed and Kate soon understood he was hoping to trade one favour for another when he said, 'You could make Ruby a sandwich to get her through the travelling.'

Kate couldn't warm to Ruby, but she wouldn't let the girl go hungry. She made her a cheese sandwich, which she packed in a bag with some cherries and a slice of gooseberry tart. There was a bottle of ginger beer in the larder, which reminded Kate of Leo and gave her a little lift of joy as she remembered the picnic they'd shared. That went into the bag too.

'Thanks,' Ruby said, then added for effect, 'Everyone in this family is so generous!'

Kenny gave Kate a look that said clearly: *See how lovely she is? You shouldn't be so mean to her.*

'Actually,' Kate said, 'seeing as you're going to the shops, and we're such a generous family, Kenny, you

221

could buy some things to send to the twins. Cigarettes, another pack of playing cards as they lost the last pack I sent, and socks. They always need socks.'

She didn't offer her own money. It was time someone else in the family paid out. 'Ernie?' Kenny said.

Their father took no notice, probably pretending he hadn't heard so he could save a shilling or two.

'Ernie!' Kenny repeated sharply.

Ernie muttered a curse but got up and fetched his cash box. He took some coins out and slapped them on the table.

Only a few coins but Kenny didn't argue. 'Vinnie?' he said.

'You don't expect me to—'

Kenny *did* expect him to help make up the shortfall.

Grumbling, Vinnie handed over some money and Kenny headed for the kitchen door, doubtless to harness Pete to the cart. 'I shan't be long,' he told Ernie, who scowled.

'You'd better not be.'

Ruby followed Kenny outside, swinging her hips in a dress that did full justice to her figure.

Soon Kate and Pearl were alone. Kate washed and dried the breakfast dishes, stirred the washing that was soaking in the dolly and then smiled at Pearl. 'Let's work in the kitchen garden this morning.'

Away from Ruby's influence, Pearl worked diligently, and when the time came for Kate to go indoors to prepare the mid-morning tea, she had no hesitation in saying, 'You deserve a break, Pearl. Come in and sit down for a few extra minutes.'

Pearl looked pleased. She always looked pleased by

praise, and Kate guessed she'd spent her life hearing mostly criticism. 'Don't mind if I do.'

They washed at the kitchen sink; then Pearl sat at the table as Kate made tea and cut bread. 'Have an extra slice before the others come,' Kate invited. 'I won't tell if you won't.'

Pearl's plain face lit up again. She reached for a slice of bread and smoothed on some margarine, the butter rations not stretching to cover elevenses. Kate was glad to make Pearl happy.

'Ruby seems to be a good sister,' Kate remarked, watching Pearl for signs that she was party to a deception.

Pearl chomped on her bread, then said, 'The best. She writes the longest letters to him and sends him little treats when she can.'

'It must upset her to know that her brother is miserable.'

'It's awful,' Pearl agreed, and words suddenly spilled out with feeling. 'He's with a married couple who don't want him and don't even try to hide it from him. They never call him Timmy but the Boy or You or even the Nuisance. They don't give him enough blankets and he's always hungry too. Poor Ruby's at her wits' end. She wants to see Timmy today but she also wants to see this couple so she can tell them to look after him properly or she'll report them for cruelty.'

Kate was in no doubt that Pearl believed this. Perhaps it was true.

'Do you know, they even took the stamps she sent to Timmy so he could write back to her?' Pearl added. 'They said he must have lost them but he was sure he'd kept them safe. Ruby only found out because she sent more stamps. This time she sent them to Mrs Harris herself so she couldn't pretend Timmy had lost them again.'

'That was clever.'

'Ruby *is* clever. I'm so lucky to have her as my friend.'

Seeing the postman outside, Kate went to greet him, thoughts of a letter from Leo quickening her heartbeat. He handed over a small bundle of letters, but Kate had to spend a minute or two chatting before she could glance down at them. At last the postman went on his way and Kate looked through the envelopes. Bill for Ernie ... Another bill for Ernie ... A letter for Pearl ... A letter for Kate with her name and address typed on the envelope ... Could this be it? A letter from Leo?

She hid it in her pocket, then returned to the kitchen to put Ernie's bills on the table and hand Pearl her letter.

'Thanks,' Pearl said, but her expression was gloomy as she stared down at the envelope.

'News from home?' Kate asked.

'Looks like it.' Her big hands tore into the envelope and pulled out the letter. 'It's from my mother and sister.'

'I'd have liked a sister.'

'Not one like Helen, you wouldn't. She and my mother make a pair. Neither of them thinks much of clumsy old me.'

There was lifetime of slights behind Pearl's words.

'If they don't appreciate you just because you're

different, they're fools. Imagine Helen on this farm. I suspect she wouldn't be half as useful as you.'

Pearl laughed, sounding surprised as though she'd never considered that she might have an advantage before.

Kate hoped she was making headway with Pearl but the arrival of the Fletcher men put an end to the conversation. Pearl sat up straighter, wiped tell-tale crumbs from her mouth and stuck the butter knife into the margarine to hide the fact that it had already been used.

Towards evening Kenny slipped outside without a word to anyone and moments later Kate heard him in the cart, doubtless on his way to collect Ruby from the bus stop. He was gone a long time and Kate began to wonder if they'd gone to the Wheatsheaf. The thought annoyed her as she had the evening meal to serve and didn't know whether to wait for them.

'Are you trying to starve us?' Vinnie grumbled after a while.

'Obviously, I'm waiting for Kenny and Ruby,' Kate snapped back.

'It's their bad luck if they don't bother turning up. More for the rest of us.' The thought of eating Kenny's share clearly cheered Vinnie. So much for brotherly love.

Kate had just decided to serve the supper when she heard the jangle of Pete's harness and the creak of cartwheels. At last!

Ruby came in smiling. 'Thank you so much for giving me the day off, Mr Fletcher,' she cried. 'It was wonderful to see Timmy.'

Kenny came in too, and Vinnie sent him a grudging look. 'You've kept us waiting.'

'Sorry, that was my fault,' Ruby said. 'Well, not my fault exactly. The bus ran late due to a puncture and Kenny was sweet enough to wait for me.'

Ernie sent his eldest son a scowl and muttered, 'Sweet!' as though sweetness was an unmanly failing.

'We're here now,' Kenny pointed out, then glared at Kate. 'What are you waiting for?'

They all sat at the table and Kate served a casserole of sliced sausages and vegetables with potatoes on top. Ruby kept up an account of her day, but Kate still didn't know whether she was telling the truth or performing a pantomime. If it was a pantomime, it was a detailed one.

'Mrs Harris is such a witch,' Ruby said. 'She didn't even offer me a glass of water, and I'd been travelling for hours. And when I mentioned that Timmy sometimes says he's cold and hungry she called him a liar. An *ungrateful* liar who didn't appreciate her generosity in giving him a home and feeding him despite the inconvenience. She's horrible, Pearl.'

'Timmy must have been glad to see you, though.'

'He was. We went for a walk and it was lovely. But I hated leaving him with that witch. Timmy hated being left too. He tried to be brave but in the end he cried. I told him I'd try to visit him again soon.'

Ruby had achieved little in the way of extra work on Thursday, as far as Kate had seen, and the work that was carried out on Sunday appeared to owe more to the helping hands of Kenny and Pearl than Ruby's own efforts.

'I'm so sorry,' Alice said when Kate snatched a few

minutes out of her Sunday evening to visit her. 'Is she any help at all?'

'Sometimes, but the way she distracts both Kenny and Pearl rather cancels out half of her usefulness.'

'What can you do?'

'I don't know. Kenny won't hear a word against her.'

'How do Ernie and Vinnie feel about that?'

'Ernie calls Kenny a fool. I think Vinnie's jealous. He seems to be setting his sights on Pearl, so he doesn't feel left out.'

'Is she setting her sights on him?'

'She's certainly flattered by the attention – I don't think any man has taken an interest in her before. I doubt Vinnie's ready to be serious, though, so I hope she isn't serious either. I wouldn't like her to be hurt.'

'I can't think how I might help so I'll just hope it all settles down,' Alice said.

It was enough. Kate wasn't expecting Alice to change the situation. The relief came from simply talking to someone who cared. Kate was tempted to mention Leo too but didn't feel quite ready yet. If she saw Leo again, then perhaps she'd tell Alice about him, because a second meeting would surely suggest that his interest was more than just a passing fancy. It would cost him some trouble to see her, after all.

Feeling she'd been hogging the conversation, Kate changed the subject. 'Have you heard from Daniel?'

'He was well last time he wrote, thank goodness.'

'And the bookshop? I'm sorry I haven't called in on it recently.'

'It's a slow business trying to persuade people to donate to a hamper for the Forsyths but we're getting there.'

'I haven't signed up yet, but I intend to give something.'

'Fresh vegetables from the farm would be welcome if you can manage them. Don't buy anything.'

Alice knew that Kate earned little.

Cycling home from Alice's cottage in the long summery twilight, Kate thought over the letter she'd received from Leo and had read so many times that it had imprinted on her memory.

*Dear Kate,*

*I hope you approve of the typed envelope. I used five cigarettes to bribe a clerk to type it for me but I think he'd have done it for nothing as he found the whole situation intriguing. Not that I told him about you, but he guessed there was someone special involved and I think it amused him to think of me sneaking around behind a strict father's back.*

*I hope you arrived home safely from our tryst in Beech Lane and didn't get into trouble for being late. I was loath to part from you as I enjoyed our picnic so much and I can't wait to see you again – if you'd like to see me? Unfortunately, my duties make it tricky for me to plan things in advance – I may be called into action at short notice – but let me know if you'd like to see me again and I'll try my best to get over to Churchwood as soon as possible. Forgive me if it takes me some time, though, and forgive me even more if I have to let you down at the last minute. It isn't as though I'll be able to tell you if I can't come as you're not on the telephone and I imagine you wouldn't welcome a telegram.*

She wouldn't welcome a telegram. Someone turning up at the door with an urgent message for her was bound to rouse the curiosity of her family or the girls.

*Know that there's nothing I want more than to be with you. I'm sorry if that comes across as rather strong since we've only met twice. Please don't run away, though, because I'll never push you to go faster than is comfortable for you.*
*Best wishes,*
*Leo Kinsella*

Reading it, Kate had felt emotions circling inside her like dancers skipping around a maypole. Chief amongst them was delight, as though the world was full of promise, even with all the troubles on the farm. Even so, she delayed writing back for a couple of days. She didn't want to look desperate and neither did she wish to lose her head over a man she barely knew. Trying to be cautious, Kate told herself that it wouldn't be the end of the world if no letter came from him in reply. It would be disappointing, though. Deeply disappointing.

# CHAPTER TWENTY-EIGHT

## *Alice*

*I'll be thinking of you*, Daniel had written in his last letter, *and I'll be keeping my fingers crossed that the Forsyths fit in better than expected.*

Alice was keeping her fingers crossed too, though more in hope than expectation. She looked at the hamper that had been arranged for the new vicar and his wife and thought that, thanks to the persuasive powers of May and the rest of the bookshop team, Churchwood had been generous after all. Amongst other things there was wine, sherry, tins of soup, jars of preserves, fresh vegetables and fruit, and half a dozen eggs from Alice's hens. If the Forsyths didn't appreciate it, they'd be an ungrateful pair.

A rumble out in the road announced the arrival of Bert in his truck, here to transport the heavy hamper to the vicarage. All members of the bookshop team were going along to present it, apart from Kate, who couldn't spare the time.

'Afternoon, young Alice,' Bert said as she opened the door to him.

He collected the hamper from the dining room and paused to survey it just as Alice had done. 'If the Forsyths don't appreciate it—'

'They'll be an ungrateful pair,' Alice finished. 'That's just what I was thinking. Is Naomi with you?'

'On her way.'

Naomi arrived as Bert placed the hamper in the truck. She still looked under strain. 'Tooth hurting again?' Alice asked.

Naomi flushed as though the weakness of it embarrassed her. 'No more than an occasional niggle, but thank you for asking.'

Bert was watching her thoughtfully too. Was he also thinking that Cecil Wade was troubling Naomi more than her tooth? Cecil had been strutting around the village, as smug as could be, doubtless congratulating himself on pleasing the archdeacon and planning to become the Forsyths' closest ally. It was spiteful to hope that the Forsyths would give Cecil the cold shoulder but, after the way Cecil had treated Naomi, Alice hoped it anyway.

They climbed into the truck and headed for the village green to meet May and Janet. 'It looks wonderful,' Janet said, admiring the hamper as Bert heaved it out of the truck.

'Especially taking rationing into account,' May added.

Removal men had been at the vicarage for several hours carrying in the Forsyths' possessions. Now they were closing the van and preparing to move off. 'Ready?' Alice asked the team, and they walked up the path to the vicarage door.

Mrs Forsyth answered Alice's knock.

'We don't wish to intrude when you must be extremely busy, but on behalf of the bookshop we want to welcome you to Churchwood and present you with a gift,' Alice said.

Bert stepped forward with the hamper.

'Many people who come to the bookshop contributed,' Alice continued. 'That's what the bookshop is all about – the community helping and supporting each other.'

'How kind,' Mrs Forsyth said, but she was looking at the hamper as though expecting a slug to crawl out of the strawberries.

'What's this?' Reverend Forsyth appeared behind his wife's shoulder, and she moved aside to let him join her in the doorway.

'It's a gift from the bookshop,' May told him.

'Many people contributed,' Janet added.

'How – er – generous. Do you wish to come in? You'll excuse us for being in some disarray as we only arrived a few hours ago.'

'We won't come in today,' Bert answered. 'We know you must be busy. If I could just . . .'

He held out the hamper and Reverend Forsyth took it into his arms.

'It will be lovely to see you in the bookshop once you've settled in,' Alice said. 'We're looking forward to showing you more of what we do and how we help.'

'Ah yes, the bookshop.' Reverend Forsyth made it sound like the naughty pupil in an otherwise well-behaved class.

'We hope you'll come to love it as much as we do,' Naomi said.

He smiled thinly.

'We have a bookshop session tomorrow afternoon,'

Alice told him. 'If you're settled in by then, it would be wonderful to see you. And Mrs Forsyth, of course.'

Naomi took up the cause again. 'Once you understand what we're about, I'm sure you'll—'

Reverend Forsyth cut across her. 'Tomorrow may not be possible as we have many other demands on our time.'

'Of course.'

'But rest assured, the bookshop is in my thoughts. You could say that it's a priority for me.'

Alice didn't like the sound of that. From the looks on their faces, neither did the others.

The conversation had come to an end. 'We hope you enjoy the hamper,' Alice said, and the team returned to the truck in silence.

'It'll suit me if he has so many demands on his time that he never sets foot in the bookshop,' May said then. 'What a superior kind of person he thinks he is! Did it not occur to him that people had made sacrifices to donate to that hamper?'

'His wife is awful too,' Janet agreed. 'So haughty!'

Alice hadn't warmed to their supercilious attitude either. 'I agree, but I still think the best way of saving the bookshop is to try to win them round with friendliness and hope the bookshop works its magic on them.'

No one had a better idea to offer so Alice continued: 'It might be wise to avoid provoking them if we can. I suggest we only bring out the sorts of stories the Forsyths might approve of at our next few sessions. I know that might feel as though we're giving in to narrow-mindedness, but we're fighting for the bookshop's life.'

'Well, when you put it like that,' Janet agreed.

# CHAPTER TWENTY-NINE

## *Naomi*

Janet and May walked off, and Bert turned to Alice and Naomi. 'Can I give you ladies a lift home?'

'I've some shopping to do,' Alice told him, 'but thanks anyway.'

She walked off too, leaving Naomi alone with Bert. It was as good a time as any to tell him of her failed visit to London. Accepting the lift, she got into the truck and recounted what had happened. 'Are you going to tell me I behaved like a fool?' she asked.

'Well, I don't think *I'd* employ you if I ever needed a detective,' he teased, though his twinkling eyes took the sting out of it. 'Seriously, though, I still think a professional investigator might be the best man for the job, but I understand why you don't like the thought of it.'

'It's all so sordid.'

'That's as may be. The question to ask is whether it's a price worth paying for the information you want. Information that might bring you peace of mind.'

Or blow her marriage to smithereens.

'Have you kept the newspaper I gave you?' he asked.

'Yes.' Naomi had put it in a drawer in her sitting

room and covered it with some of her bookshop paperwork.

Bert nodded his approval. 'Hold on to it so you've got it to hand when the right moment comes.'

The right moment being when she reached desperation point.

They arrived at Foxfield and Bert drew the truck to a halt. 'You know where to find me if you want another chat, even if you haven't made your mind up about the best thing to be done.'

'I appreciate it, Bert. Really I do.'

One thing was certain. Naomi needed to pull herself together. She'd been useless with the Forsyths and as an excuse for her low spirits the feigned toothache was wearing thin.

'Helloooooo! Naomi!'

Oh, no. It was Marjorie. Naomi should have guessed that her gossip-loving friend would be desperate to hear about the Forsyths.

Taking a deep breath, Naomi got out of the truck, waved to Bert and waited for Marjorie to draw near.

'I saw you at the Forsyths' door.' Marjorie's mud-coloured eyes were bright with anticipation. 'What are they like?'

'The same as they were when they interrupted the bookshop with the archdeacon.'

'But their things. You must have seen their things.'

'Do you mean their furniture?'

'Furniture, ornaments . . . everything. I expect the Forsyths have heirlooms that have been in their families for years and years.'

'I didn't go inside the house.'

'You must have seen into the hall.'

'Marjorie, I didn't look.'

'You didn't see anything?' It was inexplicable to Marjorie, whose eyes would have darted everywhere. 'You must have noticed what Mrs Forsyth was wearing, though. I couldn't see her dress properly from where I was standing. Did it look expensive?'

'I'm sorry to disappoint you, but I didn't look at the dress either.'

'Oh.' Marjorie was deflated.

'I'm sure the Forsyths will waste no time in meeting the congregation, so you'll see them soon enough.'

'I suppose so.' But Marjorie had hoped for advance information. She looked gloomy for a moment, then rallied herself, looking at the Foxfield door as though hoping to be invited inside.

'Goodness, look at the time!' Naomi said hastily. 'Sykes wants to talk to me about some plans for the garden.' Sykes was the Foxfield gardener-cum-handyman. Before petrol rationing, he'd also driven Naomi around in Alexander's Daimler when she was allowed to use it.

'I could—'

'Goodbye then, Marjorie. I hope you're coming to the bookshop tomorrow. The Forsyths may be there.'

With that Naomi turned and set off, walking around the house towards the rear garden. It was a relief to hear the crunch of gravel as Marjorie walked back along the drive. Ducking behind a laurel bush, Naomi waited until the coast was clear, then returned to the front door and let herself into the house. It was mean to deny Marjorie a cup of tea and a chat, but Naomi couldn't have coped with her today.

*

236

Deep sleep eluded her again that night. Naomi woke from a troubled doze feeling fuzzy-headed and heavy-limbed. But she'd let the bookshop down yesterday and she was determined to do better today, especially if the Forsyths called in.

'I don't know about you, but I'm ready to defend the bookshop tooth and nail,' she said as she helped to set out chairs and tables. The words were addressed to her friends, though Naomi suspected the person she was really trying to convince was herself. The truth was that she felt physically weak and her once-sharp thoughts had become like blind spectres shambling around her mind.

When the hall was ready, they all stood back to take it in. It looked much the same as usual – from a distance. It was the detail that was just a little different. Newspapers and some wholesome magazines were still on show, but the steamier and more frivolous books and comics were nowhere in sight. The wooden Noah's Ark with the carved animals was always present but today Alice had placed it in a prominent position with a book containing the story of the ark beside it. 'For today's story time,' she'd explained.

Other books with religious themes were on display, too. *Bible Stories for Children*, *The Young Jesus*, *The Story of David and Goliath* . . . 'I'm hoping to show the Forsyths that we're not an ungodly lot,' Alice had explained. 'It's just that we don't push religion down people's throats, and we welcome everyone, whatever their beliefs.'

'You haven't hidden all the non-religious books, I see.' May picked up Beatrix Potter's *The Tale of Mrs Tiggy-Winkle*.

'I won't pretend we don't allow that sort of book. I've included a mix of titles, just not the ones most likely to offend the Forsyths.'

'Compromise,' Bert said.

'Precisely.'

People began to arrive – mothers with babies and young children for story time; people for Janet's knitting club; other people for Bert's horticulture tips . . .

'I loved this book,' Naomi heard Mrs Hutchings say as she took a book from her bag and passed it to Mrs Hayes. 'The hero was an absolute dreamboat and when he kissed Marianne I swear I—'

'Shall I take that?' Naomi reached for the book in question, a steamy romance featuring a cover on which a tall and impossibly handsome man held a golden-haired beauty in his arms. 'I'll mark it down as returned and check it out for you later, if you want it, Ada. We're about to begin.'

She slipped the book into her bag, vowing to keep an eye out in case other 'unsuitable' books were returned today.

It was starting to look as though the Forsyths wouldn't appear when the door opened and in they came. Both being tall and dark-haired, and both wearing clothing that was dark even if it was well cut, they seemed to cast a shadow over the bookshop like rainclouds sweeping over a picnic. The chatter in the room quietened and then turned silent except for one little boy who asked, 'Who are those people, Mummy?' before his mother told him to shush.

'Good morning to you all,' Reverend Forsyth said. 'I'm afraid my wife and I have a luncheon engagement with the archdeacon so we can't stay, but we wanted to look in before we left.'

His face was stern as he glanced around the room. Mrs Forsyth's face was prim.

'We'll return for a longer time as soon as our schedule permits,' he said, making it sound as though his intervention in this den of iniquity couldn't come soon enough.

'That's good,' Bert called, deliberately misunderstanding him. 'We'll be glad to welcome you to the bookshop we all value so highly.'

'That's right,' someone else called. Wilfred Phipps, Naomi's almost-ally on the church council. 'The bookshop brings our community together.'

'We positively favour bringing our church community together,' Reverend Forsyth assured him. 'But changes ... I think we'll be making changes. God's business on God's premises, do you see?'

With that the Forsyths withdrew and once again Naomi had done nothing to help. She wanted to follow them outside to try to build some sort of relationship before too much harm was done but she was down on her knees with little Joey Buxton and by the time she got up the Forsyths would have gone.

She cursed herself for a fool. A slow-witted, slow-bodied fool. She'd meant to do so much to help the bookshop today but she'd done nothing.

She urgently needed to get her life back into its familiar groove. Did that mean she was desperate enough to enlist the help of a private detective? Very nearly.

# CHAPTER THIRTY

## *Kate*

The sound of feminine giggles drifted down from the hay loft as Kate walked past the barn. Ruby must be up there with Kenny, and they wouldn't be working because there was nothing up there except the hay that was used on the farm to stop boots and tyres from sinking into mud, or sometimes sold to other farmers as animal feed or bedding.

Kate continued to the kitchen garden and picked some beans. Returning, she found Vinnie chasing Pearl round the yard. 'Stop messing about!' Pearl protested, but she looked pleased by the attention. She squealed as Vinnie caught hold of her.

'I win, so you owe me a kiss,' he said, looking up because Pearl was taller.

'Don't be so silly.' She stamped on his toe with one of her big feet.

'Ow!' Vinnie yelled, hopping.

Pearl ran towards the house, laughing and looking over her shoulder as though hoping he'd follow.

'I'll get you for that!' Vinnie cried, running after her.

Dodging him, Pearl raced away with Vinnie in pursuit.

Kate took the beans into the house and Ernie came in after her, his lip curled in bad temper.

'That's your fault,' he accused her, dipping his head towards the silliness in the farmyard. 'You brought them girls here.'

The gall of him! 'Yes, I did bring them here, and they're helping.' Not as much as she'd like, but the farm would be struggling even more without them. 'How would you have got on in Five Acre Field without Pearl to help you yesterday?' Separated from Ruby, Pearl had worked hard. 'Anyway, you should be blaming your sons for the silliness out there.'

Ernie only scowled and threw himself into a chair at the table, reaching for the newspaper someone had brought back from the Wheatsheaf. But when the boys came in, he sent them a contemptuous snarl. 'Idiots! Mooning over a pair of girls like that!'

Kenny looked annoyed. His feelings for Ruby appeared to be growing ever more serious.

Vinnie simply grinned. 'Just having a bit of fun.'

Ernie wasn't happy with his sons larking around with girls, but he'd be furious if he thought Kate was involved with a man. She hugged her secret to her like a cosy blanket. Leo had written to say he'd be back in the lane tonight and hoped she'd manage to meet him.

*Sorry for the short notice, but I have the chance to borrow the motorbike again and I'm so keen to see you that I'll wait in the lane for hours if necessary. They're forecasting rain but I won't let that put me off and I hope you won't be put off by it either. I'll aim to arrive at seven.*

Kate glanced up at the grey-clouded sky numerous times that day, relieved that the rain was holding off. At half past six she unlocked the bicycle and rode off without a word to anyone. It wasn't as though her family ever showed consideration for her, and she didn't want to risk being held up.

She called in at The Linnets first, finding Alice at home. 'Just a quick visit,' Kate said as Alice led her into the kitchen, something she'd said many times since they'd become friends. 'I'm sorry I haven't been down to the bookshop recently. Have the Forsyths been back?'

'They made a brief appearance and announced that they plan to make changes. No details yet, but I suspect we're not going to like them.'

'They're going to ram their piety down people's throats,' Kate guessed, sitting down after Alice waved a hand in invitation.

'Probably.'

'Which will leave people who aren't religious with nowhere to go. Surely a decent vicar would welcome everyone? Didn't Jesus mix with sinners?'

'He did indeed.'

Kate hadn't been brought up to go to church but if anyone was going to persuade her to try it that person would be someone like Adam, who led by example instead of condemnation.

'What can we do?' she asked.

'Try to preserve as much of the bookshop's identity as possible,' Alice replied. 'I can't think of a better plan.'

Neither could Kate. Of course, she couldn't visit Alice without mentioning the person dearest to her friend's heart. 'Any news from Daniel?'

242

'I'm not expecting another letter for a little while yet,' Alice told her, smiling in anticipation of the moment the letter actually arrived.

Kate understood that feeling now. She, too, felt ready to burst at the thought of Leo's letters. For a moment she considered telling Alice about him, but she still felt shy, and besides, she'd already lingered longer than planned.

'Tea?' Alice offered.

'No time.' Kate got to her feet. 'Give Daniel my love when you next write to him.'

The girls hugged. 'Don't bother seeing me out,' Kate said, hoping to avoid awkward questions about where she was going since she wouldn't be heading back up Brimbles Lane.

It was ten minutes to seven according to the clock in Alice's kitchen. Kate pedalled quickly as she headed for Beech Lane, bracing herself for disappointment if Leo didn't appear.

*Please understand that, if I fail to arrive, it'll be because I've been pressed into duty or there's a problem with the motorbike,* Leo had added. *It won't be because I don't want to see you because there's nothing I want more.*

But he *was* there, and Kate's heart swelled with joy. He was leaning against a tree, helmet and goggles off and his eyes warm as he watched her approach.

'You've made a flight lieutenant very happy,' he said, taking her bicycle and wheeling it behind the same tree as before.

His words were delicious, but also embarrassing and she wished she knew how to be more sophisticated. 'I hope I'm not late?' she said, because she couldn't think of anything cleverer to say.

243

'Not at all. I was early.' He grinned at her. 'Enthusiastic, you see?'

More embarrassment. She looked up at the sky to hide her blush, casting around for something to say. She could mention the weather but that would surely bore him.

'Shall we ride on the bike or go for walk?' Leo asked.

'I don't mind.' Goodness, could she sound more dull-witted?

Luckily Leo appeared not to think so. 'If you really don't mind, let's walk. It'll be easier to talk.'

He moved the motorbike behind another bush and then offered his arm. Kate had never walked arm in arm with a man before. She felt stiff and self-conscious and in danger of bumping into him until she realized she had to match her steps to his and vice versa. If Leo noticed her awkwardness, he was too gallant to comment. They walked up the lane a little way and Kate began to relax and enjoy his closeness.

Then the rain started. A fat drop landed on Kate's nose and Leo must have felt a drop too because he came to a halt, saying, 'Looks as though the clouds have decided to drench us after all.'

Those first drops were succeeded by many more. They chilled the air and landed like small weapons on their heads and clothes and the surface of the lane, which rapidly darkened with wetness.

'The copse,' he said, gesturing ahead where there was a belt of trees.

He let go of her arm but offered a hand instead. Taking it, Kate ran to the trees with him, barely noticing the rain because she was so aware of the firm, warm pressure of his fingers wrapped around hers. He was grinning when they reached the trees, his eyes aglow with life and good humour. Kate took her hand back shyly and fought for some poise. 'Shame about the rain,' she said, only to wish she could grab the words back. The weather again. So boring!

'I don't know about that,' Leo told her. 'Rain has its compensations.'

Was he thinking that it had given him an excuse to take her hand?

'That log over there looks dry,' he said. 'Almost dry anyway.'

It was sheltered by a canopy of leaves. They sat, and Leo whipped off his jacket to hold it over both of their heads. 'In case of drips,' he explained.

He looked at her for a moment, then said, 'How have you been? How are your land girls?'

Kate talked about Ruby and Pearl as positively as possible, not wanting to lie but not wanting to criticize either. She didn't tell him that romance was flourishing at Brimbles Farm in case it came across as a hint that she wanted romance too. Kate *did* want it but felt horribly self-conscious about appearing to flirt.

'How has flying been since I last saw you?' she asked.

He told her about his Spitfire and RAF comrades, but she sensed he preferred her to talk. It was understandable. Leo might think highly of his nimble little aircraft, but he was flying to kill and risked being killed in return.

'Do you like the farm?' he wanted to know.

'I hope I won't be doing farm work for ever. But as for the countryside itself, I love it.'

She told him about the sunsets and sunrises over the fields with their myriad shades of pink, red, yellow and violet. She also described the way the winds made the grasses sway like dancers and the trees shimmer like sparkling fairies. Then there was the supple softness of new growth, the soaring flights of birds and the rich smell of the earth after rain.

She realized he was paying more attention to her face than her words and promptly shut up.

'Don't stop,' he said. 'I like to see how passionate you are about nature.'

She shrugged but didn't continue, feeling tongue-tied under his scrutiny – and excited by it too.

'Do you think you might be able to come out with me one day?' Leo said. 'For more than a snatched hour or so, I mean?'

Oh, dear. He must wish he'd been dancing or eating dinner in a fine restaurant instead of sitting here getting wet. 'Perhaps,' she said, 'but I can't promise to get away. I'm sorry. Obviously, you'd prefer to spend your free time having fun instead of sheltering under a jacket.'

'You couldn't be more wrong. I could have plenty of so-called fun in the bars and dances near the base.'

'You could?' Kate felt the stabbing knife of jealousy.

'Yes. But I'd rather see *you*, rain or no rain.'

'Oh.'

'Let me know if you think you can get away from

the farm for an afternoon or evening. But don't worry if it isn't possible. As long as I'm with you, I'm happy.'

They sat for a while longer until the rain eased off, signalling to Kate that she should get home. They headed back towards the bikes, and it felt natural now for Leo to take her hand.

This time he kissed her when they said goodbye. It was the gentlest of kisses but the touch of his lips on hers ignited a fire inside her. The urgency of it frightened her a little. 'Don't worry,' he said, drawing back. 'I meant it when I said you're worth waiting for.'

Kate felt weightless with happiness as she cycled home. Not even when Ernie launched into a long tirade against girls who shirked their work did the brightness fade from her mood. She still had her problems, but being in love gave her the sensation of floating atop a choppy sea. Well, perhaps she wasn't in love exactly. It was still too soon for that. But there was promise in the air, sparkling and vivid.

The feeling was fragile, though. For all his talk of contentment in seeing her in snatched moments and uncomfortable conditions, would the situation pall in comparison to the bright lights of bars and the possibility of dances with other young women?

She was a little reassured by the letter that came from him on Saturday morning. *I felt as light as air itself after we met*, he wrote.

Me too, me too, Kate thought.

*It was as though I no longer needed my Spitfire because I had wings of my own. I have to force myself back to earth to get on with daily life but I only have to think of you to start gliding upwards again.*

247

'You look pleased with yourself,' Ruby said, catching Kate smiling as she thought over the letter later.

'Just thinking about all the work I've done today.'

It wasn't a clever retort, and Ruby would doubtless take it as a criticism of her poorer work efforts. But Kate had found it impossible to resist. Sure enough, Ruby's painted face hardened, and she went off with a flounce.

Kate didn't want Ruby to know anything about Leo, but she did want to confide in someone.

She cycled down to The Linnets the following afternoon. Entering the garden by the side gate, she saw Alice down by the trees, staring up at them as though watching a bird.

'I've met a man,' Kate blurted as she headed towards her friend. 'He's called Leo Kinsella and he's a flight lieutenant in the RAF. I've only seen him three times, but I like him. A lot.'

Alice turned. 'Hello, Kate. That's lovely news. I couldn't be happier for you.'

She was smiling but Kate was appalled to see that tears were sliding down Alice's face.

'What it is?' Kate demanded. 'What's happened?'

'It . . .' Alice couldn't speak. She took a deep breath and tried again. 'It's Daniel. He's been taken prisoner.'

# CHAPTER THIRTY-ONE

## *Alice*

Kate's arms went around her, and Alice sobbed against her friend's shoulder. After all the months of separation, the daily worry over Daniel's well-being, the trauma of awaiting his rescue from the beaches of Dunkirk . . . Now this terrible news. Questions jostled for space in Alice's head. Was he hurt? How would he be treated? What if he fell sick? How would he cope emotionally? And how long would his captivity last? The 1914 war had continued for four long years. There were no signs that this war would be shorter, and it might well be longer. Would she ever see Daniel again?

Alice had tried to be brave but this . . . It was too much.

'I'm so sorry,' Kate said. 'Sorry about Daniel and this whole rotten war. Cry as much as you need. It'll help.'

Alice did cry for a while. But eventually the sobs subsided. She drew back from Kate to blow her nose on an already sodden handkerchief. 'I know I should be grateful that the news isn't worse. Daniel could have been seriously injured or . . .' She couldn't say the word, but Kate nodded to show she understood.

'When did you hear?'

'About an hour ago. Daniel's parents sent a tele-gram. Not that they had much information. They don't know how he came to be captured or where he's being held.'

'You'll be able to get letters to him eventually? Receive letters from him too?'

'I hope so.' Alice took a deep breath to try to steady herself. She was aware of her father watching them through the French windows of his study.

'Let me make you a cup of tea,' Kate suggested, and she steered Alice back up the garden and into the kitchen.

Alice's father joined them. 'It's a bad business,' he said. 'But plenty of men were taken prisoner during the 1914 war and came home when it was over.'

He smiled at Alice, and she made a valiant effort to smile back, though they both knew that not all men who'd been imprisoned in the earlier war had made it back to England. Poor food, sickness, war strain . . . But there was nothing to be gained by voicing the fearful possibilities. They could only hope that Dan-iel would come through.

'Do you mind if I make free with your kitchen?' Kate asked him. 'I offered to make tea.'

'That's kind.'

He smiled at Alice again, and she had to blink away more tears at the love she saw in his eyes. Then he withdrew tactfully, leaving the girls to talk alone.

Kate made the tea, having been here often enough to know which cupboards and drawers held cups, spoons and tea, and also to know that milk was kept on a marble slab in the larder. As Kate got everything ready, Alice sat at the small square table.

Daniel was alive. That was the most important thing. If he sat out the war as a prisoner, he might actually be safer than if he were still engaged in fighting. Alice was going to miss him dreadfully, though.

Kate took tea to Alice's father in his study, then returned to the kitchen and sat down. She looked awkward. Fidgety. It was always a struggle for Kate to talk about personal matters, but Alice knew she wanted desperately to help.

'I won't pretend to understand exactly what you're going through,' Kate finally said. 'I've no experience of such things. But you and Daniel have courage, bravest people I know. What's happened is worrying and frightening, not to mention heart-wrenching. But you'll both find a way to cope.'

'I don't feel strong *or* brave right now,' Alice answered. 'But yes, I'll have to find a way to cope for Daniel's sake. It won't help him if I crumble to pieces.'

'He'll find a way to cope for your sake too. And one day you'll be reunited. Hopefully soon.'

'You're a good friend, Kate.'

'I don't feel I am. Not at the moment.'

'Only because you have so little time to spare.' Alice sat quietly for a moment longer, then straightened her shoulders. 'Tell me about this man you've met.'

Kate blushed. 'I've only met him three times. Once by chance and twice by arrangement.'

'But you like him.'

'I do.'

Kate confided a little about Leo.

'His cousin is at Stratton House?' Alice asked.

'Anthony Kinsella.'

Alice nodded in recognition. 'He's just been moved

251

nearer his family to convalesce, but I remember him well. Nice man. Your Leo sounds a nice man too, and talking of people having courage . . .'

'He must be both of those things to fly a Spitfire into combat,' Kate agreed. She hesitated, then added, 'Please don't think I'm comparing my feelings for Leo to yours for Daniel. I've only just met Leo while you've loved Daniel for years.'

'It isn't a competition, Kate. It's wonderful that you care about Leo, and it's natural for you to worry about his safety.'

'He's in danger every time he flies.'

'We're in this war together and we'll support each other through it. That's what friends do. Now, how are you getting on with Ruby and Pearl?'

Kate pulled a face and told Alice about the last few days on the farm. Then – inevitably – she glanced at the clock on the mantelpiece and announced that she had to leave. She got up and rubbed her hands down the front of her breeches, looking awkward again. 'Take care of yourself, Alice. Don't feel you have to rush around looking after other people. Not for a while anyway.'

'If I stay at home brooding, I might feel worse.'

'Just don't overdo it.'

Alice's father said much the same thing the following morning when he took one look at her strained, wan face and drew her into his arms. 'Bad night?'

'I didn't have the best sleep.'

'Daniel's situation will take some getting used to. You should rest today.'

'I'd prefer to go to the hospital. I can be useful

252

there. Besides, I'd rather tell people about Daniel sooner than later.'

'Better to get it over with?'

'I think so.' It was going to be difficult to talk about Daniel as a prisoner of war. She'd have to steel herself not to cry.

Tom the porter was the first person she saw as she walked into the hospital. 'Morning, Alice,' he said chirpily. Then he noticed her expression.

'It's Daniel,' Alice explained. 'He's been taken prisoner.'

'Oh, Alice. That's rotten news.'

'At least he's alive. And uninjured, as far as I know.'

'Two things to be grateful for. And the war won't last for ever.'

'I keep reminding myself of that.'

Alice moved to Ward One, running into Babs Carter in the corridor. Babs folded Alice into a hug when she heard the news. Matron came out of her office so Alice explained the situation to her too.

'I'm very sorry,' Matron said.

'But it could be worse,' Alice finished, guessing that Matron must be thinking of her patients, some of whom had life-changing injuries and might even die as a result of them.

'Don't feel you have to stay today if you're not up to it,' Matron said kindly.

Alice straightened her shoulders. 'I'm up to it.'

'Good girl.' Matron patted Alice's arm and moved on.

Alice collected and distributed books, wrote a couple of letters for patients and read a story called 'The Cheat' about betting fraud in horseracing and an enterprising lad whose intrepid actions led to the gang being arrested.

She was glad she'd made the effort to go but felt exhausted walking home.

'Rest,' her father urged when she reached the cottage.

But the bookshop was due to open that afternoon. 'I'm expected, and besides, it'll give me a chance to tell several people about Daniel at the same time.'

She didn't want to have to keep repeating the story. Every telling meant a battle to hold back her tears.

'Very well, but you don't need to stay for the entire afternoon.'

'The Forsyths might turn up.'

'Then let someone else deal with them. You won't help anyone if you fall ill.'

'I'm not ill. I'm just . . .' Oh, what were the words?

'Under terrible emotional strain,' her father finished. 'And that can lead to illness. Trust me. I'm a doctor. Or rather I *was*.' He smiled at his own dry humour.

Alice smiled back though there was little energy behind it. 'I'll certainly consider it,' she said, wanting to please him so he could return to his studies with an untroubled mind.

On arriving at the bookshop, there was no need to announce that she'd received bad news. Naomi took one look at Alice's pale face and moved towards her saying, 'Heavens, what's happened?'

Bert, May and Janet gathered around her too. Tears stung Alice's eyes like needles and prickles of pain tightened her throat, but she managed to break the news of Daniel's imprisonment and was grateful for the comforting hugs she received.

'At least he's safe,' Bert said.

'That's one of the things I keep telling myself.'

'You should go home,' Naomi advised. 'Get some rest.'

Alice was thinking that perhaps she actually would go home when the door opened, and Reverend Forsyth entered with his wife. 'Good afternoon,' he said.

There was a determined light in his eyes that sent unease rippling through Alice's stomach. The darting glances she exchanged with the others suggested it was having the same effect on them.

# CHAPTER THIRTY-TWO

## *Naomi*

Bert was the first to speak. 'Afternoon, vicar,' he said, his voice taking on the growl of someone who was ready for a fight. 'Mrs Forsyth.'

Naomi roused herself to take the initiative. Alice might be their natural leader but the poor girl looked too exhausted to do anything. 'Yes, good afternoon, Reverend Forsyth. Mrs Forsyth too, of course. We've met before but you must have been meeting a lot of people so a reminder of our names can't hurt. I'm Naomi Harrington. These are Alice Lovell, Bert Makepiece, May Janicki and Janet Collins. We're the bookshop organizing team along with Kate Fletcher, though we run it on democratic lines. All suggestions are welcome here.'

The others nodded, and Janet said, 'It's nice to see you,' which wasn't true but was doubtless intended to be tactful.

'We're here to observe,' the vicar announced. He was holding a black leather-bound notebook and a good-quality pen peeped out of the breast pocket of his jacket. 'As I'm sure you can imagine, it's been a busy time for us, being new to the parish, but we've learned a lot about it over the past week and we'd like to take things forward. Would it be convenient for you all to stay behind after today's session has ended so we can have a talk?'

Naomi looked round at her friends again. 'Most of us can stay. I think Alice might—'

'I'll stay too,' Alice said.

This meeting couldn't have come at a worse time for her. At her best, Alice was clever and clear-minded. She never shouted or disparaged others and made her points calmly and rationally. But today she needed her friends to fight on her behalf. Not that Naomi was feeling in fine fettle either. If only she could sleep! Every night she got into bed feeling exhausted, only to be tormented by thoughts of Cecil Wade and – even worse – Alexander's possible betrayal. Visits home and phone calls from him were increasingly rare but Naomi found that her nerves were wound so tightly by his presence and even his voice that they were in danger of bursting. And when he was away her thoughts became obsessed with wondering about what he was doing and whom he was seeing. Her situation didn't compare to poor Alice's, though, so she needed to stay strong and focused.

'Sit down,' Naomi invited. 'We'll be opening in a few minutes so people should begin to trickle in soon.'

'Speak of the d—' Bert began, only to pull back. It must have occurred to him that the vicar and his lady might not want the devil mentioned in a building that belonged to the Church. 'Here they come now,' he said instead.

The vicar and his lady smiled at the arrivals but it seemed to Naomi that the smiles were of the distant, we-know-best variety. The wary looks they received in return weren't lost on her either.

When everyone had found somewhere to sit, Alice addressed the room. 'It's lovely to see you all and we're particularly pleased to have our new vicar and his wife with us today. As you may have seen from the notice outside, we have story time for little ones today, to be followed by crafts, and we hope some of your older children will join us after they've finished school. We also have a sewing session to make items for our fundraising. I believe lavender bags, tray cloths and pyjama cases are planned.'

'That's right,' Janet called.

'For those who enjoy games, we've brought dominoes and the draughts board.' Alice was looking at Wilfred Phipps and William Treloar, who both loved board games. 'Edna and Joan are on tea-making duty.'

'We haven't forgotten,' Edna assured her.

How strong and bright Edna was looking. Only months ago, Edna's desperate attempt to end her life had played a major part in inspiring Alice to set up the bookshop to meet the villagers' need for companionship and support. Now Edna was a living testament to its success.

'Let's begin,' Alice said.

Alice looked even paler now so Naomi approached the vicar and his wife again. 'I hope you'll see this as an opportunity to get to know some of the parishioners. Perhaps you'd like to join in with the sewing, Mrs Forsyth?'

'My wife and I will merely observe today, thank you, Mrs . . . er . . .'

'Harrington. If that's what you prefer, then of course there's no need to join in any of the activities. Do wander around, though. We're a friendly sort of place and you'll be able to see how much everyone loves the bookshop.'

The Forsyths' smiles were thin.

Naomi moved away and saw Mrs Blackstock waving from the table where the books were on display. 'Not many out for us to borrow today,' Mrs Blackstock observed.

'We're being a little careful at the moment,' Naomi explained in a low voice. 'Just until our vicar recognizes that our bookshop is good for the village.'

'I was hoping for that book Hilda Roberts liked so much. The one about the Italian count and the servant girl.'

'*Sunset Kiss*?'

'That's the one.'

'I'll pop it round to you at home but not a word to anyone else.'

'I promise, though it's silly to have to hide it away when it's so harmless. Reading a book like that doesn't make me want to throw over my Jacob. Very happily married, we are. But a little bit of daydreaming about counts and palaces in that lovely-sounding place – Tuscany, isn't it? – helps a body to get through the ironing or scrubbing the front step.'

'Hopefully, our new vicar will come to understand that.'

There was an eruption of happy chatter as older children spilled in after being released from school. It was break time and Naomi took cups of tea to the Forsyths. 'Perhaps now you'd like to circulate,' she suggested.

'I think my husband is the best judge of how a vicar should behave in his parish,' Mrs Forsyth told her.

It felt like a rebuke and Naomi's face flamed. 'Of course,' she said, hoping she hadn't made things worse.

She moved away but kept an eye on the Forsyths for the rest of the afternoon. They hadn't moved before the break, and they didn't move after it. The black notebook remained on Reverend Forsyth's lap and the smart pen remained in his jacket breast pocket.

Naomi thought it was to the bookshop's credit that so many people helped to tidy things away at the end of the afternoon. Books and toys were put into boxes, the floor was swept and the kitchen left gleaming – all without anyone needing to be asked to help. If they could spare a few minutes, they did.

'Thanks a lot,' Godfrey Michaels said, as he filed out with Jonah Kerrigan, 'though it put me off my game to see the Forsyths' beady eyes watching me.'

'He's just sour because I beat him. Three times,' Jonah said, but even he looked towards the Forsyths with disapproval. 'Here's hoping they leave us alone and get on with their other business in future.'

The Forsyths were at the door bidding people farewell but there was little warmth in their manner. 'Have you ever seen a pair so convinced of their own rightness?' Bert murmured into Naomi's ear.

She hadn't, though she felt a pang as she remembered that she too had been an I-know-best sort of person once. It had been Naomi's way of running from her insecurities, though, and she couldn't see any sign of insecurity in the new vicar and his wife.

When only the Forsyths and the organizing team remained, Reverend Forsyth asked them to sit at a table. He took the chair at the head with his wife at his side. 'Well,' he began, but Bert – clearly out of patience – cut across him.

'I hope you're not going to shut us down. You must have seen how much people enjoyed themselves today.'

'My dear man, I've no intention of shutting you down, as you put it.'

'I hope you're not going to change us either.' Bert folded his arms across his middle, his expression truculent.

'I think we're fortunate that St Luke's has a hall in which we can bring people together,' Reverend Forsyth said. 'I intend that we should continue to do so. But tone and – er – content need to be adjusted. Now, I've observed and I've thought about the best way forward and I've reached some conclusions.'

He opened the notebook but as he hadn't written a word in it while he'd been so-called observing, it was obvious that he'd decided what he wanted in advance.

'Firstly, the name needs to change to something more appropriate than a shop. We're not a common marketplace, after all.' He shuddered as though the thought disgusted him.

'Selling books helps with fundraising and keeping the stock of books healthy,' Alice pointed out. 'People sometimes donate the books they buy so others can read them, both here and at the military hospital.'

'The name needs to reflect what the church and the hall are about,' Reverend Forsyth insisted. 'I suggest Bible Study at St Luke's. Or would you prefer St Luke's Bible Study Group? Do speak up. I like to run things on democratic lines.'

No, he didn't. The last thing he wanted was alternative opinions.

Alice tried anyway. 'What about St Luke's Books? Or St Luke's Community Get-Togethers?'

'Both excellent ideas,' Naomi approved, but the Forsyths only winced.

'If none of you have a strong preference for St Luke's Bible Study Group, I suggest we opt for Bible Study at St Luke's.'

'I agree,' Mrs Forsyth announced, as though her husband could do no wrong. 'That name allows for a number of groups, from small children to adults.'

'Indeed it does, my dear,' Reverend Forsyth said. 'Moving on, the banner outside the hall also needs to be changed. For one thing, the name isn't correct any more.'

'And for another thing?' Bert asked.

'We need something more . . . respectful to the church.'

'We like the style of banner we've already got,' May protested. 'It's bright and cheerful.'

'But disrespectful, do you see?'

'Not really,' May told him. 'God created colours, didn't he? And I can't believe he objects to people being cheerful.'

'You're a member of our congregation, Mrs . . . er . . . ?'

'Janicki. May Janicki. I don't come to church services, no. But—'

'Thank you for sharing your view, Mrs Janicki. Time is marching on so we must move on too – to the content of the sessions.'

'We have a variety of activities on offer,' Alice said.

She was looking taut and focused but exhausted too. 'We try to appeal to everyone, from the very young to the more mature.'

'We shall continue to do so, Miss . . . er . . .'

'Lovell. Alice Lovell.'

'My wife and I have worked out a programme which we think will bring an interesting and respectful slant to the sessions while also providing spiritual enrichment.' He turned to Mrs Forsyth. 'Would you like to explain, my dear?'

'Certainly. We're planning stories, colouring and crafts for younger children with each activity reflecting a Bible story. For older children, there'll be classes which will help them when they come to be confirmed in their faith. And for adults we'll have proper Bible study groups.'

'What about fun?' Bert asked.

'Fun, as you call it, is for people's private living rooms – if that is what they seek in life,' Reverend Forsyth said. 'In a building dedicated to God's work we prefer to offer rewards that run much deeper than cheap and tawdry entertainment: spiritual satisfaction and fulfilment. We believe our programme will deliver both – to those who approach it with the right spirit. There may be people in the village who are interested only in frivolity but it's hardly the job of St Luke's to encourage them in that way of living.'

'Can't a person have a serious side *and* a fun side?' Bert challenged.

'I hope that most of us find enjoyment in life, Mr . . . er . . . ?'

'Makepiece. Bert Makepiece.'

'I hope that most of us find enjoyment in life without being foolish in our behaviour.'

'Miserable old grump,' May muttered.

'The bookshop fundraises for other causes as well as itself,' Alice pointed out. 'The homeless, people injured in the bombings . . . We collect things like old clothes and toys for the needy . . . Sometimes we make them too.'

'Naturally, good works will continue, but through the agency of the church,' Reverend Forsyth said, and his wife gave an approving nod.

The meeting ended with Mrs Forsyth undertaking to write up a programme for the next month.

At that moment Cecil Wade sauntered in. 'I heard you and your delightful lady were here, Reverend Forsyth.' He bowed towards the delightful lady. 'Have you shared the good news about your plans?'

'We have.'

'They're going to make these meetings worth attending.'

Cecil rocked on his heels, terrifically pleased with himself. He might not be on first-name terms with the Forsyths yet, but he was working on it. Wretched man.

'Time to go,' Bert announced.

He got up and Naomi, Alice, May and Janet did likewise.

'That was depressing,' Bert said once they were outside.

Alice looked strained and vexed. 'I feel I should have done more.'

'No, *I* should have done more,' Naomi insisted. 'You're still in shock.'

'Let's not blame ourselves or each other,' Bert insisted. 'We had our suspicions about the Forsyths all along and now we know those suspicions were well founded. The question is: what are we going to do next?'

'I don't know,' Alice said, 'but we can't just sit back and let our bookshop be ruined.'

'Quite right,' Bert approved. 'I vote we all go home and meet in a day or two when we've had a chance to think.'

'That sounds sensible,' Janet said.

'Come to Foxfield tomorrow evening,' Naomi suggested. 'We can talk again then.'

Naomi hoped the others would have some ideas because she had none. She felt useless and dull-witted. Frustrated, too, because she was still letting the bookshop down.

She needed a good night's sleep urgently and there was only one way of getting it as far as she could see – by getting to the bottom of Alexander's situation once and for all. If she could satisfy herself that he was faithful, she could put the uncertainty and distress behind her and start living properly again.

The time had come to speak to a private detective. Today was Suki's day off so if Naomi made a call she was unlikely to be overheard. Tomorrow Suki would be back at work and Naomi would have lost her chance.

Back at home, she opened the drawer into which she'd placed Bert's newspaper and turned to the classified advertisements. It was two minutes to five. If she didn't telephone now, the detectives' offices might have closed.

Choosing the first advertisement, she picked up the telephone and made the call.

'J. Webber, Enquiry Agent,' a female voice said. A secretary, probably.

Naomi opened her mouth to reply only to be struck dumb by indecision.

She couldn't.

She must.

'I have a situation,' she finally said.

'You think Mr Webber might help with it?'

'Perhaps.'

'Let's make an appointment so you can discuss it with him. Naturally, consultations are strictly confidential.'

'Erm . . . Yes. Thank you.'

An appointment was made for Thursday, 3 July.

Naomi had to sit down after the call ended. The thought of seeing this Mr Webber made her feel unclean and frightened of the consequences of what he might discover. But the frayed state of her nerves was frightening her too.

At least the appointment was more than a week away. She had plenty of time in which to decide whether to keep it or cancel it.

# CHAPTER THIRTY-THREE

## *Kate*

Kenny's venture into romance wasn't only disrupting work on the farm. It was adding to Kate's workload in other ways too. Feeding wet washing through the mangle, Kate realized he was changing his shirts more often, and yesterday he'd helped himself to a clean towel after complaining that Vinnie had left filth on the one he'd been using before. Kate was all in favour of cleanliness, but this behaviour was out of character and Kate knew he wouldn't give a moment's thought to the extra burden on her.

She finished at the mangle, hung the squeezed washing on the line to dry and headed back indoors to find Ernie snarling at Kenny and telling him, 'The answer's no!'

No to what?

'He wouldn't be any trouble. He's just a lad.'

'Lads want feeding.'

'Not at your expense. Ruby will pay for his keep out of her wages and he'll bring his own ration book.'

The penny dropped. Kate should have foreseen this. It explained why Ruby – surely the most unlikely farmhand that ever lived – had chosen to be a land girl. She'd wanted to carve out a place where she could bring her brother.

'How many more times!' Ernie roared. 'The answer's no!'

Kenny stomped to the kitchen door and went out in a huff but not before firing a glare in Kate's direction as though blaming her for Ernie's reaction.

Kate hadn't said a word against Ruby to Ernie. But she couldn't deny that the thought of the boy at Brimbles Farm filled her with dread. It wasn't that she wished Timmy to stay in a place that made him unhappy – the thought of any child being unhappy touched Kate's heart, especially as she was no stranger to misery herself – but work on the farm was overwhelming and Ruby was already failing to do her share of it. Looking after a child would almost certainly mean she'd give even less time and effort to her work, and if Timmy Turner were half as troublesome as his sister, he'd cause havoc. Arguments too. Kenny might accept a spirited child on the premises because he was in thrall to Ruby, but it was impossible to imagine Ernie and Vinnie having an ounce of tolerance.

Where would the boy sleep, anyway? There were no spare beds. And what would happen about his education? The village school was almost two miles away. Was he old enough to get there and back by himself?

Kate wilted under the thoughts that raced through her mind. Was it selfish to think of her own situation too? She was already getting up ridiculously early each morning and working late into the evenings so she could snatch a few minutes here or an hour there to see Alice or Leo. It wasn't just for her own sake that Kate wanted to see Alice. Never lacking in courage, Alice was turning a brave face to the world, but her well-being was under attack on two fronts at once – Daniel's imprisonment and the ruin of the bookshop – and she needed the support of her friends. Kate's visits to Alice were rushed and she was doing nothing at all to help with the bookshop, though the Forsyths' plans sounded dreadful and would surely signal the death knell of the sort of jolly community gatherings that made the bookshop both special and useful.

'Clearly the Forsyths want to make their own decisions for the foreseeable future,' Alice had told her. 'But even if it takes a while to persuade them, we're going to keep suggesting more variety and fun in the programme.'

'Might they lose interest in the bookshop? Or whatever they're calling it now?'

'Who knows? I suspect they're proud people, so I think we'll have to be subtle and gradual in getting back to normal.'

It was all so vague, and here was Kate not even setting foot inside the bookshop any more. Not that the Forsyths would be interested in her opinion.

Then there was Leo. Kate wanted time to see him for a meal or a dance so she could feel carefree and full of laughter for once.

Not that she thought her wishes were more important than a young boy's happiness, but they were ingredients in a mix of other concerns. Besides, Kate wasn't entirely convinced by Ruby's tale of woe – it might be at least a partial invention to give weight to her plea to bring Timmy here.

Kenny tried to broach the subject with Ernie again later that afternoon, obviously not realizing that Kate was by the chicken coop. He'd barely got a word out before Ernie yelled at him: 'Don't start that again!'

Ernie stalked away and Kenny kicked a stone in frustration.

Was that to be the end of the idea?

It wasn't.

Too clever to sulk, Ruby spent the evening looking sorrowful and giving the occasional sigh but also being a model of considerate behaviour.

'I need to iron a blouse. Can I iron anything for anyone else?' she asked before dinner.

'I seem to have more meat than you, Ernie. Have some of mine . . .' she said as they ate.

'I'll dry the dishes tonight,' she offered afterwards. 'I know it isn't part of my job but it's nice to be helpful.'

Later, Ernie asked Kenny for a Woodbine. Kenny scowled and passed one over reluctantly. 'Pull yourself together, man,' Ernie snapped.

Ruby was all oil on troubled waters. 'It's sweet of you to care about poor little Timmy, Kenny, but it's understandable that your father might not want a child around the place, even one as quiet and helpful as Timmy. As healthy too, because he's never ill. It's a shame that Brimbles Farm won't benefit from the unpaid help, though.'

She'd hit the bullseye with skinflint Ernie. 'What do you mean, unpaid help?' he demanded.

Ruby widened her eyes in innocent-looking surprise at the fact that he hadn't considered this before. 'Timmy helps on a nearby farm after school. He isn't a big lad but he's quick and nimble, and he loves farming. He started doing it to get away from the awful couple who are supposed to be looking after him, but he likes it so much that he's declared he wants to be a farmer when he grows up.'

'He isn't paid?'

'Not a penny, though the farmer's wife gives him food now and then. He doesn't get much to eat where he's living.'

'Humph,' Ernie said, and he drank his tea in thoughtful silence.

Kate didn't miss the conspiratorial look that passed between Ruby and Kenny. They'd sown the seed in Ernie's mind. Now they had to wait to see if it took root.

In the meantime, it was business as usual for Kate. She went about her work with her body on the farm but her thoughts on Alice, Leo and the bookshop. One afternoon she looked up to see planes flying overhead. Spitfires? They certainly had the look of the Spitfires she'd seen pictured in a newspaper. Was Leo flying one of them and, if so, did he realize he was flying over Churchwood? Was he thinking of her? Perhaps even looking down at her?

Had she been alone, she might have blown him a kiss. But Ruby was nearby.

She overheard no more discussions about Timmy Turner, but Ruby had an air of sly expectation about her while Kenny was being remarkably polite to Ernie.

Two days later, Ruby ran into Kenny's arms in the barn. Ernie had succumbed to the lure of free labour and Timmy was coming to live on Brimbles Farm as soon as it could be arranged.

Would he be the sweet and helpful boy Ruby had described? Or would he be trouble like his sister?

271

# CHAPTER THIRTY-FOUR

*Alice*

Opening her atlas, Alice turned to a map of Africa and traced the outlines of the northern countries. Was Daniel imprisoned somewhere there? Or had he been taken across the Mediterranean to a camp in Germany, Poland or some other part of German-controlled territory?

Nothing had been heard from Daniel himself and no more information had come from the War Office or the Red Cross. Alice supposed it could take a while for prisoners to be transported to camps far from where they were captured but not knowing if he was well and coping made the situation even harder to bear. She was trying to get on with her own life but didn't feel she was making a good job of it despite the kindness that was coming her way.

Her father's gentleness was expected, but Mr Parkinson, too, was showing compassion. 'Forgive me if I'm speaking out of turn, Miss Lovell, but are you quite well?' he'd asked, when she'd gone to work only to struggle to concentrate.

She'd opened her mouth to assure him that she was fine, but she'd seen real concern in his eyes. Changing her mind, she'd told him about Daniel's imprisonment.

'You have my sympathy, Miss Lovell,' he'd said. 'If you need time away to come to terms with your news, please take as much as you need. My memoirs are far from urgent.'

'I'd rather work than sit at home brooding, but if you feel my work isn't satisfactory, I'll—'

'My dear, I'm not criticizing your work. And as you often stay late, I think it only fair that you should feel able to . . . let your mind drift a little at this difficult time. Was your young man serving in Africa?'

Alice confirmed he was and found herself telling Mr Parkinson more about the man she loved.

'He sounds a fine young man.'

'He is. My father thinks so too.'

'I sense that means high praise indeed.'

'My father isn't only kind but also clever and principled. I think it would have grieved him if I'd agreed to marry someone he didn't consider a fine young man.'

'He's a retired doctor, I think you said.'

'A retired doctor who's chosen to study ancient civilizations now he has time for it.'

Mr Parkinson wanted to know more. 'So he's a fellow book lover who's interested in history,' he mused, after Alice had told him about her father's book collection and studies. 'How fascinating.'

It was a relief to know she didn't have to pretend to be fine all the time at work.

With the patients at Stratton House, she managed to put on a show of business as usual, but in short bursts that left her feeling exhausted. Like her friends in the village, her nursing friends had rallied round with sympathy and support, but Alice hated feeling close to tears whenever she was shown kindness. Even Matron had caught her walking dejectedly along the corridor and said, 'In my office. Now, please.'

Once inside, she'd insisted that Alice sit down, and she'd even fetched her a cup of tea. Matron never usually fetched tea for anyone.

'I'm sorry to be so feeble,' Alice had said.

'Nonsense. You're here to cheer the men up and you're succeeding at that as well as ever. If you slump a little afterwards, it's only to be expected. You're still reeling from the news, but you have a strong back-bone, Alice. You won't buckle.'

Alice certainly hoped not but she wished she could feel stronger sooner. After all, she wasn't the only one who was going through challenging times. Kate in particular was on Alice's mind. Not only was Kate facing troubles at home, she was also in the throes of her first romance. Alice should be making more effort to persuade her to talk about her feelings – something Kate never found easy.

Not seeing Kate in the fields when she next passed Brimbles Farm, Alice walked up towards the farm-house, refusing to be intimidated if she encountered the Fletcher men. Luck was on her side because she saw none of them before finding Kate in the farm-yard. 'I know it's hard for you to come to me so I thought I'd come to you,' Alice explained. 'But if it isn't convenient . . .'

'If I wait until it's convenient, I'll never see you. Let's go to the orchard.'

They could be more private behind the screen of trees, and there was an old log there that they used as a seat. Sitting side by side, Alice dug in her bag for two slices of apple pie and Kate took one.

'Thanks! Any news about Daniel?' she asked.

'Not yet. Any news about Ruby's brother?'

'He's coming on Saturday. Ruby is going to collect him.'

'Another day off?'

'Do I sound mean, begrudging her the time to collect a small boy who's apparently unhappy?'

'No, because you can't trust Ruby to be honest.'

'I'll be able to judge the Timmy situation for myself once he's here. He might be a sweet boy.'

'Let's hope so. Where will he sleep?'

'With Ruby. She says they've often shared a bed and Pearl doesn't seem to object to having another person in the room.'

'Is Kenny still bewitched by Ruby?'

'Utterly, though I can't help wondering if she's just been using him to get Timmy here. I've no experience of courting so I can't judge what's real and what's pretence.'

Alice smiled. 'Perhaps you're getting a little experience of courting.'

A pink tinge warmed Kate's clear skin. 'You mean Leo.'

'Mmm.'

'I do like him. Rather a lot.' Coming from Kate that was a big admission. Having grown up without love or even affection, she tended to hide her vulnerability behind a show of indifference.

'If he values you, then I like him too because it shows he's a sensible man,' Alice said.

Kate shrugged. She never believed compliments.

'Will you be seeing him again soon?'

'He says he's trying to organize both free time and the loan of the motorbike. Actually, he says he's thinking of buying a motorbike if he can get hold of one.'

'He's keen to see you.'

'He'd like to take me out somewhere instead of snatching a few rushed minutes here and there. I'd love to go out with him, but can you imagine the fuss Ernie and the boys would make if they saw me leaving the farm in a dress?'

'You could come to the cottage to change and Leo could pick you up from there. Better still, you could go to Naomi's house – then he could ride around the back and no one need see you getting on the bike.'

'That's a wonderful idea. But at the moment I can barely grab a free hour, let alone a whole afternoon or evening.'

Alice grew serious. 'I really think you should take the time whether it's convenient to the farm or not. I wasted more than a year when I thought Daniel only wanted me because he felt guilty about my hand. We could have been happy in that year. Now we know we love each other but Daniel is trapped hundreds, maybe thousands, of miles away and heaven only knows when we'll see each other again. We need to seize hold of happiness while we can.'

'You're right.' Kate was suddenly decisive. 'If Ernie and the boys find out I'm seeing Leo . . . Well, they've been mad at me before and they're never pleasant even when they're not mad.'

'Tell them you're going somewhere with Naomi and me if they ask.'

Alice walked home, hoping she'd done just a little bit of good for Kate. She arrived at the cottage just as Adam Potts arrived too. 'Adam! How lovely to see you. Do come in.'

'I heard about Daniel,' he told her. 'I may not be your vicar but I'm here in a personal capacity to let you know you're in my thoughts and prayers.'

Inside, Alice told her father that Adam was visiting and then led him into the kitchen, gesturing for him to sit at the little square table. Julian Forsyth would doubtless expect the formality of the dining room, but there was no need to stand on ceremony with Adam. He slotted comfortably into any situation. Alice noticed a button hanging off his jacket. 'You're going to lose that,' she warned.

'Oops.' He tugged it off.

'Would you like me to sew it back on?'

'Mrs Evershed will do it.' Mrs Evershed was the housekeeper at his lodgings.

'I can help you to a piece of pie, though?'

Adam grinned. 'Now that I won't refuse.'

They talked about Daniel for a while, and Adam reassured Alice that she could call on him any time she wanted to talk. 'As a friend.'

'Thank you. I'm coping, I think, though it isn't easy. But how are you, Adam?'

'Perfectly well, thanks. I'm sorry I can't be with you all in Churchwood, but I know I tried my hardest in the interview, so I'm not punishing myself for having failed.'

'Have you seen the Forsyths since they moved in?'

'I have.'

She didn't press him to share his impression of

them. The careful neutrality with which he'd spoken told her all she needed to know anyway. If he'd warmed to them, he would have said so.

She guessed that delicacy was preventing him from asking about the bookshop, so she volunteered some information. 'We're now called Bible Study at St Luke's. Our cheerful banner and many of our books have been packed away. That's bad enough, but the worst thing is that numbers are already falling off dramatically. People tell us they can't relax any more. They feel they're being judged, and where's the fun in that? We're trying to persuade them to be patient. We hope to improve things over time.'

'Time often makes a difference. Reverend Forsyth might find other projects and interests to wean him away from the bookshop.'

'There's Mrs Forsyth too, and she's as bad as her husband. Neither have any idea of tolerance and compromise. Mrs Phillips told me that one look from Mrs Forsyth's beady eyes sends her all aquiver, and Jonah Kerrigan said he won't come to the bookshop any more as a protest against both Forsyths.'

'So you're giving up?'

'Not yet.'

But even that was a step in the wrong direction. Once she'd have answered, 'Never!'

# CHAPTER THIRTY-FIVE

## *Naomi*

The office of Jack Webber, Private Enquiry Agent, was to be found at 26 Jackson Street, near Covent Garden flower market. It was a narrow street with shops on both sides. In between the shops were more doors that opened directly on to the pavement. It was clear from the nameplates beside them that these doors led to businesses on the upper floors. Walking along the pavement, Naomi saw the names of a dentist, a solicitor, a theatrical agent, a bookkeeping service, an employment agent, a property-letting agent and other names that gave no clue about the nature of the owner's businesses.

Her pace slowed as she drew near number twenty-six. She gave the black-painted door a glance but didn't stop. Instead, she quickened her pace again as though fearing she might be contaminated by Mr Webber's seediness. She walked to the end of the row of shops, stared sightlessly into a stationer's, then walked back, just slowly enough to register nameplates indicating that number twenty-six was also home to a photographer and a dress-alteration service. Naomi comforted herself with the thought that anyone who saw her enter might assume she was there to have a garment altered.

Not that she'd decided whether or not to enter. It was fifteen minutes before her appointment time, so she crossed the road and walked along the street on the opposite pavement. This time she looked at the windows on the upper floors. The photographer's name appeared in gold letters on the first-floor window but she couldn't see the names of Jack Webber or the dressmaker on the other windows.

Naomi walked to the end of the road again, still revolted at the thought of sharing her sordid suspicions with a stranger. Perhaps she should simply tell Mr Webber's secretary that she'd made a mistake and pay for the time wasted on her appointment. But once the relief of avoiding the meeting had worn off, she'd return to the ceaseless, gnawing uncertainty that was plaguing her peace of mind and sapping her health.

Three minutes before her appointment time, she entered number twenty-six and found herself in a tiny hall that contained only a staircase to the upper floors.

Naomi climbed to the first floor to find that she was required to climb higher to reach Mr Webber's office. She was breathless when she arrived and still couldn't decide what to do. The door had a glass window inset into the upper half and here Mr Webber's name appeared in black paint.

The secretary must have spotted Naomi through the glass because she opened the door suddenly from the inside. 'Mrs Harrington? Come in, please.'

Naomi entered an outer office. 'The thing is—' she began, but never got the chance to finish.

'Mr Webber is ready for you,' the secretary

announced, and she opened a door to an inner office.

It was too late to avoid him now. Naomi walked through the door, and he got up from behind a desk. He was a little below medium height, slim and wiry with oiled dark hair and the sort of narrow moustache she'd imagined. His suit was smart enough but tasteless to Naomi's eyes, the cream stripes in the brown fabric being so broad that they looked flashy. She wanted to turn tail and flee.

'Mrs Harrington,' he said, offering a hand.

'Mr Webber.' His handshake was a little too vigorous for comfort. 'The thing is,' she tried again, 'I think I've made a mistake. I'm sorry to have wasted your time, but—'

'You're not the first to take fright and you won't be the last,' he said. 'A lot of people who walk through my door are nervous. It's natural. People only come to me when they've got a problem, and sharing problems can be tricky. Why don't you sit down and, until you're ready to tell me about your problem, I'll tell you what I can do to help?'

Naomi wanted to flee more than ever but she didn't wish to be rude. She sat on the edge of the visitor's chair, and he sat down behind his desk.

'Tea?' he offered.

'No, thank you.' Tea would anchor her here for several minutes at least. Naomi preferred to stay poised for flight, holding her handbag on her lap and clutching the handle in both hands.

In contrast, Jack Webber lolled back in his chair, one thin leg crossed over the other, confidence oozing from him along with the calculating glee of a hunter.

'First, let me assure you that my services are confidential and extremely discreet,' he began. 'I've experience of a wide variety of cases. I've proven thieving by members of staff, investigated the backgrounds of gold-digging suitors, looked into business fraud, exposed a child-beating nanny, and often uncovered grounds for divorce.'

Naomi must have blushed when he mentioned divorce because his sharp eyes narrowed.

'Of course, not everyone who learns their spouse is unfaithful wants a divorce. They might simply want to threaten a divorce if the spouse doesn't come to heel, or negotiate something to their advantage. A better allowance ... More freedom ... Sometimes, the mere threat of a divorce is enough, especially if the parties are likely to be of interest to the more scandal-hungry Sunday newspapers.'

He let that sink in before continuing: 'As I said, discretion is important, especially as not all suspicions are well founded. No one wants to make their situation worse with false accusations, do they?'

Naomi certainly didn't.

'I carry out surveillance, often in disguise, and I take photographs as evidence. Good-quality photographs.'

The thought of seeing incriminating photographs of Alexander made Naomi feel queasy.

'Now. How might I help *you*, Mrs Harrington?'

He couldn't. Or rather Naomi wouldn't give him a chance. Not just yet. She got to her feet. 'I'm afraid I don't feel ready to ... Perhaps I'll be ready in a week or two but today ...' She shook her head, shuddering.

'There's no need to be hasty,' he said, sitting up straighter.

'I'm sorry I've wasted your time. Please tell me what I owe and perhaps I'll see you when I'm . . . another time.'

'See my secretary,' he said, subsiding in obvious disappointment.

'Thank you.'

The secretary looked surprised to see Naomi emerge so quickly. 'I've decided not to proceed for the moment,' Naomi explained. 'Could I settle my bill for Mr Webber's time?'

'Mr Webber's fees are based on an hourly rate.'

'I'm happy to pay for a full hour.' She was reaching for her purse as she spoke. 'No need for a receipt, thank you.' She didn't want to be carrying around evidence that she'd consulted him.

She got outside and breathed in deeply. What a wasted journey. Naomi was back where she'd started. Or was she?

Not quite. She knew she couldn't go on without learning the truth about Alexander and she knew she might have to overcome her scruples to employ the services of Mr Webber or someone else of his calling. But she decided on one last attempt to get to the heart of the problem herself.

# CHAPTER THIRTY-SIX

## *Kate*

They were here. Kate caught a glimpse of the cart through the kitchen window but moved away, not wanting to be seen staring in case it made Timmy feel uncomfortable – or his sister took it as a sign that Kate resented his presence.

She waited until the kitchen door opened, then turned with a smile. Ruby entered with her brother at her side, her expression suggesting she was ready to do battle at the first sign of Timmy being unwelcome. Like his sister, Timmy was short for his age. *Un*like her, he was all skinny limbs and knobbly knees with a scab on one and a bruise on the other. His light brown hair was greasy too, looking as if it had been cut by scissors last used to trim the rind off bacon.

He was far from being a handsome child. His mouth was too wide and his teeth too big, though he might grow into them over time. But Kate's heart softened at the wariness in his blue eyes and the clothes he wore – a hand-knitted jumper that was too small, patched short trousers that were too big, and scuffed brown lace-up shoes. Kate knew all too well what it was like to have no decent clothes.

'This is Timmy,' Ruby announced. 'Timmy, this is Kate.'

She could have been introducing a nasty spider, but whatever Ruby had said about her, Kate wouldn't let it affect her behaviour to the boy. Suspecting he was unfamiliar with social niceties, she didn't offer to shake his hand but spoke warmly instead. 'Welcome to Brimbles Farm.'

He glanced up at his sister as though unsure how to respond but the awkward moment passed as Pearl and Vinnie came in. 'Hello, Timmy,' Pearl said. Even with a child she looked ill at ease, her arms and legs moving in the uncoordinated way that signalled her nervousness. 'I'm Pearl. Ruby's friend. You're bunking in with me as well as her.'

Pearl offered a handshake then thought better of it and stuffed both hands into the pockets of her breeches.

'I'm Vinnie. I expect you've heard about me.' Vinnie stepped forward and gave Timmy a playful punch on the shoulder, which only made him look more nervous.

Ernie came in then and Ruby nudged Timmy forward, nodding as though to say, *This is him. You know what to do.*

'Hello, Mr Fletcher. I'm Timmy,' the boy said, obviously having practised the speech. 'Thank you for letting me come to stay.'

'Humph,' Ernie said, then turned on Kate. 'Where's the tea?'

'It's coming.' She kept her voice calm to avoid unsettling the boy with an exhibition of Fletcher sniping so soon after his arrival, but she knew it could only be a matter of time before the grousing began. 'Would you prefer a glass of milk?' she asked Timmy.

He nodded but Ernie sent a sour look Kate's way. She hoped he wasn't going to begrudge every crumb the boy ate and every drop he sipped.

Kenny was the last to enter. He glanced around the group, his fists clenched in anticipation of anyone upsetting his sweetheart or her brother. Seeing nothing objectionable in the scene, he relaxed and looked over at the table. Kate had already added a seventh chair for Timmy, so he gestured for Ruby and her brother to sit.

Kate carried the big teapot to the table where mugs and plates had already been laid out. She followed the teapot with bread and margarine, and a glass of milk for Timmy.

The boy's eyes widened hungrily at the sight of the bread, but he waited for another signal from Ruby before he reached for a slice. There was no jam in the house – Kate was saving sugar to make more – but she put a jar of honey on the table instead. 'Only a scraping,' Ruby told her brother.

He was careful to take only a small quantity. Even so pleasure broke out like sunshine on his urchin face as he tasted it, holding it in his mouth to savour it before chewing and swallowing. The milk was drunk with enjoyment too, Timmy wiping his mouth on the back of his hand after every slurp.

Ruby watched him carefully at first, but then some of the tension left her and she said, 'It was so kind of you to let me take time off to collect Timmy today, Mr Fletcher. You can be sure I'll make up for it. Timmy will help me. Won't you, Tim?'

Mouth full of bread, he nodded.

The conversation turned to the birds that were

stealing the seed from Five Acre Field. 'We should take the guns out,' Ernie said.

But a few shots over the field wouldn't deter the birds for long.

'That old scarecrow isn't doing its job any more,' Kenny said. 'The birds have grown used to it.'

Ruby perked up at that. 'I could give it a new look and make another scarecrow too. Another two or three, maybe. Timmy could help me with that too. You'd like that, Tim?'

Again, he nodded.

'I could help as well,' Pearl offered.

Kate hoped the tall girl wasn't going to feel pushed aside now Timmy was here to take up Ruby's attention.

'New scarecrows are a good idea,' Kenny said, looking around as though challenging anyone to disagree. 'I'm sure I can find some old clothes to dress them up in.'

'Back to work,' Ernie instructed, getting up.

Kenny, Vinnie and Pearl got up too.

'I'll take Timmy's things upstairs then be right out,' Ruby said.

Timmy's things were in a battered old satchel. Ruby took him upstairs, watched by Pearl, who appeared to be hoping for an invitation to join them. When no invitation came, she went out looking dejected.

As Kate cleared the table and washed the dishes she could hear voices murmuring upstairs. 'Did I say the right thing?' Timmy asked Ruby.

'You did well. Don't forget that it's the old man who'll decide whether you can stay so don't annoy him. Be nice to Kenny too. He's on our side.'

They didn't spend long upstairs. Ruby appeared to be anxious for Timmy to create a good first impression because she took him out with her as she returned to work. 'Can I see the chickens?' Kate heard him ask before the door closed behind them.

'Another time. The old man needs to see us working first.'

Kate put the dishes away, then went out to work in the kitchen garden. After a while she heard Ruby and Timmy by the chickens. 'Ere, look, Ruby, there's loads of 'em. Cor, that one's huge!'

His cockney accent was stronger than his sister's. Ruby tended to half cover hers with a drawl, which she probably considered to be more sophisticated.

Kate liked Timmy's enthusiasm and thus far she'd seen nothing objectionable in him. But would it last?

He looked hungrily at the stew and potatoes Kate placed on the table that evening, but Ruby served him only modest portions of each, her look warning him not to ask for more. He ate every last speck on his plate, apart from a small smear of gravy, though Kate guessed he'd have licked that up too if he hadn't thought his sister would tell him off for bad manners. Usually, the Fletcher men and Pearl tucked into anything that was left in the serving dishes. Tonight, Kate grabbed the dish first and gave Timmy an extra spoonful before anyone else could tuck in. Ruby sent her an uncertain look as though wondering if Kate had some sort of ulterior motive. But Kate simply thought a hungry young boy needed food, and she'd been careful to serve him without drawing the watchful eye of Ernie.

Work began on the new scarecrows later that

evening. Kenny and Vinnie brought in old clothes that might once have come Kate's way. How typical of them to decide that the sort of clothes they expected their sister to wear were raggedy enough for scarecrows. Then they went out to the barn and returned with hay to stuff into the clothes. Kate sat over some mending, listening to the laughter as the scarecrows came into being. Glancing up now and again, she caught the look of love on Ruby's face as she watched Timmy enjoying himself. Clearly, there was good inside Ruby, but she was as distant from Kate as ever.

Pearl, on the other hand, was desperate for approval. 'Look, Kate!' she said, holding up her scarecrow.

'It's terrific,' Kate told her. 'It might be helpful to hang something metal on it. Old chains and things like that. The noise they make in the wind will help to scare off the birds.'

'Got any metal, Vinnie?' Pearl asked.

'We can look for old chains tomorrow.'

Timmy let out a loud laugh at something Kenny said, then clapped a hand over his mouth and looked fearfully at Ernie who uttered another disapproving 'Humph!' and snapped open a page of his newspaper.

'It's getting late,' Ruby said. 'Time for bed, Tim. We can finish our scarecrow tomorrow. Say goodnight.'

'Goodnight,' Timmy said, mainly addressing Ernie, who ignored him.

Ruby took Timmy upstairs, returning a few minutes later to put the half-completed scarecrow in a corner and sweep up the stray wisps of hay, having never gone anywhere near the broom before.

When Kate went to bed, she lay back and thought over Timmy's arrival and what it might mean for Brimbles Farm. Questions circulated round her head:

Would Timmy follow his sister's lead in being hostile to Kate?

Would he help around the farm enough to reconcile Ernie to his presence? (Kate's feelings rebelled against the thought of another child being forced to work as hard as she had growing up, but Ernie wouldn't take kindly to being misled about the boy's usefulness.)

Would the natural high spirits and noise of a child irritate Ernie so much that he insisted on Timmy leaving anyway?

Would caring for Timmy mean Ruby worked even less hard than usual?

What if Ruby and Kenny fell out? Romances didn't always prosper.

What if Pearl felt so pushed aside that she asked to be moved to a different farm or went into a sulk and decided she wouldn't work hard if Ruby didn't?

Finally, selfishly but irresistibly, how would Kate's life be affected by all this?

Kate pushed the worries aside to focus on pleasanter thoughts. All being well, she'd see Leo again tomorrow. It would be another secret snatched meeting in the now-familiar Beech Lane, but she had news for him.

'It's all arranged,' Alice had told her. 'You can change at Foxfield and Leo can pick you up from there. Naomi is happy for you to use her phone to call him and he can use it to leave messages for you.

Or you can arrange to be at Foxfield when he's due to ring.'

'That's kind of her. Kind of you to arrange it too.'

'We're both happy that you have some joy in your life.'

Kate still felt embarrassed that her friends knew she was seeing a man. She'd be even more embarrassed if she ever had to tell them that Leo had lost interest. But overall, it was nice to know they were on her side.

'Don't let an opportunity to spend time with Leo pass you by because it isn't convenient,' Alice had repeated. 'When we've less idea than ever of what the future holds, we need to think of now. This minute. Seize your chance to be happy, Kate.'

All the seizing in the world wouldn't give Alice even five minutes with poor, imprisoned Daniel, possibly for years and years. Leo was vulnerable to capture by the enemy too – or worse. Kate really should seize her chance to be happy with him, even if it was only temporarily.

Sunday had never been a day of rest for the Fletchers on Brimbles Farm. Mornings began the same as other days – with work. The only difference was that the work tended to slacken off towards the end of the afternoon, though it sometimes picked up again after an hour or two of relative idleness.

The morning after Timmy's arrival, Kate was up first as usual, trying to get on top of her work to ensure she was free to meet Leo later. Ernie appeared next, after shouting crudely at Vinnie to stop being lazy and get up. Kenny must already have stirred.

Kate had the first pot of tea of the day waiting for everyone. Breakfast would follow later when the farm had some work under its belt. Pearl wasn't far behind the Fletcher men, even though she wasn't required to work today, then Ruby came down with Timmy, both blinking like owls disturbed from deep sleep. Ruby's expression was moody – mornings didn't agree with her – but wary too.

'Tea or milk?' Kate asked Timmy, thinking it was a pity that he hadn't been allowed at least a little longer in bed.

'He'll have tea,' Ruby snapped, then added a belated 'Please.'

Did she think Kate would try to get Timmy sent away? Kate could think of no other reason for her attitude.

Sitting at the table, Ruby made a visible effort to rouse herself out of her stupor. 'What would you like me to do today, Mr Fletcher? I'm keen to make up for the time I was away yesterday.'

Kate didn't think Ruby was keen at all but needed to stay in Ernie's good books – in so far as Ernie had any good books.

'I could finish off the scarecrow if that would help?'

'You can get down to Five Acre Field,' Ernie told her, scuppering the idea of an easy time in the kitchen.

'I'll be glad to,' Ruby lied. 'Timmy can help.'

'I'm going to finish my scarecrow,' Pearl announced.

'I'll give you a hand,' Vinnie told her, only to receive a glare from Ernie and add hastily, 'After my other work, I mean.'

They all trooped outside, Timmy yawning, leaving

292

Pearl obviously at a loose end now the others had gone. It was clear she'd rather be outdoors than finishing her scarecrow by herself. Alone, Kate washed the cups quickly, then mixed vinegar with water to spray on to some of the plants in the kitchen garden that were looking infested. Working her way along the neat rows of vegetables, she noticed slugs and snails that needed removing later. Not that she liked to kill them. She preferred to put them in a bucket, which she emptied into the hedgerow across the lane to give the creatures a chance of finding new homes.

Breakfast followed – porridge sweetened with honey, followed by one rasher of bacon and one egg per person. Gone were the days of plenty when Fred 'n' Frank had tried to out-eat each other by stuffing their faces with numerous rashers and several eggs. The thought of her absent brothers softened Kate and she decided she'd write to them again later, even if they only replied with mocking stories about each other and pleas of *Send more cigs* and *We need more grub!*

Modest as the breakfast was, Timmy looked thrilled at the sight of it. 'Mind your manners,' Ruby warned him.

'Can I really have bacon? And an egg? A real egg? I only had bread at the 'arrises' 'ouse. Sometimes it had dripping on it, but not always.'

Poor kid.

Breakfast over, Kate washed up again, then went out armed with a bucket to see to the snails and slugs. Pearl wandered out after her, hands stuffed in pockets and feet planted wide as she stood nearby. Usually, Pearl spent Sundays with Ruby.

'There's one,' she said, pointing to a snail. 'Want me to get the little blighter for you?'

'Only if it's no trouble.'

Pearl picked up the snail and put it in the bucket.

Kate was thinking that life was complicated. A week ago, she'd have been glad to see Ruby pack her bags and leave as it might have been possible to get a more useful land girl to replace her. Timmy's arrival had made things trickier – getting rid of Ruby would also mean uprooting her brother and Kate wanted to give him a chance. It would be interesting to know how the land lay between Ruby and Pearl, though.

'Timmy seems a nice boy,' Kate said casually.

'He is. He's lucky to have a sister who looks out for him.' There was wistfulness in her expression. Perhaps she was already feeling herself to be of decreasing importance to her friend.

It wasn't long before Kate had to go indoors again, this time to prepare the lunch. On Sundays it was the main meal of the day. She had some steak and kidney keeping cool in the larder though the quantity was small and there was Timmy's mouth to feed too. His ration book hadn't been registered in Churchwood yet, but Kate hoped Ernie wouldn't have thought of that. Kate made enough pastry for three pies. Into the steak and kidney pie went the carrots and turnips she used to bulk out the meat these days. Another pie contained vegetables and a small quantity of minced beef left from the previous day and into the third went rhubarb – unsweetened due to the sugar shortage but still likely to be tasty served with custard.

Kate never suggested that the girls help around the house, but Pearl offered to lay the table anyway. She wasn't a great reader and was terrible at knitting and sewing, so needed something else to fill her time off. 'I'll put the wireless on, shall I?' she said.

'I don't see why not.'

As she waited for the meal to cook, Kate scrubbed some shirt cuffs and collars at the sink, then put them to soak in the dolly. She also wiped finger marks off doors and chairs and watered the herbs she grew on window ledges. Juggling tasks to make use of every minute was the only way she could stay on top of her work.

Pearl danced along with the wireless after fiddling with its knobs to find a programme she liked. Her dancing reminded Kate of a shuffling carthorse but she was pleased to see that it made the big girl look happier.

Pearl stopped dancing abruptly when the others filed into the kitchen, and her plain face turned red as she realized she must have been seen through the window. Vinnie walked up to Pearl and performed some strange gyration that he must have thought was dancing, but Kate was glad to see that Pearl's only response was to send a watchful look in Ernie's direction. Maybe one day Vinnie would grow into a decent human being but until then Pearl was better off without him bruising her heart.

After lunch there was more washing up for Kate – it never seemed to end – but finally she cleaned herself up as best she could, slipped outside and cycled to meet Leo.

He wasn't there. A hollow opened up inside her as she wondered if he'd been kept at the base, but a ten-minute wait brought the phut-phut of the motorbike to her ears. A minute later, Leo leapt off the bike and folded her in his arms.

'I think I may be able to come out with you one day,' Kate told him. 'If you'd still like that?'

'Like it? I'd love it!' There was something intense in his eyes that made her wonder if he was halfway to falling in love with her the same way she was halfway to falling in love with him.

The thought gave her a skittery sensation inside – excitement mixed with fear because this was the great unknown to Kate and the thought of throwing caution to the winds and admitting her feelings would feel like throwing herself off a precipice.

He smiled, released her and dug in the pocket of his flying jacket. 'Look what I've got.'

'Chocolate! What luxury.'

They walked for a while, Leo slipping her arm through his; then they sat on some grass and shared the chocolate. Kate would have liked to save some for Timmy but it would only have led to questions about where she'd got it.

They talked about what had happened in their lives since they'd last met and, all too soon, it was time to part. They agreed that Leo should look into arranging for them to go out together to a dance or something similar as soon as possible. In the meantime, they'd meet up again on the evening of next Sunday, all being well. Arrangements were always subject to Leo's duties and Kate's ability to leave the farm.

'I can't wait,' he murmured as they said their good-byes; then he kissed her on the lips. Only gently – a soft, sweet nuzzle – but it promised much, and as Kate cycled home again, she felt as though she were soaring high in a gilded flying chariot instead of dodging potholes on an old bicycle.

# CHAPTER THIRTY-SEVEN

## *Alice*

'Are any of you coming to the bookshop?' Alice asked in the grocer's shop. The women present glanced doubtfully at one another.

Mrs Hutchings was the first to speak. 'You know how much we used to love it, Alice.'

'But it isn't the same any more,' Mrs Hayes finished.

'That big banner you used to put up outside – the one with all the letters in different colours – sort of set the scene,' Mrs Hutchings added. 'Everything was bright and cheerful then.'

Mrs Hayes nodded. 'Now there's just that little board outside – white chalk on a black background. It reminds me of school, and that's how it feels when we go inside. Everyone has to be on their best behaviour. We much preferred just relaxing over a cuppa and a chat.'

'It's still about bringing Churchwood together,' Alice pointed out.

Elsie Fuller joined in. 'I was there a day or two ago when Mrs Forsyth asked us to knit blankets for the poor while she read Bible stories to us. Hilda here ran into problems with her knitting, so I leaned across to explain where she'd gone wrong and Mrs Forsyth stopped talking and stared at me. "May I help you with something?" she asked me, all pretend sweetness. I explained what I'd been telling Hilda – only whispering, mind, not talking loud – and she asked me if I thought chatting was . . . Oh, what was the word?'

' "Appropriate",' Hilda Roberts supplied.

'That's right. She asked if chatting was appropriate when I was listening to the Bible. I don't mind telling you that I went red in the face and I haven't blushed in years. Embarrassed, I was. And it wasn't as though I was doing anything that hadn't been done a hundred times in the old bookshop. We never had to stay silent there.'

Hilda nodded and took up the story. 'Mrs Forsyth said I should have waited until the end of the story then raised my hand to ask for help. That woman's voice has daggers in it even when she speaks quietly.'

'I know things have changed,' Alice soothed, 'but the only way we'll get our old bookshop back – or something that resembles it – is to let the Forsyths settle in and work on persuading them little by little to allow some of the old ways to creep back. That way they won't feel undermined.'

A moment of silence followed. 'All right,' Mrs Hutchings said then, 'I'll give it one more chance, but the moment that woman embarrasses me the way she embarrassed poor Elsie is the moment I'll be off.'

'Thank you, Mrs Hutchings.'

'I'll come too,' Mrs Hayes said, 'on the same condition.'

'Elsie?' Alice asked.

Elsie looked at Hilda, who nodded. 'If you really think we might get our old bookshop back, it's worth trying to put up with that snooty madam,' Elsie said. 'But we'll sit near the door so we can get away quickly if she picks on us again.'

'I'm grateful,' Alice told them.

'Why did the Forsyths have to change something that was working so well?' Mrs Hutchings lamented. 'It's a mystery to me.'

Answers sprang into Alice's mind: because the Forsyths were smug, because they refused to listen, because they were the sort of people who thought they always knew best . . . But she simply smiled, told the women she'd see them in the hall soon, and left to help get the bookshop ready.

Naomi was walking up from Foxfield. Alice waited for her on the village green. 'I've been trying to talk some of our ladies into coming along,' she said.

'Did you have any luck?'

'They said they'll come today.'

'But they might not come again.'

'Not unless things change.'

Naomi looked just as depressed as Alice at the thought of the bookshop going into a terminal decline.

They reached the hall. 'I suggest we put out fewer chairs than usual,' Naomi said. 'There's no point in giving ourselves more work if they're not going to be needed. No news of Daniel, I suppose?'

'Not yet.'

'Come and use my telephone any time if you want to speak to his parents.'

'You're wonderfully kind, Naomi.' But she still looked strained to Alice. 'How are you? Is your tooth still bothering you? I saw you catching the bus the other day. Did you need another visit to the dentist?'

'No, I . . . went to London to see an old acquaintance.'

'That must have been nice.'

'Mmm. Twenty chairs will probably be enough. I suspect some of those will go unused.'

Naomi was proven right. There were more chairs than people. The session began as usual with informal milling around the tables where once a wide variety of books, newspapers and magazines had been available. Now there were only the books that had passed muster with the Forsyths. 'No romances, I suppose,' Mrs Hayes whispered to Alice.

'Not today, I'm afraid.'

Mrs Forsyth was trying to force a worthy book of sermons on to Hilda Roberts.

'Maybe next time,' Hilda said, and Alice wondered if Hilda felt safe in saying that because there wasn't going to be a next time.

Eventually, Mrs Forsyth instructed everyone to sit. With obvious wariness, they did so. Some hadn't bothered to remove their coats. Others sat with handbags perched on their laps. Alice thought back to the days of old when people had lolled in their chairs, chatting and laughing.

'Today I'd like to look again at the Bible passage on which my husband gave such an uplifting sermon in church on Sunday.'

'Was it uplifting?' Alice heard Elsie Fuller whisper to Mrs Palfrey.

'I wouldn't know. I fell asleep.'

Mrs Forsyth stared at them until, shamefaced, they sat to attention.

It was the same when Edna Hall burrowed in her

301

pocket for a paper bag of mint imperials. Sugar shortage or not, Edna always had mint imperials about her person. 'I'm eking them out,' she'd told Alice. 'One mint each day.'

Once again, Mrs Forsyth stopped talking until Edna, blushing, returned the bag to her pocket and sat quietly.

'What a disaster,' Naomi declared to Alice when the session finished and the few people who'd attended trooped out, sending Alice looks that said as clearly as words, *We* did *try*.

'Did you hear that Bert has cancelled his men's evening session?' Alice said.

'I did. No games or beer allowed. He asked around a few of his regulars but none of them thought the new style of meeting was worth turning out for. You can imagine how Humphrey Guscott expressed himself.'

'Pithily,' Alice said. Humphrey's use of language was colourful to say the least.

Mrs Forsyth came over. 'What a worthwhile meeting that was. I'm sure I gave those ladies plenty to think about.'

'I'm sure you did,' Alice answered.

The vicar's wife went on her way and Alice turned back to Naomi. 'Let's hope we have better luck with the children's story time. Mrs Forsyth surely can't object to children making a noise.'

'I wouldn't bet money on it,' Naomi said gloomily. Then she changed the subject, looking oddly awkward about it. 'I may be away for a couple of days soon. I'm not sure when.'

'Are you seeing your friend again?'

'I'm going to London, yes.' Was she feeling

awkward because she feared it might appear that she too was deserting the bookshop? 'I'll let you know which days I'll be away.'

'I hope you have a lovely time, but look after yourself, won't you?' Alice said.

Maybe some fun in London was the very thing Naomi needed. She hadn't been herself for months.

The children's story time was equally disastrous. 'How that woman expects a two-year-old to stay silent is a mystery – unless she wants the kids scared half to death,' Pam Cooper said.

'She hasn't got kids of her own. That's the problem,' Maggie Larkin pointed out, only to reconsider and add, 'Except that you haven't got kids yet either, Alice, and you're great with them.'

'The difference is that Alice is nice,' Pam said. 'I don't know why Mrs Forsyth wants to come to these story times if she's got no liking for little ones. No understanding of them, anyway.'

'She likes the sound of her own voice,' Maggie suggested.

'Mrs Forsyth might lose interest after a while,' Alice ventured, hoping to keep the mums and other family members coming to the bookshop before it disintegrated.

'It's possible,' Maggie conceded, but it was apparent that she considered it unlikely.

Alice's spirits were low as she walked home. It didn't help that she arrived to find that there was still no letter from Daniel.

# CHAPTER THIRTY-EIGHT

## *Naomi*

Not for the first time Naomi regretted that Brimbles Farm was so far from Foxfield. Long walks hurt her feet and today it would feel more of a trudge than ever because she was bringing disappointing news. 'Of course I'll take telephone messages for Kate,' she'd told Alice, delighted to hear that Kate had a young man in her life.

The girl deserved some joy, though Naomi wished that the young man in question had a safer job than piloting a fighter plane. How brave those young men were!

'And of course she can use my house as a place to change and meet him,' she'd added.

'I can pass on any messages when I walk by Kate's farm on the way to the hospital,' Alice had said.

Today was Saturday, though, and Naomi knew Alice was spending the afternoon with May and the Kovac children. Not wanting to disturb her, Naomi was taking the message herself. She needed the exercise, but oh, how she wished she had better feet.

Not relishing the thought of encountering the Fletcher men, she was pleased to see the taller land girl at work in one of the fields. 'Excuse me!' Naomi called.

The girl looked up and came over.

'Is Kate at home?' Naomi asked. 'If she is, would you mind fetching her for me?'

'Don't mind at all.'

'Thank you.'

The big girl ambled off. There wasn't an elegant bone in her body, but Naomi sympathized with her for that, having no natural elegance herself.

Kate came quickly and the land girl returned to her work. 'You've heard from Leo?' Kate asked, and the anxiety in her lovely face touched Naomi's heart.

'He telephoned not long ago. It isn't good news, I'm afraid. He won't be able to meet you tomorrow after all, but he insisted I should stress that it's due to circumstances beyond his control.'

'I understand.' Kate looked woebegone but managed a weak smile. 'Leo is at the beck and call of his duties, but without the war bringing him to visit his cousin in Stratton House we might never have met.'

'He said he'll be in touch again soon.'

Kate nodded. 'Can I offer you tea? Or a glass of water?'

'Thank you, but I'm sure you need to get back to work. How is it? With the land girls, I mean?'

'Pearl isn't bad, but she'd be a lot better without Ruby's influence. They're still friends, though I suspect Pearl feels a little neglected now Ruby is focused on Kenny and her brother.'

'Has the boy settled in?'

'Well enough. He's a sweet boy at heart, I think.'

'Is he taking up much of Ruby's working time?'

'She takes him to school in the mornings and collects him in the afternoons. She uses my bicycle to

305

make it quicker and insists it's only until he's confident about walking alone. Afterwards, she puts on a show of making up the lost time, but there's a big gap between what she says she's going to do and what she actually achieves, even with Pearl and Kenny helping.'

'How does your father feel about all this?'

'He grumbles constantly – but he's never been Mr Charming.'

'It must be hard on you, having to do more than your fair share of work while Ruby gets away with doing only a half-share.'

Kate shrugged. 'I'd rather Timmy was happy than miserable. And I'm making time to see Leo – when he can see me. I'm sorry I haven't been down to the bookshop, though.'

'You're not missing much.'

'Alice says it's going from bad to worse.'

'She's right. It's incredible to think that it was such a thriving venture less than a month ago.'

'Now it's dying.'

'Extraordinarily quickly. And not just because the fun has gone out of it. The Forsyths have a knack of making people feel small. Cecil Wade's presence doesn't help.'

'That pompous fool!'

'He comes quite often and minces about as though he's in heaven already. And he's even worse than the Forsyths at belittling people.' They exchanged sour looks at the thought of Cecil Wade. 'I'd better head for home,' Naomi said then. 'It's been lovely to see you, Kate, though I'm sorry I didn't bring happier news. Look after yourself, won't you?'

'You too, Naomi.'

Guessing that Kate was about to comment on her jaded appearance, Naomi gave her a quick hug and walked away.

Kate wasn't the only one who was disappointed by Leo's news. Naomi was frustrated by it too. Had she not felt she should stay at home to welcome him the first time he came to meet Kate at her house, Naomi would have gone to London again, having decided that Alexander might be more likely meet any secret lover on a Saturday or Sunday when there'd be fewer colleagues, clients and general acquaintances around. Now she'd have to wait for next weekend.

# CHAPTER THIRTY-NINE

## *Kate*

The thought that Leo might worry about how she was feeling now he'd let her down preyed on Kate's mind. Appallingly aware of how a split second of distraction could cost a pilot his life, she wanted him to keep all of his attention on flying his plane and evading the enemy, at least while he was in the air. The Blitz appeared to be over at last, but the RAF was still busy taking the fight over Europe and protecting shipping too.

In bed that evening she wrote to assure him that she understood that duty had called. She got up early the next morning to post the letter in the village to be sure it was collected as early as possible on Monday, and was back home before anyone else had stirred.

On Wednesday a letter came in reply.

*Dear Kate,*

*I'm so sorry I couldn't meet you as planned. I'm torn between hoping you weren't too disappointed and hoping you minded a lot because you like me a lot. I trust my message wasn't too much of an inconvenience to your friend, Naomi. I'm looking forward to meeting her and your other friends, too – Alice, especially.*

*May I hope to see you next Saturday? I'd like to bring you back to Hollerton. A pub in the village nearest the base is holding a dance and I'd love to twirl you round the dance floor and show you off to my friends. Ralph in particular can't wait to meet you . . .*

Goodness. Kate hugged the letter briefly to her chest and then hid it away.

That afternoon she decided it was high time she went into the village to visit the sorry wreck the bookshop had become. She missed it dreadfully – or rather she missed the old days.

'Where do you think you're going?' Ernie demanded as she wheeled the bicycle out of the barn.

'I'm taking a break. I worked all of Saturday and all of Sunday. I'm due some time off and I'm only taking a couple of hours.'

He wrapped his filthy fingers around the handlebars. 'It's the middle of the working day. You're paid to work, not shirk.'

'And I'll be working into the evening. If you're looking for someone to nag, go and vent your spleen on Vinnie. He's lounging around in Two Acre Field with a packet of Woodbines. Or go and see what Kenny is up to. I can assure you it isn't work.'

She snatched the handlebars out of his grasp and rode off.

It saddened her to walk up to the door of the Sunday School Hall and see that the cheerful banner was gone from above the door. Normally a buzz of chatter and laughter reached outwards from the meeting room, but today she walked into a place of whispers and tension. Then one voice announced crisply, 'It's time to begin,' as though any conversations not led by the speaker were trivial and time-wasting. The speaker was, of course, Mrs Forsyth.

'Kate!' May rushed forward to fold her friend into her arms. 'It's lovely to see you at last.'

'It certainly is,' Alice agreed.

Naomi and Janet sent Kate little waves and the few other people who were present smiled at her.

'Really, ladies, where are your priorities?' Mrs Forsyth chided. 'I'm sure ... Kate, is it? ... Kate is welcome, but I'm equally sure she doesn't wish to be a disruptive influence.'

Her cold gaze skewered Kate accusingly as they all sat down. May sent Kate a rueful look in sympathy.

The session was even worse than expected. Gone was the merry bustle of the local community. Instead, attendance had dropped by more than half, and no one looked glad to be there. Kate felt her old rebelliousness rising up. She stuck her legs out in an ungainly fashion, unable to resist the temptation to provoke Mrs Forsyth's further disapproval.

But in time her thoughts drifted to the happier subject of Leo, and May had to poke her in the ribs to get her attention when Mrs Forsyth asked Kate a question. 'I'm afraid I don't know the answer,' Kate admitted.

'It would help if you bothered to listen.'

'It's annoying when people don't bother to listen, isn't it?' Kate said pointedly, the Forsyths being the worst offenders.

Afterwards, when Mrs Forsyth had left – leaving the tidying up to others – Kate apologized. 'I'm sorry. I can't have helped by being cheeky.'

310

'You only said what we were all thinking,' Alice assured her.

'Even so . . . Goodness, it's a desperate situation, isn't it? But I've no idea what can be done to change it.'

Neither had anyone else.

Kate took Naomi aside for a moment. 'Please say no if it isn't convenient, but there's a chance that Leo might be able to meet me on Saturday.'

'Saturday?'

Did Naomi look dismayed? 'Please don't feel obliged to—'

'No, no. Saturday will be fine. Really, Kate. I'll keep my fingers crossed that he manages to get the time off.'

Kate spent the following days bracing herself for another disappointment, but none had come by the time she set out for Foxfield on her bicycle, her change of clothes in a bag over her shoulder. Had Leo sent a message that hadn't reached her yet?

'The telephone hasn't rung,' Naomi assured her when she arrived.

Naomi's bedroom was at least four times the size of Kate's tiny room at home and much more luxurious, with carpet underfoot, an enormous bed with a satin eiderdown, and a dressing table on which sat silver-backed brushes, a leather jewellery box and sparkling glass bottles of perfumes and lotions. Nearby was a bathroom with an enormous claw-footed bath, pristine white sink and toilet, another dressing table and a chair – a world away from the tin bath and outside lavatory at Brimbles Farm.

'Use as much hot water as you'd like and take as long as you need,' Naomi said, but Kate didn't linger long, wanting to spend every possible moment with Leo if he arrived early.

She heard the phut-phut of a motorbike as she made her way down the grand staircase and, after a consenting nod from Naomi, opened the door to him.

'You're a sight for sore eyes,' he said, taking in Kate's appearance in the dress and shoes May had given her, their russet and forest-green colours doing wonders for Kate's chestnut hair, which hung in loose waves past her shoulders.

He stepped forward and kissed her cheek. 'It's wonderful to see you, Kate. I hated letting you down last time.'

'It couldn't be helped and you're here now. That's what matters.'

He was as attractive as she'd remembered, tall and loose-limbed with a face that might have missed out on classical handsomeness but more than compensated for it by being full of character and glowing good humour. 'It's wonderful to have the chance to show you off to my friends at last,' he said. 'Tonight's going to be particularly special. Ralph has just become engaged to his childhood sweetheart. Ruth's coming to the dance too. It'll be great for you girls to meet.'

Surely this meant that Leo really was serious about her? Kate hoped she wouldn't let him down. 'Talking of meeting friends, come and meet Naomi.'

She must have been hovering nearby as she stepped into the hall. She shook Leo's hand and Kate was

312

pleased to see the approval in her expression. 'You're taking Kate into Bedfordshire, I understand.'

'To a dance. Please don't worry: I won't ride the bike fast even in daylight and I'll ride it even more carefully when I bring her back in the blackout. Oh, and in case you're wondering, I'm not misappropriating RAF petrol. The bike belongs to a fellow pilot and the petrol comes from his mother's house, which, by smiling good fortune, isn't far from the base. His father foresaw the war and built up a petrol supply before it was even declared, only to die before he could use it. My friend is glad to let me have some in return for a few drinks in the mess because he's afraid a bomb might fall on it and blow his poor mother to kingdom come.'

'Can I offer you some refreshment?' Naomi asked.

'Thank you, but I hope you won't mind if I whisk Kate away?'

'Of course not. Enjoy yourselves.'

'I'm sure *I* will,' Leo said, sending Kate a look that made her blush.

'I need to put my breeches back on,' Kate said, fearing her dress would be neither decent nor warm on the bike.

'I'll lend you a scarf for your hair,' Naomi offered.

She led Kate into the sitting room where Kate slipped the breeches on under her dress and fastened the scarf beneath her chin.

'I don't think I'll win prizes for fashion,' Kate said, rejoining Leo.

'I know nothing about fashion, but you'll get first prize from me.'

They said goodbye to Naomi and then left the house on the bike. 'I said we'd call on my friend Alice,' Kate told Leo, but when they arrived there was no need to knock on the cottage door because Alice was already standing outside.

'I heard the motorbike,' she explained.

Alice, too, looked approvingly at Leo when they were introduced, and accepted his sympathies over Daniel's imprisonment with typical stoicism. She didn't keep Leo chatting for long, though. 'Go!' she urged. 'Go and have a lovely time, but look after my friend, Leo. She's very dear to me.'

Kate gave Alice a quick hug and waved as Leo started the bike and moved them off.

The motorbike was exhilarating, and Kate was glad she had no need to worry about either her modesty or her hair. Instead, she enjoyed the firm breadth of Leo's back in front of her and the closeness of her arms around his waist.

Nervousness still prickled inside her. She'd scrubbed her fingernails and rubbed some lotion of Naomi's into her hands, but there was no escaping their work-worn roughness. Would Leo's friends consider her to be a country bumpkin without an ounce of wit or sophistication, and with nothing to say that wasn't about the price of seed and the best way to grow green beans?

'Nearly there,' Leo shouted back after a while, and the nervous prickles intensified.

They reached the village of Hollerton, which gave the base its name. Leo brought the motorbike to a halt outside a pub called the Crown. Kate was puzzled. Wasn't the dance at the Red Lion? 'I can't expect you to dance the evening away with no food inside you, and the Crown offers better food,' Leo explained. 'Not that it's a gourmet restaurant but the food's still good.'

Kate unfastened the headscarf but looked down at her breeches, wondering what to do about taking them off.

'There's a bush down there,' Leo said, pointing along the side of the pub. 'I'll turn my back and keep guard.'

Five minutes later, the breeches were packed in her bag and Kate was sitting opposite Leo, studying the Crown's menu on a blackboard beside the bar. A waitress came over and gestured towards it. 'Lamb chops would be my choice. There's no fish because we can't get any even though it isn't rationed, but there's sausages in onion gravy, shepherd's pie or steak and kidney pie. More kidneys than steak but tasty all the same.'

'Kate?' Leo prompted.

She'd never been to a café before, let alone a restaurant. It felt overwhelmingly glamorous, and the food sounded heavenly. 'I'll have the chops, please.'

'Same for me, please,' Leo said, and he ordered wine as well.

'Don't worry,' he told Kate. 'I won't get squiffy and ride you into a ditch on the way home, but a glass of wine with our meal will make this occasion feel even more special.'

Kate's cheeks warmed under the gleam from his eyes.

She swallowed and tried for some poise. 'Tell me about the people I'll be meeting. I know about Ralph and his fiancée, Ruth, but who else will be there?'

He duly told her about his fellow pilots and crew, and Kate tried to commit the names to memory: Rex, Andrew, Laurence . . .

The meal was delicious and the wine – a rich red – helped Kate to relax. She'd brought some of her hard-won wages with her, but Leo insisted on paying the bill and the tip as well.

Afterwards, they walked on to the Red Lion, their ears picking up the sounds of music as they approached. The dance was taking place in a barn to the rear.

Walking in, Kate saw couples dancing with merry abandon in the middle while more people crowded round the bar at the far end or sat at the tables that lined the walls on both sides.

'Leo!' A voice reached them above the tones of Glenn Miller whose 'Pennsylvania 6-5000' was playing on the gramophone.

Leo waved to a group that was sitting around a couple of the tables and led Kate over. 'This must be the lovely Kate,' a man said, getting to his feet. 'Even lovelier than I imagined. You're a lucky man, Leo Kinsella.'

'Ralph Sheridan,' Leo told Kate.

Ralph shook her hand before kissing it gallantly, and if he noticed the roughness of her fingers it didn't show on his face. He was tall like Leo. Brown-haired, brown-eyed and handsome, with something of Leo's good humour about him. It was easy to see why the two men had been friends for so many years. 'I hear you've just got engaged,' Kate said.

'I have indeed. To this lovely lady.' He gestured to

the young woman who'd been sitting beside him, and she got up with a welcoming smile.

'Kate, this is Ruth, my fiancée,' Ralph continued. 'Ruth, this is Kate, the girl with whom Leo is besotted.'

Kate laughed, for surely Ralph was exaggerating. It still gave her a happy feeling inside.

'It's wonderful to meet you,' Ruth told her. She was pretty in a homely way, and Kate warmed to her immediately.

'Congratulations to both of you.'

More introductions followed – more RAF personnel and some girls as well. A Betty, a Jean, a Veronica . . . All were friendly.

Seats were shuffled to make room for Kate and Leo while Rex went to the bar for more drinks. A new song came on the gramophone: 'One O'Clock Jump'.

'Kate,' Ralph said, 'will you do me the honour of—'

'Not a chance,' Leo interrupted. 'Kate's first dance is going to be with me.' He frowned suddenly. 'If that's what you'd like too, Kate?'

It was. They got up and Kate felt the warmth of Leo's hand at the small of her back as he guided her on to the dance floor. There he took her in his arms, grinning down at her. 'Having fun?'

'I certainly am.' He was a wonderful dancer.

Kate danced with Leo's friends too and chatted with the girls. They all fizzed with life, dancing, drinking and laughing as though determined to squeeze every possible moment of enjoyment out of the evening.

'I'd like to keep you here for ever,' Leo told her when they danced again. 'But I need to get you home.'

She'd already stayed later than planned. 'I'm sorry to drag you away.'

'I don't mind. It means I'll be alone with you again before I have to part with you.'

They said their goodbyes, and Kate was encouraged to come back soon, especially by Ralph and Ruth.

Outside, the air was cooler. Refreshing. They walked back along the now-quiet street to the motorbike. Kate returned to the bush to slip on her breeches and change her dress for her working clothes of shirt, ancient jumper and jacket. 'You still look beautiful to me,' he told her.

She tied the headscarf back over her hair and got on the bike behind Leo. 'Warm enough?' he asked.

'I will be.' With her arms around Leo's waist, she'd share his warmth.

He rode as carefully as he'd promised but all too soon they were back in Brimbles Lane. They'd told Naomi that Kate would collect her bicycle early the next morning so Leo could take Kate straight home. Not wanting to alert anyone to his presence, she asked him to stop the motorbike well short of the farmhouse. They both got off, and Leo raised his hands to her shoulders. 'Perhaps this is premature but I'm falling in love with you, Kate Fletcher.'

She smiled because she felt the same.

He kissed her and the nuzzle of his lips felt like velvet until he deepened the kiss and Kate groaned inwardly in pleasure. 'I don't want to leave,' he told her when the kiss was finally over, but they both knew he hadn't a choice.

She'd walked around the farm at night for as long

as she could remember but Leo still insisted on walking her closer to the farmhouse. In the shadow of a tree, they stopped again and looked up at the sky, admiring the myriad stars that shone silver-white against a background of indigo. 'A shooting star!' Kate said, pointing.

'Lovely,' he agreed.

He kissed her again then released her.

'Stay safe,' she told him. 'Please stay safe.'

# CHAPTER FORTY

## *Alice*

Alice was out collecting eggs and talking to the chickens when she heard Kate's voice whispering to her from the lane. 'Is that you, Alice?'

Alice went to meet her. 'I didn't think you'd be up so early,' Kate said as she came into the garden through the side gate.

'It's a beautiful morning,' Alice told her.

The truth was that Alice had a lot on her mind but there was nothing to be gained by going over old worries, and besides, she was eager to hear about Kate's outing with Leo. She needed only one look at her friend's face to know that the evening had been wonderful. Kate was blushing adorably. 'I've been collecting my bike from Naomi's,' she said.

'So I see.' Alice waited; then she smiled and said, 'Well? How was the dance?'

'It was nice.'

'Nice?'

Kate's composure cracked. 'Oh, Alice! It was so much better than nice. It was the best night of my life. Leo is such fun! He's interesting too. And kind. He loves a joke but he's always kind.'

There hadn't been much kindness in Kate's life,

growing up. 'I'm delighted for you,' Alice told her. 'You'll be seeing him again?'

'When he can get away from the base. Hopefully soon.'

'I'll keep my fingers crossed for it to be very soon,' Alice assured her.

'The bookshop . . .' Kate began.

'I've called a meeting for this afternoon. I don't expect you to come, though.'

'I don't think I can manage this afternoon,' Kate said regretfully.

They parted with a hug. Alice was delighted to see her friend looking so happy.

May was beaming too when she arrived at The Linnets for the meeting. The reason for her smile stood beside her. Marek Janicki. Her husband, home on leave.

'It's lovely to see you, Marek,' Alice told him.

'Is lovely to be back in England. I am sorry about Daniel, though.' Marek still spoke with an accent, having lived to adulthood in Poland.

'Thank you. I'm sure you and May want to spend this precious leave together so please don't feel obliged to sit through this meeting, May.'

'I want to stay.'

'I want her to stay also,' Marek said. 'The bookshop . . . the friends . . . have made a big difference to my May and the children. I will leave May here and go for a walk. Remind myself of beautiful England. I will collect May later.'

They waved him off and then settled in the cottage dining room – Alice, May, Naomi, Bert and Janet.

'The reason I've called this meeting is because I'm not sure how much longer we can go on hoping the Forsyths will change,' Alice began. 'They're even worse than expected and attendance has dropped drastically.'

'The daft thing is that a lot of people would happily go along to a Bible study group if it wasn't so dull and patronizing, and if they could have the fun of the old bookshop, too,' Bert said. 'Even folk who weren't interested in the Bible got to know the Christian "love thy neighbour" stuff just by being part of the bookshop community. But they've fallen by the way-side now. They're not coming to the meetings and they're not coming to church either.'

It was true. All of it was true.

'Mabel Thompson said she was made to feel she'd committed a crime just for sneezing when Reverend Forsyth called in to read a Bible story,' Janet reported.

'Pam Cooper said she had to stop coming because Mrs Forsyth made it clear she disapproved of her walking around shushing her newborn,' May said.

'And William Treloar went without a hot drink for two days when he fell ill with a stomach bug. No one knew about it,' Naomi reported.

'I was wrong to hope the Forsyths would gradually unwind,' Alice admitted. 'I suggest we make up a . . . a delegation, if you like, to call on them formally and explain how the village is suffering.'

'They won't like it,' Bert warned. 'But I don't think that should stop us because it's looking as though plain speaking is all we have left if we're to stop the rot.'

'It might look threatening if we all go,' Janet said.

'I agree,' Bert told her. 'I vote for young Alice here

to go, along with Naomi as she's done so much for the church over the years.'

'I vote for Alice and Naomi too,' May said. 'The Forsyths will never listen to me, seeing as I don't go to church.'

'If you really think I'll be of any use,' Naomi said uncertainly.

'We do,' everyone chorused.

Alice felt a wave of anger towards Cecil Wade for damaging Naomi's confidence but now wasn't the time to dwell on it. 'I'd like Bert to come too,' Alice said. 'Reverend Forsyth thinks highly of his wife but that may be because her thoughts always echo his. He might not take kindly to being challenged by women, so your presence could be invaluable, Bert.'

'Count me in then.'

'When would you like us to call on them?' Naomi asked. 'It's just that I'm expecting to go to London on Friday and I may spend the night there.'

'Are you seeing your dentist again?' Janet asked.

'No, I'm . . . seeing an old friend now the worst of the bombing is over.'

Janet shuddered. 'You're braver than me, Naomi. I'd still worry about air raids.'

Naomi gave a small smile.

'Don't forget your gas mask,' Janet added. 'Horrible, smelly things, but they might mean the difference between life and death.'

They decided to call on the Forsyths the following morning.

It was Reverend Forsyth who opened the vicarage door to Alice's knock. 'I wonder if we might have a word with you?' she asked. 'With Mrs Forsyth too, if she's at home?'

Alice had kept her voice light and friendly, but Reverend Forsyth's expression had hardened at the sight of them. 'Very well. Come in.'

He led the way into his study. Papers on a desk suggested he'd been interrupted while working there. Mrs Forsyth was sitting on a sofa with a notebook and pen, but got up as they entered and said, 'Good morning.'

'I'm sorry if we're disturbing you.' Alice was desperate to try to establish at least some level of goodwill.

'It's our duty to be available to parishioners,' Reverend Forsyth said, and his wife added, 'May we offer you tea?'

'Save your ration. Tea is precious these days, isn't it?' Naomi said, and Alice guessed that she, too, was trying to build some rapport.

'It's our duty to offer hospitality, no matter the inconvenience.' Mrs Forsyth could have been correcting a small child.

'I only meant . . .' Naomi shook her head and gave up.

They all sat down, the Forsyths on one sofa, the bookshop contingent on the other, like opponents about to go into battle. Alice ran a nervous tongue around her lips, wishing she could find a way to persuade these people that they needed to change their approach. 'I wonder how you feel the study group idea has been received?' she asked.

'My husband is doing a splendid job,' Mrs Forsyth said, laying a protective hand over his.

'As is my wife,' he replied.

'It's just that numbers seem to be dropping off and we wondered if they might be boosted by introducing more variety into the programme,' Alice ventured.

Reverend Forsyth sighed. 'Are you suggesting a return to the old ways, Miss Lovell?'

'Some of the old ways,' Alice admitted. 'A compromise, if you like.'

'We most certainly do not like.'

'I'm not sure why you feel so strongly about the way we used to do things,' Alice said, sounding puzzled. 'We provided a service that brought the community together. Where was the harm if some of the time was spent relaxing over a cup of tea and a chat?'

'What we saw was godless, vulgar and corrupting.'

'Corrupting?' Naomi questioned. 'Reverend Forsyth, you go too far.'

Outrage stiffened him further. 'May I remind you that I came to this parish to lead the community? The problem as I see it is that, as a group, you don't want to be led along a proper path. You want to be leaders yourselves so you're undermining my mission – and my wife's mission – by opposing all our attempts to turn Churchwood into a sober, right-thinking sort of place that welcomes real leadership from those best qualified to deliver it.'

'That's unfair!' Alice protested. 'We want to work with you, not against you.'

'But only on your terms, Miss Lovell. Those terms – and that attitude of resistance – simply won't do.'

'People are missing out on all the things that were good about this village,' Alice argued, 'the sense of community especially. It lifted spirits and allowed people to give each other practical help, too. Why, only the other day I heard that one resident had been unwell and didn't receive the support he needed because no one knew he was sick. In the old days of the bookshop, his absence would have been noticed. People would have investigated and rallied round.'

'Miss Lovell, you're being absurd. It grieves me to have to use such a term, but circumstances require it. We're not against community spirit. We want to build it. But it needs to be serious and God-fearing. As I believe I've said before, if people want to waste their time with mindless chatter or disgusting books, then they're free to do so in their own homes. Church property shouldn't be used for such things.'

'I think we've heard enough,' Bert said. 'I thought young Alice was being optimistic in wanting to reason with you, but at least she tried. If something bad happens and someone slips through the community safety net you've slashed to ribbons, we'll know where to point the finger of blame. You've been warned.'

'Are you threatening us, Mr Makepiece?'

'Merely making it clear where the blame will lie.'

'I'll thank you to leave now,' Reverend Forsyth said.

'Oh, I'm leaving. In fact, I can't get away from your arrogance quickly enough.'

Bert pushed his bulky frame upright. Alice and Naomi stood, too.

'I'm sorry it's come to this,' Alice said, then followed Bert to the door, Naomi joining her.

'I apologize if I made things worse,' Bert said outside.

'The situation was at rock bottom already,' Alice told him.

'I can't see the Forsyths ever having a change of heart about the bookshop,' Naomi said.

'Neither can I,' Alice agreed. 'Which means the bookshop is officially dead and buried.'

The way home took all three of them in the same direction. They reached The Linnets first, where Alice was desperately relieved to say her goodbyes and then retreat to her room where she could let the tears fall freely.

# CHAPTER FORTY-ONE

## *Naomi*

'Should I pack any evening dresses?' Suki asked.

'No, thank you, dear. Celia and I have an informal couple of days in mind.'

'That'll be nice, madam. Cosy.'

'In fact, I'd like my case to be as light as possible. There may not many porters at the station with the war on, so I need to be able to manage my case by myself.'

'Of course, madam.'

'All I really need is a change of blouse, stockings and underwear, and some night things.'

Suki hesitated. 'You will take care, madam? I know you say the air raids have mostly stopped, but they can always start up again.'

'Bless you, Suki. I assure you I shan't take any unnecessary risks.'

Suki smiled and left the sitting room. Naomi felt bad for lying to the little maid. It was true that Naomi was going to London, but Celia was an invention and Naomi would be staying in a hotel instead of her imaginary friend's house. Of course, if Alexander came for one of his rare weekends at home, she wouldn't be going anywhere.

Naomi waited until Thursday evening before telephoning Alexander as he hadn't bothered ringing her. He was telephoning less and less as the war went on, only ringing if he was coming home. This time she wanted to be sure about his intentions.

She caught him just before his office closed for the day. 'I imagine you already have plans, but I just wanted to make sure before I commit to seeing my friend Celia. You remember Celia? You met her at the Frobishers' four or five years ago.'

'I don't remember her, and yes, I have plans for this weekend.'

'Anything interesting?'

'Just seeing clients and playing golf.'

'I hope you have an enjoyable time. Goodbye, Alexander.'

It gave her a small burst of power to be the one to end the call, though the surge was a spark that flared briefly and then died. Alexander wouldn't have cared that she rang off first. Probably, he hadn't even noticed. But at least she now knew he wouldn't be returning to Foxfield.

Despite wanting to travel light, Naomi's case felt heavy, and she was glad Bert had offered to give her a lift to the bus stop. He'd actually offered to accompany her to London, but, much as she appreciated his kindness, she'd turned the offer down. He had a living to earn and it didn't seem fair to drag him away from his business for what might be a complete waste of time.

'Perhaps I'll come along if you decide to see the private detective, after all,' he said.

Did that mean he thought this amateur attempt to follow Alexander again was a waste of effort? Probably, but Naomi wanted one last try at it.

Wishing her good luck, he waved her off on the bus.

Arriving in London, she decided to check in to a hotel straight away so she could leave her case in her room. In staying Friday night, she hoped to give herself the best chance of learning Alexander's movements once his work had finished for the weekend. She found a small and relatively inexpensive hotel in Bloomsbury. Not knowing how much she'd spend on taxis, she was keen to economize on other expenses. Besides, she was unlikely to see anyone she knew at the Ruston.

'Just the one night, madam?' she was asked.

'Yes, please. Is the room likely to be available tomorrow night as well should I need to stay in London longer?'

'I believe so, madam. We have several vacant rooms at present.'

Naomi guessed that many people were still too afraid of air raids to come to London unless they had a compelling reason.

Her room would have earned a sneer from Alexander. It was plain and even a little threadbare. Positioned only one floor up at a front corner of the building, it overlooked another hotel – Brewster's – which had a small garden square at the side of it. The garden must once have been a place to sit or stroll but now it was a Dig for Victory garden, given over to growing vegetables.

In addition to the bed, Naomi's room held a wardrobe, armchair and small table, and the bathroom was only a short walk along the corridor. It was far from luxurious but sufficient for Naomi's needs.

After all, she wasn't here to be pampered. She was here to confront the dismal failure of her marriage.

It was a depressing thought, but at least that failure hadn't made her cynical about other romances. Certainly not Alice's relationship with Daniel. The love between those two was obvious for all to see and Naomi hoped fervently that they'd soon be reunited.

Then there was Kate and her young man. Naomi had seen Kate only briefly when she called to thank Naomi for the use of her house and telephone. Kate could be fierce and even a little frightening at times, but she'd blushed an endearing shade of pink when she spoke about her rapturous evening at the dance. It wasn't easy for Kate to open up about her feelings and Naomi felt honoured to be in on the secret of her romance.

She liked what she'd seen of Leo Kinsella too. All credit to him for seeing past Kate's country bumpkin appearance and soil-filled fingernails to the vibrant and intelligent person she was beneath them. Of course, he had to be a strong-minded man to fly fighter planes when the toll the war was taking on the lives of young airmen was grim.

By lunchtime Naomi was back in the alley near Alexander's office. He might be more likely to meet a lover on a Saturday or Sunday but it was possible that he'd leave London early this afternoon in order to meet her and Naomi didn't want to risk missing his departure. After half an hour she saw him emerge and followed him at a distance to a nearby restaurant. Unfortunately, there were curtains on the lower half of the windows so Naomi couldn't see if he was meeting someone or eating alone. There was a café on the other side of the street. She went inside and sat at a table by the window to rest her feet, picking at a sandwich and keeping a close eye on the restaurant door.

She paid her bill early but sat over a second cup of tea only to realize that ordering it had been unwise as she soon needed a bathroom. She was absent from her watching post for less than five minutes but still fretted about the possibility of having missed Alexander's departure. Jack Webber wouldn't have made such an amateur mistake, but Naomi still recoiled from the thought of appointing him as her investigator. She'd need to be desperate, though if she continued making stupid errors she might become desperate sooner rather than later.

'May I fetch you anything else?' the waitress asked.

Oh, heavens. Was Naomi going to have to order another cup of tea just to keep her table? She could always order it and not drink it, though that would feel wasteful. She was spared the necessity when she noticed movement across the road. Alexander was leaving the restaurant. A man walked out behind him and they shook hands briskly. A client? A business acquaintance?

Naomi realized the waitress was waiting for an answer. 'Thank you but no, I'm leaving.'

She placed a sixpence beneath the saucer as a tip and put on her coat while letting Alexander get ahead of her. Then she hastened after him. But he didn't meet anyone else. He simply returned to work.

It was half past two and, as it was a Friday, Naomi thought there was a chance he might begin his

332

weekend early, but she was probably safe for an hour or two. She took another look around war-torn London, donating a few coins into a collection box for injured servicemen and stopping to chat briefly with a woman in the green uniform of the Women's Voluntary Service who was dispensing tea from an urn on the back of a small trailer. 'That's very welcome, missis,' a passing air raid warden told her as he sipped from a metal cup.

Towards four o'clock, Naomi hailed a taxi and directed the driver to return her to Clark Street. 'Pull in here, please,' she instructed before they reached Alexander's office. 'I need to wait now, possibly for quite a while, but I expect to pay your full rate for the time spent.'

The driver shrugged as though to say, *Well, if you've got money to waste, I'm happy to take it off your hands.*

He reached for a newspaper and settled down to read it, but after almost an hour had passed he grew restless. Eventually, he turned to her. 'Do you think you might hurry the person you're waiting for along a bit?'

Hardly. Alexander couldn't know she was here.

'Only my missis ain't well and I said I'd be home in time to give the little 'uns their tea.'

Bother. If Naomi gave up this taxi, it might not be easy to find another now the streets were filling with workers making their way home. But the thought of the driver's poor, sick wife struggling with small children nudged at her conscience.

'I'm sorry to have kept you so long,' she said. 'How much do I owe you?'

She paid him what he asked, added a tip and got out. Up ahead of her, Alexander stepped through his office door. Oh, no. Had he seen her? Heart thumping, she scuttled into a nearby porch. She risked a peep and saw Alexander getting into a taxi. Looking around, she saw another taxi coming along. Naomi ran for it, hoping Alexander would be too busy giving his driver directions to notice her.

'Where to, madam?' the taxi driver asked her.

She was too agitated even to try to be subtle. 'Follow the taxi that's in front of us, please.'

'Seriously?'

She wanted to snap that it might be a joke to him, but it wasn't a joke to her. Holding back, she merely said, 'Yes, seriously.'

Her severe expression must have got through to him because he turned away, saying, 'Right you are, madam,' and set off after Alexander.

He was a skilful driver who managed to stick close to Alexander's vehicle despite the busy traffic. Naomi soon suspected that Alexander was returning to the flat and this proved to be the case. But it didn't follow that he'd be staying there all evening. And even if he did remain at home, he might not be alone.

Instructing her driver to pull in to the kerb, she watched as her husband paid his driver and then headed into James Mansions with a jauntiness he never showed at Foxfield.

'Will that be all, madam?' her driver asked.

'Would it inconvenience you to wait a while?'

'Not if you're paying.'

He sat back as though to catch up on some sleep. Meanwhile, Naomi watched the windows of the flat, hoping that the long summer daylight hours would keep the curtains open for some time.

She watched the door too, scrutinizing the few people who entered or left. Alexander wasn't amongst those who left, but could a lover be amongst those who entered? That woman there, perhaps. She was tall, slender and fashionable in a smart grey dress and jacket with an immaculate hat, handbag and shoes. There was no way of knowing.

The hours ticked by. At eight o'clock the curtains were pulled across the drawing-room windows by – she suspected but couldn't be sure at a distance – Alexander himself. When nine o'clock came, Naomi decided it was unlikely that he'd be going out tonight. She roused her driver with a tap on the window and directed him to take her to her hotel. She winced when she paid the fare. This surveillance was costing her dear and might cost still more if she had to buy the services of Jack Webber – but she had to know the truth.

She reserved her room for another night and asked for a glass of brandy to be brought to her. Kicking her shoes off, she closed her curtains against the advancing darkness, switched on the lamps and got on to the bed still dressed to drink the brandy. She hadn't eaten since picking at that lunchtime sandwich, but it was too late to ask for food even if she had an appetite – which she hadn't. She'd been losing weight for a while. Not dramatically, as she'd forced herself to eat to avoid her staff speculating about her health, but her skirts were feeling looser. Not so long ago that fact would have delighted her. Now it worried her because it was a sign of strain.

Out in the street a driver tooted a horn urgently. There came a screech of brakes, followed by the loud bang of a vehicle crashing into something. Naomi's hotel? Or the building next door?

Had anyone been hurt? Naomi sat up with a view to investigating but paused when she heard voices. 'You fool!' one of them accused. 'What did you think you were doing, riding a motorbike round a corner so quickly in a blackout?'

'Weren't my fault.' This voice sounded cockney. 'If you'd stuck to one side of the road instead of coming up the middle, I'd 'ave missed yer.'

'Don't talk nonsense, man. If—'

The words were cut off by an almighty boom that lifted Naomi in her bed, sucked the air from her lungs – the sound from her ears too – and then sent the bed crashing downwards through the floor.

# CHAPTER FORTY-TWO

## *Naomi*

How much time had passed? Naomi didn't know. Instinct had made her dive under the covers and press a pillow over her head as the bed fell then came to a crashing halt, only to fall and halt again. Now she lay curled up and braced for a further fall – or for death and destruction to rain down on her in the form of masonry, furniture and glass plummeting from the rooms above hers.

Her hearing returned in the form of a painful, high-pitched buzz that quickly became a background to creaks, rattles, thumps and horrible yawning sounds as debris detached from whatever had been holding it and fell around her. Something heavy thudded on to the bed just below her curled-up legs. What felt like smaller chunks of plaster bounced on to the pillow over her head but did no damage – as far as she could tell.

Gradually human sounds reached her ears – shouts and cries, along with the clamouring bells of fire engines, ambulances or both. Would someone search for her? Find her? Hoping they'd come soon, she tried to steady her racing heart and panicking thoughts by breathing deeply, but even here under the covers the air smelt and tasted of thick dust that made her cough and fear suffocation.

She tensed as more debris thudded and rattled around her. Would someone find her before it was too late? Another thought struck her. Bombs – and surely the explosion had been a bomb – were often followed by incendiary devices that caused raging infernos. Would she have survived the bombing only to burn to death instead? Was it really dust that filled her nostrils? Or dust mixed with smoke?

At last a voice called, sounding nearer. 'Hello! Anyone down there?'

'Yes!' It emerged as a dust-filled croak and ended with a cough. She tried again, fighting her way out of the bedclothes. 'Yes!'

Looking up, she saw a man peering down at her over the edge of what looked like a chasm. In the light of his torch, Naomi could see that he was wearing a tin hat. The letter W on the front signified that he was an air raid warden. She could also see the scene of devastation for the first time. Her bed had fallen to the ground floor and then into the cellar. A door had been blown off its hinges, revealing the remains of smashed bottles in the wine store beyond it. A chair from the lounge had fallen on to her bed. And above that . . . Naomi gulped at the sight of what was above that. Blackness, but not the darkness of the night sky. It was the darkness of upper floors.

The bomb must have blown a hole in the hotel from the cellar to Naomi's first-floor bedroom, but the upper floors had been left unsupported and gravity might bring them crashing down at any moment.

She could neither see nor hear crackling flames but, clearly, she was still in desperate danger.

'Are you hurt?' the warden called.

Naomi shielded her eyes as the torch was directed on to her face. 'I don't think so.'

Which was remarkable in the circumstances.

He disappeared, leaving Naomi feeling alone and horribly vulnerable, but soon he and another warden were scrambling down on ropes. 'Sure you're unhurt?' the first one asked. 'Only we don't want to do more damage getting you out.'

'I'm sure,' Naomi assured him, shuddering as more debris rattled down from above.

It was ridiculous to think of dignity when her life had been – and still was – in danger, but Naomi felt mortified at being seen in her stockinged feet with her hair wild and doubtless filled with dust.

'What about that cut?'

'What cut?'

He gestured to her forehead.

Naomi touched the back of her hand to it and realized she was bleeding. 'It's nothing.'

He called up the crater and more ropes were thrown down with a harness attached. 'Let's be having you,' the warden said, and, cheeks burning with humiliation, she got off the bed. She was surprised to see more glass shards glinting on the sheet. Drops of blood too, for she had more small cuts elsewhere.

She was helped into the harness.

'My case!' she cried, spotting it. 'And my shoe!'

But she shouldn't be worrying these men about personal possessions at a time like this. They were risking their lives to save hers. 'Sorry,' she said.

'It's all right, love. It's the shock,' the second warden said, then he yelled upwards again. 'Right you are, chaps!'

Naomi found herself being lifted off the ground. She closed her eyes and clung to the ropes, afraid but also wishing she was less sturdy and easier to haul. After only moments hands were guiding her to safety. The harness was removed and a blanket was wrapped around her before she was steered on to a stretcher. 'Thank you! Thank you, so much,' she gabbled. Absurdly, her teeth were chattering though the night was warm.

Two new men carried her to the pavement across the street. 'It was a bomb?' she managed to ask.

'Spect so,' one told her. 'There must be hundreds – maybe even thousands – of unexploded bombs all over London, left over from the Blitz.'

At least it hadn't been an air raid. She glanced across the road and saw that she'd been right about the damage the bomb had caused. One lower corner of the hotel looked as though it had been gouged out by a monster. It was the same with the building next door. The bomb must have fallen between them and lain hidden for months until the collision between the car and motorbike had dislodged it or set off vibrations that had made it explode. The car had been blown on to its side and a man she took to be the owner was staring at it in dismay. At least he hadn't been hurt.

'Let's take a look at you, madam,' someone said.

Naomi looked around to see a woman in dark uniform. The letters LAAS appeared on a badge stitched to the front of her hat. 'Ambulance Service,' she

340

explained. 'London Auxiliary. We'll soon have you in hospital.'

'Thank you, but I don't need hospital,' Naomi assured her.

It struck Naomi then that she was far from home in ruined clothes, with no shoes and no money. What was she to do?

'If she isn't going to hospital, bring her in here,' someone else said.

Bring her in where?

The stretcher was picked up again and Naomi was taken into the hotel on the opposite side of the road from the Ruston. What was the name of it? Brewster's, she recalled.

Inside someone was sweeping glass from a broken window but no other damage appeared to have been sustained. 'Has anyone been hurt?' Naomi asked.

'Not seriously,' someone told her. 'A miracle when you think about it.'

The warden she'd first seen came up. 'Yours, I believe.' He set her suitcase beside her – sadly battered and scuffed but intact – and the single shoe she'd spotted. Not that it was any use without its partner.

'Thank you so much!'

'Got the other shoe!' his colleague cried, following. 'These, too – which I'm sure you'll be glad to have back.'

He passed over her handbag – dusty and scratched – and also her gas mask in its now-dented tin.

'Thank you so much!' She was saying the same words over and over, touched by the kindness of strangers and perhaps a little hysterical too. She

341

began to feel a fraud, lying on a stretcher, and got up to be helped to a seat and given brandy. It steadied her a little.

'Is there anyone we should telephone for you?' a woman asked.

Naomi saw nothing to be gained by reporting what had happened to anyone in Churchwood. There'd be time for that when she returned. 'No, thank you, but this is a hotel, I believe?'

'Brewster's, madam.'

'Might I have a room for the night? I have money.'

'There's no need to pay. The bomb wasn't your fault.'

'It wasn't the fault of Brewster's either. Really, I insist on paying.'

She was allocated a room and helped up to it, touched again by the compassion of the hotel staff who waited for her to undress, then took away her clothes and shoes for laundering and polishing. She'd lost her coat and umbrella but, miraculously, the contents of her suitcase had survived.

She was glad to sink into a hot bath and wash the grubbiness from her body and hair. But when she went to bed, sleep was further from her than ever. She must have dozed eventually because she woke clinging on to the bed and believing she was falling, falling, falling, while her ears rang from a boom and a painful, high-pitched buzzing.

She was up early the next morning. She felt shaky, stiff, and sore from the small cuts and the dust that must have blown into her eyes. But she'd come to London for a purpose and, bomb or no bomb, she was going to see it through.

# CHAPTER FORTY-THREE

## *Naomi*

Few people were stirring when Naomi went downstairs and asked the hotel to hold her room for the day. Breakfast wasn't yet being served at Brewster's so she decided to head towards Euston Road, certain that cafés would be open near the train station. Waiting for the doorman to call her a taxi, she studied the ruined corner of the Ruston again, and fought down a wave of weakness at the memory of what had happened and how very much worse she might have fared. The upper floors were now being supported on props and it looked likely that the Ruston wouldn't be accommodating guests for some time to come.

A taxi approached, the doorman called it over and she left him with a tip.

In a tiny café near Euston Station, she ordered scrambled eggs. Powdered eggs, but still food. Not that she was hungry, but she wouldn't be able to get through the day without fuel inside her. She also sipped on a cup of tea, but, fearing she might need the bathroom at an inconvenient moment, she left most of it behind. She also bought a bun in a paper bag and slipped it into her bag for later.

By seven she was in another taxi outside James Mansions, not wanting to miss Alexander if he left the flat early. The closed curtains suggested he hadn't yet risen – or so she hoped. Was there a woman lying beside him in Naomi's bed? Naomi pushed the thought away. There was nothing to be gained by torturing herself, and besides, she needed to concentrate on the comings and goings at the door.

Half an hour later the curtains were opened in the drawing room and kitchen. It wasn't possible to see what was happening in the bedroom and bathroom as they overlooked the rear of the building.

Not until midday did Alexander emerge, and he was alone. He hailed a taxi and Naomi instructed her driver to follow it, ignoring the knowing look he gave her. Alexander's taxi led them to Bloomsbury and pulled up outside Marcroft's Hotel, not far from the Ruston and Brewster's where Naomi had spent her ill-fated night. She watched Alexander pay off his taxi, walk up the hotel steps with the sort of bounce she rarely saw in him and pass through the open doors.

'You'll never find out what he's up to if you sit here,' Naomi's driver pointed out.

He was right but she was feeling the urge to flee. What would she do if she walked in and saw him with another woman? There was much about her life that she liked – her house, her friends . . . Why not simply focus on enjoying what she had instead of wasting energy on what she didn't? Wasn't ignorance bliss?

No, actually. For months she'd tried to persuade herself to close her eyes to whatever was happening in Alexander's life, but it hadn't worked. She *had* to know.

The driver coughed as though to remind her of his

presence. Naomi scrabbled in her bag, took out her purse and handed over both the eye-watering fare and a large tip.

The driver's eyes widened. 'Thanks, missis. Eddie Gumtree's the name. Look me up next time you want your 'usband followed.'

Naomi got out and stood on the pavement, looking up at the hotel, a small but exclusive-looking concern that occupied several properties in a tall Georgian terrace. It occurred to her that if Alexander came out again, he couldn't fail to see her. The thought sent her scurrying up the steps in search of cover. A commissionaire in green-and-gold livery bowed as she entered. Naomi attempted a stiff smile, continued into the foyer and scooted behind a large potted palm.

It was a large room, furnished with sofas and armchairs. Alexander wasn't sitting in any of them and neither had he approached the mahogany reception desk, but Naomi realized the staff member who stood behind it was watching her curiously. Straightening, she stepped from behind the plant while sending him a smile that she hoped would reassure him that she was a sane, confident woman, then stepped from behind the plant.

What next? A pair of double doors with glass set into their upper halves appeared to lead into a restaurant. Naomi moved towards them and peered through the glass, readying herself to duck back out of sight if she spotted Alexander. She *did* spot him. At least she thought she did. It was impossible to be sure based on a glimpse of a dark-suited shoulder and one long leg.

Concentrating on trying to identify the man, she

didn't notice the waiter approaching from inside the restaurant until he stood only inches away on the far side of the glass. He opened the doors. 'Madam requires luncheon?'

Naomi's mouth opened and closed a couple of times before she got out, 'That's right.'

'Let me show you to a table.'

'That one.' She pointed to a small table that was not only in a corner but could also be reached without crossing the line of sight of the man who might be Alexander. It also offered the camouflage of another potted palm. 'Please,' she added, seeing that her vehemence had startled him.

'Certainly, madam.'

He ushered her to the table, and she sat down quickly, moving her chair to gain more coverage from the plant. The waiter offered her a menu, but she was too flustered to read it.

'Just something light, please.'

'We have plaice.' The waiter's tone was proud because fish was hard to come by now German U-boats were playing havoc with British fishing fleets.

'Yes, plaice. Excellent.'

'The soup is—'

'No soup, thank you. But a glass of wine would be welcome.' It might help to steady her nerves. 'The house white wine will be acceptable.'

Naomi was relieved when he bowed and walked away because she feared he was drawing attention to her.

Carefully, she peered between the palm fronds and felt a jolt as she saw the man was definitely Alexander. She could see his patrician profile, with the large but distinguished nose that gave him the appearance of looking down on people. A fitting nose really, as he often felt people to be beneath his notice, not least Naomi's friends.

But who were the others with him? He sat at a circular table with four chairs around it, and all four were occupied. Opposite him sat a woman. Not in the first flush of youth – perhaps in her late thirties – though time had treated her kindly. Her figure might once have been slimmer but there was something soft and feminine in its slight roundness now. She'd also retained the fair-haired, blue-eyed prettiness that must have made her stunning in her youth.

On one side of her was a girl of around fifteen or so – too long and angular to be pretty, though adulthood might bring her elegance. On the other side sat a boy. Naomi couldn't see his face but guessed him to be a little older and not yet comfortable with his long thin legs and arms.

It was unlikely that a woman who was having an affair with Alexander would bring her children along to a tryst with him. Perhaps she was a client, a widow needing advice on her financial affairs. Should Naomi sidle away now and put this nonsensical surveillance behind her? Alexander would be furious if he discovered she was following him, particularly if he caught her while a client was present.

She began to get up, intending to cancel her order on her way out, but she'd left it too late. The waiter arrived at her table with a silver tray on which stood her glass of wine.

'Thank you,' Naomi told him. 'I hadn't realized it was so late and I have an appointment soon. If you could bring my bill so it's ready for when I leave . . . ?'

347

'Certainly, madam.'

She took a sip of wine but in her agitated state began to choke. Water. She needed water but she didn't dare to make a fuss by calling the waiter over in case Alexander turned and saw her. She got through the choking in silence, then took out a handkerchief to dab at her eyes, which had filled with tears.

'Oh, Papa!' she heard.

Naomi froze. *Papa*?

It was the gangly boy who'd spoken. But surely she'd misheard? Perhaps his sister was called Poppy or—

The boy turned to Alexander and for the first time Naomi saw his face in profile. The nose was large. A patrician nose. Almost identical to Alexander's.

Now the girl spoke. 'Could we go shopping after lunch, Papa? I need a new pen.'

She too had something of Alexander in her thin face and long frame.

Naomi felt nausea rise in her throat. She grabbed her bag, found her purse and threw some money on to the table – far more than was needed – then moved swiftly to the door.

'The cloakroom?' she asked at the reception desk and hastened in the direction indicated, bursting into a cubicle just in time to vomit into the toilet.

She'd have been appalled enough to learn that Alexander was having an affair, even if it had begun only recently. To learn that for twenty years, if not longer – perhaps all through their twenty-six-year marriage – Alexander had had a secret family ... There were no words for the level of devastation Naomi felt.

She had to get away from this place. She wiped her

mouth, pulled the toilet chain and left the cubicle to dampen a handkerchief at a sink and wipe away the sheen of perspiration that had coated her face in sickly clamminess. She didn't linger, though, fearful that Alexander's woman or daughter might appear at any moment. Instead, she opened the door a crack, checked that the coast was clear, then made her way out of the hotel and into a world that had shifted on its axis.

Her legs were unsteady and her emotions in turmoil. With no thought of a destination but only of putting distance between herself and Marcroft's Hotel, she set off along the road, then turned down another street at the first opportunity. The weakness worsened to trembling. She needed to sit down, but where? On someone's doorstep? Hardly.

She pressed onwards, regretting that she hadn't asked the hotel doorman to hail a taxi for her, but there was no way she was going back. She entered one of London's leafy squares and was relieved to see that the garden in the middle wasn't closed off by railings. Inside she found a bench and sat down.

The initial shock was wearing off, but other emotions were rushing in to take its place. Anger, for one. How dare Alexander treat her as a source of cash instead of a living, breathing human being with feelings? Humiliation too. What kind of fool could be married to a man for more than a quarter of a century without realizing he was building a family elsewhere? And then there was hurt. To be used and abused with such utter disrespect – with contempt, in fact – was more than wounding, it was devastating.

Had he and his woman laughed at Naomi behind

her back? Mocked her attempts to entice and please him?

Another emotion jostled for space inside her: a lacerating sense of loss for the children she'd never had – and would never have now she was forty-six.

'As far as I can tell, you're perfectly normal,' a gynaecologist had told her when she'd been married for three years with no sign of a child and felt desperate enough to submit to a probing and embarrassing examination. 'Sometimes these things can take a while.'

He'd paused, then added: 'Of course, sometimes the problem can lie with the husband. Perhaps Mr Harrington would like to come and see me.'

Mr Harrington had not liked to go and see him. 'For heaven's sake, Naomi,' he'd said. 'Aren't I enough for you?'

'Of course you are,' she'd assured him hastily, not liking to see him so irritated.

'Well, then.'

A few years later she'd seen a different gynaecologist. He too had found no obvious reason why she shouldn't conceive a child. And he too had suggested that Alexander attend for examination. 'Of course, some men don't like to entertain the idea that their bodies might be functioning less than perfectly. A man and his virility . . .' He'd smiled ruefully as though it was a problem he'd encountered often.

Then he'd given a delicate cough. 'Of course, I'm assuming relations between you and your husband are . . . normal?'

Naomi had blushed scarlet. 'Yes,' she'd rushed to say. 'Oh, certainly.'

350

But the truth was that she'd had no idea what normal meant when it came to marital relations. Even so she'd suspected that Alexander's infrequent visits to her bedroom – sometimes many months apart – hadn't constituted what the doctor would consider normal for two people who wanted a baby.

Alexander's lack of interest in having a child with Naomi made sense now she knew he'd preferred to become a parent with the pretty fair-haired woman instead. All those years of desperate longing – the rivers of tears Naomi had shed – and meanwhile Alexander had been fathering two children elsewhere.

Doubtless, he'd have held them in his arms as babies, admiring their tiny, cherubic faces and pink fingernails. A year or so later he'd have held out his arms to encourage their first steps and they'd have nestled their soft faces into his neck or looked up at him with wide-eyed wonder as he'd read them stories. A few years further on he'd have shared conversations with them as he'd guided them through the world.

Back in Churchwood, Naomi had meant nothing more than a bank to him, a bank he could draw upon to top up his own income and provide a home for this family. Had Naomi paid for the medical care that had brought those children into the world? Had she paid for their fees at prestigious schools? Had she even paid for the woman's smart hat?

Pain racked Naomi's body and she couldn't stop herself from doubling over as sobs broke out. How could Alexander be so heartless? Her entire adult life felt wasted. A mockery. She'd lost her chance of a child because Alexander wanted only to use her.

Gradually the sobs subsided, leaving a headache behind. She got to her feet unsteadily and set off in search of the train station as she needed to get away from London and Alexander as soon as possible. But she hadn't gone far before she had to lean a hand against a lamppost, feeling in danger of collapse.

'Hey, missis!'

Oh, no. Attention was the last thing her battered dignity needed. A taxi had pulled in to the kerb. The driver was looking out and something about him stirred her memory. Of course. It was the same cabbie as this morning, but she was in no mood for a chat.

Intending to assure him that she was fine, Naomi pushed away from the lamppost only to feel herself swaying. She reached for the lamppost again.

The taxi door opened. Closed. Footsteps approached; then the driver was at her side. 'Come on, missis. In you get.'

'No, really—'

'Don't argue. You're in no fit state.'

He helped her into the back of the taxi. 'Saw what you didn't want to see, I suppose. Some 'usbands are like that. Some wives too. We're better off without 'em.'

Unfaithfulness was bad enough, but what Alexander had done went far beyond that. It was as though he'd swept over her life and razed it down to bare earth. Barren earth.

'A hot cuppa won't mend what's just been broken but it won't hurt either,' the driver said.

'The station,' Naomi told him. 'I can get tea near the station. St Pancras, if you please, but first I need to call at Brewster's Hotel.'

'Right you are.'

He drove to Brewster's and made sure her legs didn't buckle when she stepped on to the pavement. He waited while she paid her bill and fetched her case, and then he drove her to the station.

'No charge, missis,' he said when she offered money. 'You were generous enough before and one good turn deserves another.'

'You're very kind.' And kindness at this most vulnerable moment had more tears forming in her eyes.

She got out of the taxi before he could see them.

'Need a hand to a café?' he asked.

'Thank you, but I'll manage.'

'Promise you'll get that cuppa?'

'I will.'

She did buy it, too, cradling the warm cup in her hands as though trying to draw comfort from it. None came.

The thought of returning to Churchwood in this state filled her with dread – until she remembered that she'd be able to blame her ravaged appearance on last night's explosion. After all, she'd arrive at home with cuts and bruises to her person as well as a battered suitcase, gas-mask holder and handbag.

She wouldn't mention Alexander to anyone. Her friends would be all kind concern, but Naomi couldn't bear their sympathy just now. Not when every cell in her body was smarting with humiliation and hurt. What she needed was to take to her bed and retire from the world to lick her wounds until she decided on a way forward.

In time she hauled her stiff body to her feet, caught the train to St Albans, and from there took the bus that was headed to Churchwood, thankful to see only strangers. Thoughts whirled around her head. All those evenings and weekends when Alexander had said he was seeing clients or playing golf . . . How many had he spent with his secret family? Sometimes he'd been away for a week or more. He'd told her he was visiting far-flung golf courses but doubtless he'd been taking holidays with that woman and their children, building sandcastles on beaches and strolling along promenades to enjoy the bracing sea air. How easily the lies had slipped through his treacherous lips.

Reaching the village, Naomi got off the bus and set off for Foxfield. She'd never been a good walker but today she felt as though she'd aged another forty years in just a few hours. Her progress was slow and laboured.

'Lovely evening,' William Treloar called from his garden.

'Yes, lovely,' Naomi called back, but she continued trudging onwards.

It was a relief to step between the Foxfield gate-posts at last. She let herself into the house to give herself a few more seconds in which to brace herself before she had to face the staff. Suki must have heard her, though, because she hastened out of the kitchen, only to pull up short. 'Oh, madam! What's happened?'

Basil came out of the sitting room too, looking at his mistress with mournful, anxious eyes. Naomi took a deep breath. 'I had an unfortunate experience with an unexploded bomb. There's nothing seriously wrong with me but I'd like to rest for a while.'

'Of course, madam. Shall I bring you some tea?'

'No, thank you, Suki. I think I'll just sleep.'

She climbed the stairs on leaden feet, faithful Basil beside her. Naomi wanted no other company. Not now and perhaps not for a very long time indeed.

# CHAPTER FORTY-FOUR

## *Kate*

Life really did know how to take with one hand while giving with the other.

Kate had been appalled to hear that there was no longer any hope for the bookshop. Alice had walked up Brimbles Lane to tell her.

'I'm so sorry, Alice,' Kate had said. 'You put such a lot of work into starting it, and it's done so much good to so many people. I'm one of them.'

Having spent the first nineteen years of her life feeling angry, miserable and lonely, meeting Alice and making more friends through the bookshop had made Kate happy and given her some confidence. Without that confidence, she would have run a mile from Leo Kinsella.

The bookshop had also given purpose and pleasure to Alice. It was cruel of the Fates to snatch that from her at the same time as she was parted from Daniel.

On the other hand, the Fates had brought Leo into Kate's life. The very thought of him gave her joy, and in the days since the dance at the Red Lion, her mind had returned countless times to the warmth of his smile, the glow of his eyes, and his kisses. Especially his kisses.

She'd felt changed by them somehow. More womanly and more mature, though she'd hoped she looked unchanged when she walked into the farm-house kitchen after the dance.

Ernie had wasted no time in being the first to speak. 'Where've you been?' he'd snarled.

'With friends,' Kate had retorted, judging it better to appear truculent. 'You wouldn't know anything about friends, though. Not having any of your own.'

'You'd better not be doing something you shouldn't.'

Kate had only rolled her eyes to show Ernie he was being ridiculous.

She'd walked to the kitchen sink to fill a glass with water and realized someone had washed up the dishes. Kate had left potatoes and a vegetable pie cooking in the oven when she'd left, announcing that they'd all have to fend for themselves for once, but she'd expected to return to a sink full of dirty dishes.

'Ruby and I cleared up,' Pearl had said proudly. 'I washed and she dried. And guess what? I didn't break anything.'

'It was Ruby's idea,' Kenny had said, and Ruby had preened with self-satisfaction.

'Just trying to be helpful.'

Putting on an act in front of Ernie, more likely. Still, she and Pearl had saved Kate a job and for that she'd been grateful. 'Thank you.'

She'd got a few things ready for the morning then gone up to bed, lying back to relive the evening and cherish the feeling of being cocooned in velvet happiness.

A week had passed since then, a week in which she'd exchanged more letters with Leo, delighted to receive confirmation that he was as enthusiastic about her as she was about him. Kate worried for him, though. Twice in that week she'd seen planes passing overhead. Each time she'd wondered if Leo was among the pilots and whether they were merely practising or out on missions. Would someone at the base have been counting the planes as they left and then counting them again as they returned, hoping that the numbers would balance?

Throwing grain to the chickens this Sunday morning, she heard the bells of St Luke's. Would many people be going along to the service? Kate had never been to a service in her life but might have been tempted with someone like Adam as vicar. She'd have felt comfortable with Adam, knowing he'd excuse her ignorance of rituals and make her feel welcome. The Forsyths had the opposite effect on her. They were all too ready to find fault and deplore it.

The day continued as most Sundays did, Kate working as hard as ever to earn the right to snatch moments of free time in which to see Leo when he was next able to come to Churchwood, and also to see the friends she was neglecting. Alice must be feeling the bookshop's ending terribly. May must be missing Marek now his leave had ended, and Naomi had been out of sorts for weeks. Hopefully, her visit to London would have done her some good.

After lunch, Kenny and Ruby went off without saying where they were going and hadn't returned by the time Kate brewed tea and cut bread and jam for everyone else. 'Tuck in, Tim,' Pearl urged, having been left in charge of the boy for the afternoon.

She reached an eager hand to the bread and Timmy took a slice too, but slowly, with none of his usual enthusiasm for food. Kate frowned and studied him more closely. Was she imagining that he looked flushed and heavy-eyed? 'Are you feeling unwell, Timmy?' she asked.

Pearl swelled up defensively, shooting a wary glance in Ernie's direction as Kate's question had made him turn suspicious eyes to the boy. Ernie wouldn't welcome illness in the house. 'Timmy's fine,' Pearl insisted. 'Aren't you, Tim?'

He nodded.

'Told you,' Pearl crowed. 'Eat up, Timmy.'

Kate wasn't as easily satisfied. 'Have you checked if he's running a temperature?'

'Eh?' Pearl looked alarmed.

'Does his forehead feel hot to the touch?'

Pearl stretched a cautious fingertip to Timmy's head.

'You need to use more than one finger,' Kate told her. 'Do you want me to—'

'I can do it.' She pressed her palm against him. 'Feels fine to me. Anyway, Ruby wouldn't have gone out if Timmy were sickening for something.'

'That's right, I wouldn't.' Ruby swept into the room, obviously annoyed at having her sisterly qualities doubted.

Kate sighed. What rotten timing. 'I simply pointed out that Timmy looks unwell.'

'Meaning that I'm too useless to notice if my brother is sick. Well, he's perfectly fine.' Ruby sat down beside him and cuddled him. 'For your information, Timmy had a bad dream last night. It woke him up and now he's feeling tired.'

'You see?' Kenny said, as though Kate had been motivated by malice.

So much for trying to help. Kate would mind her own business in future.

Timmy still wasn't back to his energetic self by morning as far as Kate could tell but at least he could have a lazy day at home, the school summer holiday having recently begun. That morning Kate worked in a field that bordered Brimbles Lane to be sure of catching Alice if she passed on her way to the hospital. Spotting her, Kate ran over. 'How are you, Alice?'

'Coping.' Her mouth twisted ruefully. 'We have to cope, don't we? I still have my job and I still have my visits to the hospital to keep me busy.'

'How have the patients taken the news about the bookshop?'

'With disappointment. They loved getting out to bookshop socials and so did the staff. At least I can keep books circulating round the hospital, though without bookshop fundraising it'll be hard to buy new ones or replace any that fall apart or go missing.'

'It's such a shame,' Kate said, but they both knew that lamenting the situation wouldn't change it.

'Have you heard any more from Leo?' Alice asked.

'I've had a letter. Hopefully, I'll see him again soon. Hopefully, you'll have news of Daniel soon, too.'

'Hopefully,' Alice echoed. 'I imagine you haven't heard about Naomi yet?'

'Is she back from London? Did she have a nice time?'

'The answer to your first question is yes, but the

answer to your second question is no. Apparently, she was caught by an unexploded bomb going off.'

'*What?*'

'She escaped with minor cuts and bruises, according to Suki, but she's badly shaken up.'

'Who wouldn't be?'

'I haven't seen her yet. She was keeping to her bed when I took flowers round.'

'Poor thing. You'll let me know if you hear more? And you'll give her my love if you see her?'

'Of course I will.'

Alice continued to Stratton House and Kate returned to work, thinking that she'd drop some soft fruits off for Naomi at the first opportunity. Anything to make Naomi feel comforted.

Kate was outside later that afternoon when she saw Timmy crossing the farmyard to the house. His steps were slow and his shoulders were hunched miserably. Either something had happened to upset him or he really was unwell. Kate worked for a few minutes longer, then went inside to make the tea.

Ruby was already there though it wasn't yet her break time. She was whispering something to Timmy, but she turned and tilted her chin defiantly. 'I know there's work to be done and I'll make up the time so there's no need to look disapproving.'

'I wasn't aware that I *was* looking disapproving.'

Ruby didn't answer.

'If Timmy isn't well, I could ask my friend Alice's father to come up. He's a retired doctor.'

'Is he indeed? There's no need for a doctor, retired or otherwise. As I said before Timmy arrived, he's never ill. Not seriously anyway.'

Was pride keeping Ruby from admitting that her brother was unwell? Or did she fear Ernie would send Timmy away if she failed to deliver on her promise of his good health? For Timmy's sake, Kate hoped neither was true, and that Ruby was simply the best judge of her brother's condition.

'Sit at the table and draw,' Ruby told him. 'You know you like drawing.'

Timmy sat down while Ruby fetched a sheet of scrap paper and a pencil from the dresser. The boy was facing away from Kate so she couldn't see his face but she took it as a good sign when he picked the pencil up and began to draw what looked from a distance to be a horse.

Pearl and the Fletcher men came in for tea and Ruby went with them when they returned to work. Kate washed up, then stood looking at the back of Timmy's head. 'You'll call one of us if you don't feel well?' she asked.

Timmy nodded but said nothing and Kate went out to work too. But even as she mended chicken wire, worry about him wouldn't leave her. Eventually, she crept up to the house to peer through the kitchen window. Timmy wasn't drawing any more. He had his arms on the table and he was resting his head on them.

Kate stepped inside and walked around the table so she could see his face. 'Timmy, I know you're trying to be brave but you're really not well, are you?'

He shook his head, fighting back tears. Then he began to cough.

Ruby must have noticed Kate's return because she burst into the kitchen. 'What are you doing?'

'Talking to your brother. This is your idea of a child who's fine?'

Ruby crossed to Timmy, folded him into her arms then tested his temperature with a hand against his forehead. 'Oh,' she said.

'Yes, oh,' Kate echoed.

Timmy coughed again and his eyes streamed. 'I don't feel well,' he said.

'You've got a cold,' Ruby told him. 'You must have caught it from Colin at school. Didn't you say he'd caught a cold when he visited his cousin? In Luton, wasn't it?'

Timmy managed a nod.

'Do you want me to fetch Dr Lovell?' Kate asked.

'For a cold? I can manage.'

'Please yourself.'

'Let's get you tucked up in bed,' Ruby told her brother.

He got up slowly.

'I can't work any more today,' Ruby said, sounding vexed with the situation. 'I need to look after him.'

'Clearly,' Kate agreed, then took pity on Ruby and added, 'It's nearly the end of the working day anyway.'

Kate finished off her outside work and made the dinner. Pearl and the Fletcher men drifted in. 'Pearl, would you mind asking Ruby if she's coming down for dinner or if she'd prefer a tray upstairs?' Kate asked. 'Timmy too. I can boil him an egg if he hasn't much appetite.'

Pearl went upstairs and returned a few minutes later. 'She says I'm to take a tray up for both of them.'

Pearl was to take the tray. Not Kate.

'She doesn't want to be a bother,' Pearl added, with a wary glance at Ernie, who was scowling.

Doubtless, the words *No work, no pay* were circulating in his mind.

Kate prepared a tray for Ruby and Pearl took it up, returning to eat her own dinner. Afterwards, Kate stacked the dishes ready for washing. 'Pearl, could you go up and fetch Ruby and Timmy's plates, please? If they've finished eating.'

'I'll go.' Kenny got up and left the room.

When he returned his expression was sombre.

'I'm going to fetch Dr Lovell,' Kate said.

She grabbed her jacket and ran out to the bicycle, cursing herself for not insisting on calling the doctor earlier.

Minutes later she knocked on the cottage door. Alice opened it. 'Kate! What a lovely—'

'Sorry, Alice, but I need your father. Little Timmy is ill.'

Dr Lovell must have overheard because he emerged from his study. 'The child is at the farm? I'll fetch my bag and be right with you.'

'Is there anything I can do to help?' Alice asked.

'I don't know, to be honest. But come anyway, if you can. I can drop you and your father home in the trap.'

Soon they were walking at speed up Brimbles Lane. 'You go on ahead, Kate. Tell the boy's sister we're on our way,' Dr Lovell said.

Kate got back on to her bicycle and hastened off. Kenny was looking out for her anxiously. 'The doctor's coming now,' she told him. 'How's Timmy?'

'He doesn't look good to me, and Ruby is worried.'

Dr Lovell went straight upstairs when he arrived, Kate and Alice following. 'Well, young man, let's have a look at you,' he told Timmy.

'What is it?' Ruby demanded. 'What's wrong with him?'

He took Timmy's temperature, listened to his chest, studied his face and looked inside his mouth. Then he tucked Timmy up again. 'You'll do,' Dr Lovell told the boy, but his face was sober as he beckoned everyone else to follow him from the room.

Outside on the landing, he turned to Ruby. 'It's measles,' he announced.

'Measles? But Timmy hasn't got a rash. I'd have noticed.'

'He has white spots in his mouth and the rash will follow.'

'Right,' Ruby said, swallowing. 'But measles isn't serious? I had it when I was a kid. I don't remember much about it, but I got well again, so Timmy will get well again too, yes?'

'Most children who catch measles recover with no lasting damage,' Dr Lovell said.

'But some don't?' There was an edge of panic in Ruby's voice and her eyes were wild with it.

'Timmy is . . . what? Seven?'

'Yes, seven. Can you give him some medicine? I'll pay anything.'

'There isn't any medicine for measles. But he's past the age when measles is of most concern, and I'm sure you'll nurse him well.'

'What must I do?'

'Close the curtains to protect his eyes from the light. Give him as much water as he can take. Keep his temperature down with cool flannels. And call me if there's any change. Or call Dr Lambert from Barton. He's the local doctor. I'm retired so you may prefer—'

'I'll call you, if that's all right? You're closer and . . . Well, I suppose I trust you.'

'Thank you. There'll be no fee so don't let money hold you back from asking for help. I'll look in on him again soon.'

'Thank you.'

'Just one more thing. I suggest you notify your parents and ask them to come.'

Ruby stiffened at that suggestion. Did she fear her parents would blame her for letting Timmy fall sick?

Kate saw Alice and her father to the door. 'Ruby's parents can stay with us at the cottage as you haven't room for them here,' Alice said. 'They needn't worry about the cost and trouble of finding accommodation.'

'I'll tell her. Thank you for coming so quickly.'

Neither Alice nor her father wanted Kate to bother taking them home in the trap, so she went back upstairs. Ruby looked surprised by Alice's offer – grateful, even – but seemed no less reluctant to get her parents involved. 'It isn't your fault that Timmy's ill,' Kate pointed out.

Ruby only shrugged.

'Ernie will have to know that Timmy's ill and you're not working today. There's no way of keeping it from him.'

'It may actually be a few days before I can work again,' Ruby said, her expression a mix of worry, disappointment and vexation, 'but I'll make up for it.' She looked at Kate with an echo of her old hostility

366

but with something approaching sincerity too. 'You don't need to point out that I've promised that before. This time I mean it.'

'If your parents come, they can nurse Timmy,' Kate said.

While Ernie wouldn't like strangers at the farm, he'd prefer their presence in the house to Ruby's absence from the fields. Kate sensed that Ruby was very much aware of that fact. But it didn't appear to lessen her determination to look after Timmy herself.

Kate headed for the bedroom door. 'Help yourself to anything you need in the way of food, drinks, towels and such,' she said, then went to tell Ernie the joyful news that his workforce was depleted for the foreseeable future.

# CHAPTER FORTY-FIVE

## *Alice*

'Timmy must have caught the measles from someone else,' Alice's father pointed out as they walked home from Brimbles Farm. 'It takes about ten days from infection before symptoms develop so he must have been mixing with other children at school and else-where. It's likely that other children have caught it too. We need to track them down to ensure they're getting the care they need.'

'I'll get straight on to it,' Alice assured him.

As the school had just closed for the summer, she started with May. 'How are Rosa, Samuel and Zofia faring?'

'Now you mention it, Samuel isn't feeling all that marvellous.'

Alice advised her of the symptoms to look out for and how to nurse the boy. 'Thank goodness you called,' May said. 'I don't know the first thing about measles, or nursing.'

'I've drawn up a list of other Churchwood children so I can warn all the families. Could you run an eye over it to check I haven't missed anyone out? You could check if I've got the addresses right too.'

May took hold of Alice's list. 'I can't think of any other families. The Larkins are at number eight, not number six. I don't know the number of the Palmers' house but it's the one with pink roses growing across the front.'

'Thank you,' Alice said, feeling she was making progress. 'I'll leave you to look after Samuel now but don't hesitate to ask if you want my father to call, or if you'd like me to take Rosa and Zofia off your hands for a while.'

She called on Janet next. Janet's children were grown, but she had grandchildren in Churchwood and had lived in the village all of her life. 'We'll reach more families faster if I help,' Janet said. 'Let's divide the list between us.'

'You're a treasure, Janet.'

'Pulling together is what Churchwood does best. Or rather what it used to do best.'

They agreed to meet up later that afternoon so they could go through the list again and work out which families hadn't yet been visited.

It was tiring work. Leaving Janet to visit the families closest to home, Alice went further afield, worried about the people who didn't have neighbours nearby so might struggle to call for help. Few people had telephones.

She headed first for the cottage of Hattie Maddocks, the young widow who lived with her mother and three children on the very outskirts of Churchwood. Alice had helped her family through illness once before and she was glad that she'd called again because Hattie almost fell on her neck in relief. 'I've been praying for someone to call. My mother has gone to stay at my sister's, and I don't see anyone now the school has closed and the bookshop too. My

Sal's sick again and I can't leave her to get to the shops.'

'I'm here to help.' Alice explained about the measles that might be circulating around the village.

'We haven't had measles in Churchwood since I was a girl,' Hattie said. 'I expect all the children will go down with it together. Oh, heavens!'

'You must need some shopping,' Alice said, and with Hattie's help she drew up a list.

Returning to the village to buy supplies, Alice was pleased to see Bert pull up beside her in his truck. 'What's this I'm hearing about measles?' he asked.

Alice filled him in. 'I've just been shopping for the Maddocks family.'

'Pass that basket to me and I'll head up there in the truck. It'll save your feet and leave you free to call on other families. You know more about sickness and nursing than I do.'

'Thank you. I'm meeting Janet later. Perhaps you'd like to join us?'

'I would. We need to start pulling together again.'

'Naomi . . . ?' Alice began.

'I'm not sure she's up to helping out just now.'

'I haven't seen her since she returned from London. Perhaps I'll call again just to see how she is, but I won't ask her to help.'

'Until later then,' Bert said, and he moved off in the truck.

By the end of the afternoon, it was clear that several children were already ill, and it was probable that more would fall ill soon. Bert and Janet came along to The Linnets and Alice's father joined them. A few minutes later, so did Adam Potts. 'Rumours have reached Barton of a measles outbreak,' he said. 'Is there anything I can do to help? In a personal capacity, I mean. I don't want to tread on Reverend Forsyth's toes.'

Looks passed between Alice, Bert and Janet. None of them had even thought to involve the Forsyths. 'I reckon that says everything that needs to be said about our feelings for the new vicar and his lady,' Bert said. 'But I'm sure I speak for all of us when I say we'll welcome your kind of support, young Adam. Folk will want practical help and comfort more than preaching just now.'

They drew up more lists – of families who needed visits from Dr Lovell, families who needed help with shopping, families who needed someone to sit with their sick child while they caught up on sleep, and families who needed help with their other children.

'I'm sure folk will trust us with their ration books, and we can explain in the shops why we've got them,' Bert said. 'We've got a lot to do but we'll manage.'

Alice called at Foxfield again later.

'I'm afraid madam still can't be disturbed,' Suki told her.

'I understand. You'll tell her that her friends are thinking of her and wishing her well?'

'Of course, miss.'

'Please give her these flowers too.' Alice had picked another posy of blooms from the cottage garden. Naomi had many more flowers in her own garden, but it was the thought that counted. 'Don't hesitate to call my father out to Mrs Harrington if she doesn't improve. In fact, perhaps my father should look her over anyway.'

'It's kind of you to suggest it, miss. I've suggested it too, but madam says all she needs is peace and quiet.'

'Very well. But if she hasn't improved by tomorrow . . .'

Kate called at the cottage later that evening and heard all about the plans that had been put in place to help Churchwood through the crisis. 'Ruby is following your father's advice to the last detail,' she reported. 'For all her faults, she really cares about Timmy. Do say if this isn't convenient but I wonder . . . If Ruby doesn't change her mind about getting her parents here, might you give Pearl a bed for a few nights? It'll be hard for her to sleep in the same room as a sick child.'

'Of course,' Alice said. 'I should have thought of it myself. In fact, send her along tonight. We can swap things round tomorrow if Ruby changes her mind.'

'Thanks. I'm sorry I can't help here in the village.'

'You're doing more than your fair share of work on the farm. At least we can try to keep Pearl in fine fettle so you don't have her work to do as well.'

'You're a wonderful friend, Alice Lovell.'

'So are you, Kate Fletcher.'

They parted with a hug.

Alone again, Alice's mind boggled at the thought of big, awkward Pearl in the little cottage. It was the sort of thing she'd have liked to mention in a letter to Daniel – along with an account of the response to the measles crisis – but she still had no idea where he was. If only she could be sure that his heart was still beating steadily, wherever he was in the world.

# CHAPTER FORTY-SIX

## *Naomi*

What was it that Suki had just said? She was talking to the cleaning lady down in the hall and a word had reached Naomi's ears that had sounded horribly like 'measles'. She hoped none of the village children were sick.

When Suki came upstairs Naomi called to her.

'Do you want some tea, madam?'

'In a moment. Did I hear you mention measles?'

'I didn't mean to disturb you.' Poor Suki looked stricken.

'Never mind that,' Naomi waved a hand dismissively. 'What's this about measles?'

'It's going around the village.'

'Oh, heavens. Why did no one tell me before?'

'We didn't want to worry you. Anyway, other people are helping out.'

'People?'

'Miss Lovell and her father. Mr Makepiece. Mrs Collins. Not Mrs Janicki as her little boy is sick.'

In other words, the bookshop team. Except for May and Kate, who couldn't help. And Naomi, who'd been lying in bed feeling sorry for herself. 'It's time I got up.'

'Are you sure it isn't too soon, madam? You're still looking pale.'

It wasn't too soon. It was much too late. 'Quite sure, thank you, Suki.' Naomi gestured towards her dressing gown. 'Would you—?'

Someone knocked on the Foxfield front door. 'Shall I go down and answer, madam?'

'Yes, please. But if it's Miss Plym . . .'

'I'll tell her you're still not ready for visitors.'

Suki left and Naomi's conscience struck her. Marjorie had been calling daily and doubtless she meant well but Naomi couldn't face her chatter just at this moment even though she was bracing herself to brave the world again.

She still crumpled inside every time she thought of Alexander's betrayal and the chance she'd lost of marrying a better man if one had come along. The chance she'd lost of having children, too. Boys . . . girls . . . she wouldn't have minded which. Naomi would have cherished any child. It was impossible to imagine this grief would ever ease but it felt cowardly to hide away when other people might need her help. It felt especially cowardly – fraudulent, too – to hide away under the pretext of being sent into shock by a bomb. After all, she'd barely been touched by it. Naomi couldn't help feeling bereft about Alexander, but she could certainly avoid the shame of feeling a coward and a fraud.

Getting out of bed, she wrapped herself in her dressing gown.

A rap came on her door, and Suki entered. 'Dr Lovell to see you, madam.'

'Suki, I don't—'

Too late. Dr Lovell was already walking in. 'Don't blame your maid,' he said, as Suki retreated. 'It was my daughter who insisted I came. Just to be sure nothing serious was troubling you.'

'I've been a little tired, that's all.' Naomi was uncomfortably conscious of her unbrushed hair and pasty face. What a fright she must look.

'That's far from being all. Please sit down, Naomi, and let me examine you.'

'There's really no need. I'm not ill.'

'Why don't I be the judge of that?'

Naomi didn't like to refuse. Not after he'd gone to the bother of calling on her. She sat back down on the bed in surrender.

'I agree with you,' Dr Lovell said a few minutes later. 'You're not sick in your body but in your soul. Am I right?'

Naomi couldn't answer at first. Tears prickled behind her eyelids and her throat grew tight. But she took a deep breath and said, 'I won't insult you by denying it. I'm finding my way through it, however.'

'Don't worry, I shan't pry. But there's something to be said for old proverbs like a trouble shared being a trouble halved. Not literally, of course. But talking really can make a difference. You have friends in Churchwood, Naomi. I hope you'll confide in one of them.'

'Perhaps I shall.'

'Don't fear that I'll mention your troubles to anyone. Not even my daughter. I take my duty of confidentiality seriously.'

'Thank you.' Naomi was grateful, but she needed

375

more thinking time before she shared the sorry story of her marriage. Changing the subject, she asked, 'How are the measles children?'

Dr Lovell took his glasses off and wiped them on a handkerchief. 'I'm worried about a couple of them but not to the point of sending them to hospital, though I won't hesitate to do so if I feel it's necessary. I've seen measles cause terrible damage in children. One little lad I knew went blind and another girl lost her life. But unless something changes, I'm hopeful Churchwood's children will be fine.'

'That's good to hear. Not that it should stop me from getting up and helping.'

'I think it will do you good to get out and about. As long as you don't overdo it.'

'I'll be careful. Alice is the person to speak to about helping, I suppose?'

He smiled. 'You know my daughter!'

'I'll call on her soon.'

She had one other person to call on first. Naomi bathed, dressed and made her way downstairs to ask for some food – the first she'd had in a while. It was ridiculous how a few days in bed had weakened her. She needed to rebuild her strength – for the sake of the village and for her own sake too. She couldn't reach a decision about Alexander while her mind was fuzzy.

'Perhaps you could bring some of the flowers down from my room?' she asked Suki.

Churchwood's gardens and residents had been generous with sending bouquets and posies to wish Naomi a rapid recovery. Several had been accompanied by notes, including one that said:

*I've heard about the German bomb but I can't help wondering if you've been laid low by a different sort of bomb too. Telephone me or send word by young Suki if you'd like me to visit, otherwise I'll wait here for when you're ready to talk about what happened in London.*

It was signed from Bert.

Again, she watched from over the hedge that bordered his side of the lane between their properties as he worked in his market garden. 'Hmm,' he said, when he noticed her. 'You're looking as weak as a newborn kitten, woman.'

They went into his cosy house and Bert made tea as Naomi settled in one of the armchairs beside the hearth. 'It was just as you suspected?' he asked, bringing the tea over and sitting in the other armchair.

'It was worse. Alexander has ...' She struggled against another rush of overwhelming emotion.

Bert leaned down and stroked Elizabeth, his cat, doubtless trying to give Naomi the time she needed to regain control.

'Alexander has a secret family,' she finally got out.

The news brought Bert's head up in outrage. 'A *what*? Well, I'll be—' He broke off as though not wanting to waste words on the man he was so disgusted by. 'There's no doubt?'

'None at all. The children are almost grown so he's had this secret family for most of our marriage. Maybe even longer.'

Bert's lip curled and his breath came angrily, leaving her in no doubt of what he'd like to do to Alexander Harrington. 'And to think that man looks down on Churchwood folk when he's the worst scoundrel of all. Humph!' He spent a moment or two in high dudgeon, then took a big breath and spoke more calmly. 'Have you decided what to do about it?'

'I need to let it sink in first.'

'And get your strength back too,' he advised.

'In the meantime—'

'I won't say a word to anyone.'

'Thank you.'

'Not', he added warmly, 'that you've anything to be ashamed of. The shame is all on that iceberg you had the misfortune to marry.'

Perhaps so, but Naomi still felt foolish – stupid – for being so taken in.

'You know where to find me if you want to talk some more,' he said when she got up to leave.

'I do, and I'm grateful.'

'Don't let that long stick of ice bully you. He'll have me to answer to if he does.'

Naomi smiled at the thought of earthy Bert squaring up to fastidious Alexander. 'That's good to hear,' she said.

Naomi visited Alice next and was touched by the welcome she received. Alice threw down the tea towel she was using to dry dishes and held Naomi close instead. 'I've been so worried about you!' she said.

'I'm a lot better now and I'm here to be of some help.'

'Are you sure you're up to it?' Alice asked.

'Your father gave me a clean bill of health,' Naomi declared. 'You're a naughty girl for sending him over but I appreciate the concern behind it.'

'Whatever you do will be welcome,' Alice said

gratefully. 'I'll admit that I've been struggling to cope with work and the hospital on top of this crisis. I also have Pearl staying while Timmy isn't well.'

'The land girl? Goodness.'

'I fear for the china and glass when she's here, but her heart is in the right place. I think she's lonely, which is why she latched on to Ruby and defended her so staunchly even when Ruby was in the wrong. I hope that's all in the past now, though. Kate's kindness seems to be getting through to Ruby at last.'

'So it should. Now then' – Naomi drew herself up in a ready-for-business stance – 'tell me where I'm needed most.'

Naomi was allocated some visits and wasted no time in heading into the village to start on them.

Marjorie came out of the grocer's as Naomi approached. 'I've been so worried about you!' she cried, folding her into an awkward hug. 'Suki guarded you like a dragon, even though I told her you wouldn't mind *me* visiting.'

'She did what she thought best, and as you can see, I'm well again now.'

'You must have been terrified when the bomb went off. I'm looking forward to hearing all about it. Perhaps I could come to Foxfield for tea. Or even dinner. It's been an age since we had a cosy chat.'

'I'll arrange it soon, but let's get through this measles crisis first.'

Bert drew up in his van and Naomi managed to shake Marjorie off to talk to him. 'It's like old times, with us all working together again,' Naomi said.

'Churchwood at its best,' he agreed, giving her an approving nod. 'Where are you headed now?'

'The Bramley family on Chestnut Street.'

'I won't keep you, then. Welcome back, woman. And don't dwell too much on what happened in London. You'll see your way forward soon enough.'

He left her with a wink of encouragement.

Naomi was passing baskets of shopping to Bert for delivery to the measles families the following day when Lavinia Forsyth approached.

'Terrible business, this measles,' Mrs Forsyth observed.

'Isn't it?' Bert said. 'Luckily, young Alice Lovell rallied people around.'

'Ah, yes. Miss Lovell.' Mrs Forsyth frowned, disapproving as ever. 'She should have come to my husband and me for help. We're the spiritual leaders in the village.'

Naomi stared at her, feeling irritated. 'Mrs Forsyth, is it really such a mystery why Alice didn't come to you for help?'

Naomi's forthright tone had Mrs Forsyth blinking. 'Naturally, as the vicar and his wife, we expect not only to be consulted but also to lead.'

'Lead how, exactly?' On the edge of her vision Naomi caught an encouraging nod from Bert. 'The families don't need you to preach the Bible at them. They need you to *live* the Bible instead. Through kindness, sympathy, fellow feeling and practical help. Why did you need Alice to tell you about the crisis anyway? Why didn't you find out about it for yourselves?'

'We couldn't have predicted measles, Mrs Harrington.'

'Perhaps not, but misfortune was bound to strike the village in some form or other over time. People fall ill. They're bereaved. They worry about money and food and all sorts of things. A decent vicar and his wife would know that and be on the watch for it.'

'Mrs Harrington, you need to look to your tone!'

'I'm being offensive, am I?' Naomi was aware that Bert was grinning now. 'I'm afraid I don't care. In fact, I'm going to go further and say that not only should a decent vicar and his wife be on the watch for troubles in their congregation, they should also build the sorts of relationships that make people turn to them for help. No one turns to you for help because you don't listen to them. Instead, you judge them. We couldn't have made it clearer that the bookshop helped the villagers to keep an eye on each other, but you ignored us. You think you're doing good here in Churchwood but you're not. Attendance at church services has fallen off since you came. And I don't know anyone who enjoys the Bible study groups except for Cecil Wade, and he's another pompous idiot.'

'*Another* one? Are you calling my husband and me pompous idiots?'

'I'm being offensive again, aren't I? I'm not normally so outspoken but I haven't been quite well. To answer your question, though, I suppose I *am* calling you and Reverend Forsyth pompous idiots.'

'Bravo,' Bert said, not bothering to hide his smile. 'I couldn't have put it better myself. It's a pity things have come to a slanging match in the street, Mrs Forsyth, but you've brought it on yourself. I think it best if I go to young Adam's church in Barton from now on. I suspect I won't be the only one.'

Mrs Forsyth looked outraged. Then she turned on her heel and walked away.

'Oh dear,' Naomi said. 'Perhaps I shouldn't have been so harsh on her.'

'You said nothing that didn't need saying. In fact, I'm proud of you, woman.'

Naomi wasn't at all sure she was proud of herself. But as the day wore on, she found she couldn't regret speaking up. She was sick and tired of people trampling over others – the Forsyths, the archdeacon and, not least, Alexander. She was exhausted by it all, but the burn of anger was getting hotter.

# CHAPTER FORTY-SEVEN

## *Kate*

'Thanks,' Ruby said, as Kate carried a tray into the room they now all thought of as Timmy's, 'but I could have come down for it.'

Kate shrugged to show that it hadn't been a bother. 'How is he?'

'Dr Lovell says he's through the worst. You're feeling a bit better, aren't you, Tim?'

The boy still looked wan but managed a weak smile.

'That's good to hear,' Kate said, and gestured to the food she'd brought. 'Soup, bread, cheese and apples. I'll come back for the tray later.'

'Let me bring it down. I need to move about more.'

Kate saw that she meant it. Ruby had barely stirred from Timmy's bedside for days. 'You might feel better for some fresh air too,' Kate recommended.

Ruby nodded and muttered, 'Thanks,' again. A truce was still in place, even if it wasn't an entirely relaxed one yet.

Kate had just returned to the kitchen from the garden with vegetables for that night's dinner when Ruby came down with the tray. 'That soup was tasty,' she said. 'Timmy managed nearly all of his bowl.'

'Progress.' Kate was pleased. 'Do you want me to—'

'I'll wash the dishes.' Ruby did so with practised

efficiency, protecting her fingernails by instinct as far as Kate could tell.

'Tea?' Kate offered.

It wasn't time for the mid-afternoon break but she thought Ruby might welcome a cup and a chance to breathe some fresh air. When the tea was made, Kate suggested taking it outside. 'We can leave the door open so you'll hear Timmy if he calls.'

'His window's open anyway so we'll hear him from above.'

There was no such thing as a proper bench in the farmyard, but a plank of wood supported on old bricks made a decent enough seat. Ruby looked tired in the daylight despite her usual cosmetics. She'd nursed her brother well.

'Pearl appears to be happy enough staying with Alice,' Kate reported.

'She said she feels like Gulliver in Lilliput but she's been made welcome and she hasn't broken anything. Not yet anyway.'

'It isn't too late to invite your parents to visit,' Kate pointed out, thinking they couldn't object to the way Ruby had nursed their boy. 'Pearl's in Alice's spare room but Naomi is well again now and she's said your parents can stay with her. Even if only your mother comes, it'll give you a break and—'

Ruby's mouth had tightened. 'She doesn't need to come. She knows I'm looking after Timmy.'

'She might like to come anyway. Just to see you both.'

Kate had little experience of mothering but it seemed to her that most, if not all, of the mothers in Churchwood loved to see their children. 'You've been wonderful with Timmy. You've looked after him like a mother instead of just a sister and—' She broke off as understanding crashed into her head. 'Oh!'

'Whatever you're thinking, forget it because it isn't true,' Ruby said, panicking, but she'd given herself away because how could she have guessed what Kate was thinking?

'You're Timmy's mother,' Kate said slowly.

'No,' Ruby denied. 'That's nonsense.'

But it all made sense now. Ruby had joined the Women's Land Army to be near her evacuated son, then manoeuvred permission for Timmy to join her at Brimbles Farm. And when that son had fallen ill, she'd been fierce in taking on the responsibility for his care.

Ruby swallowed and then sighed as though bracing herself for trouble. 'Are you going to get rid of us?'

'Get rid of you?'

'I'm used to it by now.' Ruby's voice was bitter. 'I've lost jobs because I'm an unmarried mother. My own father calls me a tart. My mother makes it plain that she's ashamed of me, and as for people in general . . . Sneers, dirty looks – I've had them all. Men think I'm easy game. But women are even worse, looking down their snooty noses at me . . . That's why . . . Well, that's why I expected snooty looks from you.'

'Ruby, I've had sneers and disgusted looks from people for most of my life. I have friends in the village now, but that began only a year or so ago. Before then I was loathed for being one of the Fletchers. Churchwood's problem family. Filthy, uncouth and – in the case of my brothers – fond of a brawl.'

'But you look so . . .'

'What?'

'Elegant, I suppose. You're tall but you're not clumsy like Pearl. You move like a dancer. You're beautiful, too, in a natural sort of way. You don't need to paint your face to look attractive and you're . . . Well, you're a good person. Everything I'm not. I suppose I was jealous of you. Nervous of you, too, as I was afraid you'd see through me. It made me . . . not as nice as I should have been.'

Ruby looked down as though cringing at her behaviour but then a thought seemed to strike her and she looked up again, grinning wickedly. 'Actually, I don't wear cosmetics just to look better. I also wear them to stick my tongue out at all the stuffy, snooty women who look down on me.'

Kate understood that feeling. Hadn't she used bold, taunting looks to set the Churchwood gossips twittering back in those lonely days when she had no friends? 'I won't judge your appearance and I won't judge you for Timmy either because I don't know the circumstances,' Kate said.

Ruby shrugged. 'I used to work in a hairdresser's. I got taken on as an apprentice and I loved it. When I realized the owner liked me, I was flattered at first. He took me out for my sixteenth birthday and . . . that's when it happened. I didn't mind too much when he first kissed me because I thought it meant I was special to him. But he went much further, holding me so tightly that I couldn't push him away and kissing me so hard that I couldn't tell him to stop and . . . Well, it was all over quickly. Afterwards, he threatened me with the sack if I told anyone what had happened and I was too scared to know what to do. Scared of him.

Scared of telling my mum and dad . . . It turned out that the owner was engaged to marry someone else. When his fiancée came to the salon she seemed to suspect that something had happened. She spent the whole time glowering at me and the next day I was sacked anyway.'

'Has he helped to support Timmy?'

Ruby laughed. 'He denied Timmy was anything to do with him. He said the baby could be anyone's.'

'You weren't tempted to give Timmy up for adoption?'

'My parents wanted that. But I love Timmy and he's been worth all the struggle.' Ruby paused; then she said, 'I suppose you think it was selfish of me to keep him when he could have gone to a couple who'd give him everything I can't, not least respectability.'

'I think he's a lucky boy to have a mother who loves him so much,' Kate said, feeling only admiration for the way Ruby had coped.

The land girl looked startled at that.

'Does Timmy know you're his real mother?'

'Yes, but he also knows it's important to hide it. He could hardly *not* know when my parents can barely look at him.'

'I'm sorry I suggested inviting them to stay. That must have made a difficult situation worse. Does Pearl know the truth?'

Ruby shook her head. 'She's a great girl but I couldn't risk her being so shocked she no longer wanted to be my friend. It must look an odd sort of friendship to outsiders. But we've helped each other. She's helped me to be a land girl of sorts and I've helped her to feel less lonely. I'm rather fond of her.'

'I'll keep your secret,' Kate assured Ruby, but there was someone else involved whose feelings needed to be considered. Kate hesitated then asked, 'Where does Kenny fit into all of this?'

'You think I'm using him.'

'Are you?'

'I suppose that's how it started. The way I saw it, men had used me to get what they wanted, so why shouldn't I use them to get what I wanted? I could see Kenny liked the look of me, so I played up to him and it worked. It got Timmy here. But I've grown fond of Kenny too. I won't say I'm in love with him because it'll take a lot to get me to love any man after what I've been through. But fondness . . . Yes, I'm fond of him. That's not a bad place to start from, is it?'

'You need to talk to him about Timmy. Explain. It isn't fair to go on deceiving him.'

'No.' Ruby attempted a smile but it ended as a rueful grimace. 'Maybe I should just pack my bags and leave before he throws me out.'

'He might surprise you. Heck, he might surprise *me*. I've never had much respect for my brothers, but Kenny is the best of a bad bunch and he's very taken with Timmy.'

'All right, I'll talk to him.'

'Tell him that your secret's safe with me and I see no reason why Ernie and Vinnie need to know the truth.'

Ruby nodded. 'Thank you. But can I wait until tomorrow? Just to give Timmy a bit more time to get better in case things don't go our way?'

'Of course.' Kate smiled. 'I'm not your enemy, Ruby.'

'I can see that now. I wish I'd seen it before.'

\*

The following evening Kate took advantage of the long summer daylight to cycle down to Alice's. 'I'm feeling cut off up at the farm. I want to hear the news.'

Alice filled her in on the measles crisis – 'I think we're getting on top of it' – and also on Naomi's exchange with Mrs Forsyth, which Bert had reported with relish.

'Good for Naomi!' Kate said.

'I'm not convinced she's as well as she makes out – something's troubling her – but she's throwing herself into helping the village. How's life on the farm?'

'Improving. I'm getting along with Ruby much better now.'

'She's told you, then?'

Kate was puzzled. 'Told me what?'

'That she's Timmy's mother. I'm right, aren't I?'

Kate stared at her. 'Yes, but how did you guess?'

'Instinct, I suppose. Many of my father's patients were mothers and I've seen how they behaved when their children were sick.'

'Clever old you. I've told her I'll keep the secret and I'm sure you'll do the same. The only person who needed to know was Kenny and he's been remarkably good about it.'

'It must be a relief to Ruby not to have to pretend with everyone.'

'She still has to pretend with most people, but yes, her conscience isn't troubling her over Kenny any more.' Kate shrugged, then said, 'You'd have told me if there was any news of Daniel.'

'You'd have seen me dancing round in circles of joy. I know he may be perfectly safe in a prisoner-of-war camp, but I'd give anything for a letter that confirmed it. I hope Leo is still keeping in touch?'

'We write, and I hope he'll be able to get over soon.'

'I'm glad,' Alice said.

Kate left soon afterwards. She locked the bike up in the barn, then headed towards the farmhouse to cook the evening meal. She'd got a small amount of minced beef from the butcher and planned to make it into a hash with mashed potato and mustard to give it a kick. Luckily, there were always vegetables of one sort or another to serve with it – an advantage of living on a farm.

A distant phut-phut of a motorbike reached her ears. Leo? Had he got the use of the motorbike unexpectedly? Kate felt a thrill of excitement coupled with anxiety because she didn't want him anywhere near her family. She raced through the orchard to meet him, glad she'd cleaned up before going down to Alice's.

She hesitated before pushing through the hedgerow to the lane; then, seeing the rider really was Leo, she stepped out and prepared to greet him with a smile.

Leo brought the bike to a halt, got off and walked towards her, reaching up to remove his helmet and goggles. One look at his dear face told Kate something terrible had happened.

Her blood began to pound in her ears. Her mouth felt dry, her legs weak as she hastened to meet him. 'What is it, Leo? What's happened?'

'It's Ralph.' He swallowed hard to get the words past trembling lips. 'He's dead.'

'Oh, no! I'm so sorry.' She wrapped her arms around Leo, wishing she could take away some of the hurt. Poor Ralph and poor everyone who loved him, Ruth and Leo especially.

Leo held her close for a moment as though squeezing every last drop of comfort from her. Then he released her and backed away, leaving her puzzled. 'I came to tell you in person because this . . . because *we* . . . Well, we can't go on,' he said.

Shock and dread nearly scooped Kate's legs from under her. She took a step forward, her hands itching to pull him back so he could tell her he didn't mean what she feared he meant.

'Ruth is devastated,' Leo continued. 'I don't want that to happen to you. It's best to break off now, before things get serious.'

They were already serious. For Kate.

'The life of a fighter pilot in wartime is fragile. No girl should put her feelings at risk by becoming attached to such a man when it's probably only a matter of time before . . . And no man should let her. Not if he cares for her.'

'Leo, please.'

'I'm being posted overseas anyway – North Africa – so this will be a clean break. Much the best thing even if . . . even if it hurts. Goodbye, Kate. I wish things could have been different, but I can't change our circumstances. I can only do the honourable thing and let you live your life without the sort of grief that Ruth's suffering.'

'I'll suffer anyway!' Kate cried.

'For a little while, perhaps. But in time . . .' His expression was bleak as he appeared to stare into the future. Then he pulled himself straighter. 'I'm setting you free to *save* you, Kate. I want you to be happy because you deserve it. You're wonderful, and you should never listen to anyone who tells you otherwise. It's been a privilege to know you. A joy. But now I have to walk away.'

He tugged her close for a final short, sharp embrace, then walked back to the motorbike and got on.

'Don't go,' Kate pleaded, but he was already firing the engine, not bothering with the helmet and goggles as though desperate to get away.

He turned the bike and, after one last look at her, he rode out of her life.

# CHAPTER FORTY-EIGHT

## *Alice*

'Miss Lovell! Alice!'

Having just set out to visit one of the measles families, Alice turned to see an obviously agitated Ruby running after her. 'What is it?' she asked, hastening back. 'Has Timmy taken a turn for the worse?'

Ruby came to a breathless halt, bending forward at the waist and heaving air into her lungs. 'Timmy's fine. It's Kate.'

'Is she unwell?'

'I don't know what's wrong.' Ruby straightened up again. 'I only know it's bad. Someone came on a motorbike. He looked like an RAF man from a distance. Kate went to meet him then ran into the orchard and sort of . . . collapsed in tears. I asked if there was anything I could do to help but she waved me away. You're her friend, though. You might have better luck.'

'I'll come straight away.' The measles families were doing well and Kate's need was clearly greater.

Alice raced to the farm with Ruby beside her. Had the visitor been Leo or someone on Leo's behalf? Bringing devastating news of him, perhaps? 'The orchard, you said?'

'That's where I last saw her,' Ruby confirmed; then

she paused before adding, 'I hope I've done the right thing in fetching you.'

'You have.'

'I'll go back to the house, out of the way. Let me know if there's anything I can do to help.'

'Thank you, Ruby.'

Alice made her way into the orchard. Kate was hunched over on her knees with her face in her hands. Getting down beside her, Alice gathered her friend into her arms. Kate resisted at first but finally loosened, burrowing into Alice's embrace and sobbing. Alice rocked her and stroked her hair, desperate to know what had happened but aware that she had to wait until Kate was able to talk.

'What is it?' Alice asked when the sobs finally eased.

'Leo came. He . . . he broke things off with me.'

'Oh no! Did he give a reason?'

'He said . . . He told me his best friend had been killed. Ralph. I met him at the dance. Now Ralph's fiancée is grieving, and Leo . . .' Kate swallowed against another rush of tears.

'He doesn't want to put you in the position of grieving for him if the worst should happen?' Alice guessed.

'Something like that.'

It was understandable that Leo wished to save Kate from pain. Understandable, too, if he thought her pain would cut deeper the longer their relationship continued. It was admirable, even. Not that Alice agreed with it. She feared for Daniel daily but believed that it was a price worth paying for the love they shared. 'He must have been in shock if he'd only just lost his friend,' she ventured. 'Perhaps on reflection . . .'

Kate shook her head. 'He's being posted to Africa. He wants a clean break.'

'Then I'm desperately sorry.'

Alice let Kate cry some more; then she said, 'Wait here while I have a word with Ruby. You're coming home with me.'

'I can't.'

'You can and you will, if only for tonight. Work will have to wait.'

Alice found Ruby hovering by the farmhouse. 'Is it the chap she's been seeing?' Ruby asked. 'She's never mentioned him, but I suspected she was seeing someone.'

'A pilot,' Alice confirmed. 'Sadly, he's broken things off.'

'Poor Kate.'

'Indeed. We all rallied round when Timmy fell ill. I hope we can all rally round now to help Kate to come to terms with her disappointment.'

Ruby stood taller. 'I won't let her down. What do you want me to do?'

'Don't tell Kate's father and brothers about Leo. Kate wouldn't like it. But could you make up Kate's bed for Pearl so Kate can take her place at the cottage tonight? If you and Pearl could try to cover Kate's work for a day or two, that would be helpful too.'

'We'll do our best.'

'Thank you.' Alice touched Ruby's arm gratefully before walking away.

She hadn't gone far before she heard Ernie accosting Ruby. 'What did *she* want?'

*She* was doubtless Alice.

'None of your business,' Ruby snapped.

*Well done, Ruby,* Alice thought. The land girl looked like becoming a useful ally.

Returning to the orchard, Alice helped Kate to get up. How pale she looked! How heartbroken! They said little as they walked down to the cottage. Once there, Alice installed Kate at the small kitchen table, put the kettle on for tea and went to tell her father what had happened. 'Does Kate need my help too?' he asked.

'Your sympathy only at this stage. She isn't hysterical. Just terribly upset.'

'Call if you need me.'

Back in the kitchen, Alice made the tea, took a cup in to her father and then sat beside Kate. 'Drink,' she urged.

Kate wrapped her hands around the cup as though seeking comfort in the warmth. 'I'm sorry I'm making a fuss. I know I'd only met Leo a few times.'

'But you liked him.'

Kate nodded and wiped away more tears. 'He was a breath of fresh air. Kind and fun, and so full of life! He made *me* feel full of life, too. And special. Leo always made me feel special.'

'You *are* special.'

Kate shrugged and it troubled Alice to think that her friend's confidence might suffer from Leo's rejection when it had taken so long for that confidence to grow.

'It was too soon to know if we might have had a future together,' Kate said.

'But you hoped for it all the same.'

'It was stupid of me.'

'Not stupid at all. If it hadn't been for the war, you might have had a chance.'

Yet if it hadn't been for the war Kate and Leo might never have met. Life was ever complicated.

Alice wondered how Leo was feeling. Sad, because he'd inflicted pain on Kate? Honourable, because he believed he'd done the right thing? Or relieved because all he'd really wanted was to be free of the relationship? Alice didn't know him well enough to guess and speculating about it wouldn't help Kate.

Deciding that what her friend needed now was quiet, Alice suggested moving into the back garden, hoping there might be something soothing in its peacefulness. They'd got up to head outside when there was a knock on the front door. 'If that's one of our friends, shall I tell them what's happened?' Alice asked, trying to save Kate from having to explain about the break-up as each retelling would surely give her pain.

'I'd appreciate that.'

The visitor was Naomi, who went straight to Kate and hugged her after Alice told her about Leo. 'I'm so sorry, my dear.'

'Thank you.' Tears were shimmering in Kate's eyes again. 'I'm hardly the first person to discover that romance can end in disappointment and I'm sure I won't be the last.'

'That doesn't stop it from hurting.' Naomi gave Kate a final sympathetic pat, then turned to Alice. 'I only called to tell you that little Henry Avery is almost back to his old self, so his mother is happy to do her own shopping from now on. I think she'll welcome the chance to get out and about.'

'That's good to hear.'

'There's a new invalid, however. Pam Cooper's girl, Lucy. But don't worry about it. I'll keep in touch with Pam.'

In other words, Alice could concentrate on looking after Kate.

'Take care,' Alice urged, because Naomi still wasn't looking particularly well.

Naomi left and, fetching cushions, Alice took Kate into the garden.

Pearl returned, looking nervous, as though she wanted to say the right thing to Kate but feared she might make a hash of it. 'I'll fetch my stuff and clear out,' she told Alice. 'Should I say anything to Kate or leave her alone?'

'A kind word wouldn't hurt,' Alice said, taking Pearl outside where she shuffled her feet awkwardly.

'Ruby told me about your chap. I'm sorry.'

'It's kind of you to care, Pearl. I'm sorry to mess you about with the sleeping arrangements.'

'That's no bother, and don't worry about work. Ruby's on top of the cooking and she's got some washing soaking. I'll see to the chickens tonight.'

'You're wonderful,' Kate told her.

Pearl blushed and then made a speedy exit.

Dr Lovell appeared. 'I don't want to disturb you, Alice, but this just arrived and I thought it might be important.'

It was a telegram. Oh no. Was more bad news to follow, this time about Daniel?

Alice ripped the envelope open and the message inside had her rocking back on her heels in shock.

'Alice?' Kate got up from her seat as though preparing to steady her.

'It's from Daniel,' Alice said. 'He's coming home.'

But how could that be? Surely the telegram wasn't some sort of cruel hoax?

# CHAPTER FORTY-NINE

## *Alice*

*COMING HOME DARLING GIRL. MORE NEWS TO FOLLOW. DANIEL X.*

Alice read the telegram over and over. Dare she hope that it really was from Daniel? That he really was coming home?

'It looks genuine to me,' her father said. 'Heaven knows how it's come about but I'm sure we'll hear eventually. In the meantime, let's just be thankful.'

'Yes,' Alice agreed, allowing joy to surge through her at last. Daniel was coming home! She didn't know when, but he was on his way or almost on his way. It was wonderful.

'I'm so pleased,' Kate said.

Kate! Alice's conscience burst into life. Alice had forgotten her friend's troubles momentarily. How unfortunate that Kate had witnessed Alice receiving the most glorious news on a day that had brought her only rejection.

'Don't look so stricken,' Kate said. 'I don't begrudge you your happiness.'

'I feel I'm rubbing salt in your pain.'

'I'm glad for you. For Daniel, too.'

For Kate's sake Alice tried hard to keep a lid on

her joy for the rest of the evening, though she couldn't ignore her own curiosity, or the occasional doubt. Try as she might, she couldn't help wondering how Daniel was free or entirely suppress her doubts about the telegram's authenticity.

'Go to Naomi's and telephone Daniel's parents,' Kate finally suggested, which was an excellent idea though Alice felt bad that her agitation had been obvious.

Naomi – still looking tired – assured Alice that she was glad to help.

Alice got through to Daniel's mother. 'We've received a telegram too,' Mrs Irvine said.

'You're sure it's genuine?'

Clearly, that possibility hadn't occurred to her. But after a moment of shock she rallied. 'He called us by the names he used as a boy: Mumkins and Dadkins. He uses them as a joke now but no one else is likely to know that.'

Alice's relief almost took her breath away.

'We've left messages with his regiment and the War Office asking for more information,' Mrs Irvine continued. 'We'll let you know if we hear back.'

'I'll let you know if I hear anything too.'

Alice slept little that night as excitement bubbled inside her. Kate slept little too, judging from her wan appearance in the morning, but she was quietly dignified and made no mention of her struggles.

'Thanks for letting me stay last night,' she said instead. 'It helped enormously, but I'll go back home today.'

Was Alice's happiness too much for Kate to bear?

'I'm needed on the farm,' Kate pointed out. 'You have to go to work, too.'

That was true. Mr Parkinson was expecting Alice. 'Come back if you can't cope at home,' she urged. 'If I'm still out, my father will let you in.'

Watching her friend set off down Brimbles Lane, Alice was glad that Ruby and Pearl were on Kate's side now. Hopefully, they'd shield her from the worst of the Fletcher men's harshness. Vowing to look in on Kate as soon as possible, Alice changed the linen on the spare bed ready for Pearl and then hastened into the village to catch the bus to St Albans.

'My word, you've a spring in your step today, Alice,' Mr Parkinson said as she breezed into his room.

He'd got into the way of calling her Alice ever since she'd confided in him over Daniel's imprisonment. He was a nice man and, based on Alice's reports about him, her father thought so too. Each man had described the other's work as fascinating, and she'd begun to wonder if they might actually welcome meeting up. It would be lovely for her father to have a friend. Lovely for Mr Parkinson, too, perhaps. Maybe she should invite her employer to tea at the cottage one day soon.

Not just now, though, as she wasn't sure when Daniel might arrive. She explained about the telegram and was touched by Mr Parkinson's delight.

'What uplifting news!' he said. 'I couldn't be more delighted.'

For the next few hours Alice tried hard to concentrate on Mr Parkinson's memoirs but time and again her thoughts strayed to Daniel and whether she'd find another telegram or telephone message waiting for her at home.

'I'm sorry if I've been distracted,' she said when she finally got ready to leave.

'It would take a harder man than I to find fault on a day like this, especially when you're normally such an exemplary worker. You've earned the right to lose focus for a few hours.'

On impulse Alice bent to kiss his cheek.

'Now, now!' he protested, but his pleasure was obvious.

She arrived home to find there was no news at all about Daniel. She hadn't forgotten Kate, of course, and was glad to have Pearl staying as the land girl would be able to fill Alice in on her friend's mood.

'Gosh, I'm no good with emotions and stuff,' Pearl said when asked to report. 'I'd say she's working as hard as ever – maybe even harder – but isn't in top form on the inside, if you know what I mean?'

Alice did know and called on Kate the following day on her way to the hospital. Pearl's description had been spot-on. Kate was busy and outwardly calm but there was a fragile air about her. 'I've had a letter from Leo,' she said.

'Oh?' Alice felt a leap of hope but it withered instantly. Kate wouldn't be sad if the news was good.

'Read it.' Kate pulled it from her pocket and held it out.

'I'm not sure I should read anything personal.'

'Don't worry about that.'

Alice took the letter, still feeling she was intruding.

*Dear Kate,*

*I'm writing to offer heartfelt apologies if I've hurt you.
I never set out to do so and can only say I'm sorry I let
my heart rule my head. A better man than I would
have realized much earlier that romance has no place
in wartime. Not for a fighter pilot, anyway. I can only
hope that I've spared you from greater hurt in the
future.*

*You're an incredible girl, Kate. It's been a privilege
to know you and I wish you all the joy and happiness
you so deserve.*

*Fondest regards,*

*Leo x*

Alice wasn't sure what to make of it. 'I think he
really cared for you,' she said, though it certainly
appeared to draw a line under the relationship.

Kate shrugged, tilting her chin as though bracing
herself to be brave. 'Maybe he did, maybe he didn't.
It's over now.'

'I'm sorry.' Alice had said it many times before but
there were no better words.

'I'll survive. You're off to the hospital, I assume?
You'll see people there with far worse problems than
mine.'

Alice would indeed see men who were broken in
body and sometimes in spirit, but that didn't make
Kate's heartache any easier.

'Have you heard when Daniel will be arriving?'
Kate asked.

'Not yet.'

'Hopefully soon.'

Alice continued to the hospital, where Tom, Babs,

404

Pauline and Matron were all delighted to hear that Daniel was somehow on his way. Afterwards, Alice rushed home again but there was still no more news.

Thursday passed in a similar fashion. 'You're going to need the spare bed in case Daniel turns up,' Pearl pointed out. 'I'll clear off in the morning. Ruby's happy for us both to bunk in with Timmy again but I might sleep in the barn instead.'

'I don't want you to be uncomfortable,' Alice argued.

'Won't bother me to sleep on a bed of hay. I'm hardly a delicate princess.'

'You're a good friend and that's infinitely more important.'

The compliment had Pearl blushing. 'I only became a land girl to get away from home, but . . .' Her voice trailed off as though she didn't know how to put her feelings into speech.

Guessing at what Pearl was trying to say, Alice smiled. 'I'm glad you came to Churchwood, Pearl.'

'Crikey.'

Friday came. Still no news. Still more waiting.

Until evening, when a knock on the door had Alice jumping to her feet. Could the caller be Naomi bringing a telephone message?

It wasn't Naomi on the doorstep. It was Daniel – painfully thin, hair overgrown and with stubble on his chin. But smiling. 'Hello, darling girl.'

Alice burst into tears and launched herself against his chest.

'I'm going to take this as a sign that you're pleased to see me,' he said, laughing and kissing her hair before lifting her chin and kissing her lips.

405

Alice stopped crying enough to kiss him back, exulting in the nearness of him.

'I've waited such a long time for that kiss,' Daniel finally said. 'I feel better already.'

They went inside where Alice's father was hovering discreetly.

Hands were shaken. Hugs exchanged. And Alice busied herself with making tea and warming stew for Daniel, uncaring that the stew had been intended for the evening meal for her father and herself. 'I'm sorry to be eating your rations,' Daniel said.

'You're welcome to them,' Alice told him.

Her father went out to retrieve the bag Daniel had forgotten after dropping it on the front step in his haste to kiss her. 'I'll take it upstairs,' he called, and Alice knew he was being tactful in leaving her and Daniel alone.

'I have so many questions!' she told him. 'But I don't want to bombard you with them.'

'Ask away. I'll let you know if I'm feeling swamped.'

'How did you come to be released?'

'I wasn't released. I escaped.'

'Escaped?' Alice was torn between admiration and horror. He could have been shot.

'I was captured in North Africa along with a lot of others. Conditions weren't great in the camp there – baking hot and not very sanitary – but we exchanged one kind of hazard for another when we were shipped across the Mediterranean. We didn't know if we'd be sunk by a torpedo or bombed from above. We got there in the end, though, and after that we travelled overland, assuming our ultimate destination was to be Germany, though no one told us. It was a slow process. They held us in temporary camps along the way. I was crammed into the back of a lorry one day with about twenty other chaps when it suddenly veered off the road and crashed into a ditch. I don't know exactly what happened, but a German-speaking captain interpreted the shouting and commotion and explained that the driver had collapsed. A stroke, perhaps. In the chaos some of us slipped away.'

'No one saw you?'

'Oh, they saw us. Shot at us, too.'

Alice shuddered at the thought of what might have happened but reminded herself that Daniel had lived to tell the tale.

'We scattered in different directions and ran like crazy,' Daniel continued. 'We were out in the countryside, and I headed for a wood. I thought it would offer the best cover. But when I burst through on the other side, the earth suddenly dropped by twenty or thirty feet and I realized I'd made a serious mistake. I fell – couldn't stop myself.'

Alice winced again.

'I fell through bushes and over rocks, and landed with my chest on a particularly vicious rock. I was fairly battered and I guessed some ribs were broken. Guards were coming after me through the woods but getting up to run on was . . . well, it was impossible. The only thing I could manage was to shuffle into the hollow beneath an overhanging rock. If the guards had climbed down the incline, they would have seen me. But they were distracted by shouts and gunfire from what sounded like a couple of hundred yards away. They ran towards it and never came back.'

'Thank heavens for that!' Alice exhaled slowly in relief. 'You managed to get up eventually?' she asked.

'I'd like to say I was the hero of my own rescue but I lay in that hollow for what felt like hours. It wasn't just my ribs. I'd banged my head badly too – the word *dizzy* doesn't quite describe it. I felt sick every time I moved. When I heard footsteps in the darkness – a man and a dog – I thought a guard had come back.'

'It wasn't a guard?'

'A local farmer. The dog found me, and the farmer carried me to his home. Hid me in a small cellar under his cow byre. The entrance was covered with wood and earth, and I could hear the cows walking over my head.'

'Was he German?'

'An Austrian, who hated that his country had been forcibly united with Germany. Anyway, luck was on my side because he knew people – resistance workers – who were willing to get me out when I was well enough.'

He took hold of Alice's hand. 'I thought of trying to get a message to you, to let you know I was safe, but I had no guarantee of staying safe and I thought it would be cruel to get your hopes up only to have them dashed again if I didn't make it home. I got here by a combination of hikes, cycle rides and boats, passed from one resistance worker to another. They're incredibly brave people.'

'I'd like to meet them and shake their hands,' Alice said fervently.

'Perhaps one day you will. Right now, I've got some

time off to recover before I return to active service, and I'd like to put it to the best possible use.'

'Which is?'

He reached for her hand and kissed it. 'Marrying you, of course. There won't be time for a grand wedding but I don't care about that. I just want you to be my wife sooner rather than later. What do you say?'

Alice flung her arms around him. 'I say yes!'

# CHAPTER FIFTY

## *Naomi*

Poor Kate. Knowing how it felt to be let down in love, Naomi had taken a bunch of summer flowers up to Brimbles Farm, steeling herself to brave the Fletcher men should they be around. She'd been relieved to learn they were at work in distant fields. She'd found Kate looking pale but all her friends could do was trust to time to take the edge off her disappointment and comfort her in the meantime.

The walk home took Naomi past the side of The Linnets. Lucky Alice! Naomi had been thrilled to hear of Daniel's return and their plan to marry as soon as possible by special licence, instead of waiting to hear the banns read in church over several weeks.

She reached the Foxfield front door as a shiny black car swept on to the gravel drive. Seeing Alexander in the passenger seat, Naomi stiffened. She hadn't laid eyes on him or even spoken to him since coming face to face with his betrayal in Marcroft's Hotel.

The car came to a halt and Alexander got out, leaning back inside to speak to the man who'd given him a lift. 'Thank you, Charles. Next time the luck may go your way.'

'I doubt it. You're too good a golfer, Harrington.'

The man drove off, and Alexander approached the

door. He spared Naomi a nod by way of a greeting and asked, 'Do you have a key or are you waiting for the maid to answer?'

Naomi used her key, then stepped into the hall and on into the sitting room. She didn't expect Alexander to follow, and he didn't. Instead, she heard him move into the study. No *How are you, dear*? Not even *Hello*.

How smug he was. How arrogant.

She closed the sitting-room door and sat down, her chest heaving with emotion until Suki arrived to offer tea and to ask if the master would prefer a tray in his study tonight.

'A tray, please, Suki.'

Naomi didn't bother asking Alexander what he wanted. She simply couldn't bear to look at him across the dining table.

She didn't see him again before she went to bed. Lying back against her pillows she reminded herself that she had the power of choice over what to do about her marriage. By morning she knew how she was going to use it.

He entered the breakfast room, nodded at Naomi, arranged a newspaper in front of his plate and began to eat.

'Please don't come here again,' Naomi said.

He glanced up, irritated by the interruption. 'What are you talking about?'

'I'm saying I don't want you here at Foxfield. Not ever. I want a separation. I might even want a divorce.'

He sighed but couldn't disguise his impatience. 'You're upset because I'm rarely here these days. Is that it? You want to see more of me?'

Naomi laughed. She couldn't help it. 'I don't want

to see *more* of you, Alexander. I don't want to see you *at all.* Ideally, I'd never see you again, though that might be too much to hope for as we must have financial affairs to sort out.'

'I don't understand.'

'I've been a fool. For years and years I've been a fool, pathetically grateful for any crumb of attention you threw my way. But that's over now. The thing is, Alexander, I *know*. I was there.'

'Where? I wish you'd stop talking in riddles.'

'At Marcroft's Hotel. Where you met your family for lunch.'

She saw the shock register in his face before he quickly masked it. 'The last time I was in Marcroft's was . . . let me see . . . around two weeks ago. I met a client there. A widow and her children.'

'Since when do clients' children call you "Papa"? Since when do clients' children look just like you?'

Now he was well and truly caught. His face drained of colour and his cruel mouth slackened as he struggled to find words that might somehow save him.

'Don't make yourself ridiculous by trying to talk your way out of it. The fact is that you betrayed me many years ago and you've been betraying me ever since. Who is she? What's her name?'

It was typical of Alexander to turn resentful, though he was the guilty one. 'What difference will it make if I tell you her name?'

Perhaps none. It was the betrayal itself that mattered rather than the identity of the stranger he'd involved in it. But Naomi wanted to know all the same. 'If you don't tell me, I'll find out another way. Don't make the mistake of thinking I've no way of finding out. I've already seen an enquiry agent. Jack Webber of Covent Garden. Do you want him probing into your grubby affairs?'

Alexander swallowed, thwarted and hating it. 'Her name is Amelia Ashmore. The children are William and Eliza. But they've all taken the name of Harrington.'

'You haven't married this woman?'

'How could I marry her?'

'There's such a thing as bigamy.'

'That would be criminal.'

So he wouldn't commit a crime, but every other sort of deception was fair game to him? 'How long have you been together?'

'Really, Naomi, I don't think these questions can possibly be helpful.'

'How long?'

'Twenty years. Almost twenty-one.'

He'd never bothered to mark the anniversary of his marriage to Naomi but he remembered when he met this Amelia Ashmore. Would he have married Amelia instead if he'd met her first? Or would he always have wanted access to the sort of money he'd gained in marrying Naomi? He was a greedy man and money mattered to him.

'Where does she live?'

'It doesn't matter where she lives.'

Naomi simply waited for an answer.

Alexander sighed, annoyed. 'In Surrey. She lives in Surrey. A town called Virginia Water.'

Which meant he had Naomi to the north of London and this woman and her children to the south. 'Was it my money that bought her house?'

'Naomi, I work for a living. I'm a professional man. A successful man.'

Which didn't actually answer the question. 'Where did you meet her?'

'At a golfing event.'

'Did she know you already had a wife?'

'Not at first. But eventually . . . Naturally, I told her.'

'By then you were so much in love you couldn't resist each other?' Naomi's tone was sarcastic. Bitter.

It made Alexander's lip curl in distaste.

'Why didn't you divorce me? Or ask me to divorce you?' Naomi had never considered herself attractive to men. But if she'd been freed from her marriage all those years ago at least she'd have had a chance to meet someone else and be happy. She'd have had a chance to have the children she craved.

'I didn't want to hurt you,' Alexander said, and the insincerity of it made her burst out laughing even as she wept inside.

'You wanted my money,' she sneered.

'No,' he said, but even Alexander had the grace to flush a little at the obvious lie.

Desolation swept through her at the thought of all the years she'd wasted on this lying, selfish, arrogant man. But Naomi couldn't change the past. She could only influence the future. 'What I want now is a separation,' she repeated. 'Perhaps a divorce.'

'Obviously, you need time to come to terms with what you've . . . discovered.'

'I've had all the time I need.'

'But a separation . . . These things have consequences. You haven't had a chance to think them through. There's no need to rush into something you might later regret.'

'You're thinking of yourself, not me. You're thinking of money. Your reputation, too. Some clients might not take kindly to having an adulterer as their stockbroker. Your earnings might suffer.'

Naomi had no idea how much Alexander actually earned. Certainly, he presented the appearance of a successful man, but appearances could be misleading. With Naomi's fortune at his disposal, he might never have pushed himself in his career but merely seen it as a symbol of his status in the world.

'You'll lose out, too, if we split our assets,' he pointed out. 'You may have to give up this house and you've always said how much you love it.'

'I do love it. But if losing Foxfield is the price I have to pay for breaking free from you, then I'll pay it. Gladly.'

Bold words. Naomi would be devastated to lose her home.

The veneer of civilization dropped from Alexander's face. 'Don't imagine I'll be generous if we have to divide our assets.'

'I don't expect you to be generous. I suspect you've been siphoning off my money ever since we married, but don't try to fleece me again. Oh, I know you have a family to support. Those children of yours didn't ask to be born and they shouldn't be punished financially because their father is beneath contempt. But you're a greedy man, Alexander. You won't get a penny more than is reasonable. Don't assume I'm too stupid to stop you getting what you want. I've already spoken to a lawyer.'

The news came as another shock to Alexander.

'Yes, to Ambrose Goodison. I can see from your face that you've heard of him. He's one of the best lawyers in London when it comes to marital break-downs so be warned. If you try to cheat me out of a single penny, I'll set him on to you like a dog. I might even go to the newspapers and that really wouldn't be good for your business. I suggest you cooperate so we can end this sorry period in our lives as discreetly as possible. In the meantime, please pack your things and leave. Right now. If you can't carry all of them, I'll have them sent to the flat.'

'I don't have petrol for the car.'

'Then you'll have to catch the bus and the train like an ordinary person. I suggest you get used to it. You'll be far from poor after our separation, but you won't be as rich as before. You must know the saying about cutting your coat according to your cloth.'

'You'll be poorer too and you won't be able to bear a scandal.'

'You're wrong. I have friends, you see. Loyal, genuine friends who'll be by my side no matter what happens.' She took a sip of her tea, then looked at Alexander as though surprised to see him still there. 'Do you need help with your packing?'

He threw his napkin on to the table and got up so forcefully that his chair toppled over. 'You'll regret this,' he said.

'I doubt it. I feel . . . liberated.'

He left the room and Naomi returned her cup to her saucer because her fingers were trembling. In fact, she was trembling all over. What she'd done felt enormous. Frightening. But she'd done it and, so far at least, she couldn't regret it.

She heard Alexander crashing about upstairs and in his study. 'Is everything all right, madam?' a worried-looking Suki asked when she came to clear the breakfast table.

'Everything is fine. Or it will be.'

Suki smiled, but uncertainly.

Naomi would tell her about the separation soon enough, but not quite yet.

Alexander left the house without a word, slamming the door behind him and sending gravel flying through the air as he stormed down the drive. Naomi didn't bother getting up for a final view of him through the window.

She went to her sitting room and sat doing nothing for some time then decided to go out. She had her coat on and was heading for the front door when someone knocked on it. 'I'll answer,' Naomi called to Suki.

She opened the door and blinked in surprise. 'Mrs Forsyth!'

'Good morning, Mrs Harrington. Might I trouble you for five minutes of your time?'

'Certainly.' Naomi ushered Mrs Forsyth into the sitting room, wondering at the cause of the subdued look on the woman's face. 'Please sit down. Would you like tea?'

'No, thank you. I just . . .' Mrs Forsyth twisted her fingers together. 'I came to tell you that we're leaving.'

'Leaving?'

'My husband and I have realized that our mission

doesn't lie in Churchwood after all. Country air doesn't suit my husband's health after the warmth of Africa, and a small parish church doesn't make the most of his talents.'

'I see,' Naomi said, knowing an excuse when she heard it. 'Does he have another position in mind?'

'We feel it would be wise to take our time instead of rushing into something new, but we're leaving Churchwood anyway. As soon as possible.'

'Cecil Wade will be disappointed.'

'But you won't be. Neither will anyone else.'

'I won't deny that we've had our differences,' Naomi admitted.

'We hoped to do so much good here. We really did.'

The woman looked genuinely dismayed by their failure, and Naomi's heart softened a little. 'I'm sure. Let's just say that you and Churchwood weren't a good fit. I hope you'll find a better fit elsewhere.'

'Thank you. Well, I won't keep you. I can see you're on your way out.'

'Is it known generally that you're leaving?'

'My husband spoke to the Diocese first, of course. Then he spoke to the churchwardens. I'm sure they'll call a church council meeting soon to discuss the future.'

'Will we have to go through another round of applications and interviews, do you think?'

'The Diocese will advise on procedure but we've only been here a few weeks and there was another applicant who might still want the position.'

'Adam Potts,' Naomi said, feeling a renewal of hope that he might become Churchwood's vicar after all.

'Indeed. It may be that he'll be offered the role without needing to go through the process all over again.'

Naomi nodded, encouraged.

'Goodbye then, Mrs Harrington. I'm sure I'll see you again before we leave, but a personal word ... That's what I wanted.'

'I appreciate it.'

Mrs Forsyth left and within minutes Naomi also left to go to Bert's. She walked slowly, dazedly, thinking of all that had happened – Kate's broken romance, Alice's forthcoming wedding, the Forsyths' departure and her own momentous decision to part from Alexander. Doubtless the separation wouldn't be plain sailing – Alexander had the capacity for spite – but still ... no regrets.

'Unless I'm much mistaken, you're here with news,' Bert said, inviting her inside.

'The Forsyths are leaving,' Naomi told him as they walked into the house.

'Permanently?'

'For ever.'

'That's good to hear.'

'I don't know exactly when they're going but Mrs Forsyth said it would be soon.'

'So we might have young Adam as our vicar, after all.'

'Let's hope so.'

Bert nodded in satisfaction and then gave her one of his all-seeing looks. 'And your other news?'

'I've told Alexander I want to separate from him.'

His sigh suggested even more satisfaction. 'That's good to hear, too. I never got to know your husband well – hardly at all, in fact – but I knew enough to feel that you deserved better, even with his good looks and swanky clothes. Not a nice man, your Alexander. Glass of sherry to celebrate?'

'Why not?'

'Sit yourself down then.'

Naomi sat in one of the fireside armchairs. Bert's cat looked up from the hearth rug she was kneading contentedly, then laid her head back down. Naomi felt that she too was kneading contentedly, in her mind if not with her fingernails.

Bert handed her a glass and sat opposite her. 'Cheers,' he said.

'Cheers.'

'You're looking better already.'

'I'm feeling better,' Naomi said by way of explanation.

Much as she enjoyed sitting in Bert's homely kitchen, she didn't stay long as she had another errand to run. If she was going to lose Foxfield, then she wanted to give it one last, glorious performance as her home.

She knocked on the door of The Linnets. Alice answered and invited her to walk through the cottage to the garden where Daniel was sitting. Naomi wasted no time in telling them both about the Forsyths leaving.

Unsurprisingly, they were thrilled, though Alice looked guilty after her first cry of delight. 'It's awful to be glad when people have failed and know they've failed. They must be unhappy about it,' she said.

'They were given every chance to work with us instead of against us,' Naomi pointed out.

Daniel nodded. 'Maybe they've learned an important lesson about listening to people instead of trampling over their wishes and preferences.'

'You're right,' Alice admitted. 'It's just . . .'

'That you have a soft heart,' Daniel said, smiling and reaching for her hand.

'Hopefully, this means Adam will be able to marry us,' Alice said, brightening.

'Your wedding is one of the reasons for my call,' Naomi said. 'But first let me tell you about my own marriage.'

They were full of concern when she explained about the separation. Not that she confided the details of Alexander's secret family. In time, she'd be ready to share the truth but just now she was still adjusting to it. Besides, the centre of attention belonged to these lovely people. Having no wish to draw any of that attention to herself or sour their happy mood, she simply said, 'He wasn't the man I thought,' and Alice and Daniel were too considerate to press for more information.

Taking a deep breath, Naomi added, 'It's possible that I'll lose Foxfield.'

'Oh, no!' Alice cried.

'It's a price I'm willing to pay, if necessary, but I'd like to have one last party in case that possibility becomes a certainty. One last joyful celebration to remember for always. What I'm trying to say is that I'd love for you to hold your wedding reception at Foxfield. If that's what you'd like?'

Alice gasped and looked at Daniel. 'Yes, please,' they chorused and Naomi found herself folded into hugs from both of them.

# CHAPTER FIFTY-ONE

## *Kate*

Alice's wedding day dawned fair with a promise of sunshine. Rising early was normal for Kate but since breaking up with Leo she'd slept little and on this summer morning she'd been up while Churchwood was still in darkness. She'd made a cup of tea and taken it to the small stream that ran between two of the fields. Sitting on a rock, she'd watched the indigo sky lighten to grey and then to a softly gleaming pearl. Now shades of gold heralded the appearance of the sun over the distant horizon and around her nature stirred into the new day. A lark soared overhead while only a few yards away a kingfisher darted into the water in a flash of blue feathers to catch its breakfast.

It was a beautiful morning. Kate understood that in her head but in her heart she only felt hurt. She was finding it impossible to imagine ever again feeling about a man the way she had felt about Leo.

Not that she was giving in to the lowness or making more of it than was justified. On the contrary, she was reminding herself again and again that she'd only met Leo a few times and that many people in the world were struggling with far greater challenges than a heart bruised by a short romance – the men and women who were fighting in the war or supporting the war effort miles from their loved ones; the injured; the bereaved; those left with nowhere to live . . .

Closer to home there was Naomi, carrying the failure of her marriage with dignity and selflessness. Kate had never warmed to the austere chill given off by Alexander Harrington but the news that Naomi was separating from him had still come as a shock. Naomi hadn't explained the reasons for it yet. 'All in good time. Let's focus on Alice and Daniel first,' she'd said. 'I'm only telling close friends about the separation for the time being so please keep it to yourself.'

Perhaps Alexander had been unfaithful. If so, it must have been a crushing discovery after so many years of marriage.

Whatever Naomi's reasons, if she could shoulder her heartache with courage, so would Kate. She was struggling to feel genuine happiness but was counting her blessings over and over. She had health and energy. She had a roof over her head and food to eat. She had friends – wonderful friends – and even her family was showing signs of improvement. Certainly, Kenny was changing for the better and even Vinnie appeared to have realized that spitefulness wasn't a route to popularity. It was hard to picture Ernie ever showing affection or generosity, but miracles happened sometimes and only yesterday she'd received a letter from the twins that suggested their absence from home was giving them pause for thought about family life.

*Thanks for the parcel, our Kate*, Fred had written.

*My mate Robbie was jealous because his sister never sends him anything except a letter now and then, even*

*though she isn't short of a bob or two. I hope you're get-*
*ting Ernie and the boys to pay for some of the things*
*you send as you really are short of a bob or two. Think-*
*ing about that put me in mind of the time Vinnie took*
*the chain and padlock for your bicycle and Frank and*
*me tricked you out of sixpence each by pretending we*
*knew where it was hidden. It seemed funny at the time*
*but I don't suppose it was funny to you. What I'm try-*
*ing to say is that I'm sorry.*

Frank had added some scrawl on the end. *We're told*
*to do our own sewing here and I've nearly stabbed myself to*
*death patching up a tear in my sleeve. I used to think stuff*
*like sewing was easy women's work but it's horrid. Maybe*
*you can show me how to do a better job of it when we finally*
*get leave.*

Both boys had signed off with love. Progress indeed.

As always, Alice was being kindness itself. 'I want
you to come to my wedding and I want you to be my
bridesmaid,' she'd said. 'But if it might be too much
to endure just now, I'll understand.'

Kate couldn't have wished Alice and Daniel more joy,
but the thought of attending a crowded, jolly event
where she'd have to keep a smile in place for hours
daunted and drained her. She'd have to bear it, though,
because she'd be a poor friend to Alice if she didn't. 'I
wouldn't miss the wedding for anything,' she'd insisted.
'And I'll be honoured to be your bridesmaid.'

Bert, May and Janet had all rallied round and even
at Brimbles Farm Kate was finding kindness. 'What's
wrong with Kate?' she'd heard Kenny ask Ruby. 'She'd
better not be falling sick because we're already struggling with the work.'

Ernie's antennae had prickled to attention at that, but Ruby had handled both men magnificently.

'Kate needs a bit of peace and quiet,' she'd told them. 'If there's extra work to be done, it's down to you and the rest of us to do it. You know Kate does more than her fair share.'

Ernie had scowled but Kenny had given Kate an uncertain look. And when Vinnie had begun to tease her, Kenny had told him to shut up. Pearl had waded in, too, with 'Stop being such a pain in the neck, Vinnie.'

Chastened, Vinnie had said no more.

Watching the dawn break now, Kate was grateful to both land girls. They were working hard and insisting on pitching in around the house as well.

A fox slunk across a field, shoulders low to the ground. A distant deer scanned the scene and then darted soundlessly into a copse. The sky deepened its shade of blue and warmth eased the cool tingle of the air.

Kate was to go to Naomi's to dress for the wedding. 'Come and have a long, leisurely bath then May will help with your hair,' Naomi had said.

There was work to be done before then, though. Kate saw no benefit in moping. It wouldn't bring Leo back and it was easier to be out in a field weeping than indoors trying not to weep.

Getting up, she cast another long look at the countryside morning before walking back to the house. She checked on the chickens and collected the eggs but decided against letting the chickens out of their run when a fox was nearby. There was plenty of space inside the wire for them to take air and exercise.

She also took fresh hay, a few oats and a pail of clean water to Pete in his field, then went inside to make breakfast.

'I could have done that,' Ruby protested when she came downstairs later and saw Kate frying bacon. 'I may not be much good at farm work but I can cook.'

'I'm the other way round,' Pearl said, following her into the room. 'I can't cook to save my life but I'm handy with spades and shovels.'

They all ate the breakfast Kate cooked and went to work in the fields, Kate included.

It was almost noon when Ruby told Kate, 'You'd better be going soon.'

'Going where?' Ernie had sneaked up as though warned by instinct that work had stopped.

'You know where she's going,' Ruby reminded him, no longer sucking up to him now she was sure of Kenny. 'It's her friend's wedding. And before you complain about the work, Pearl and me are putting in overtime to make up for Kate.'

'I hope you're not—'

'Expecting to be paid for it? No. But you'd better pay Kate her usual wage or we'll all be out on strike.'

Kate smiled gratefully as Ruby sent her a wink.

After a quick wash and brush-up Kate set off on the walk down Brimbles Lane, steeling herself to be brave for Alice's sake. 'How is our bride?' she asked Naomi once Suki had answered the door to her knock. 'Any wedding-day nerves?'

'Alice and Daniel are so well suited that nerves don't stand a chance,' Naomi answered.

'Good.'

Naomi touched a hand to Kate's arm in

426

recognition that this was hard for her. In return, Kate squeezed Naomi's fingers, knowing that she had her troubles too.

They went upstairs together. In Naomi's bedroom Alice sat in her dressing gown while May arranged her hair in loose waves. 'You're looking lovely already,' Kate told Alice, who'd never been more radiant.

'It's sweet of you to say so,' Alice answered gratefully, but even on her wedding day she was concerned for Kate. 'How are you?' she asked.

'Coping.'

Was Alice convinced? Probably not, but she was sensitive enough to know that if Kate were to keep her tears in check, she needed no one to mention Leo.

'Naomi tells me there's plenty of hot water for your bath,' Alice said.

Kate went to bathe and wash her hair, allowing her guard to slip for a few minutes as she cried into the steamy water. But she was back in command of herself when she emerged to find May ready to go to work on her hair.

Kate was wearing a dress of May's for the wedding. It was made of forest-green crêpe, which May insisted showed off Kate's long chestnut hair beautifully. Both girls were tall and slender so the dress was an excellent fit. Once Kate was ready, it was Alice's turn to dress.

May had made Alice's wedding dress from a length of ivory satin that had been lying unused in May's London factory. Alice's slight frame suited the dress's simple style – a fitted bodice that fastened up the front with satin-covered buttons, long sleeves and a skirt which flared out from Alice's tiny waist and reached to the floor. The veil her mother had worn for her wedding was fixed to Alice's hair and a small spray of tiny white rosebuds and gypsophila from Naomi's garden was arranged on top.

Something old, something new, something borrowed, something blue . . . So the old wedding rhyme went. Alice's veil was something old while her dress was something new. Naomi's pearl necklace contributed something borrowed and a tiny cornflower hidden in Alice's bouquet of white roses and gypsophila was something blue.

More flowers had been arranged in jars on the small tables that had been placed in the garden for the party. All of the flowers and greenery had come from Naomi's garden, Bert's market garden and numerous other gardens around Churchwood. The food was to be a picnic made up of contributions from well-wishers too.

A knock on the Foxfield door signalled the arrival of Dr Lovell. He was dressed in a suit and had dampened down his hair, though doubtless it would fluff out like a dandelion clock again as soon as it dried. Naomi pinned a rose to his lapel and then he took his daughter in his arms. 'My beautiful girl! I couldn't be prouder of you. Or happier for you.'

They all walked to the church. Naomi, May and Kate went first, leaving Alice and her father to follow. Adam Potts met them at the church door in his curate's robes, looking delighted at the prospect of joining together two dear friends.

The others entered the church, but Kate remained outside until Alice arrived, arm in arm with her father and looking adorable. Kate spent a moment straightening her friend's veil before they processed down the aisle, past rows of happy-looking guests – people from the village; Alice's nursing friends; Daniel's parents, sister and nephews; and Alice's Mr Parkinson, who looked extraordinarily touched to be invited.

Daniel stood at the front, watching his beloved with a warm glow in his dark eyes.

Kate's breath caught in her throat as she thought that Leo would never wait for her with such love in his eyes. Would he even survive the war? Kate would probably never know, but she hoped so. She might never see him again, but she hoped fervently that he'd live. And perhaps that was what love was all about – wanting the best for someone even if they had nothing to give in return.

On that thought Kate took a steadying breath and settled down to listen to the service. It was beautiful because there was joy in the air. Adam spread it all around the church with his welcome and spoke every word of the ritual as though it had been written especially for the couple before him. Hymns were sung, vows exchanged, a ring placed on Alice's finger and the register signed. Then they processed out of church and Alice stood with Daniel looking enchanting as rice was thrown over them as confetti.

'Time to head to Foxfield for the party,' Naomi announced, and it appeared as though everyone in the village was trooping along the street.

Alice had even invited the people at Brimbles Farm to join the party once they were able to escape the farm for a while. Ernie had only sneered, of course, but Ruby, Pearl and Timmy had been keen to accept.

Even Kenny and Vinnie had accepted, looking both pleased and bemused by the invitation. 'You'd better smarten yourselves up,' Ruby had warned them.

'You'd better behave yourselves too,' Pearl had added. 'Mind your manners and don't dare to start a fight or I'll drag you back to the farm by the scruffs of your necks.'

Kate fixed a smile to her face and took a glass of Bert's home-made wine. She talked and danced and ate enough of the food to stop people from worrying about her. And she reminded herself constantly that she was blessed to be here amongst friends – people she cared about and who cared about her.

She looked at Alice and Daniel, glad to see how they positively glowed with happiness. Glad, too, to see how much Alice was cherished by Daniel's family and how much affection Dr Lovell had for his new son-in-law. Dr Lovell appeared to be making friends with Mr Parkinson, too. That was something to be glad about – it would relieve Alice's mind to know her father wasn't lonely.

Naomi was smiling at the dancers and encouraging them along. Bert stood at her side, her friend and supporter in troubled times. May was dancing with the Kovac children, while Janet walked around, bursting with pride as she showed off her son, Charlie, who was home on leave. It was a privilege indeed to be part of this community.

Kate glanced up at the sky, gloriously blue as the sun shone down on them. Was Leo flying in that sky over Africa right now? 'Stay safe,' she whispered.

She raised her glass to take another sip of wine, only to freeze as she saw someone standing near some bushes as though he'd just then walked round from the front of house and come to a sudden halt as he surveyed the wedding party in apparent surprise. Her breath caught in her throat as the possibilities raced through her mind. A trick of the light? A ghost? A mirage?

His gaze fell on her and he sent her a look of deep yearning. And Kate knew then that Leo really was here, tall and smart in his blue uniform but looking uncertain. She moved towards him, leaving her glass on a table as she passed. Her thoughts and emotions raced like wild things stampeding and crashing together.

Not yet within touching distance, she stopped walking to search his face for some sort of clue to explain his presence.

'Forgive me?' he asked.

For leaving her? Was it only forgiveness he wanted or . . . something more? Kate hardly dared to hope.

'I love you, Kate Fletcher,' he said, 'I can't bear to think that you might not love me in return.'

'But—'

'I thought I was being selfish in drawing you into a relationship. I felt I had no right to lead you into grief if something happened and I didn't make it through the war. Ralph's death seemed like a warning.'

'What's changed?' Kate asked.

'*I've* changed. I've come to my senses – after a strict telling off from Ralph's Ruth. Yes, she's devastated by what happened to Ralph, but she insists she doesn't regret the time they had together – she'll treasure it always, in fact – and it comforts her to remember that Ralph died knowing how much she loved him.'

It all made sense to Kate.

'I've hated keeping away from you,' he said. 'I know it's too much to expect you to love me after what I did, but do you think you might come to—'

'Of course I love you!' Kate cried.

Leo looked as though he was unable to trust his own ears. Then a slow smile broke out across his lips, and he sighed. 'That's good to hear,' he said, his voice gravelly with emotion.

He held out a hand. Kate took it and he drew her closer. Wrapping his arms around her, he breathed in deeply. 'I love you so much!'

With that he kissed her. Kate snaked her arms around his neck and kissed him back, revelling in the bliss of being so close to him.

How much time passed before she remembered she was in someone else's garden in full view of dozens of revellers? Kate didn't know but eventually she eased back and turned, hoping no one had noticed the kiss.

They had noticed it: Alice, Daniel and the other guests. They were grinning broadly. The Brimbles Farm party had just arrived and Kenny stood staring at his sister in shock. Vinnie's mouth had actually dropped open and, as Kate watched, Pearl reached out and closed it again.

Kate felt herself blushing furiously. Then Alice and Daniel stepped forward to usher her and Leo into the crowd. Glasses were handed round and Leo was introduced to everyone, including Kenny and Vinnie, who were marched up by Ruby and Pearl. Neither Fletcher man disgraced himself. In fact, Kate thought they looked a little awed. To his credit, Leo took the Fletcher men in his stride.

Amongst all the cries of 'Pleased to meet you' and 'Welcome to Churchwood', whispers came thick and fast into Kate's ear – from Alice, Naomi, May, Janet, Ruby, Pearl . . . 'So happy for you, Kate!'

Then Adam Potts spoke up. 'This is a day for celebration so I thought you might like to hear my news too. I've been offered the vicar's post here in Churchwood. Which means the bookshop is back in business.'

There were cheers and cries of delight. 'We're going to need more wine so we can celebrate in style,' Naomi said to Bert as glasses were looking empty.

'Then give me a hand in fetching some, woman.'

Bert and Naomi headed towards his crates of homemade delights.

'Happy?' Leo asked Kate softly.

She smiled up at him. 'I've never been happier.'

Then she looked around at her friends with a feeling of deep satisfaction. None of them could know what the future held. They could only treasure the present. And just now it seemed to Kate that Churchwood glowed with joy.

# Acknowledgements

I consider myself to be blessed in having some fantastic teams in my corner, supporting my writing career.

In no particular order, they are:

Transworld and the wider Penguin Random House: Wow! What wonderful people! Particular thanks are due to my amazingly helpful and insightful editor, Alice Rodgers; to my copy-editor and safety net, Richenda Todd; to designer, Richard Ogle and photographer, Larry Rostant, for producing book covers that I love; to Vivien Thompson, and to Phil Evans in the production team; and to Hana Sparkes, Sophie MacVeigh and everyone else involved in marketing and promoting my books.

The Kate Nash Literary Agency: Another wow! It's a privilege to work with an agent who combines humour and friendliness with ambition and a can-do/will-do attitude. The rest of the agency team are fabulous too – Justin, Bethany, Saskia, Sophie . . .

My family and friends: Special hugs are due to my daughters, Olivia and Isobel, who always tell me I can succeed and never accuse me of being a writing bore. More hugs are due to my friends for their unfailing encouragement and support. Friendship is a theme that runs through all of my books, probably because I believe it can be transformational. My friends mean such a lot to me.

Readers and reviewers: Thank you, thank you, THANK YOU for buying, reading, reviewing and telling the world about my books. You've made my childhood dream come true.

# About the Author

**Lesley Eames** is an author of historical sagas, her preferred writing place being the kitchen due to its proximity to the kettle. Lesley loves tea, as do many of her characters. Having previously written sagas set around the time of the First World War and into the Roaring Twenties, she has ventured into the Second World War period with *The Wartime Bookshop* series.

Originally from the northwest of England (Manchester), Lesley's home is now Hertfordshire where *The Wartime Bookshop*'s fictional village of Churchwood is set. Along her journey as a writer, Lesley has been thrilled to have had ninety short stories published and to have enjoyed success in competitions in genres as varied as crime writing and writing for children. She is particularly honoured to have won the Festival of Romance New Talent Award and the Romantic Novelists' Association's Elizabeth Goudge Cup and to have been twice shortlisted in the UK Romantic Novel Awards (RONAs).

Learn more by visiting her website:
www.lesleyeames.com
Or follow her on Facebook:
www.facebook.com/LesleyEamesWriter

Don't miss the start of *The Wartime Bookshop* series . . .

**The Wartime Bookshop**
**Book 1 in *The Wartime Bookshop* series**

**Alice** is nursing an injured hand and a broken heart when she moves to the village of Churchwood at the start of WWII. She is desperate to be independent but worries that her injuries will make that impossible.

**Kate** lives with her family on Brimbles Farm, where her father and brothers treat her no better than a servant. With no mother or sisters, and shunned by the locals, Kate longs for a friend of her own.

**Naomi** is looked up to for owning the best house in the village. But privately, she carries the hurts of childlessness, a husband who has little time for her and some deep-rooted insecurities.

**With war raging overseas, and difficulties to overcome at home, friendship is needed now more than ever. Can the war effort and a shared love of books bring these women – and the community of Churchwood – together?**

**AVAILABLE NOW**

And pre-order the next two books in the series . . .

## Christmas at the Wartime Bookshop
### Book 3 in *The Wartime Bookshop* series

**Naomi** is fighting to free herself from Alexander Harrington – the man who married her for her money then kept a secret family behind her back. It could be the start of a whole new life for her, but after years of Alexander controlling – and draining – her finances, two questions remain to be answered: how much of her money is left, and will she be able to achieve the independence she craves?

**Alice**'s dreams came true when she married sweetheart Daniel. Now he has returned to the war and Alice misses him terribly, but she is delighted to discover that she's carrying his child. Will she, Daniel and the baby make it through the war unscathed?

For **Kate**, life with her dysfunctional family on Brimbles Farm has never been easy but she now has Land Girls Pearl and Ruby to help, giving her more time for her friends. She's also in love with pilot Leo. But what sort of shadow will be cast over the lives of all at Brimbles Farm when her brother returns from the war with terrible injuries? And why has Leo stopped writing?

**AVAILABLE OCTOBER 2023**

# As good as Elaine Everest or your money back

We hope you enjoyed this book as much as we did. If, however, you don't agree with us that it is as good as Elaine Everest and would like a refund, then please send your copy of the book with your original receipt, and your contact details including your full address, together with the reasons why you don't think it is as good as Elaine Everest to the following address:

**Lesley Eames Money-Back Offer**
Marketing Department
Transworld Publishers
Penguin Random House UK
One Embassy Gardens
8 Viaduct Gardens
London
SW11 7BW